The
Seven Heroes
and
Five Gallants

by Shi Yukun and Yu Yue
Translated by Song Shouquan
English Text Edited by
Esther Samson and Lance Samson

Panda Books

First Edition 2005

ISBN 7-119-03354-9

© Foreign Languages Press, Beijing, China, 2005

Published by Foreign Languages Press

24 Baiwanzhuang Road, Beijing 100037, China

Website: http://www.flp.com.cn

E-mail Address: info@flp.com.cn

sales@flp.com.cn

Distributed by China International Book Trading Corporation

35 Chegongzhuang Xilu, Beijing 100044, China

P.O. Box 399, Beijing, China

Printed in the People's Republic of China

Yumo

北俠紫髯伯歐陽春

Ouyang Chun, the Northern Hero

南俠御貓展昭

Zhan Zhao, the Southern Hero

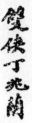

Ding Zhaolan

雙俠丁兆蕙

Ding Zhaohui

小諸葛沈仲元

Shen Zhongyuan

黑妖狐智化

Zhi Hua, the Black Fox

小俠艾虎

Ai Hu

鑽天鼠盧方

Lu Fang, the Sky Rat

微地鼠韓彰

Han Zhang, the Earth Rat

穿山鼠徐慶

Xu Qing, the Mountain Rat

翻江鼠蔣平

Jiang Ping, the River Rat

錦毛鼠白玉堂

Bai Yutang, the Sleek Rat

飛叉太保鍾雄

Zhong Xiong, the Marvellous Trident-Thrower

鐵面金剛沙龍

Sha Long, the Iron-Face Guardian

沙鳳仙 秋葵

Phoenix Sprite and Autumn Sunflower

丁月華

Moon Flower

甘玉蘭

Jade Orchid

龐吉

Pang Ji

襄陽王

The Prince of Xiangyang

神手大聖鄧車

Deng Che

花胡蜨花沖

Hua Chong

宋仁宗

Emperor Renzong

玉宸宮李太后

Empress Dowager Li

陳林

Chen Lin

寇珠

Kou Zhu

郭槐

Guo Huai

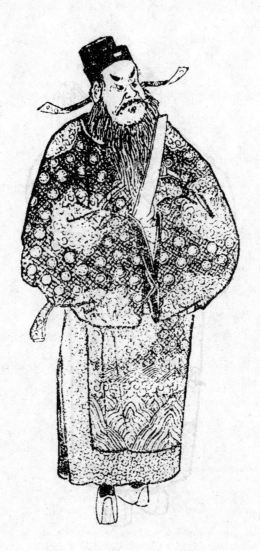

包孝肅

Bao Zheng

顏春敏

Yan Shenmin

公孫策

Gongsun Ce

CONTENTS

PREFACE

LATE in the Qing Dynasty (1644-1911) a large number of novels about chivalrous heroes and complicated legal cases appeared in Chinese literature. Incorporating the deeds of heroes with legal cases, these novels describe both how upright, incorruptible officials settle legal cases and how gallant heroes get rid of despots and champion the good. Such stories cater to the tastes of ordinary people, particularly townsfolk, and this accounts for their popularity. *The Seven Heroes and Five Gallants* is a representative work of this kind, though at first it did not bear its current title. The following is an account of its development and the different titles it has borne.

Between the reign of Xianfeng (1821-1851) and that of Tongzhi (1851-1874), a master performer of *danxianr* — story-telling accompanied by a stringed instrument — emerged among the storytellers. Shi Yukun, styled Zhenzhi, was a native of Tianjin. He told many stories with excellence, but it was *The Cases of Lord Bao* that won him great fame. Once he told them in a juggling hall that had been abandoned for years and attracted a huge audience of thousands. As later generations praised him:

It's with help of Lord Bao, a settler of legal cases
That Shi Yukun of our day has won great successes.

The stories of how Lord Bao dealt with complicated legal cases have spread far and wide. They can be found in many of the *huaben* — books for prompting story-tellers of the Song Dynasty (960-1279), dramas of the Yuan Dynasty (1271-1386) and novels of legal cases of the Ming Dynasty (1368-1644). *The Cases of Longtu* narrated by Shi Yukun, had been set down intermittently by himself. To cater to the taste of his audience, he drew on material of previous times and adopted popular legends in his book. With the spread of his fame, *The Cases of Longtu* became popular, too. Some bookstores had his prompt book copied and printed for sale. In this way *The Cases of Longtu* became *Hearsay Tales of Longtu*, a novel in chapters, each with a verse heading, by an "Anonymous Author". "Hearsay" in the title suggests that it is a record of Shi Yukun's oral narrative. But Shi Yukun's singsong verses and nonsense remarks in interludes were cut out in the book.

At the beginning of the reign of Guangxu (1875-1908), a scholar styled "Wenzhu Zhuren" re-edited the *Hearsay Tales of Longtu* and renamed it *The Romance of Loyal and Gallant Men*. He explained his intention in the preface:

> The original title of this novel was *The Cases of Longtu* or *The Cases of Lord Bao*. The novel proper contains thirty-odd chapters and over sixty sequels have been added. Since it is a legendary book, it is not surprising that there are supernatural elements. I have renovated it by preserving the good parts and omitting the descriptions of evil spirits, and offer to readers a literary work about justice and honesty in praise of loyal, upright officials and gallant heroes, among whom are countless chaste ladies, loyal servants and maids, officials and runners, ordinary people and monks ready to champion the good. So I have used "loyal and gallant", attributes to these characters, in the title of the book, which has a hundred and twenty chapters altogether.

The prompt book of Shi Yukun indeed contained descriptions of "evil spirits", such as the monster that appeared when the Prince of Xiangyang was suppressed, the black ape that kidnapped Zhi Hua who was later rescued by a deity, and the brass net trap of spider spirits that killed Bai Yutang. All these incidents had been deleted by Wenzhu Zhuren.

Later *The Romance of Loyal and Gallant Men* was published under a new title, *The Book of Three Heroes and Five Gallants*. The three heroes in the title are Zhan Zhao the Southern Hero, Ouyang Chun the Northern Hero, Ding Zhaolan and Ding Zhaohui the Twin Heroes, while the five gallants are Lu Fang, Han Zhang, Xu Qing, Jiang Ping and Bai Yutang. These are the characters of whom the reader has the deepest impressions.

The book was again revised by a man styled as "Ru Mi Daoren" and then handed down to a man styled as "Tui Si Zhuren". The latter had it printed with movable type by the Juzhentang printing house in Beijing in 1879. The book caused a sensation and was soon avidly read throughout the city.

By the fifteenth year (1889) of Guangxu's reign, the novel reached Suzhou, where Yu Yue, a scholar without employment, obtained a copy from his friend. Being a serious scholar, he at first thought he would find it commonplace, but after browsing through it, he was completely fascinated by it. His scholastic temperament, however, got the upper hand: he found absurd the substitution of a cat for the prince in the first chapter, "The Prince Is Substituted by a Cat; the Imperial Concubine Is Rescued by a Loyal Courtier", so he rewrote it to conform to Song history. Furthermore, he contended that since the Southern Hero, Northern Hero and the twins made four heroes instead of three, the "three heroes" in the title was incorrect. He picked out Ai Hu the Young Hero, Zhi Hua the Black Fox, Shen Zhongyuan the Young Zhuge (Sage) and included them in the list of heroes, renaming the work accordingly, *The Seven Heroes and Five Gallants*.

Yu Yue was rather pedantic and in rewriting the novel, carried his scholarship too far. First, he rewrote the story of the cat substituted for the prince. According to the original story, two concubines Li and Liu of Emperor Renzong of the Song Dynasty became pregnant at the same time. The emperor declared that the concubine who first gave birth to a prince would be made empress. Li was the first, but Liu was cunning and crafty. In order to become the empress, she had somebody substitute a skinned cat for Li's baby boy and spread the rumour that Li had given birth to a monster. The emperor abandoned Li and made Liu the empress. Liu, however, made a further attempt to put Li to death. With the help of a loyal courtier Li escaped from the palace. The baby was rescued by palace maids and eunuchs and later became the crown prince. This story had appeared in the dramas of the Yuan Dynasty. Shi Yukun simply adopted it from earlier stories about Bao. The story is fictitious and does not follow history. Yu Yue rewrote the first chapter to conform to history but left untouched a later chapter which is relevant. As a result, the reader inevitably comes across a discrepancy in the fifteenth chapter where Bao airs grievances on behalf of Imperial Concubine Li.

Moreover, Yu Yue was over-scrupulous in renaming the book. "Three . . . and five . . . " is idiomatic usage in Chinese. In its original sense, it denotes the numerals three and five, like the "three sage kings and five emperors" of ancient China. Used connotatively, "three . . . and five . . . " mean "many" or "numerous", as in the phrase "in groups of three or five" (in threes and fours). In the title *The Book of Three Heroes and Five Gallants* "three . . . and five . . . " are used both in the original and in the connotative sense, that is, the three heroes and five gallants point both to the named characters and at the same time to all the heroes in the story. Even in its original sense, it is correct to count the Southern Hero, Northern Hero and Twin Heroes as three heroes instead of four. We have "three virtuous kings" in ancient Chinese history:

King Yu of the Xia Dynasty, King Tang of the Shang Dynasty and Kings Wenwang and Wuwang of the Zhou Dynasty. They are four kings, not three. But Kings Wenwang and Wuwang both belong to the Zhou Dynasty, so they are counted as one and not two. In the story of the heroes, Ding Zhaolan and Ding Zhaohui are twins, so why should they not count as one? The usage of "three ... and five ..." reveals the richness of Chinese culture. "Seven Heroes and Five Gallants" is technically correct but less imaginative.

Despite his pedantry, Yu Yue made a notable contribution to the distribution of the novel. His revised edition of *The Seven Heroes and Five Gallants* was read widely in south China and soon throughout the country. Since then two versions of the same story existed concurrently: *The Book of Three Heroes and Five Gallants* and *The Seven Heroes and Five Gallants*.

All this shows that the book underwent a slow process of formation before it was turned from a prompt book for story-tellers into a novel in chapters. The features of story-telling fade while it gains quality as a literary work.

Although there have been many stories or dramas about gallant heroes and upright, incorruptible officials since the Song Dynasty, *The Seven Heroes and Five Gallants* is probably the first novel to combine both elements. Later, more novels of this type appeared, like *The Cases of Lord Peng* and *The Cases of Lord Shi*. Lu Xun sums up the characteristics of these stories in this way: "There were many stories of this type about brave and gallant men in towns or villages who championed the good, killed tyrants and achieved great deeds for the state. These gallants invariably worked for some outstanding official. In this case it was Bao Zheng..."*

Artistically, *The Seven Heroes and Five Gallants* has marvellous descriptions of characters and complex plots.

---

* Lu Xun, *A Brief History of Chinese Fiction*, 3rd ed., Beijing: Foreign Languages Press, 1976, pp. 340–341.

As the reader is aware, *The Seven Heroes and Five Gallants* e-
volved from a prompt book for story-tellers. Shi Yukun was a native story-teller of great artistic attainments. Though the singsong
lines have been cut out and the text polished by scholars, the novel
still retains some of the artistic features of the folk art of story-
telling. Lu Xun says it mimics voices of people and describes objects much in the way of prompt books for story-tellers. In his
preface to the novel Yu Yue admires it for the "remarkable plot
and the romantic imagination revealed. The characters are drawn
with a wealth of detail while the descriptions are apt and vivid".
Wenzhu Zhuren also praises it for "offering vivid details in flaw-
lessly knit episodes" (Preface to *The Book of Three Heroes and Five
Gallants*). Apart from vivid details, the novel is full of suspense.
In Chapter 87, Jiang Ping and Ai Hu are in the same boat when
the former plunges into the river to save a drowning man. Not
knowing where Jiang Ping is, Ai Hu is worried. Here the readers
too, worry about Jiang Ping. But the author simply follows the
thread of Ai Hu and thus keeps the readers waiting in suspense until Chapter 97 for the outcome of Jiang Ping, where the author re-
sumes Jiang Ping's story. This device usually adopted in story-
telling is successfully used in *The Seven Heroes and Five Gallants*
and adds brilliant touches to it.

Secondly, *The Seven Heroes and Five Gallants* arranges the plots
in its own peculiar way. It consists of three parts: Chapters 1
through 27 are largely about the legal cases settled by Lord Bao;
Chapters 28 through 78 are about the trouble caused by the five
"rats" in the eastern capital and adventures of the heroes and gallant men; while Chapter 79 till the end narrate Yan Shenmin's ex-
pedition to Xiangyang and the surrender of Zhong Xiong. In this
way, the principal and subordinate parts are arranged in a coherent whole with the main parts shown in relief, thus ensuring that
the reader's attention is captured and that he will read on eagerly
till the end. Had episodes about cases handled by Lord Bao been in-

serted in the narration of the trouble caused by the five "rats" in the eastern capital, the reader's attention would have been diverted.

At the same time, the author displays his skill in arranging plot within the main frame of the novel. Lesser events cluster around major events while still lesser ones are arranged within the lesser; thus a multi-level, multi-plot structure is formed. As the main plot reaches a climax all relevant characters and subplots are clearly displayed. For example, from the main plot of "five rats making trouble in the eastern capital" emerges Bai Yutang's sworn brother Yan Shenmin who comes to the home of Liu Hong for his wedding, and from this event occurs a murder caused by the breach of the marriage contract by the Liu family. The complex plot reveals the author's well-conceived plan: Bai Yutang brings Yan Shenmin into the story and the murder trial involves the appearance of Lord Bao at court — thus Yan Shenmin is woven into the main plot of the novel and the ground for the next major event is laid.

Thirdly, the novel presents a panoply of characters of various types. It is remarkable in that there is not only a lively depiction of the main characters like upright and selfless Lord Bao, the courageous, arrogant master of martial arts, Bai Yutang, the wise Jiang Ping and the young but clever and ambitious Ai Hu, there are also detailed and impressive descriptions of ordinary people. Zhao Hu is an example. The author displays Zhao's warm-heartedness and concern. In Chapter 22 when Zhan Zhao displays his skills in the Prowess-Display Building, others only cheer him on and encourage him, it is left to the thoughtful fourth brother, Zhao Hu, to offer the hero a cup of warm wine. "It will pep you up," he says. Thus his thoughtfulness is outlined in a few sentences. In the episode where Zhi Hua steals the crown from the palace, the author deliberately adds a poor foreman, Wang Da. Feeling sympathy for Zhi Hua, who is disguised as a clumsy and foolish poor man, he takes every care of him. In this way the author depicts the good nature of Wang Da and at the same time reveals the wit and resourcefulness of Zhi Hua. This shows the author's close observation of everyday life and his faculty to manipulate the language. Therefore though there are many characters in the novel, none of them are identical. Finishing the novel the reader has a clear picture of the numerous characters in his mind. As Lu Xun says, "The outlaws are described vividly, and the descriptions of the ways of the world and humorous remarks all add bright colour to the heroes."

Last but not least, the fact that the novel evolves from a prompt book for story-tellers and is therefore full of colloquialisms is a salient feature. Story-telling is a verbal art. The story-teller has to command linguistic skills. He has to know the colloquial expressions of the people on the one hand, and on the other he has to be able to imitate different regional dialects. The novel fully displays the author's faculty in both fields. In Chapters 111 and 112, Zhi Hua dresses himself as a fisherman and cracks jokes with the guards at the gate of the Army Mountain Fortress. At first glance the author seems to be parading his glib tongue, but then the reader realises that the witty remarks of Zhi Hua relax the vigilance of the guard of the heavily-guarded fortress. This displays the quick wit of Zhi Hua. In the novel regional dialects like those of Shanxi and southern China are used in many places. Each dialect helps to express the personality of the characters of a special region. The straightforwardness of Shanxi people and the shrewdness of the southerners are stressed in a few words in vernacular. The author is indeed well versed with regard to language.

Although *The Seven Heroes and Five Gallants* has not achieved the status in Chinese literature of famous novels like *Shui Hu Zhuan* (translated variously as *Outlaws of the Marsh* and *The Water Margin*) and the *Romance of the Three Kingdoms*, it has its merits and exerts an influence on other works.

Originating in the Northern Song Dynasty, tales about Lord Bao had become wide-spread among the people in the Southern Song

Dynasty, and they first flourished in the dramas of the Yuan Dynasty and matured fully in the novels of the Ming and Qing dynasties. In the prompt books of the Song and Yuan dynasties and the dramas of the Yuan Dynasty the tales were separate episodes, even *The Cases of Lord Bao* of the Ming Dynasty was but a collection of a dozen separate episodes. In those tales the image of Lord Bao is one-dimensional. In *The Seven Heroes and Five Gallants*, however, the tales of Lord Bao are knit into an evolving and changing string of episodes and the characters are depicted in multiple dimensions. Thus the full round character of the upright and incorruptible Lord Bao has been added to the legacy of literary images in Chinese literature.

After *The Seven Heroes and Five Gallants*, there appeared a great number of stories about chivalrous heroes and complicated legal cases. Despite their inferior quality, these stories comprised a new school which has exerted a direct influence on modern novels of chivalrous heroes.

The Seven Heroes and Five Gallants has undergone many reprintings and enjoys a large readership in China. The English translation will enable more readers to know the charm of Chinese novels and share with Chinese readers gems from the Chinese literary legacy.

Written by *Deng Shaoji* and *Wang Jun*
Translated by *Wen Jingen*
April 10, 1996, Beijing

MAJOR CHARACTERS

Bao Zheng: Lord Bao who, from humble beginnings, rises to high office at the imperial court and gathers around him a group of brave men to fight corruption among those in power.

THE SEVEN HEROES

Ouyang Chun: known as Northern Hero.

Ai Hu: adopted son of Northern Hero.

Zhan Zhao: known as Southern Hero.

Ding Twins: Ding Zhaolan and Ding Zhaohui, whose sister marries Southern Hero.

Shen Zhongyuan: former cohort of Ma Qiang, who later joins the heroes.

Zhi Hua: known as Black Fox.

THE FIVE GALLANTS

Bai Yutang: known as Sleek Rat, Gallant Number Five.

Han Zhang: known as Earth Rat, Gallant Number Two.

Jiang Ping: known as River Rat, Gallant Number Four.

Lu Fang: known as Sky Rat, Gallant Number One.

Xu Qing: known as Mountain Rat, Gallant Number Three.

CHAPTER 1

Bao Zheng — the Legends and the Facts.
How They Relate to the Seven Heroes and Five Gallants.

THERE are many stories of great personages and unusual events from China's long history which have been passed down through the centuries.

Some are recorded in the formal histories of the dynasties, but many are only recalled in folk ballads or in plays and operas performed through the ages by troupes of actors. It is often difficult to sort out the facts from the myths. Chinese historians used to discount the word-of-mouth stories as mere inventions, but many of the events and characters in them have remained popular to this day.

Even 800 years ago, society was aware that popular reputation could count for more than the sober facts of a person's life. Lu Fangweng, also known as Lu You (1125-1210), a great poet of the Southern Song Dynasty, summarised the point in a poem in which he wrote: "What does the official obituary matter — just listen to the ballad about Adviser Cai." He was referring to a ballad from nearly a thousand years earlier which told the story of Cai Bojie, who in the Han Dynasty became renowned for achieving the unusual feat of marrying into the family of Prime Minister Niu — and his career was assured.

The tale of Adviser Cai was but one of many from the Han Dy-

nasty which became firm favourites with ordinary people for centuries thereafter. Indeed, *The History of the Han Dynasty* says
that there were 950 tales of marvels from the Zhou Dynasty,
which ruled from 1100-221 B.C. Long-famous tales from the Xia,
Shang and Zhou dynasties included one about Yao, who was sent
to prison, about Sun, who was put to death in the wilds, about Tai
Jia, who killed Prime Minister Yi Yin, and a romantic one about
the woman from Lishan Mountain who later became queen.

Perhaps one of the most long-lasting tales in which myth and
fact have become almost inextricably intertwined concerns Lord
Bao, also known as Bao Longtu (Longtu means dragon pattern).
In folklore he was credited with being an immortal who lived
throughout the Tang, Song, Yuan and Ming dynasties — a span of
some thousand years.

The elusiveness of the basic facts of his life is referred to in one
of the 200 poems in *The Small Penglai Mountain*, a collection of
partly didactic poems by Yu Yue (1821-1907), also called Yinfu or
Master Quyuan, who was a palace graduate in the reign of the
Qing Emperor Daoguang and worked as a compiler in the Hanlin
Academy.

"With the name of Lord Bao, *The Seven Heroes and Five Gallants* is begun," wrote Yu Yue, referring also to "The history of
the cases of Longtu." Alluding to Lord Bao's reputation as an immortal who had manifested himself in many reigns over the centuries, Yu wrote these lines:

Dynasties of events seem always new,
Though the Tang, Song, Yuan and Ming are past and gone.
Most of the ancients are old friends of mine,
But half of the stories are fictitious and untrue.

In fact Lord Bao came to prominence in the Song Dynasty. One
book about him, *The Cases of Longtu*, gave a version of his life. It
said that he could preside over the trials of living beings by day,

and those of the nether world at night. He was regarded as an embodiment of King Yama.

A biography of Lord Bao can be found in Volume 316 of *The History of the Song Dynasty*. He was born in Hefei, in Luzhou Prefecture; his given name was Zheng and courtesy name Xiren. After passing the imperial examinations he was appointed Supreme Court Judge and Magistrate of Jianchang County. Later, he resigned to look after his elderly parents. When they died, he mourned at their graveside for a long time before accepting the position of Magistrate of Tianchang County. Later he was transferred to Duanzhou and became the Censor in the Imperial Government, an assistant in the Ministry of the Interior. Afterwards he was appointed Commissioner of Transport east of the capital, was transferred to Shaanxi Province, then to Hubei, and later became Vice-Minister of the Interior, Adviser of the Tianzhang Library, a member of the Censorate, Scholar of the Longtu Academy, High Commissioner of Transport in the Hebei region, and was then sent to Yingzhou.

After the death of his son, he begged to be transferred to Bian Principality, then to Yangzhou, Luzhou, Chizhou and the prefecture of Jiangning. Next he was appointed Prefect of Kaifeng, Adviser, Censor and promoted to the rank of Scholar of the Privy Council to take charge of the three Ministries of Finance, Interior, Salt and Iron, and was made Vice-President of the Privy Council and finally Vice-Minister of the Rites. He died when he was sixty-four. This is the official career of Bao Zheng.

Because he had been the Adviser of the Tianzhang Library, he was known as "Adviser Bao", and because he had been the Scholar of the Longtu Academy he was later called "Bao Longtu". Because he had been in charge of Kaifeng Prefecture, some memorabilia associated with him are still there today. He presided over Kaifeng for only a short period, but many remarkable events took place there during this time. Although his official career took him from Magistrate of Tianchang County through Prefect of Jiangning, many of his posts were never referred to, as if he had only been the prefect of Kaifeng. This was due to want of study of his biography.

According to his biography, Bao Zheng was so resolute and firm in governing that even the imperial relatives and eunuchs had to desist from their evil ways. So the people in the capital held him in high regard, saying: "Before any bribe is extorted, Bao Zheng the King of Yama turns up to prevent it."

This did not mean that he conjured up spirits and ghosts, but referred to his honest and upright behaviour in the government.

So the references to him as an embodiment of the legendary King Yama were merely a reflection of his sterling qualities and prodigious energy.

The biography says that Bao Zheng abhorred harsh judgements and advocated leniency and kindness. Though he was disgusted by evildoers, he was not averse to showing them consideration. From this, one can see that as an official Bao Zheng did not merely put emphasis on strictness and impartiality.

When he was the Magistrate of Tianchang County, a man complained that his ox's tongue had been cut off. Bao Zheng suggested: "The ox cannot live on without its tongue. Better slaughter it and sell the beef to make money." The man took his advice and left. Before long another man came to bring a lawsuit against the first man's slaughter of his cattle. Bao Zheng retorted: "Why do you accuse him of slaughter after you've cut off the tongue of his ox?" As Bao Zheng had hit the nail on the head with this remark, the man hurriedly kowtowed and pleaded guilty.

This story was recorded in his biography. It proved that Bao Zheng was outstanding at solving cases. Accordingly, *The Cases of Longtu* was based on this talent of his.

In the great variety of dramas of the Yuan Dynasty there was a fabricated story that Bao Zheng had tried the case of Empress Dowager Li. But there is no smoke without fire. According to the history of the Song Dynasty, the imperial concubine Li Chen had formerly been a maid of Empress Dowager Zhang Xian. She was assigned as chambermaid to Emperor Zhenzong and became pregnant by him. She gave birth to a son, Renzong. The empress dowager took the boy as her own son and when he ascended the throne his real mother was retired into the obscurity of the imperial concubines of the previous reign. He only learnt the truth of his birth when the empress dowager died, by which time his mother had been dead for many years. The grief-stricken emperor conferred the posthumous title of empress dowager on her.

This was supposed to be the source of the story entitled "The Cat Substituted for the Crown Prince" though in reality no such case had existed. Since the chambermaid had been ill-treated by the empress dowager, her death gave rise to various rumours which clash with the account in the *Records of Bribery* by Wang Zhi of the Song Dynasty. According to this account, a woman of the Wang family, who claimed in the law court to have slept with Emperor Shenzong, and to have given him a son, produced an embroidered waistband from the imperial palace as proof. After careful investigation, the story was judged to be a fabrication and Bao Zheng sentenced the woman and her son to death. The matter had no connection with the case of the ill-treated maid and did not conform to the Yuan drama of trying the case of the empress dowager. Later a poem was composed which read:

Histories spread are incredible;
So are the romances newly invented.
Pockmark Liu and Pockmark Li
Slander people of the past and of today.

The Seven Heroes and Five Gallants was originally entitled *The Cases of Longtu* with Bao Zheng as the protagonist. "The Cat Substituted for the Crown Prince" was the most stirring case among those tried by him in that account.

It was said that two imperial concubines of Emperor Zhenzong named Liu and Li were both with child. During the Mid-Autumn Festival, all three were enjoying themselves in the garden, watching the full moon.

A little tipsy, the emperor told them that although he was very happy about their pregnancies the eunuch astrologer had reported that the Dog Star was encroaching on the Imperial Constellation and would be harmful to the coming crown prince. He gave each of the concubines a jade seal, a scarf embroided with dragons to quell the Dog and a golden ball with a pearl inside.

He ordered the eunuch Chen Lin to take the balls to the department in charge of seals to have the concubines' names engraved on them. Soon Chen Lin returned with the name of the imperial consort Li of the Jade Dawn Palace exquisitely carved on the one, and the name of Liu of the Gold Flower Palace on the other. Holding the precious objects in their hands, the two concubines knelt down in front of the emperor and kowtowed.

The emperor, still under the influence of wine, rashly promised that whoever gave him a son would be made an empress.

This aroused the imperial concubine Liu's greed and jealousy. She returned to her palace and plotted with the major-domo, Guo Huai, to kill Li, her rival. She was overheard by her maid named Kou Zhu who, because she had a strong sense of justice, decided to become very watchful.

One day while in the company of Li, the emperor remembered that the next day was the birthday of the Eighth Prince who resided in the Southern Green Palace. He instructed the eunuch Chen Lin to take some fruit from the royal garden as a gift. Soon after the eunuch left, the imperial concubine Li felt the first birth pains and the emperor hastily summuned the other imperial concubine, Liu, to take care of her. Together with her major-domo and a midwife they brought in a box with a dead skinned cat inside and substituted it for the newly-born son. They wrapped the baby in an embroidered scarf and put him in a wicker basket and ordered the maid Kou Zhu to throw the basket into the water under the Gold

Water Bridge. She did not have the heart to drown the prince but was prepared to perish with him in the stream. Just then the emperor's eunuch Chen,Lin returned from the royal garden holding a filigree box. Relieved, she knew the little prince would be saved.

Chen Lin took the baby to the palace of the Eighth Prince and with tears related the story to him and his princess, Lady Dai, who decided to keep him with their own sons.

When the imperial concubine falsely reported that her rival had borne a monster, the emperor decreed that Li should be sent into exile. Fortunately the head steward of the palace named Qin Feng was a kind and compassionate man and she was whisked away to another palace where she lived in peace and safety. As for the other imperial concubine, Liu, she also bore a son and was granted the title of empress. Unfortunately the young crown prince died when he was only six years old. The emperor was grief-stricken and when the Eighth Prince came to console him he was asked how many sons he had. In reply, the Eighth Prince told him that his third son was exactly the same age as the late crown prince. So the young boy was immediately sent for. In fact he was the original crown prince and father and son became so close they could not bear to be separated from each other. From then on he was kept at the palace. Eventually, when the old emperor died, the crown prince succeeded to the throne and became Emperor Renzong.

Long before that, when the boy first came to the imperial palace, he did not attract Empress Liu's attention. But gradually she became suspicious. She called in the maid Kou Zhu and tortured her but she did not confess and eventually killed herself by dashing her head against a stone step. Liu suspected that the crown prince's mother was still alive and might cause trouble. So she made another false accusation, alleging that Li had secretly cursed the emperor. The emperor issued a decree granting Li the privilege of committing suicide. On hearing this, the chief steward Qin Feng informed her of the plot and another eunuch called Yu

Zhong nobly offered to die in her place when she was removed to the eunuchs' quarters to await her fate. He twisted his hair into a bun, put on her dress and lay on the bed. When the decree arrived the supervisor was invited by Qin Feng to have a rest and when the "suicide" was reported, the supervisor gave the corpse a cursory glance and left. The body of Yu Zhong was buried with due ceremony according to the rules. Li took on the identity of the martyr eunuch and pretending sickness was immediately moved out of the palace. Qin Feng sent her to his home in Chenzhou. Much later he was murdered by the treacherous Guo Huai.

This was the story of "The Cat Substituted for the Crown Prince", which the reader will learn more of in Chapters 15-19.

CHAPTER 2

The God of Literature Appears in a Dream as the Loyal Official is Born. The God of Thunder Shows His Power When the Fox Shelters from a Disaster.

IN the Bao Family Village in Hefei County, south of the Yangtze River there lived a squire named Bao Huai, who was a wealthy but generous man. He was known as "The Philanthropist" or "Millionaire Bao". His wife gave birth to two sons; the elder was called Bao Shan and the younger named Bao Hai. Bao Shan had a newly-born son and was a kind and honest man with a virtuous wife; whereas his younger brother, Bao Hai, was crafty and dishonest, married to an ill-natured woman who was childless. Fortunately the old squire managed his household well and the elder son treated his brother with tact and kindness so the family led a peaceful life. They were farmers, diligent and frugal despite not being descended from a scholarly background.

Unexpectedly the squire's wife was with child again that year. The squire thought that as he already had two sons and a grandson, a third child so late in life would just be another encumbrance. How could his wife, nearly fifty, bear the pain of childbirth and then the rigours of nursing a baby?

One day while sitting in his study brooding over these matters, he fell asleep and dreamed that clouds floated in and then a sudden bright red light flashed through the room and a monster appeared.

It had a pair of horns, blue face and red hair, big mouth and sharp fangs. With a silver ingot in its left hand and a cinnabar writing brush in its right, it danced before him. The squire cried out and woke, his heart pounding. At that moment, a maid-servant came in and announced that his wife had just been delivered of a son.

The squire drew a deep breath and sighed: "Bad, too bad! What bad luck to have such a monster. What ill fate awaits us?"

He went to his wife, said a few words to her but did not as much as glance at the little baby.

All was not well in the younger brother's household either. Bao Hai's wife grumbled: "Now the property will have to be divided into three portions instead of two. We have to think of a way out."

Bao Hai, equally worried, replied: "Father has told me that he dreamed of a monster with red hair and blue face descending from above. He is terribly afraid, for the baby was born at the same moment. The monster must be the watermelon demon from our eastern field."

"Terrible!" his wife exclaimed and then goaded him: "If it is kept at home, it is bound to make trouble. An ancient book says many families were brought to ruin by the advent of a monster. We've got to tell the old man to abandon it in the wilds; that will save us having to divide the property into three portions."

Relieved at his wife's suggestion, the second son told his father what should be done — without mentioning the real reason behind it.

His father, already deeply troubled, agreed at once.

"You do the job quickly and tell your mother that the baby died just after it was born."

Bao Hai removed the baby and put it in a tea basket and took it to a pit overgrown with weeds behind the Bright Screen Mountain. He was just about to take the baby out of the basket when he saw the green eyes of a tiger gleaming in the thicket. He dropped the basket and ran away.

He went straight to his room and threw himself onto the bed. "Terrible, terrible!" he stuttered.

In answer to his wife's questions he told her about the tiger. "What a pity I didn't bring back the tea basket."

His wife laughed scornfully. "You're just like the man who gleans sesame seeds in the field but spills buckets of sesame oil on the ground — you pay more attention to trifling matters than to the important. How much does the basket cost? Won't a share of your family property have been saved?"

"That's true," Bao Hai chortled. "Suffer a light loss and you'll gain a big advantage. I'm really lucky to have such a wife as you. The tiger must have eaten the baby by now."

They were unaware of listening ears outside the window. As Bao Shan's wife was passing by, she overheard what they had said and hurried back to her room unable to restrain her tears.

She told her husband who said consolingly: "Don't be so upset. The Bright Screen Mountain is only five or six *li* away. I'll go and see what I can do."

When Bao Shan reached the spot he found the pit overgrown with weeds and while searching found an empty basket. At first he thought that the baby had been eaten but further on he found the naked baby lying on a thick layer of weeds. He tucked the baby inside his gown and returned home.

His wife was overjoyed at the sight of the Bao Number Three Brother and held him close as the hungry baby nuzzled against her. She undid her tunic and fed him.

"We've rescued our brother," said Bao Shan, "but another new-born baby is bound to arouse suspicion."

His wife suggested that they put their own son with foster-parents and she would suckle the new baby.

As luck would have it there was a woman in the village who had just lost her baby. She had abundant breast milk and was delighted to have the son of Bao Shan.

The seasons changed and went and in a flash six years went by.

The boy addressed his brother and sister-in-law as father and mother. They called him Darky. He was a strange child who never cried or smiled. A silent child with a sullen face. He ignored people who teased him and was not much liked except by Bao Shan and his wife.

When it was the birthday of the squire's wife there was a small family dinner. Her daughter-in-law accompanied by Darky came to offer their best wishes. After making a curtsey she stood aside as the boy ran to the old lady and knelt down and respectfully kowtowed to her three times. She beamed with pleasure and embraced him saying: "I gave birth to a child six years ago. He would be just his age if he had lived."

As they were alone, Bao Shan's wife went down on her knees and confessed. "Forgive me, mother. This is the boy you bore. I was afraid you were too old and did not have enough milk to nurse him. So I secretly brought him up in my own home. I won't presume to keep the truth from you any longer."

Out of a sense of loyalty she did not want to reveal how her brother-in-law and his wife had conspired to kill the child.

The old lady exclaimed that she was a virtuous woman and asked what had happened to her grandson as a result.

He was reunited with the family and the squire was happy, regretting the wrong he had done his wife.

Darky lived with his real mother who loved him dearly and changed his name to Black the Third. Bao Hai and his wife, thwarted in their conspiracy, waited for two years before inveigling the squire again: "We country people should be hardworking and not loaf about. What future is there for him if he's only fond of eating and averse to work? Black the Third is nine years old and should learn to tend the cattle from shepherds like Changbao, the son of Old Zhou the farmhand. In this way he can learn some skills and won't become an idler."

The couple accepted the advice and asked Old Zhou to take good care of their son. The farmhand instructed his own son, Changbao: "Humour the young master otherwise you'll be sorry."

The third son went out every day to tend the sheep and cattle outside the village near the river or by the foot of the Bright Screen Mountain. One day as he sat under a tree enjoying the view and meditating, dark clouds suddenly closed in, thunder rumbled and lightning flashed across the sky. He hurried to an old temple in a cleft on the mountain to shelter from the storm. He was sitting cross-legged in front of the altar when he felt an arm steal round his waist. Turning, he saw a girl looking frightened and blushing in embarrassment.

"I wonder who she is. She must be frightened of the storm just like I was. It is more likely for such a delicate girl."

He unbuttoned his jacket to cover her as the thunder roared louder than ever outside. The sun was setting by the time the rain and thunder stopped and he turned to look — but the girl had disappeared. Full of wonder, he went out of the temple and told Changbao to drive their cattle home.

At the entrance to the village he saw Autumn Fragrance, the maid-servant of his second sister-in-law, approaching with a dish of fried cake.

"My mistress made this especially for you," she said.

He was just going to eat the cake when he felt a tingling in his fingers and dropped it. Changbao's dog snatched it and took off; his young master wanted to chase it but Black the Third said the cake would not be fit to eat and they should see to the cattle.

As they entered Old Zhou's room, Changbao went to pen up the animals and suddenly called out: "Aiya! Why are the dog's eyes, ears and mouth bleeding?"

They hurried out to the courtyard and found the dog was dead.

Old Zhou realised it had been poisoned and asked what it had eaten. When he was told that it had eaten a cake sent by the sister-in-law, the old shepherd warned Black the Third to be on his guard against anything she gave him to eat in future.

Black the Third did not believe him; instead he blamed him for trying to sow discord between him and his second sister-in-law. In a huff he left for home.

A few days later Autumn Fragrance was sent to him and said that her mistress had something urgent on which she wanted to consult him. When Black the Third complied she told him that Autumn Fragrance had carelessly dropped her gold hairpin in the well and was afraid that the old lady would be cross at the loss of this valuable ornament. The mouth of the well was too narrow for others to enter and besides, if she asked other people to retrieve it, they might talk.

"Third Brother, you're small," she said. "Go down and feel around for it and save me from blame."

He naively agreed.

She bade her maid to fetch a rope and they took Black the Third to the well in the back garden.

Having tied the rope round his waist they let him down inch by inch. Half-way down he heard them shouting down to him: "Sorry, we can't hold it any longer!"

He felt the rope go and fell to the bottom of the well. Luckily it held no water and he was not hurt. The truth then dawned on him.

"Old Zhou is right," he said. "Second Sister-in-Law is really trying to kill me. No one knows where I am. How can I find my way out?"

He caught a glimpse of light and wondered whether it was the gold hairpin. He made a grab at it but the light moved farther away. Amazed, he ran after it. But the farther he went, the farther it moved and he could not catch it. His face dripped with sweat.

"Strange!" he thought. "How could there be so long a path in the well?"

He kept on following and a few *li* away the light came to a stop and he grabbed it. It turned out to be a tiny antique mirror. He could make out nothing in the dark and was full of foreboding.

Suddenly he saw light ahead again and tucking the mirror inside his jacket carried on to discover he was at the entrance to a ditch outside the back wall of a threshing floor.

He was furious but contained his anger and went to see his elder sister-in-law to tell her the whole story. Though it gave her much pain, she could only console him and advise him to be wary. As he left, he gave her the mirror.

She realised that it was his word against his brother and sister-in-law and worried that they might succeed one day. She sighed at the thought that they were prepared to seize a larger share of the family property at the expense of all moral principles.

When her husband returned she told him the whole story. He shook his head and exclaimed: "What nonsense! The boy must have missed his step while larking about and fallen into the well and made up that story. If he is kept in, he will stay out of trouble." Secretly he was worried and remembered what his brother and sister-in-law had done before. But as an elder brother he was obliged to turn a blind eye, so as to keep peace in the family. "If I exposed them it would sour relations between us and bring discord," he thought.

He gave a sigh and said to his wife: "I find Number Three Brother shows great promise. We have been held back from learning to read and write. We should get a tutor for the youngest brother. If Heaven feels pity for us and he passes the imperial examinations and is appointed an official, it could change our family status. We would not be bullied by corrupt officials any more."

His wife readily agreed and said he should speak to his father to get his approval.

The next day Bao Shan explained to his father how they had suffered through lack of education and what a good idea it would be to have a tutor for Number Three Brother. "I still can't do the accounts properly and we're often cheated by others. Third Brother could keep the accounts," he said.

His father thought it was a good idea but suggested that they find someone with only a little education, enough to be able to teach sufficient characters with which to get by.

His son consulted with neighbours to recommend a learned teacher.

It was not that Bao Shan was deliberately defying his father. It was because he had noticed his young brother had extraordinary gifts and felt that he would have a great future.

The neighbours were eager to recommend a tutor for "Millionaire Bao" but had not imagined that Bao Shan would invite a well-read scholar named Ning living in the next village. He was noted for his moral integrity and erudition. But he was eccentric: he would not teach stupid pupils. During lessons he would only admit the pupil and his page-boy into the study; and he could not be dismissed within ten years — he could leave in that time only if he himself wanted to resign. On the other hand he did not care about how much he was paid. Because of all these conditions he had never been appointed as a tutor. Bao Shan agreed to the various demands and added humbly: "I am afraid my brother is a little dull. I hope you will be kind enough to take him as your pupil."

A date was set for the tutor to start.

Teacher and pupil took an instant liking to each other and it was agreed that Black the Third's page-boy should be the only other person in attendance so he could also learn to read and write.

CHAPTER 3

In the Gold Dragon Monastery the Hero Comes to the Rescue for the First Time. In Hermit Village the Fox Pays the Debt of Gratitude for the Third Time.

AFTER the introductions were over Master Ning took his seat. Black the Third presented the Confucian classic *The Great Learning* and the tutor started the first lesson with:

"The way to broaden learning is..."

"...Is to display virtues," chipped in Black the Third.

"What I want to explain is 'The way to broaden learning...'," the tutor said.

"Yes I know. Isn't the next sentence 'is to display virtues'?"

"Go on," demanded the tutor.

"To enlighten the people and aim at absolute perfection," he answered.

The tutor was surprised, then let him continue. The text he recited was correct. The tutor suspected that he must have been taught at home before, or had heard other people read the text. He did not imagine that his new pupil, when he was taught the first sentence of any book, would be able to recite the next, just as if he were recalling it.

"The world has many bright boys, but I've never met a boy who can recite a book before he's taught," the pleased tutor said to himself. "He is a child prodigy and will have a remarkable future." Smiling, he mused: "Who would have thought that due to him I'll win a reputation for myself after I've already been teaching half my lifetime. Mencius once said, 'It's one of my three joys to have a talented boy to teach.'"

Accordingly, he gave Black the Third a formal name, Bao Zheng. The character "Zheng" meant that he would rescue the people from disaster. His courtesy name was "Wen Zheng", which literally meant "literature" and "probity", and can be formed into the single character "Zheng" meaning "politics", to denote that he would become an able and good government official.

Five years elapsed. Bao Zheng was now fourteen years old, full of ideas for state policies and highly proficient in prose and poetry. The tutor urged his father to enter his name for the district examinations. But his father, a frugal man, was afraid that it would cost him a large sum.

Eldest Brother Bao Shan tried to persuade his father that the boy might make some progress if he was allowed to take the examinations.

But the old man was adamant, so Bao Shan told the tutor: "My brother's too young and he might fail."

Two more years passed. Bao Zheng had grown into a young man of sixteen. The year for the district examinations came again, and Tutor Ning lost patience.

"If you don't enter his name this time, I will," the tutor warned Bao Shan, who went to his father and in a persuasive tone said: "It's nothing but an attempt by the tutor to get an opportunity to show off. But you may as well let my brother try. His failure will surely make the tutor give up the idea."

That argument appealed to the old squire, and he agreed. Overjoyed, Bao Shan told the tutor, who entered the boy's name. It was Bao Shan who made all the preparations for he wanted the boy to succeed whereas his father did not seem to care. When the result was published, a commotion was heard before dawn broke. The old squire supposed that the yamen policemen had come to commandeer carts and labour but it was his old servant who had come to congratulate him, saying: "Our third young master has passed the examinations and has become a licentiate."

The squire sighed: "Alas, I've been deceived by this tutor. It seems our family is fated to have this confounded son I can never escape."

He lay low in his room and refused to receive the relatives and guests who had come to congratulate him. He did not even express thanks to Tutor Ning. Bao Shan was left to attend to the guests.

"I've been teaching the son of this family for several years," the tutor thought to himself, "but I haven't even been introduced to the squire yet. Now his son has become a licentiate, why doesn't the father come to me to express thanks? He's quite unreasonable. How irritating!"

Whenever he met Bao Shan he complained about his father.

Bao Shan apologised: "My father is very busy with family matters. He's sure to choose a date for a banquet. Please forgive him."

Master Ning was a well-bred man, so he reconciled himself to the situation and complained no more. After Bao Shan's repeated requests, his father agreed and invited the tutor to a feast to express his gratitude.

When the day arrived, the tutor was shown into the drawing room where the old squire made a stiff bow. Then they took seats as host and guest but a long time passed in silence. Food and drink was placed before them but the squire still looked sullen and even stopped drinking. The tutor could restrain himself no longer and said in a very formal manner:

"I've bothered your honourable family for more than six years. I have expended only slight energies in enlightening your son — his success in becoming a licentiate is due to his own intelligence."

There was another long pause before the squire muttered: "Good."

The tutor continued: "He can go far, and apart from the licentiate he could become a candidate for the provincial examination and even a palace graduate. His achievements should be credited to the moral integrity of your honourable family."

"What's our moral integrity?" the squire snorted. "No, it's our family's bad luck to have the wastrel. We'll be fortunate to escape ruin!"

"What on earth do you mean, sir?" Tutor Ning was amazed. "Your words really puzzle me. Are there any parents in the world who wouldn't hope for their children to pass the imperial examinations and become officials?"

The squire was then forced to relate the dream he had when Bao Zheng was born, shaking with horror as he spoke. The erudite tutor realised that the image in the squire's dream was the God of Literature and Bao Zheng's serious air and extreme intelligence made him feel certain that he would one day become a great man. So thinking he nodded.

"I hope you won't take too much trouble with his studies," continued the squire. "As for expenses you have incurred, please be assured you shan't get less than is due to you."

The honest tutor went red with anger as he demanded:

"So you won't let him sit for another examination?"

"No, never!" was the squire's reply.

The tutor, now in great passion, said: "Whether you'd ask me to teach your son or not was up to you to decide. But now he's my student and whether or not he sits for examinations will be my responsibility. I now know what to do."

With that, he left the room in a huff. He knew the squire would not listen to him. But his pupil would not let him down, of that he was sure. He decided he would support him and relieve the elder brother from an embarrassing situation.

Bao Zheng sat for the triennial district test, coming out first once more, and next applied as a candidate for the provincial test. His brother rejoiced but his father was downcast and sulked in his room again. Another banquet was arranged and relatives and neighbours congratulated the tutor, pupil and family. It was then decided that Bao Zheng should take part in the metropolitan examination and this time the old squire finally gave in to the pressure but decreed that the only servant his clever son could take with him on the journey to the capital was his page-boy Bao Xing, thus saving on expenses.

His elder brother secretly gave him some extra money and Master Ning also contributed a few taels of silver he had saved out of his stipend. Bao Zheng mounted his horse and rode away with his page-boy on another mount behind. They travelled from dawn to dusk, stopping only to refresh themselves.

One evening they came to a town and entered a tavern where master and servant sat together at the same table. Bao Zheng ordered two dishes and a measure of wine. He was just about to drink when he noticed a priest at the opposite table who hastily stood up when a gallant warrior entered.

"Please be seated, benefactor," said the priest.

The warrior did not sit but took out a big silver ingot and handed it to him.

"I'll see you in the evening," he said.

The priest took it and kowtowed before leaving. The warrior looked about twenty and had an impressive and kindly mien. Bao Zheng was intrigued. He rose and with his hands clasped respectfully before his chest said: "Brother, will you do me the pleasure of sitting with me so we may converse?"

The warrior accepted with good grace.

The page-boy got up and began serving them, not daring to sit any more.

Bao Zheng asked the stranger his name.

"I am Zhan Zhao, otherwise known as Xiongfei," answered the man.

They talked for a while and then after drinking a few cups of wine, the warrior stood up, saying: "You must excuse me, sir, I have other duties and must leave you now. Perhaps another time."

With that he paid the bill and left.

After the meal, Bao Zheng and his servant proceeded with their journey. As they had stayed at the tavern longer than intended, it soon got dark and they were unable to see their way. Bao Xing asked a passing cowherd where they could stay the night.

The cowherd told them that they were 20 *li* from the nearest town of Sanyuanzhen and suggested they proceed to a place called Sand Heap and find a place there to stay.

On their way to Sand Heap the two travellers passed a monastery. A tablet over the gate proclaimed: "The Gold Dragon Monastery of National Protection Built at Imperial Command."

"I prefer the monastery to staying overnight at someone's home," said Bao Zheng. "We can give them money for incense when we leave."

A monk led them to a quiet courtyard, in which there were three rooms and served them tea.

After formal introductions, the monk revealed that there were only two of them running the monastery. Later he brought them some vegetarian food. When they finished their meal, Bao Zheng told his page to save the monk time and trouble and take the empty dishes to the kitchen.

Bao Xing did not know where the kitchen was and entered a courtyard built for the monks' meditation. He caught sight of a group of young women adorned with flowers, giggling.

He heard someone say: "The west courtyard is occupied by visitors. We'll go to the back."

Bao Xing waited until the women passed and then took the crockery to the kitchen before racing back to tell his master.

As they were speaking, the young monk entered with a lantern in one hand and a teapot in the other. He looked furtive as he placed the lantern and teapot on the floor.

"We're in danger," Bao Xing said when he had left the room. "It's a bad place. Let's leave."

But the door was locked and the page became more agitated.

"We are locked in and there is no other way out," said Bao Zheng in despair.

"We can pile up these tables and chairs and you can climb over the wall while I fight these evil monks," said Bao Xing.

His master answered he had never climbed over anything since he was a child and that Bao Xing should try to escape and report his death to the family so they could avenge him. The page refused to leave, saying he would rather die than desert him.

"In that case, let us die together," said Bao Zheng. "We must be resigned to our fate."

He moved the chair to the middle door and sat before it solemnly. Bao Xing took a door bolt and stood in front of his master, waiting.

Suddenly there was the sound of a click and the staple attached to the hasp of the door fell to the ground. A man dressed in black entered. Bao Xing, terrified, dropped the bolt. But it was the warrior they had met at the tavern and Bao Zheng remembered that he had told the priest he would see him that night, so he must be a good man.

The priest had been a former inmate of the monastery and an old monk had been murdered by the two young monks when he reprimanded them for womanising. The priest, worried he might be implicated in the crime, wanted to bring a lawsuit against them but had not realised that the monks were friends of the yamen clerks and policemen and were able to bribe them. The priest was charged with making a false accusation. He was given twenty strokes and expelled from the county. As he could find no way to seek redress, he went to a forest to hang himself. But Zhan Zhao, the warrior, had come by and rescued him and while the priest waited in the tavern, he had gone to investigate. Afterwards he had gone to the tavern, where he had given the priest some silver and met Bao Zheng. Later that night, during the first watch, he had donned his black suit and leaping onto roofs and vaulting walls went to the monastery. He made his way to the chamber where he saw the wicked monks drinking and making merry with four or five women.

He heard one of them say: "It won't be too late to kill the candidate at the third watch."

The warrior decided to rescue Bao Zheng first and then slaughter the monks afterwards.

That is why he had come to the small courtyard and cutting off the lock with his sword found the two men. The warrior's appearance was indeed fortunate. They hurried to the back wall of the monastery where Zhan Zhao tied a rope round Bao Zheng's waist and pulled the young scholar over. Bao's servant followed him.

"Go now," said the warrior and vanished back into the monastery.

They reached a village just as the fifth watch was striking, and made their way to a house showing a glimmer of light.

An old man opened the door.

"We were eager to cover much ground but got up too early to make out the way," Bao Xing said. "Will you do us a favour and let us stay until daybreak?"

The old man noticed that Bao Zheng was a scholar accompanied by his page-boy and because they had no luggage thought that they must live in the neighbourhood. He showed them in.

The house had three rooms. In the outer room was a millstone with steamer trays, sieves and buckets, which indicated the old man made and sold beancurd.

Bao Zheng was ushered to a seat on the adobe bed and the old man told them he was called Meng and he had a wife but no children.

He gave them some fresh soya milk and took a three-legged low table from a recess. He lit half a candle which he stuck into a clay candlestick.

Bao Xing thought it quite luxurious for such a poor house and when he examined it carefully, he saw it was green and inscribed with "To the Underworld", for use in mourning ceremonies.

Meng only used it for guests.

The two visitors eagerly gulped down the steaming hot bean milk and afterwards they felt warm and well-fed. They were told that it was another twenty *li* to Sanyuanzhen town.

As they rested and chatted they saw flames lighting up the sky. It was the Gold Dragon Monastery blazing.

"God's justice is manifest to all," said the old man. "It is the retribution for their evils. They can never escape Heaven's punishment. You may not know, sir, that since the old monk died, the two novices defied all human and divine laws. Fiercer than bandits, they killed and kidnapped women. But I never dreamed that they would reap such a retribution."

They turned in for the night and when nearby cocks crowed, they got up and expressed their gratitude to the old man with the promise that they would repay him one day.

As they made their way towards the town, Bao Zheng's legs ached and he walked with dragging feet as they had lost the horses, luggage and money.

"It will take us days to reach our destination," he moaned. "We will never get there at such a slow pace and with no money."

His servant tried to cheer him up by pretending that he had an uncle in Sanyuanzhen from whom he would borrow money and a donkey. "We'll get there soon," he said trying to lift his spirits. "We'll just stroll along as if we were in town. It will make it more interesting then," he said.

In that way their trek did not seem so long and they reached Sanyuanzhen at noon. Then Bao Xing wondered how he was going to explain that in fact he had no uncle there but decided first to sell one of his garments to pay for a meal.

The town was crowded with people and shops of every description. Bao Xing found a tavern and ordered a meal. When they finished eating, he whispered to the scholar that he would go and find his "uncle".

He went out into the street, found a quiet corner and slipped off his black satin-lined gown and then went to find a pawn shop. But in the whole wide street there was not one to be found. He broke out into a cold sweat.

As he stood there wondering what to do he noticed a crowd of people and elbowing his way through saw a sheet of white paper spread on the ground. It was a public notice.

"What's this all about, eh?" remarked one bystander who clearly could not read. Bao Xing offered to read it: "Gentlemen, I beg to inform you that the daughter of Lord Li, of Hermit Village, has been possessed by an evil spirit. Anyone who can exorcise the demon will be given a reward of three hundred taels of silver. We shall not break our promise."

Bao Xing thought: "Why shouldn't we try this? If we succeed, it would end our hardships. If it fails, at least we would get some food and drink for a couple of days."

So he stepped forward.

CHAPTER 4

After Exorcising the Evil Spirit Bao Zheng Is Engaged to Miss Li. Blessed with Imperial Kindness He Is Appointed a Magistrate.

"HOW far is it to Hermit Village?" Bao Xing asked the man beside him.

"About three *li* from here," the man answered. "Why do you ask?"

"My young master is good at exorcising evil spirits, subduing demons and curing all kinds of illness. As a stranger, he doesn't like to show off in case unscrupulous people spread rumours to deceive others. So he isn't likely to make promises unless the person is serious and honest. He'll say he can't subdue demons. But the more he refuses, the more you must beg him. He is really testing how sincere you are before he commits himself."

"That's not difficult," said the man. "I'm prepared to throw myself into boiling water or leap into flames to get him to consent."

"In that case, let's chat no more," said Bao Xing. "Please roll up your public notice and come with me."

The onlookers, full of curiosity, followed.

At the entrance to the tavern Bao Xing appealed to them: "Villagers, if the master of law refuses to help and wants to leave, please help me to stop him."

His companion backed up this request.

The two men entered the tavern where Bao Xing told his new friend to pay the bill as it would save time later. He readily consented as the innkeeper and waiters bowed to him saying: "Mr Li, you haven't been here for such a long time."

Bao Xing's new acquaintance was called Li Bao and he was steward to the Li family.

Just before they ascended the stairs, Bao Xing told him to wait until he heard him coughing, then he was to go up as fast as possible and add his entreaties to the young master.

While waiting for his page, Bao Zheng had become impatient for his return and had imagined all kinds of mishaps. At first he thought that when he met his uncle, Bao Xing had been held up. Or perhaps he could not get the loan or a donkey. Perhaps he had become so ashamed to have made a promise he could not keep that he did not want to return. Then Bao Zheng remembered that he had never heard him speak of having a relative in this town, so perhaps he had decided to desert him at this low ebb and had run away. While he was thus speculating, Bao Xing, all smiles, came into the room.

"You ass!" he angrily scolded. "Why have you kept me waiting?"

Bao Xing calmed him down and told him about the daughter of the Li family in Hermit Village and how he had volunteered his master's services.

Bao Zheng flew into a rage. "You fool!" he shouted.

Bao Xing coughed several times and the steward entered and knelt before Bao Zheng.

"I am Li Bao, sir, ordered by my mistress to find an exorcist to save the life of her daughter. Your page says you have great magic powers. Please come and save her." He kept kowtowing and would not get up from the floor.

Bao Zheng protested that he was unable to cure her but his page interrupted him, saying: "Quick, keep on kowtowing."

Li Bao banged his head on the floor.

"Look, sir, how heartrending! Such an honest man. For pity's sake help him," Bao Xing urged.

"Don't talk rot!" Bao Zheng glared at him and turning to the steward told him he was unable to exorcise evil spirits and was continuing his journey.

Li Bao persisted and said that neighbours were waiting downstairs to stop him. "If I let you go and our mistress hears of it, the responsibility would be too heavy for me to bear."

He kowtowed again while the highly embarrassed Bao Zheng raged against Bao Xing inwardly.

"It's absurd to believe that any demon or evil spirit is involved in this case," he reflected. "I suppose I can conquer the evil spirit because I am such a paragon of virtue. I may as well go and have a look, then find a way of escaping." He turned to the steward: "I can't subdue demons, neither do I believe in evil spirits, but I will go with you to have a look at this young lady."

Overjoyed, Li Bao kowtowed again. He led the way and told the crowd waiting at the doorway: "I'm much obliged to you all, and very fortunate that my sincerity has moved the master to consent."

He bowed to them and they fell back.

"Look! No wonder he has magic powers to subdue the demon. What an awesome look he has!" they heard one of them comment. "His noble bearing alone is enough to exorcise the evil spirit."

Many of the crowd continued to follow them into Hermit Village.

Lord Li was a former high official who had retired due to his age. He had named the place Hermit Village to indicate that he intended to lead the life of a hermit.

He only had a daughter and one day while strolling in the garden she had been possessed by an evil spirit. It was hushed up at first but her mother doted on her and bade Li Bao to search far and wide for a priest or Buddhist master to find a cure.

When Li Bao announced he had brought a young Confucian scholar as the exorcist, Lord Li wondered whether a disciple of Confucius and Mencius also studied alternative teachings. So he decided to test him first.

Bao Zheng hastily rose to his feet and bowed when he saw an old man with silver hair and glowing cheeks enter the study.

"Your pupil has the honour to pay respects to Your Lordship," he greeted the old man.

Lord Li bowed in return, impressed by the young man's distinguished bearing.

Bao Zheng recounted all that had happened to him while on his way to sit for the imperial examinations. Lord Li saw that he was a scholar in great straits, outspoken and honest. But he wanted to assess how learned he was, and so gave him a test. To his amazement, the young Bao Zheng could give him ten answers to each question. Even the distinguished scholars he knew could not excel him in learning.

He was very pleased, thinking: "Judging by his mind and bearing, he has a great future."

After a while he left him and ordered his steward to take care of him and to let him sleep in his study.

He left without mentioning exorcism but his wife secretly told Li Bao to bring Bao Zheng to her daughter.

The steward asked his page what equipment would be needed.

"Three tables, a chair and covers for them. Set up an altar in the chamber of the young lady. Provide cinnabar, writing brush, yellow paper, a sword, an incense burner and candlesticks, which must be clean. He'll meditate in the second watch, then go to the altar."

At the first watch, the page entered the study where his master was sleeping exhausted after the adventures of the preceding twenty-four hours. He woke with a start and said: "You have come just in time. Make a bed for me, I'm going to sleep."

"Don't you think we have to do something first?" asked Bao

Xing. "We have to subdue the demon."

"This is all your fault, you silly ass," scolded Bao Zheng. "I can't do it."

"Just give it a try, young master," Bao Xing implored. "I've taken great trouble to find you this dwelling-place. You've had delicious food and costly wine, and I didn't think that the instant you had eaten and drunk your fill, you would want to go to sleep. The proverb says: 'You'll feel ill at ease if you have been rewarded without doing anything for the donor.' If we succeed it will be good for all parties."

Bao Zheng wanted to look even though he did not believe in evil spirits or demons and was finally persuaded to give it a try.

When he went to the young lady's room he saw the lighted lamps and the arranged tableau. He knew it was a trick played on the household by Bao Xing as he heard him instructing the steward: "No one else is allowed in, and the women mustn't peep." Bao Xing lit incense, knelt down and kowtowed three times. Bao Zheng laughed to himself as he watched him climb on the altar and then grind the cinnabar in the inkstone, dip the brush in it and tear the yellow paper into strips. As Bao Xing held the brush, he felt as if his hand was being moved by someone else. When he looked at the slip of paper, it read: "Naughty boy! You deserve a spanking!"

Taken aback, he hurriedly burned it over the lamp and went down the altar where Bao Zheng was sitting solemnly. "Young master, don't sit here, take a seat on the altar."

Bao Zheng reluctantly ascended the altar and sat in the chair. When he saw all the objects on the table, he realised how much trouble Bao Xing had taken. He could not resist the temptation to pick up the brush and dip it into the ink and spread the yellow paper. He, too, felt as if his hand was moving the brush independent from his efforts and then heard someone fall heavily down outside the room. He took up the sword and dashed out and saw the steward.

"Lord Exorcist," said the startled Li Bao. "It's horrible! As I was coming into the courtyard just now I saw a flash of white light burst out of the room. I lost my balance and fell down."

The bemused Bao Zheng returned to the chamber. Bao Xing was nowhere to be seen. He and the steward finally discovered him huddled under the table. Bao Xing craned his neck and said to Li Bao: "What did I tell you? While my master was dispelling the evil spirit, no one was allowed to watch. That is why I hid under the table. Why did you venture to disobey his command? It's lucky for you that my master possesses great magical powers."

His convincing lies spoke volumes for his quick wit.

Li Bao said by way of excuse that his master and mistress were concerned and wanted Bao Zheng to rest.

The scholar and his page returned to the study while the steward cleared the room. He noticed the writing on the yellow paper and took it to his master and mistress, thinking it was a spell.

Lord Li saw it was a poem which read: "Grateful to you for sheltering me in the mountain. I made the poisoned cake drop to the ground. Thus were we delivered from the well while searching for the hairpin; the third time rewards you with a happy union."

Mystified by the hidden meanings in the poem, Lord Li directed his steward to sound out Bao Xing about the references in it. He told him also to report whether the young master was a married man. He had been impressed by the scholar's sterling character and attainments and when he spoke to his wife she had suggested that if Bao Zheng cured their daughter, they should marry her to him.

"I was thinking the same," Lord Li answered.

Remarkably, the young lady had fully recovered from her illness the following day — much to her parents' joy.

Li Bao reported the results of his meeting with the page: the poem Bao Zheng had written on the yellow paper recorded what he had undergone and suffered in his boyhood.

"He has lived a charmed life and he isn't married," the steward said.

Lord Li was delighted and after sprucing himself up went to the study.

"It is indeed a miracle that you have saved my daughter from her serious illness," he said with a smile. "I have no son, only a daughter, and would like her to marry you."

Bao Zheng answered: "I won't presume to decide such an important question without consulting my parents, brothers and sisters-in-law."

Lord Li took the yellow paper from his sleeve and said: "Read this and you'll understand. Don't go against what is ordained."

Bao Zheng blushed and thought: "I must have been in a daze when I wrote those words." He realised that on the occasion in his youth when he had sheltered from the storm in the mountains, the young girl who mysteriously appeared by his side was a fox trying to escape disaster, and it was she who had come to his rescue time and again whenever he was in danger.

Bao Xing, standing beside him, fervently hoped he would consent to the wedding proposal, but did not dare break in on their conversation.

Lord Li urged: "Don't hesitate any longer. I now believe that the spirit did not come here to make trouble for my daughter but to act as a go-between for you two!"

Bao Zheng replied: "Now that you've showed me this undeserved kindness, I cannot decline any longer. But I shall only send betrothal gifts after I have sat the national examinations and reported the match to my family."

Food and wine were brought, and as they drank, Lord Li asked the young scholar questions about how to run a family and to rule the state. Bao Zheng's replies were fluent and the old man was so pleased with his clear and logical answers that he insisted he stay with them longer.

After three more days, scholar and servant were provided with horses, clothes and money and the steward Li Bao was ordered to accompany them.

When they reached the capital they quickly found lodgings and waited for the day to arrive when Bao Zheng was to sit the examinations.

Meanwhile at the imperial court, the old emperor Zhenzong had died and Renzong succeeded to the throne. He made the treacherous Liu, empress dowager, Lady Pang empress, the evil eunuch Guo Huai major-domo-in-chief and his father-in-law Pang Ji the grand tutor. Pang Ji was a sycophant and slanderer. Using his powerful influence, he collected a gang of flatterers and lorded it over his colleagues. He deceived the young emperor and secretly tried to usurp his authority. As he had gone through many tribulations as a young man, the emperor was clever and wise and still kept the old ministers and upright courtiers of previous reigns and Pang Ji could do nothing to them. Consequently the laws of the state were strictly observed. Because the Spring Test was approaching, the grand tutor Pang Ji was appointed by the emperor to officiate as chief examiner. He was inundated with candidates who bribed him to help them. Bao Zheng, our young hero, was the only man who relied on his learning to sit the examinations. When the results were published, because he had no powerful backers, he was ranked as the twenty-third palace graduate but failed to become a member of the Imperial Academy. Yet he was appointed magistrate of Dingyuan County. He returned home first to visit his parents and to tell them of his impending marriage. His parents were delighted and chose an auspicious day to sacrifice at the ancestral graves and express thanks to Tutor Ning. A few days later Bao Zheng took leave of his family and together with his page and Li Bao went to Dingyuan County to take up office. Before they reached the county, Bao Zheng decided to make an incognito inspection.

They stopped for a break at a tavern and saw a man enter.

"You haven't been here for ages, sir," the waiter said.

When he sat down, the waiter brought two pots of wine and two cups.

"Why do you bring me two pots and two cups?" he asked.

"Because I saw behind you just now a man with dishevelled hair whose face was covered with blood. I thought you must be mediating between two fighting parties," answered the waiter. "Now he seems to have disappeared. I must have been seeing things."

CHAPTER 5

A Carpenter's Rule Points to the Criminal.
A Black Pot Cries for Justice.

ON hearing that another man covered with blood had followed him in, the man was seized with panic. The arrogant look of a moment ago vanished. Lost in thought he sat silent for a while, then, without even touching the wine, paid the bill and left.

"Who is he?" Bao Zheng asked the waiter.

"He is Pi Xiong, head of twenty-four horse-dealers here," he replied.

Bearing the name in mind and having had his meal, Bao Zheng directed Bao Xing to tell the yamen that he would soon take office. The policemen and clerks turned out to welcome him at the gate. In the office, the man in charge handed him the seal, folders and files.

While reading the files, Bao Zheng came across the case of a man named Shen Qing, charged with murdering a monk in the Samgharama Hall of a monastery. But the account raised doubts in his mind. He called the court into session at once to try the case. The clerks and court policemen were informed that the magistrate had made an incognito inspection trip. They believed he would be very strict with them. So they bustled about and carefully got everything ready. When summoned, they filed in and stood on both sides of the law court. Bao Zheng ordered them to bring Shen

Qing from the jail. His shackles were removed and he knelt down. Bao Zheng studied the trembling prisoner prostrated before him. He did not look like a murderer.

In answer to Bao Zheng's questions, the young man sobbed out his story: "The other day I paid a visit to a relative. It was very late when I started for home and it was raining and very hard to walk on the muddy road. I'm afraid to walk in the dark and took shelter in an old monastery. At dawn I continued on my way but to my astonishment I was stopped by two patrolmen on the road who, catching sight of some blood on my back, questioned me. I told them I had stayed the night at the Samgharama Hall of the monastery. They demanded that I go back there with them. Aiya, Your Honour! When we got there, we found a monk lying dead by the side of a Buddha statue. I was accused of murdering him. I have been wronged. I am innocent," protested Shen Qing.

"How did your gown get smeared with blood?" asked Bao Zheng.

"I lay down beside a cabinet beneath the niche and the blood must have been there on the ground," replied the young man.

The magistrate nodded, ordered him to be taken back to prison and directed a sedan chair to take him to the monastery. Bao Xing followed his master on horseback.

"If he was the murderer, why was only the back of his gown smeared with blood?" Bao Zheng wondered. "The monk was stabbed, but no knife was found."

So thinking he reached the monastery. He ordered that no one but Bao Xing should follow him into the hall. There he found a damaged statue of Buddha surrounded by other broken statuettes. He looked behind the Buddha and on the floor under the cabinet noticed a bloodstained patch. He saw something on the floor, picked it up silently and put it in his sleeve before returning to his office.

The magistrate sent for the chief on duty and told him to summon the carpenters in the county to come in the morning as he wanted some important articles made.

Nine carpenters were led into the rear flower hall where Bao Zheng commanded them to make stands for his flower-pots in various fancy designs. "Each of you must draw a design first," said Bao Zheng. "The best will be chosen and rewarded."

The carpenters bowed low and took their seats at the low tables, set with brushes and inkstones, racking their brains to design something original. One of them who had only used bamboo twigs was unable to handle a writing brush; another trembled so violently in front of the official he could draw nothing. Some finished their sketches at one stroke. Bao Zheng watched them carefully. Soon they handed in their designs and he studied them closely.

Suddenly he asked one of them: "What is your name?"

"I am Wu Liang," answered the carpenter.

Bao Zheng sent the others away and ordered the policeman to take Wu Liang to the courtroom. A court session was opened with a drum-roll.

Bao Zheng struck the bench with his gavel and roared: "Wu Liang, why did you murder the monk? Confess and you'll save your skin."

Wu Liang was taken aback, and whined: "I am a simple carpenter. I know my place and abide by the law. Why should I take his life?"

"I know you wretch won't confess," answered the magistrate and ordered his men to bring the statue of the Buddha to the court.

The watching people were curious and when the statue appeared they crowded round as Bao Zheng went up to it and seemed to talk to it for a moment. It seemed very strange to see a man questioning a statue. Even Bao Xing wondered what he was doing.

Taking his seat again, the magistrate said to the carpenter: "The Buddha has just told me that you left a mark on his back when you killed the monk. Go and compare your hand with it."

Sure enough there was a six-finger impression under the shoulder of the Buddha. No one had noticed until that moment that the carpenter had six fingers on one hand and it fitted the impression. Wu Liang was terrified and the onlookers were astonished.

"His honour is psychic!" they exclaimed. "How did he find out that Wu Liang was the murderer?"

They did not know that when Bao Zheng went to the monastery, he had picked up a carpenter's pocket rule. Then he discovered the bloodstained impression of a six-fingered hand on the back of the statue.

Bao Zheng struck the table with his gavel and sternly said to Wu Liang: "Now we have enough evidence to prove your guilt. Do you still refuse to confess?"

"Out with it!" threatened the policemen on both sides.

The frightened carpenter admitted his guilt and the court clerk recorded his confession.

"The monk and I were friends. He was fond of a drink, so am I. The other day he invited me for a drink and he got drunk. I advised him to take a disciple to provide against his old age. He said: 'It's hard for me to take disciples nowadays. Actually I am not afraid of growing old, for I have saved more than twenty taels of silver.' I knew the wine had loosed his tongue. So I asked where he had hidden the silver as it might get stolen. He replied that no one would discover the hiding place but as we were great friends he told me he had hidden his silver in the head of the statue. He got more drunk so I decided to kill him and steal the money. I hit him with my axe but I've only chopped wood with it previously so the first blow did not kill him and he tried to wrest the axe from my hand. So I pinned him down and gave him a shower of axe blows until he was dead. My hands were covered with blood. When I climbed onto the cabinet to get at the statue I held onto the back of the Buddha with my left hand while I scrabbled out the silver from the head with my right. I did not realise I had left my prints. Now that Your Honour has found me out, I confess I deserve to be sentenced to death."

Bao Zheng showed the carpenter's rule to him. He identified it, admitting that it dropped to the floor when he drew his axe. He signed a confession, then was shackled and sent to prison. The young man who had been wrongly accused was given ten taels of silver and released.

About to close the court session, Magistrate Bao Zheng heard someone beating the drum and shouting his grievances. He ordered the complainant to be brought in. Two men entered, one about twenty, the other over forty. They knelt down.

"My name is Kuang," said the young man. "My uncle owns a silk shop. He had a coral fan pendant. It weighs ninety grams. But he lost it three years ago. By coincidence I came across this man and saw the very pendant hanging from his belt. I asked to look at it to make sure but did not imagine he would not only refuse but shower me with abuse, accusing me of threatening him. He held me and wouldn't let me go."

The older man, named Lu Pei, then described how Kuang had insisted the pendant belonged to him. "How dare he try to rob me in broad daylinght?" Lu Pei demanded.

Bao Zheng examined the pendant. It was certainly made of genuine lustrous pink coral. "How much did you say it weighed?" he asked the young man.

"Ninety grams," answered Kuang. "Many things are very much alike, so I may be wrong in thinking this was my uncle's pendant, but I certainly did not try to extort it from this man."

When Bao Zheng asked Lu Pei how much the pendant weighed, he answered that he did not know as a friend had given it to him.

The magistrate had the pendant weighed and it proved to be exactly ninety grams in weight.

"The pendant deservedly belongs to the young man," he told Lu Pei.

The older man protested: "We natives of Jiangsu never tell lies. Why should I have to give it to this man?" Asked who had given him the pendant he said it was a man called Pi Xiong, head of the horse-dealers.

This reminded the magistrate of the incident in the tavern and he ordered the horse-dealer to be brought before him. Pi Xiong went down on his knees and said he had found the pendant three years before.

"Have you given it to someone?" the magistrate asked.

"As I don't know who lost it, how could I give it to someone else," the man replied and said it was still at his house.

Lu Pei was then brought back into court.

"Pi Xiong denies giving the pendant to you. So tell me the truth: how did it come into your hands?"

The disconcerted Lu Pei admitted that it was actually given to him by Mrs Pi Xiong, the horse-dealer's wife.

Bao Zheng realised that there was more to all this than appeared and after more questioning and slaps on the face from the men flanking him, Lu Pei confessed he had had an affair with the wife and she had secretly given him the pendant.

Bao Zheng then sent for the wife who admitted without any ado that she had been unfaithful only because her husband had had an affair and she wanted to get her own back. His mistress was the wife of a man called Yang. She had given the pendant to the horse-dealer, who in turn gave it to his wife, who then passed it on to her lover, Lu Pei.

As Bao Zheng issued a summons for Yang's wife, another beating of the drum was heard; the plaintiffs and defendants were removed from the court while the man beating the drum entered. He was the owner of the silk shop and when he heard that his nephew had been accused of trying to steal the pendant, had immediately come to speak up for him.

He said that three years previously he had entrusted Yang to collect silk from a shop and had given him the pendant as a guarantee but Yang had died and the whereabouts of the pendant were unknown. "It is only by chance that my nephew chanced upon the pendant today and has been accused unjustly. I beg your honour to right the wrong," he pleaded.

The magistrate called for Pi Xiong and Yang's widow to be brought in.

"What illness did your husband die of?" he asked the widow.

Before she could answer, Pi Xiong broke in: "He died of a heart attack."

"Got you!" the magistrate bellowed. "How did you know her husband died of a heart attack? It is obvious you murdered him. Out with it, how did you kill him?"

"Out with it quickly!" echoed the police on both sides.

"It's true I had an affair with Mrs Yang, but I did not take his life," the horse-dealer said, alarmed.

"You are a smooth talker!" reproved Bao Zheng. "Do you remember the day when you went to the tavern and a blood-covered man followed you? When the waiter told you, you were so frightened you settled the bill in a flurry and left without drinking a drop. Now you are still trying to pull the wool over my eyes. Men, bring in the instruments of torture."

Pi Xiong was dumbfounded, musing: "Why, this official knows even what happened in the tavern. Nothing can escape him, I suppose. I'd better make a full confession so that I can avoid torture." So thinking, he bowed low and said he was willing to confess.

"I was afraid that Mr Yang might learn about our affair and part us. We plotted to get him drunk, kill him and put the body in a coffin. We then announced he had died of a heart attack. I saw the coral fan pendant there, and when I returned home gave it to my wife."

Mrs Yang was sentenced to death by dismembering her body, Pi Xiong to be decapitated, Lu Pei, who had accused the nephew, to be given forty strokes and the horse-dealer's wife to be sold to a brothel. The coral fan pendant was restored to the rightful owners. Everybody learned that Magistrate Bao Zheng had tried the case like a god. His fame spread from mouth to mouth and finally reached an old man with a strong sense of justice.

The old man, surnamed Zhang, lived in Little Sandy Nest. He had a chivalrous character and was known as Zhang the Eccentric. He had been a woodsman. When he was too old to carry firewood, he watched others weighing it and was given a share in the profits because of his past kindness to others.

One day, he had nothing much to do and he remembered that three years before a poor fellow named Zhao the Eldest owed him four hundred cash for a load of firewood. "If I don't demand payment I feel I would have let my friends down. As I've nothing to do today, I'll go to the Zhaos and see if they can pay."

He locked his door and with bamboo stick in hand walked to the Depression by East Pagoda, where the Zhao family lived.

At the entrance to the house, the old man found that it had taken on an entirely new and imposing look. He did not dare knock at the door. From neighbours he learned that Zhao the Eldest had become rich and was now addressed as "Master Zhao". The old woodsman was displeased, thinking: "Zhao has made profits at the expense of others. He has not even repaid me for the load of firewood." He wanted to know how he had become so wealthy.

He knocked at the imposing door and when the door was opened he saw that Zhao the Eldest had also been transformed. He was now smartly dressed.

"Oh it's you, brother," exclaimed Master Zhao.

"I'm no brother of yours," retorted the old man. "It's time you paid me for that load of firewood."

"Don't be like that," protested Zhao. "We're old friends, come in first."

The old man grudgingly allowed himself to be persuaded and a garishly-dressed woman came to find out who was there.

"What a shameless thing you are doing!" said Zhang. "You are keeping a prostitute! No wonder they say you have made a fortune!"

"Don't talk nonsense!" protested Zhao. "This is my wife," and he introduced her.

The woman curtsied.

Zhang excused himself for not bowing in return, pretending he had a bad back.

When the old man entered the sitting room he noticed tier upon tier of earthen pots round the room. He refused the offer of tea, saying sarcastically: "Don't pose as a well-bred gentleman and hope to get round me when you still owe me four hundred cash!"

"Set your heart at ease, brother," laughed Zhao and handed him the money which the old man pocketed.

"I'm not looking for small gains," he said, rising. "I'm old and often have to get up at night to relieve myself. Give me a small earthenware pot to offset the rest of the debt and from now on all relations between us are broken off."

Zhao was only too pleased to let the old man chose one of the pots.

The old woodsman picked up a pitch-black pot, put it under his tunic and left without even saying goodbye.

The Depression by East Pagoda was three *li* from Little Sandy Nest. Zhang the Eccentric, still resentful, walked along the road as the late autumn sun was setting. In the forest the wind soughed and the dead leaves drifted in the air. Suddenly a whirlwind arose and a feeling of cold crept over him. He could not help shivering with cold.

"Rather chilly!" he said to himself.

Inadvertently he dropped the pot from under his tunic. It rolled on the ground.

"Oh, you've hurt my back!" he heard a faint sad voice say.

Old Zhang spat twice before he picked up the pot. He wanted to run away, but he was too old to run.

"Wait a moment, uncle," the voice called.

He turned to look but there was not a soul to be seen.

"Truly, when the life of a man is declining, even the ghosts make fun of him," he grumbled. "I haven't done anything immoral in my life, how come I meet with a ghost in broad daylight? Perhaps my days are numbered."

He kept on going. At last he reached his thatched cottage. Putting down the small pot and stick, he unlocked the door and went in.

As he was tired out he said: "I don't care whether it's a ghost or not. I'm going to bed."

No sooner had he finished speaking than a voice uttered sorrowfully: "Uncle, I died a tragic death!"

"Why, I've shut the ghost in," exclaimed Zhang the Eccentric. As he was a man of integrity, he feared no spirits or ghosts. "Go on," he urged. "I'm listening."

The faint voice was heard again. "I'm called Liu from the Eight Treasure Village. I have an old mother, a wife and a son just three years old. I was in the silk trade and was riding home on a donkey with my luggage, when I put up at the Zhao house for the night. He and his wife brutally murdered me for my belongings, and mixed my blood and flesh with clay to make a pot, then had it fired. Now my old mother, wife and son will never see me again. In the underworld my wronged spirit can't rest in peace. I beg of you, old uncle, to lodge a complaint before the magistrate Bao Zheng and avenge my death."

Saying this, he wept bitterly. Deeply moved, Zhang called: "Black Pot!"

"Here, uncle," the pot answered.

"I'd like to lodge the complaint, but I'm afraid the magistrate may not grant the indictment. So you must come with me."

Zhang was sure that if he took the black pot he would be believed but nevertheless, because of his old age, made sure to remember the name and address of the murdered man by repeating them over and over again throughout the night, so the kind-hearted old man did not have a wink of sleep. He got up before day broke, took up his bamboo stick and carrying the Black Pot, headed for the Dingyuan county seat. It was still too early when he arrived and the yamen was not yet open. He sat on the ground to wait, and sang to himself to keep himself warm in the cold morning air. As soon as he heard the court gates open, he hastily picked up the pot and started to call out his complaints. He was shown into the courtroom.

"What is your grievance?" asked Bao Zheng.

The old woodsman told him the story and then said: "I have the Black Pot to prove it."

Bao Zheng called: "Black Pot!"

But there was no response. The magistrate tried again, but still no answer. Allowing for Zhang's great age, Bao Zheng controlled his displeasure and told him to go away.

Outside the door, the old man called: "Black Pot!"

"Here, uncle," it answered.

"You wanted me to lodge a complaint. Why didn't you back it up?"

"Because the door-gods stopped me. I can't pass them. Please explain it for me."

So Zhang the Eccentric shouted out his complaint once more.

"Explain to His Honour," he told the impatient guard, "that the Black Pot was stopped by the door-gods and couldn't enter."

Bao Zheng wrote some words on a sheet of paper and directed the policeman to burn it in the doorway before bringing the old man in. Zhang, carrying the pot, entered the court again, put it on the floor and knelt aside.

"Can it give an answer this time?" asked Bao Zheng.

The old man nodded and everyone pricked up their ears to listen as he called: "Black Pot!"

Still no answer. This time, the magistrate flew into a temper and striking the gavel on the table roared: "You old ass! The first time I made allowances because of your age. But now I'll teach you never again to be so impudent as to make a fool of a magistrate!"

The old woodsman was given ten strokes of the cane. He limped away, his face grimacing with pain, leaning on his bamboo stick and carrying the Black Pot under his arm. When he got outside he threw the pot on the ground.

"Ouch, you've sprained my ankle," it complained.

"This is too much," Zhang cried out in exasperation. "Why did you again not come in with me?"

"In my bare skin? I would be too embarrassed to appear before the upright magistrate. I beg you, uncle, to explain it for me once more."

"No," retorted the woodsman. "I've already received ten strokes of the cane. If I go up there again, my legs will become useless."

Black Pot implored him piteously. Zhang the Eccentric was a soft-hearted old man; he could not help picking up the pot. This time he did not dare to shout the complaint again. He slipped in through a side gate but was spotted by a cook who tried to throw him out, but he sat on the ground and shouted. Bao Zheng heard the commotion and ordered him to be brought in.

"Aren't you afraid of another thrashing?" he asked.

Zhang bowed low and said: "The Black Pot didn't want to face such an upright magistrate with no clothes on. Only after he has been given clothes will he dare to come in."

The magistrate told his page, Bao Xing, to give him a lined jacket. "Watch him," the man on duty warned. "He might make off with it."

Zhang wrapped the pot in the jacket and held it calling: "Black Pot, follow me in."

"I'm coming, uncle," it answered.

This time he was cautiously calling it time and again until he was right back in the court-room. He put it in the middle and knelt down. Once again Bao Zheng ordered his men to listen attentively. One of them muttered that the old man had lost his mind; another that the magistrate was too easy of access; a third laughed up his sleeve.

"Our master is obsessed by the madman," Bao Xing thought.

Bao Zheng called loudly: "Black Pot!"

"Here I am, Your Honour!" it answered from inside the jacket.

Everyone was astonished. On hearing the pot, Zhang the Eccentric straightened up, mightily relieved.

Bao Zheng questioned the Black Pot about the whole story. It clearly repeated it: who he was, where he had lived, who were the members of his family, what trade he had followed, where he had stayed overnight and who had murdered him. His account made everyone in the court sigh deeply. Bao Zheng directed that the old woodsman be given a reward of ten taels of silver and told him to wait for a further summons.

Bao Zheng at once sent a man with an official letter for the murdered man's family to attend. He also had Zhao the Eldest and his wife arrested. But although closely interrogated, Zhao made no confession.

After thinking it over, Bao Zheng commanded that he be taken away but he was not to see his wife.

Then he summoned the woman to the court.

"Your husband has confessed that this murder was your idea," he told her.

Mrs Zhao felt she had been betrayed by her husband and admitted that Zhao had strangled the man with a rope and they still had the silver. She was ordered to sign her confession and put her thumb-print on it. The silver was recovered from their house and Zhao was brought into court again and confronted his wife. But Zhao still would not confess and so the magistrate ordered torture: his legs were clamped between logs, but they were tightened so much that Zhao died. The body was removed and Bao Zheng reported the result to the prefecture where it was relayed to the capital.

Bao Zheng awarded the mother and the widow the remaining silver and gave them the money paid for the Zhao property which he had had sold. The mother and widow were very grateful to

Zhang the Eccentric for bringing the lawsuit and pledged to support him for the rest of his life.

CHAPTER 6

*Bao Zheng is Dismissed and Meets the Warriors and the Noble
Monk. He Subdues the Ghost of the Wronged Maid.*

AFTER the case of the Black Pot was settled, everybody knew
that the upright and unselfish Magistrate Bao Zheng settled cases
like a god. His fame spread far and wide, but it made his superiors
jealous — and because Zhao the Eldest had died under torture, he
was dismissed in accordance with the rules. Receiving the edict
from the capital, he turned over everything to the man in charge
of the seal and left for a temple. Seeing him in such reduced circumstances, Li Bao, the Li's steward, deserted him and made off
with all his baggage and silver.

People knelt down in the road as Bao Zheng took his leave. After comforting them, he mounted his horse and with his faithful
page Bao Xing following, left Dingyuan County, not knowing
where to go.

"How unfortunate I am!" Bao Zheng sighed. "I've had so many
setbacks since my boyhood. I'm too ashamed to return home. I
may as well make for the capital and see what I can do there."

They came to a wild and forbidding mountain. There was the
loud beating of a gong and a horde of bandits descended. Among
them was a stumpy swarthy man, bare-armed, who looked fierce.
Before the two travellers could utter a word, they were taken to a
hideout where they were tied up to be dealt with later. It wasn't

long before the swarthy man came running back.

"Confound it!" he gasped. "I've met someone down there who is stronger than I am. The instant I raised my weapon, I was laid low. It's lucky that I fled quickly, or I would have been done for."

Three other chieftains went down to tackle this assailant. They found a man standing on the slope. The eldest of the four men went forward and then burst out laughing.

"It's you, brother," he said, and together they all went back up the mountain.

The mountain was named Earth Dragon Crag. The bandits were formerly in the employ of the sycophantic Grand Tutor Pang but left the imperial court when they realised how corrupt he was. They drove out the bandits who used to operate from the mountain and became chieftains themselves. The four men were: Wang Chao, Ma Han, Zhang Long and Zhao Hu and they became blood-brothers.

When the new arrival entered the hideout and saw Bao and his page tied to posts he exclaimed: "Aiya! Why are you here, Your Honour?"

Bao Zheng opened his eyes and recognised the warrior who had rescued them from the monastery. The latter made the chieftains untie Bao Zheng and his page and apologise to them.

As they chatted and drank, Bao gave an account of his latest misfortune and the listeners sighed in sympathy.

"In my eyes you four are all chivalrous men," he said. "Why do you degrade yourselves by doing such dirty work?"

"Because we haven't won our spurs yet, and can do nothing but stay here for the time being," replied Wang Chao.

Zhan Zhao said: "I believe you sworn brothers from different families have met Lord Bao here only by chance. Though he has lost his position, he will be reinstated by the imperial government one day. Wouldn't it be better for you to forsake evil and return to good by rendering service to the country in future?"

Wang Chao answered that they would work like horses for the ex-magistrate if ever he was reinstated.

They drank until the fourth watch. The following day Bao Zheng and his page took leave of the men and rode on towards the capital. As they passed the Monastery of the Great Chancellor, the magistrate fell from his horse and lost consciousness. Bao Xing tried in vain to revive him, crying out his name. The commotion startled the abbot of the monastery, called Liao Ran, a noble monk well-versed in medicine and astrology. He came out and felt the patient's pulse and muttered: "Not too bad."

He got some monks to carry him to the east room and made up some herbal medicine and after a while, Bao Zheng gave a groan and opened his eyes.

A few days later he was up and about again and expressed his gratitude to the monk. Liao Ran studied his features for a while. He knew what he had been, and asked when he was born and foretold he would experience a hundred days of disaster, after which the tide would turn. Liao urged him to stay on at the monastery and disguise himself as a priest. Days passed; the time was spent pleasantly in each other's company as they played chess and composed poems. Three months went by and Liao Ran asked the magistrate to write a few words: "Reciting Scriptures in Winter to Wish Prosperity for the Country and the People." A monk was told to paste it up at the side of the entrance, and Bao Zheng went out to see. A cook carrying a basket of vegetables came by. He surveyed Bao Zheng from head to toe and watched him go in before hurrying away.

The man was cook to Prime Minister Wang Qi. An imperial decree had directed Wang Qi to find a man who resembled a portrait drawn by the emperor. The ruler had based the image on a dream he had.

The prime minister had commissioned a painter to make several copies of the picture and bade his guards, attendants and runners to look out for the man. The cook reported his find to the guard, who uncertain whether to believe the former, accompanied him to the monastery to check. In the abbot's room he saw a priest playing chess with a monk who was the exact image of the painting by the emperor. Surprised, the guard reported to the prime minister.

Wang Qi lost no time in ordering a palanquin and went to the Monastery of the Great Chancellor to burn incense, excited at the opportunity of finding able men for the state machine.

A young novice announced him while the abbot and Bao Zheng were playing chess, but the abbot turned a deaf ear.

"Better go and greet him," Bao Zheng advised.

"Why should I?" retorted Liao Ran. "I don't make up to influential persons."

"I agree with you," said Bao Zheng, "but this one is a loyal courtier and receiving him won't sully your reputation."

"I don't think his visit has anything to do with me. I am afraid it involves you," replied the abbot. So saying, he went out to the meditation hall to greet his guest, and as tea was served the prime minister was the first to break the silence. "How many priests and monks do you have here? I have vowed to provide a pair of shoes and socks for each of them and will distribute them myself."

Liao Ran brought the inmates out to receive the gifts — but Wang Qi did not see the man he was seeking.

"Are they all here?" he asked. "Is there anyone else in the monastery?"

Liao Ran, sighing, replied: "Yes, there's another. But I'm afraid he may not condescend to take your offer. If you want to see him, I think you'll have to go and talk to him."

The abbot took him to Bao Zheng who finding no other way out, stepped forward and bowed. "Let me, the dismissed official, pay respects to Your Excellency," he greeted Wang Qi.

The prime minister was surprised: the man was the very image of the portrait sent out by the emperor. He instantly bade him to be seated.

"Will you tell me who you are?"

"I am Bao Zheng, the dismissed magistrate of Dingyuan County," was the reply and Bao related the case of the Black Pot for which he had been punished.

"This is incredible. It is impossible to believe it," Wang Qi remarked.

"But what happened is a fact," Bao Zheng seriously returned. "Since ancient times there have been numerous wronged ghosts. They were embodied in the shape of vessels to pour out their complaints. Were they all incredible, too? If you try cases impartially, how can you have the heart to plead 'incredibility' and ignore them? They would suffer injustice in the nether regions for ever. I am not a man to study heresy, and the case doesn't belong in the category of heretical matters."

Prime Minister Wang Qi was very pleased to find him to be a frank, honest and upright man. He invited Bao Zheng to his mansion immediately and asked him to change into the garment of a magistrate and wait outside the cabinet room.

Then at the imperial court, after whips were cracked three times, the emperor ascended the throne and Prime Minister Wang Qi stepped forward to report whom he had found in the monastery. The emperor was delighted and summoned Bao Zheng, who kowtowed three times before him on the marble steps. The emperor was very pleased to find the very person he had seen in his dream and in answer to his questions, the magistrate gave the background to his dismissal, not glossing over his own shortcomings. Wang Qi was afraid that the emperor might take offence at his candour but the emperor took delight in the account.

"Since you were able to resolve the case of the wronged ghost of the Black Pot, you should be able to subdue the evil spirit who is making trouble in one of the palaces," said the emperor. "A wronged ghost is wailing every night now in the Jade Dawn Palace. We can't keep the palace clean and quiet. I don't know what kind of demon it is. So I order you to go and subdue it."

He ordered a high-ranking eunuch to take Bao Zheng to the Jade Dawn Palace.

The eunuch was known as Bold Yang, because he was brave and fond of martial arts. He was given an imperial sword to patrol the palace every night. Though he was ordered to take Bao Zheng, he looked down on him. First he asked his family name, then his given name and addressed him as Old Black or Old Bao. When they came to the Gate of Manifesting Kindness, Bold Yang said: "Inside here is the inner palace. Who would have thought that you, a mere seventh-rank magistrate, would find favour with His Majesty. I suppose you'll boast to your fellow villagers about it all when you return home."

When he received no answer, he protested: "I am talking to you. Why are you ignoring me, Old Black?"

"Yes, sir. What you said is right," Bao Zheng replied.

They proceeded through the Phoenix Gate, past the eunuchs standing on either side, until they reached the Jade Dawn Palace, looking splendid in gold and emerald.

They halted and Bold Yang said in hushed tones: "You're ordered by imperial decree to go in. I will wait outside at the threshold."

Bao Zheng quietly slipped in and seeing the throne bowed to it thrice and kowtowed nine times. Then he took a seat by it. Seeing his good manners, Bold Yang said to himself: "I should not have looked down on him. Though low in rank he knows state etiquette well."

Bao Zheng sat as if in the presence of the emperor. Concentrating hard, he did not glance round.

"No wonder he finds favour in His Majesty's eyes," commended Bold Yang.

At that moment the watchtower began to sound the first watch. Suddenly a gale blew up which made Bold Yang's hair stand on end. He rose to his feet, drew his sword and flourished it until he puffed with the exertion. He stepped back into the palace and sat on the threshold to get his breath. Bao Zheng gave an enigmatic smile.

Bold Yang then saw a whirlwind winding round the bamboo grove and heard faint sobs. Bao Zheng noticed the lamp going dim and Bold Yang lying prone. After a while, the eunuch rose to his feet and began walking in mincingly, like a woman. He curtseyed to him and then knelt down. The lamp brightened up again and the magistrate thought Bold Yang was playing a prank.

"Have you any complaints to make?" he demanded mockseriously.

"I am maidservant Kou Zhu," the eunuch sobbed out in a falsetto voice. "In former times I served in the Gold Flower Palace. Because I saved the crown prince, I was wronged and have now suffered in the nether world for twenty years. I am waiting for the upright official to settle my case."

Speaking with the voice of a woman, Bold Yang told how the imperial concubine Liu had conspired to destroy the imperial concubine Li.

"Now the misfortunes she suffered will soon be over," the ghost medium continued, "I am here so that you know the cause. Please investigate the case and avenge me."

Bao Zheng promised, provided the ghost went into hiding in case it scared the emperor.

The ghost agreed and then Bold Yang kowtowed before resuming his place on the threshold, where a little later he began to stretch and yawn as if waking from a deep sleep.

He saw Bao Zheng still sitting and asked in a low voice: "Has anything happened? Did you see anything? What shall I report to the emperor?"

"I have investigated the case of the ghost," said the magistrate. "You are too fond of sleep and have kept me waiting here."

"What ghost is it?" Bold Yang asked in surprise.

"The ghost of a young maid named Kou Zhu."

Bold Yang was intrigued and thought: "The case of Kou Zhu happened twenty years ago. How does he know?" He asked out loud: "Why has she been making trouble here now?"

"I'll report to His Majesty tomorrow and you can give your own account," replied Bao Zheng.

Bold Yang began to panic: "Aiya! Mr... Mr Bao, Lord ... Lord Bao. My ... my dear ... my dear brother Bao... Do you want to ruin me? Both of us were ordered to subdue the spirit. But I know nothing about it because I fell asleep, failing in my duty. Please show some consideration. My dear Mr Bao, do tell me what has happened."

Moved by his imploring, Bao Zheng relented. "When you see His Majesty tomorrow, you can report that you have tried the woman ghost. She was the late palace maid of Gold Flower Palace. She wants to be avenged and released from the depth of misery. We've agreed and she has promised that she won't return here to make trouble again."

Bold Yang was so grateful he vowed to himself that he would never be insolent to him again.

Leaving the Palace for the cabinet room, they told the story to Prime Minister Wang Qi, who took them to the emperor to repeat their findings. The emperor was delighted, and believed in the case of the Black Pot all the more strongly.

He appointed Bao Zheng to the post of Prefect of Kaifeng. He also conferred on him the title "Scholar of the World of Living Beings and of the Hell of the Dead".

So the tale that Prefect Bao was good at trying cases of living beings in the daytime and those of the dead by night spread far and wide.

Before leaving to take up his new post in Kaifeng, Prefect Bao paid his respects to Prime Minister Wang Qi, who regarded him highly, and then expressed his gratitude to Abbot Liao Ran.

He dispatched his page Bao Xing to deliver a letter home and to inquire after his old tutor, Master Ning, and then wrote another letter to Hermit Village to report his success and to announce that he was ready to marry the daughter of Lord Li.

CHAPTER 7

Prefect Bao Acquires the Wonder-Working Basin and a Lovely Wife. A Plan Is Drawn up to Entrap the Murderer.

ON his return, Bao Xing reported to his master that his parents were very well. "They were overjoyed that Your Lordship has been appointed prefect. They gave me fifty taels of silver. Your elder brother and wife were also delighted at the news and gave me thirty taels of silver. In addition your sister-in-law has returned the antique bronze mirror you found in the well. It's very bright. She had hung it on the wall but one day the maidservant, Autumn Fragrance, tripped over the doorstep and hurt her forehead. As she looked in that mirror, some blood dropped onto its surface and some vapour rose around the drop of blood. She ran panic-stricken into the room of your second sister-in-law and gouged out her right eye. Since then the maid has gone mad and has been locked up in a room as a demon. Your sister-in-law is in great pain so your second brother was too depressed to send you more than two taels of silver."

Prefect Bao did not unwrap the mirror but told his page to keep it safe.

"Tutor Ning was delighted with your letter," continued Bao Xing. "He asked me to tell you that you should handle things justly and dedicate your life to the service of the country. And he gave me many instructions as well. After I stayed there overnight, I went to Hermit Village. Lord Li, your future father-in-law, was also overjoyed at your success. He promised to send his daughter here and gave me a silver ingot, two bolts of cloth and a letter."

The letter informed Bao Zheng that Lady Li would bring her daughter to the capital within the month, so he made preparations to receive them and sent men to meet them.

He found his wife to be very quiet and stately, lacking nothing in noble manners. Among her dowry was a wonder-working basin with a hole in one side symbolising the sun and a hole in the opposite side the moon. It was a rare treasure. But Prefect Bao did not pay much attention to it. After a month, Lady Li bade farewell to her daughter and went home. She left behind her favourite servant, Li Cai, to take the place of the treacherous Li Bao.

In his new position as prefect, Bao Zheng took as his assistant a poor scholar who had failed the imperial examinations through ill luck. His name was Gongsun Ce, whom the abbot Liao Ran had recommended to Bao Zheng. The prefect was very pleased with his gentle demeanour and distinct way of speaking. During the interview he gave satisfactory answers on the classics, proving to be an able scholar who had been thwarted in his aims by misfortune.

One day when Bao Zheng was holding court, a peasant of about fifty came in shouting complaints. He said he was called Zhang Zhiren and lived in Seven Li Village. He had a brother of the same clan, Zhang Youdao, but when he went to visit him he heard he had died three days earlier. His widow said it had been a heart attack but had not informed him of the death, making the lame excuse that there had been no one to take a message to him. He was suspicious and appealed to a magistrate to have the coffin opened and a post mortem done. Because there had been no scar found on the body, the widow had created a scene and the magistrate had ordered that the accuser be beaten twenty blows. "The more I think about it," the peasant said, "the more suspicious I feel about his death. I beg Your Honour to help me."

Tears in his eyes, he prostrated himself before Prefect Bao.

Replying to questions, Zhang Zhiren described how close he and his brother had been, visiting each other regularly. "Five days before his death he came to my home. After that I did not see him for five or six days, which was why I went to see him," he said.

Prefect Bao pondered: "Five days before the man's death he was at home. On the sixth day his brother visited him, but he had by then already been dead three days. That is to say, he died only two days after his brother saw him alive and well. His death does seem suspicious."

He granted the indictment and issued a summons for the widow.

Mrs Zhang was a bold-looking woman of about twenty. When she entered the court and was questioned she whined: "My husband was a decent man. Why should his body be disturbed? He must have done something wrong in a former life. Now I am summoned here. Can he have another trick to play on me?" She knelt down in the centre of the court in a demure and humble fashion and described how her husband had complained of pains in his chest before dying.

Tears streamed down her face but Prefect Bao was not convinced and banged his gavel on the table demanding that she tell the truth about her husband's death.

"Out with it," the policemen in the court demanded.

She crawled forward, still protesting her innocence. But her excuses for not having informed her brother in law of the death did not convince the prefect. "If you confess, you won't be tortured."

"I dared not send anyone to take him a message," she cried. "When my husband was living, my brother-in-law would try to make passes at me. When he came last time, instead of being upset over his brother's death and shedding tears, he made improper suggestions to me which I dare not repeat in the presence of Your Honour. I had to cry out for help. I did not imagine that in revenge he would accuse me at the county court alleging that his brother's death was suspicious. But the post mortem found no evidence of injury on his body and he was beaten. So now he has appealed to Your Honour." With that she sobbed again. She gave a convincing performance, but Prefect Bao was not impressed. He thought: "If I confronted her with the peasant Zhang, she'll run rings round him. We have to discover the hard facts." He adjourned the case and told her to return in three days. The woman kowtowed and departed with a complaisant air.

Back in the study, he consulted with his new assistant, Gongsun Ce, showed him her statement and expressed his doubts about her veracity.

"In my opinion Zhang's suspicions about her are well based," he said.

Gongsun read her statement and commented: "Unless the facts have been found out she will never be worsted." Prefect Bao was pleased that they seemed to be thinking along the same lines and asked for suggestions.

Gongsun Ce thought this gave him the chance to repay the prefect for giving him a job and suggested that he go in disguise and investigate. Bao Xing was told to provide travelling expenses and other equipment needed for his investigation. He acquired a medicine kit, a quack's cloth banner and the garments of a priest. Carrying the medicine kit on his back, Gongsun Ce set off for Seven Li Village full of optimism.

He was soon disappointed, for he found no clue at all. As it was getting dark and he was hungry, he turned back, but took the wrong route and travelled several *li* before arriving exhausted at an inn in the town of Yulin, where he decided to put up for the night. Exhausted and hungry, he was about to have a meal when he saw a group of people arrive, leading their horses. Among them was a dark stocky man.

"Whoever is now in the room has to make way for me," the man bawled. "If I am upset, I'll pull down your inn."

One of his companions admonished him: "Don't say that, Fourth Brother. We will be served in turn. Even if you want somebody to move out, you should ask politely. Don't make trouble."

He turned to the innkeeper: "There are so many of us it would be very inconvenient if we had to be lodged in separate rooms." The inn-keeper had little choice. He went to Gongsun Ce's room and asked if he would give up his suite of three rooms and move to smaller quarters.

Gongsun Ce had not wanted the larger rooms in the first place but had been persuaded to take them by the waiter. So he was quite willing to move out but the swarthy stocky man had a change of heart and was happy with the smaller accommodation. He ordered dishes and wine and the waiter bustled in and out, forgetting Gongsun Ce's food. While he was waiting patiently, he heard them mention Prefect Bao's name and that they were on their way to Kaifeng to meet him. He went to their room and said with his hands clasped respectfully: "So you are going to Kaifeng. I'd like to introduce you to him."

The group were, of course, the bold chieftains from the Earth Dragon Crag: Wang Chao, Ma Han, Zhang Long and Zhao Hu. Learning that Bao Zheng had been appointed prefect of Kaifeng, they had left their stronghold and were on their way to keep their promise to work for him.

They had disbanded their followers and given away all their stores of provisions, gold and silver, taking only five or six varlets with them.

They talked pleasantly about martial arts and literature. Only Zhao Hu, a heavy drinker, was a little rough. Wang Chao was afraid that the drink would loosen his tongue and to prevent his crude language causing offence he quickly ordered more food. After eating their fill, they chatted and drank tea until the second watch. They decided to get up early next morning to continue their journey.

CHAPTER 8

To Save a Loyal Servant a Brute Is Removed from the Iron Immortal Monastery. A Clue Is Found in Seven Li Village as a Problem Case Is Investigated.

BECAUSE Zhao Hu had drunk too much, he was unable to take part in the conversation and fell into a deep sleep, snoring thunderously, which prompted all the company to turn in.

Zhao Hu was the first to wake up and roused his companions, shouting that they should hurry to Kaifeng Prefecture. Gongsun Ce had not slept, through worrying over his lack of success in finding any clues to the suspected murder of Zhang Youdao. Nevertheless he got up with them and they found him a horse, leaving one of their servants to take his cloth banner and medicine kit to Kaifeng on foot. The moon was still in the sky as they rode off.

As they rode past a temple in a grove of trees, they saw a woman in red sneaking into the temple. It seemed extremely suspicious to see anyone about at dawn and they decided to investigate. "If we knock at the gate at this time of the morning, what will we say to the monk?" asked Ma Han.

Wang Chao replied: "We'll say we were eager to push on with our journey but are thirsty now and would like some tea."

"If that's our plan," Gongsun Ce added, "we had better tell the servants to take the horses into the woods and wait so as not to let the monks catch sight of our weapons and make them suspicious."

As the five men walked towards the temple they saw over the entrance the sign "Iron Immortal Monastery."

"We saw a woman sneaking in just now, but didn't hear her bolting the gate," Gongsun Ce said. "But it's locked now."

Zhao Hu thumped on the gate with his fist. "Open it, priest," he bellowed.

A voice answered: "Who wants to come in at the dead of night?" The gate opened and a priest emerged.

Gongsun Ce bowed saying: "I'm sorry to disturb you, Reverend. The five of us have been travelling nonstop and are now thirsty and need some tea. We would like to take a rest in your worthy monastery. We will give a donation for incense. I hope you won't refuse our request?"

"I must report to our superior," answered the priest.

Just then a hefty priest with bushy eyebrows and a fierce look appeared.

"Since they only want tea, let them in," he said.

They found the main hall brilliantly lit and politely took their seats. They realised by the bushy-eyebrowed priest's savage countenance and the smell of liquor on his breath that he must be a bad lot.

Zhang Long and Zhao Hu stole out of the room and into the backyard but found no trace of the woman. In another courtyard they discovered a large bell, and heard somebody groaning under it.

"She's here," Zhao Hu exclaimed.

"Lift it, brother," Zhang Long ordered, "and I'll pull her out."

Rolling up his sleeves Zhao Hu clutched the mounting on top of the bell and gave it a mighty heave.

Zhang Long dragged out the person from under the bell. A surprise awaited them: it was not a woman but an old man, bound and gagged. When they freed him he told them his sad story. He was a loyal servant of a family who had become victims of the corrupt marquis Pang Yu, whose father was the grand tutor and father-in-law of the emperor. The marquis had been ordered by imperial command to relieve famine victims but had embezzled the relief funds to build a flower garden where he could debauch other men's wives.

"My master is Tian Qiyuan. His wife was such a dutiful daughter-in-law that she even cut off some of her own flesh and mixed it with herbal medicine to give to her sick mother-in-law. When she recovered, my mistress went to the temple to give thanks. Pang Yu, the marquis, saw her and had her forcibly carried off. My master was sent to prison and the old lady died of fear. The whole family has been ruined by Pang Yu and I decided to go to the capital to invoke the law against him. On the way I sought rest at this monastery but did not realise that the priests would think from the weight of my luggage that I was worth robbing. They were about to kill me when you knocked at the gate."

As he told them the story, they caught sight of a priest peering at them. Zhao Hu leapt up and felled him with a kick.

"Look at this," he said waving a barrel-like fist in front of the priest's face and pinned him down by the bell.

Meanwhile the fierce-looking priest, whose name was Xiao Daozhi, was making the tea when he noticed that Zhang Long and Zhao Hu were missing. When the priest he sent to find them did not return, he realised something was wrong. He went to his own room, divested himself of his cumbersome robe, took up a sharp bright sword and strode off to the backyard. He saw Zhao Hu pinning down the young priest and rushed up waving his sword. Zhang Long whirled round and lashed out backwards with his foot, relying on his agility to escape the constant lunging thrusts of the sword. The priest thought he had a concealed weapon and hurriedly retreated. Zhang Long tried to trip him with his outstretched leg but the wily priest leapt up and turned in midair to ward off his kick.

Even when Wang Chao and Ma Han came to Zhang Long's aid, the three unarmed men seemed unable to prevail over the priest's flashing sword and nimble footwork. He felled Zhang Long with a hard kick on the head, but the latter managed to scramble to his feet. While the others grappled with the priest, Zhang raced towards the east side of the gate as if to get their weapons, but quickly returning, he headed straight for the priest, brandishing his left hand at his face while with his right he flung some white powder into his face, choking and blinding him. Ma Han gave him a mighty kick in the groin and he fell to the ground. Zhang Long knelt on his chest and weighing him down shook his right sleeve again and again over his face. The white powder turned out to be ashes from an incense burner.

They tied the two priests up and searched the monastery but found no one else. In one of the halls was enshrined a statue of a goddess in red. Only then did they realise that it was the goddess herself who had led them to the monastery to save the old servant.

Gongsun Ce ordered four of the band to march the wicked priests to the local county seat where they would be transferred to the prefecture and charged with robbery and murder while the rest of the group, with the old servant named Tian Zhong, made their way to Kaifeng.

Gongsun Ce reported to Prefect Bao that he had not yet discovered any clue, but that he had brought Wang, Ma, Zhang and Zhao from the Earth Dragon Crag and recounted their adventure at the monastery.

He added: "Now I will go on investigating the case of Mrs Zhang."

After retrieving his medicine kit and cloth banner he disguised himself again as a priest and set off once more.

Prefect Bao instructed the old servant, Tian Zhong, to lie low lest the Pang family got wind of his whereabouts.

As Gongsun Ce journeyed to Seven Li Village he thought: "Through bad luck I have flunked every imperial examination. Now I have the chance to prove myself on this case for Kaifeng Prefecture, but Heaven knows how I will find a clue. I'm just unlucky."

The more he thought, the more frustrated he felt. Before he was aware of it, he had gone out of Seven Li Village, and when he realised his mistake, he said to himself: "Gongsun Ce, what a silly fellow you are! Walking around here in the wilderness won't tell people you are a doctor, so nobody will ask for your help and you won't find any clues."

He began sounding his bell loudly.

"Any illness must be cured promptly, don't delay," he called out. "Anyone with a serious illness will be relieved as soon as I treat it. If the patient is broke, I'll treat him free of charge."

An old woman hailed him: "My daughter-in-law has fallen ill. Please see to her."

The old woman showed him into a cottage, raised the curtain to the west room and told him to be seated on the adobe bed.

He put down his medicine kit and leant his banner and pole against the wall. The woman took a chair with its back and a leg missing.

"My family name is You," she began. "I am a widow. My son's name is Dog and he works as a farmhand for the rich family of Landlord Chen. My daughter-in-law has been ill for two weeks. She has no energy and doesn't eat. In the afternoon she has a fever. Please check her pulse and prescribe some medicine for her."

Though he was only pretending to be a doctor, Gongsun Ce had in fact studied some medicine. Despite the young woman's protestations he felt her pulse. "Your daughter-in-law has a double pulse," said Gongsun Ce.

"Oh yes, she is four or five months pregnant," replied Dame You.

"In my view, the cause of her lassitude is anger. She has been depressed for a long time and it has affected the health of her baby. If she is not cured promptly she will have a miscarriage. So before I can prescribe the right medicine, I must know all the facts."

The old lady was very impressed with his diagnosis and explained that her son was often given sums of money by his employer, the rich landlord Chen. Recently he had come back with two silver ingots. Her daughter interrupted, asking that no more should be said, but Gongsun Ce said he could not prescribe the right medicine until he knew more.

The old lady calmed her daughter-in-law and continued: "The ingots made me suspicious and I questioned my son who told me that his master, Landlord Chen, had had an affair with the wife of Zhang Youdao in Seven Li Village. Her husband had discovered them together and Chen gave my son two silver ingots to do away with him. My daughter-in-law tried to dissuade him, even went down on her knees to implore him to think better of it. But that unworthy son of mine just kicked her and went off in a huff with his silver and hasn't returned home since. Sure enough, we heard later that Zhang Youdao had died. The day the corpse was put into the coffin, they heard a noise and thought the dead had come to life again. The noise even scared away the monks saying mass. On hearing that, my daughter-in-law sank into despair. That is the real cause of her illness."

Hearing her out, Gongsun Ce wrote out a prescription. The old woman, taking it, said: "I've seen other prescriptions, and there were always quite a few lines. Why is there only one in yours?"

"It's a rare one of mine," replied Gongsun Ce. "Wrap the medicinal herbs in a sheet of soft red paper and bake them on a tile over a slow fire. Then wash them down with Shaoxing wine. The medicine will help prevent miscarriage and invigorate the circulation."

Gongsun Ce realised that if the son was sentenced to death, his mother and wife would have no one to depend on. So he thought of a scheme out of concern for their future.

"Since your son has done something for Chen, hasn't he been rewarded?" he asked.

"I heard Landlord Chen promised to give him a six-*mu* field," the old woman said.

As there had been no written pledge, Gongsun Ce offered to write one out. He wrote on a sheet of paper, signed his pseudonym and pressed his fingerprint on it and told them that one day they could go to law and claim the field.

The old woman was beside herself with joy and apologised for not paying a fee or even offering him a cup of tea.

Gongsun Ce left the cottage elated, almost as if he had passed the imperial examination, and sped back to Kaifeng Prefecture.

CHAPTER 9

A Royal Relative Is Accused and Bao Is Promoted. He Is Given an Imperial Command to Check the Famine Relief Fund and Has Royal Executioner's Axes Made Before Leaving for Chenzhou.

BACK at the Kaifeng Prefecture, Gongsun Ce reported his findings to Prefect Bao. The prefect was delighted, and thought how resourceful and persistent Gongsun must have been to solve the case.

You the Dog was arrested and brought to court, where he dropped to his knees.

"Are you You the Dog?" asked Prefect Bao.

"No, my lord," he protested. "I'm called Donkey."

"Nonsense! You are You the Dog, so why do you say your name is Donkey?"

"I was called Dog before. They said the dog is smaller than the donkey, so I changed my name to Donkey. If you don't wish to call me Donkey, call me Dog."

"Don't talk rot!" barked the policeman in the court.

"The wronged ghost of Zhang Youdao has complained to me that you and your master, Landlord Chen, plotted his murder," said Prefect Bao. "You did as you were ordered and were given two silver ingots. Take your time and tell the whole truth and I will absolve you from guilt."

You the Dog felt reassured by the prefect's kindly mien and kowtowed, saying: "After Your Honour's promise I will tell the truth. My master had an affair with Zhang Youdao's wife. One day he was caught by Zhang and did not dare go to their house again. He fell ill from longing for her and wanted Zhang to die so that he could take her into his own home.

"He asked me to find something which was not easy to find. It is called 'Corpse Tortoise' and is like a glowworm. It gives out a green light from its tail, and is found in a grave where the corpse has rotted away but the brain remains moist. He promised to give me two taels of silver and a six-*mu* field if I succeeded in finding this rare glow-worm, no matter how long it took or how many graves I had to dig up.

"As you said, sir, .'You must do what your master orders'. From then on I went out to dig in graves and finally in the seventeenth grave found the insect. You dry it, grind it into powder and sprinkle it in tea or rice. The eater will then die of a heart attack, leaving no mark except a red spot between the eyebrows. It is a very potent poison. Later I heard that Zhang Youdao had died. That is the whole truth. Please help me, Your Honour."

Prefect Bao ordered You the Dog to sign the confession and issued a warrant for the arrest of Chen the Landlord.

"When he arrives," he said, "you will confront him and I will help you."

Meanwhile Prefect Bao summoned Mrs Zhang, the old mother of You the Dog, and his wife. The landlord arrived in court; his fetters were removed and Prefect Bao asked why he had murdered Zhang Youdao.

The frightened Chen denied all knowledge of the murder but when You the Dog was summoned Chen trembled with fear. "It's true I slept with Mrs Zhang but I did not murder her husband," he protested.

Prefect Bao ordered the instruments of torture to be brought in, which terrified the landlord.

"I confess, I confess," he babbled and related how he gave the ground-up glowworm to Zhang's wife, telling her what to do.

Prefect Bao made him sign the confession and then Mrs Zhang was brought into the courtroom. At first she still looked smug but as soon as she caught sight of Landlord Chen she dropped to her knees.

"We thought no one would find out the dreadful secret," the landlord said weeping, "but who could imagine that the ghost of your husband would rise and appeal to His Honour. I have signed a confession and you had better do the same, if you do not want to be tortured."

"Bane of my life. You good-for-nothing milksop," screeched the woman, "now that you have confessed, how can I get out of it? It is true I murdered my husband and then falsely charged his brother with taking liberties with me."

Prefect Bao ordered her to put her fingerprint on the confession, and then had You the Dog's wife and mother brought into the court. The old lady pleaded they had no one but him to support them and the landlord had promised them a six-*mu* field. She produced a piece of paper from her sleeve and Prefect Bao recognised the handwriting of Gongsun Ce. He smiled to himself: "I feel I must help them to get his promise fulfilled." He turned to Chen: "You promised them a field. Why haven't you done it yet?"

Landlord Chen had no choice but to comply and when Bao asked him how he had known about the lethal "Corpse Tortoise", he said that he had learned of it from a family tutor.

The tutor was summoned to the court and asked why he told Chen about the poison.

"I often study medicinal herbs," the tutor answered. "When chatting about poisons one rainy day, I mentioned that the most poisonous was the Corpse Tortoise. I did not think my master would use it."

Prefect Bao nodded and said: "Though there was no evil intent, you are not supposed to converse with immoral persons about poisons. You should therefore be punished lightly to prevent your doing it again."

The tutor was exiled to his native place. Mrs Zhang, the adulteress, was sentenced to be sliced to death and her lover beheaded. You the Dog was to be hanged and the plaintiff, the brother of the murdered man, was cleared of any crime.

After the trial, Prefect Bao went back to his study to write a memorandum to the throne and asked Gongsun Ce to make a fair copy. Just as the latter finished copying it, Bao Xing, the page, brought him another sheet of paper.

"His Honour wants you to copy this and put it in the memorandum," he said. "He'll present them to the throne tomorrow morning."

Looking at the second piece of paper Gongsun Ce was thrown into a panic. After a pause he asked: "Do I have to just make a simple copy of it?"

"Of course. It was written by him and he wants you to make a fair copy."

Gongsun Ce was very uneasy because the insert said that the emperor was not wise in entrusting a relative of the imperial concubine with the administration of the famine relief fund in Chenzhou. It suggested that the right person for this task had not been selected. No wonder Gongsun Ce was worried about such critical remarks.

"I'll do as I'm bidden," he said to himself. "But after the memorandum is presented to the throne tomorrow, the prefect will have to resign. It's just my bad luck that I will be linked to such a matter. I will have to await the outcome."

At the fifth watch the next day Prefect Bao came to the imperial court. His memorandum was taken to the throne by the old eunuch Chen Lin. After a long while Prefect Bao was received in audience. At first the emperor had been displeased when he read the memorandum but then realised that Prefect Bao was only being outspoken and loyal to the state, so his anger turned to joy and he granted him an audience where he conferred the title of scholar of the Longtu Academy on him, in addition to his post as prefect of Kaifeng. He also ordered him to go to Chenzhou to find out how the work to relieve the distress of the people there had gone and how they fared now.

Instead of expressing his gratitude, Prefect Bao knelt and said: "I'm not powerful enough to make other officials submit. I will have great difficulty in carrying out Your Majesty's decree."

The emperor said he would give him three letters of accreditation and assured him that no one would dare to refuse to submit.

Prefect Bao expressed his gratitude and left.

Meanwhile, Gongsun Ce was on tenterhooks, thinking he might as well pack his belongings and leave, but thought that his departure would be taken in the wrong way and so decided to stay. He heard a great commotion outside and was alarmed until Bao Xing came and told him of Prefect Bao's double preferment, at which Gongsun Ce's spirits rose and the two of them handsomely rewarded the messengers who had brought the good news.

When Prefect Bao finally returned everyone kowtowed and congratulated him on his promotion.

"His Majesty has given me three letters," Prefect Bao said to Gongsun Ce. "Please read them carefully and tell me what you think."

Gongsun Ce was puzzled. He thought Prefect Bao had presented him with a catch question, and whatever he commented on the imperial letters would be used to dismiss him. So he wrote an ambiguous commentary. The Chinese word for "letter" sounds like the word for "axe", so he wrote a piece describing three axes — one shaped like a dragon, one like a tiger, the third like a dog — and how to make them. He thought Prefect Bao would be angry, but on the contrary the latter beamed with pleasure and said: "You really are a man of many talents." He at once had carpenters brought in and told Gongsun Ce to instruct them how to make detailed models of three axes that very day, to be shown to the emperor on the morrow.

Dumbfounded, Gongsun Ce added a grotesque monster's head to the handle of each axe before showing the craftsmen how to make them.

That night Prefect Bao examined the finished models and had them put in fancy yellow boxes which were taken to the court for the emperor to look at.

When Bao Zheng appeared before the emperor he reminded the ruler that he had favoured him with three "axes", and here were models which he wanted the emperor to see before he had the real ones made.

He explained their projected use: "Any official who commits a crime will be executed with them according to his rank."

The emperor comprehended that he had taken the character "letter" for "axe" and had made the three models to suppress criminal officials outside the capital. He commended his good idea and said: "You need no further instructions. After these imperial instruments of punishment have been made, start for Chenzhou as soon as possible."

Prefect Bao left the imperial court in a palanquin. In the street ten old men knelt before it with a petition, but after glancing at it, Prefect Bao tore it into shreds and threw the pieces on the ground.

"They are crafty people," he said. "How could such a thing happen? Tell the local bailiff to march them out lest they stir up trouble in the city."

With that he ordered the bearers to get going. The old men wailed: "We came a long way to the capital to pour out our grievances. We did not think that this official, too, would be afraid of his influential superior. It seems we can't find anywhere to appeal."

The bailiff told them not to cause trouble. "It's no use crying," he said. "People are wronged and sentenced to death everywhere."

Many onlookers followed them out of the city. Just outside the walls, a man on horseback galloped up.

"Since you've brought them this far," he told the bailiff, "I'll take over from here. You may go."

The bailiff left. The man on horseback was none other than Bao Xing, the prefect's loyal page, who took the old men to a secluded spot and said: "His Honour did not grant your petition because there were too many onlookers. He suggests you stay in an out-of-the-way place and when he sets off on his journey, you may accompany us. Two of your elders must come with me now so that he can ask questions."

The two elders told Prefect Bao that their petition had come from thirteen families, some of whom had been imprisoned.

In the meantime, Gongsun Ce was supervising the making of the awe-inspiring imperial executioner's axes. The four warriors, Wang Chao, Ma Han, Zhang Long and Zhao Hu were to handle them, and Gongsun Ce gave them detailed instructions on how they were to be used.

When the awesome axes had been made, Prefect Bao had them displayed to court officials. The steel was so bright and cold that it struck terror into all who saw them. Some said that all treacherous men would be scared out of their wits, but others believed that the punishment was too harsh and that Prefect Bao was heading for trouble.

When they finally set off for Chenzhou with due ceremony, the old petitioners secretly accompanied them.

When the party reached the town of Three Stars, they found it very quiet. "The local official governs the town very well," thought Prefect Bao. But all too soon, he heard someone calling out complaints and when he got off his horse to investigate, he found a woman kneeling in a hollow willow tree by the road, holding an appeal. He looked at it and asked the woman: "The appeal says that you are the only one left in your family. So who wrote it?"

"Since childhood I've read books," replied the woman. "My father and brother were senior licentiates, and my husband a licentiate too. As for me, I love writing."

Prefect Bao told Bao Xing to give her paper, ink, brush and inkstone and bade her write another document on the spot. She did it and presented it to him. Reading it, Prefect Bao nodded.

"Please go and await my summons. When I return to the residence, I'll examine the case," he said.

She kowtowed and thanked the prefect, who continued his journey.

CHAPTER 10

A Student Buys a Pig's Head and Meets with a Mishap.
In the Guise of a Beggar the Bold Man Catches a Thief.

THE woman at Three Stars Town was named Mrs Han. Her husband died when their only son, Ruilong, was sixteen. They lived in three rented rooms in Bai Family Village and were very poor. Mrs Han earned her living by sewing and taught her son to read. He studied in the east room and she worked in the west.

One night Ruilong was reading in his room when he saw the curtain on the door of the west room move and a woman in an onion green jacket and red slippers going in. He quickly followed her but only found his mother sitting alone sewing by the lamp.

She asked him whether he had finished his study for the night. "I've come for a book to look up a literary anecdote," he replied.

He went to the bookcase and quietly looked around, but saw nothing suspicious. Puzzled, he took a book and left the room. He thought a thief might have hidden in a dark corner, but Ruilong did not want to alarm his mother. He did not sleep a wink that night and the following night, while he was reading quite late, he saw the curtain on the door of his mother's room move again. The same woman, in green jacket and red slippers, slipped in. Ruilong rushed after her, shouting. Startled, his mother scolded him: "What are you so nervous about? You should be studying."

He hesitated for a moment and then told her what he had seen.

"We'd better search the room," his mother replied, taking the lamp. Her son peered under the bed and called out: "Mother, why is the earth under the bed higher than the rest of the floor?"

They examined it and found it was sandy soil and when they moved the bed away and removed the soil, they found a box. They prised open the lid.

The box was full of gold and silver. Ruilong was overjoyed. "Perhaps the treasure is looking for us," he remarked.

"Nonsense," said his mother. "It must be someone's ill-gotten gains. We should not touch it."

In their poverty, how could the young man not be tempted by the sight of so much wealth?

"Mother," he pleaded, "since ancient times many, many people have profited from finding treasure in the ground. Furthermore, we did not steal it, nor are we picking up what other people have lost. Why should it be called ill-gotten gains? Surely it was Heaven feeling pity for our miserable state which has helped us to unearth the gold and silver. Please think about it."

His mother was finally persuaded and suggested that to express their gratitude they should buy some sacrificial offerings to the god the next morning.

Delighted, Ruilong covered up the treasure with the soil and moved back the bed. He spent the night indulging in wild flights of fancy before finally falling asleep. He woke up with a start just as the sky was getting light. He got up and told his mother he was going to buy the sacrificial offerings.

It was very early and the moon was still shining, so he took his time. When he came to Zheng the butcher's shop, he saw a light and knocked at the door to buy a pig's head. The light suddenly went out and there was silence. He decided to turn back but after a few paces he heard the creak of the door opening and a voice saying: "Who wants a pig's head?"

"I'd like to buy one on credit," replied Ruilong.

"It's you, young master Han," said the butcher. "Why didn't

you bring something to carry it in?"

"I forgot," said Ruilong.

"No matter," answered the butcher, "I'll wrap the head in a piece of cloth and you can return it tomorrow."

The pig's head was very heavy and after a while Ruilong put the bundle down on the ground to catch his breath. Two night watchmen were walking towards him and noticed the bloodstained bundle and his panting aroused their suspicion.

He was still out of breath and couldn't speak clearly, so one of the watchmen untied the bundle. In the dim light they saw, instead of a pig's head, a woman's head covered with blood-matted hair. Ruilong was terrified and before he could make any explanations he was marched off to the yamen of Yexian County.

Because it was a murder case, the magistrate immediately convened the court and Ruilong was brought in. Instead of a bloodthirsty-looking murderer, the magistrate saw a mere delicate student.

When questioned, Ruilong told his story and then burst into tears. The magistrate issued a warrant for the arrest of Butcher Zheng who vehemently denied any knowledge of the woman's head or that Ruilong had been to his shop to buy a pig's head. When questioned about the ownership of the cloth, he said that the young man had borrowed it three days before.

The poor student was no match for the ruthless butcher but fortunately the magistrate could see he did not look like a murderer and he was not tortured. Instead he put them both into prison until he could think of a solution.

This was the chain of events about which Mrs Han had written the appeal which she presented to Prefect Bao as he arrived at the town. The prefect agreed to look into the affair. The magistrate waited for him outside his official residence and together they discussed the case.

Ruilong was ordered to appear first and with a tearful face he knelt down trembling and repeated his story of buying a pig's head. When the student was asked why he had gone to the butcher's at such an early hour, he had to confess about finding the treasure.

Prefect Bao nodded and thought that the boy from a poor family might be greedy but he did not look a murderer. He ordered his men to take him away and told the magistrate to send his men to look for the treasure chest. Butcher Zheng was then brought in and Prefect Bao could see by his ferocious features that he was a bad lot. Zheng stuck to his original story. The prefect flew into a fury and ordered that he be given twenty slaps in the face and flogged thirty strokes. The villain, however, still did not confess.

When the magistrate returned from Ruilong's home he reported that when they opened the chest it was only full of gold and silver paper offerings to the dead, but on searching deeper, they discovered the body of a man without a head.

"What was the cause of his death?" Bao Zheng asked the magistrate.

The magistrate was dumbfounded. "At the sight of a body with its head missing, I did not examine any other cause of death," he said. "It is very remiss of me, very remiss."

He was told to go away.

The magistrate in a cold sweat hurried out. "How strict the Imperial Commissioner is!" he said to himself. "I must be more careful next time."

Prefect Bao questioned Ruilong again, asking if the house they lived in had been left by his ancestors or built by themselves.

"No, we rent it," replied the student.

"Who had it before you?" asked the prefect.

Ruilong did not know and he and the butcher were returned to the prison while Bao Zheng adjourned the court and discussed the case with Gongsun Ce. Gongsun Ce wanted to disguise himself once more to investigate but the prefect shook his head. "That ruse may have worked in the last case but not likely for this one," he said.

Gongsun Ce went and talked with the four warriors but none could give a definite opinion and he returned to his own room.

One of the warriors, Zhao Hu, said to the other three: "Since we came to the Kaifeng office we haven't performed any service. Now the prefect has encountered a difficulty, we should try to help. I'll go out secretly and try and find some clues."

The others mocked him: "Brother, it needs care and vigilance. How can a rough fellow like you manage? You'll become a laughing stock."

Mortified, he went to his room where his attendant, who had a ready wit, said: "As the other three have no faith in you, why not change your looks so that no one can recognise you and search for clues. If you succeed you can take credit for it. If you don't, no one will know and you won't lose face."

Zhao Hu was overjoyed and told him to make preparations.

His attendant went out and after some time returned, saying: "I've taken a great deal of trouble to gather these things, fourth lord. They cost sixteen and a half taels of silver."

"I don't care about the expense, just as long as we get on with the business," rejoined Zhao Hu.

His servant untied a bundle and pulled out some ragged clothes and helped him to put them on. Then he smeared soot on Zhao's face and took two plasters which he had dyed red and green to look as if they were blood and pus and stuck them on his master's legs. He gave him a yellow earthen jar and a stick so that the tough warrior looked like a beggar wearing a variegated patchwork of clothes. His get-up looked more as if they were worth thirty-six copper cash and not the sixteen and a half taels of silver which he had been charged, but he didn't care — he had plenty of money.

His servant promised to wait for him until the first watch and Zhao Hu left for the village carrying his jar and stick. As he walked along, he felt something prick his foot and he sat down on a rock by a temple and removed his shoe to find he had trodden on a nail. He banged it on the rock and the noise disturbed a monk who thought someone was knocking at the door. When he opened it he found a beggar who shouted at him: "Hey, monk, do you know where the body of a woman and the head of a man are?"

The monk thought he was a madman and shut the door.

Zhao Hu realised his mistake and said to himself: "I am supposed to be disguised as a beggar and therefore should be begging for alms." He then cried out: "Charity, if you please! Give me a bowl or half a bowl of liquor, any kind will do."

At the beginning, it was a novelty pretending to be a beggar, but when no one paid any attention to him he began to worry.

"I'll never find a clue this way," he thought.

It was getting dark. It was the fifteenth of the lunar month and the full moon was rising from the east. As he walked towards the village he caught sight of a shadow leaping over a wall.

He decided to follow it, saying to himself: "Does a beggar have a conscience? If he doesn't he'd steal but if he had a conscience he wouldn't become a beggar." So he put down his jar and stick, flung off his worn-out old shoes and leapt barefoot onto the wall. Looking down he saw a man hiding by a stack of straw. Jumping beside him, he pinned him down.

"Don't make a sound," Zhao Hu said, "or I'll strangle you."

"Spare me, lord," the man begged. "My name is Ye Qianer. I have an old mother of eighty and cannot support her. This is the first time I have tried to steal."

Zhao was in doubt and looked around. He spotted a strip of white silk sticking out of the ground and gave it a tug. The more he pulled the longer it grew. Finally he gave the silk a yank and saw at the other end the tiny bound feet of a woman and as he pulled more her headless corpse emerged from the loose earth.

He glared at his terrified captive who confessed he was a thief but not a murderer. Zhao tied and gagged him with the strip of white silk and raced off to report to Prefect Bao. Still dressed in beggar garb, he had great difficulty in convincing the guards who he really was but finally, to great laughter from everyone including Prefect Bao, he was able to tell his story.

Prefect Bao was overjoyed and made plans to solve the case of the headless corpse.

CHAPTER 11

Prefect Bao Winds Up the Case.
A Hero Dispenses Silver.

PREFECT Bao dispatched policemen to watch over the corpse and to escort the thief Ye Qianer to the residence.

Zhao Hu was so pleased with his success that he rewarded his servant with ten taels of silver.

In court, the policemen brought in the thief who explained that it was the first time he had tried to steal: he was so desperate to support his aged mother. He denied murdering the woman and Prefect Bao ordered he be given twenty strokes. Although he was in pain, Ye Qianer only groaned saying: "I've really been unlucky this time and last time..."

Prefect Bao quickly seized on this and after being threatened with more punishment, the thief began his confession.

"In the Bai Family Village there is a rich squire named Bai Xiong. On his birthday I went to help with the dinner party, hoping to get a tip or some leftovers, but his steward Bai An was even more mean than his master and gave me neither money nor food. So I decided that night to rob him."

"You just said that you had only stolen once," Prefect Bao interrupted.

"Yes... Well, it's the first time I stole from the Bai's," the thief answered. "I knew the squire's concubine, Yurui, had many chests of valuables in her quarters, so I sneaked in and hid. I heard someone tapping at the door. Yurui opened it to the steward Bai An and they went to bed. When they eventually fell asleep, I opened one of the chests and took out a box and returned home but when I opened the box I found a head. That's why I said I had been unlucky both times."

"Was it a man's or woman's head?" asked Bao.

"It' was a man's head," he replied.

When the thief was asked what he had done with it, he replied: "I threw the head into the house of an old man called Qiu Feng, who had walloped me for stealing his pumpkin."

"So this is the third time you have stolen," said Prefect Bao.

"But the first time was to steal a pumpkin," the thief quibbled.

The prefect issued writs to apprehend Bai An, the steward, and Qiu Feng, the pumpkin owner. Ye Qianer, the thief, was put into a cell.

The next morning, the policemen who had been ordered to keep watch over the headless woman's body reported that the spot where the corpse had been buried was in the back garden of Butcher Zheng's house. The butcher, brought back before the prefect and faced with these facts, said that on the night in question he was about to slaughter a pig when he heard a knocking on the door. When he opened it he found a young girl who said she had been kidnapped and sold to a brothel. The son of the rich and powerful governor had promised to redeem her if she promised to become his concubine. She pretended to agree but got him drunk and ran away.

"She was so pretty and her head was covered with pearls and gems that I was overcome with lust," said the butcher. "But she spurned me. I picked up a knife to threaten her but in the struggle I cut her head off. I buried the body in the back and as I was taking off the jewels from her head the student Ruilong knocked at the door asking for a pig's head. So in a panic I wrapped the head in a cloth and gave it to him. When he left I felt a bit conscience-stricken but thought he would throw it away and so solve the problem for both of us."

The butcher was ordered to sign the confession and he was taken away while Qiu Feng the pumpkin owner was brought into court.

Qiu Feng admitted he had found the head of a man and in a fright had told his farmhand to bury it, who would only do so if he paid him one hundred taels of silver. They had in the end agreed on fifty.

Qiu Feng was sent back under escort to retrieve the head and the third accused, the steward Bai An, was brought in. He was a good-looking fellow dressed in flamboyant attire.

Bai An said his master treated him like his own son, which put Prefect Bao in a fury.

"What an incestuous dog!" he said, striking his gavel hard on the table. "Since your master treats you so well, why have you committed adultery with his concubine?"

Bai An denied the accusation but when Ye Qianer was brought back into court and confronted him with what he had seen, he turned pale and crawled forward on his hands and knees.

"The head belonged to a cousin of my master called Li. My master had borrowed five hundred taels of silver from him. When the cousin demanded the return of the loan, my master plied him with drink and Li, in a drunken state, said he had met an eccentric monk called Tao Rangong, who foretold Li would have bad luck. He gave him a Wandering Fairy Pillow and told him to give it to an upright prime minister. Li, not knowing much about the matter, asked my master for advice. Li said the pillow had magical properties, that inside there were magnificent gardens, jade palaces, exotic flowers and grasses. My master coveted this pillow, killed Li and told me to bury him in the storehouse. I decided to cut off the head and preserve it in the concubine's room, to use as blackmail if our affair was ever discovered. I never thought it would be stolen."

The steward said the rooms where the body was buried had become haunted, so they rented them out to Mrs Han and her son Ruilong. He signed his confession and Prefect Bao ordered the arrest of the squire Bai Xiong.

Meanwhile, the magistrate who had escorted Qiu Feng, the pumpkin grower, returned to report his findings. They had found another corpse as well as the head of Li, the squire's cousin.

The third corpse turned out to be a cousin of the farmhand who had buried Li's head. The cousin had followed him and when he demanded forty-five of the fifty taels of silver he had squeezed out of the pumpkin grower, he had killed him with his spade. The farmhand was ordered to sign his confession and he was led away.

The squire Bai Xiong next appeared in the court and admitted everything his steward had recounted. He relinquished the Wandering Fairy Pillow to Prefect Bao.

Finally the prefect announced his verdicts. The butcher, the squire and the farmhand were sentenced to death. The old pumpkin farmer was sentenced to hard labour for bribing his farmhand to bury the head. Yurui the concubine was sold into slavery. As for the student Ruilong, he had been greedy and disobeyed his mother but because of his youth and ignorance he was allowed to return home and show filial obedience to his mother by working hard. She was given twenty taels of silver by the magistrate as an official testimonial to her great pains in educating her son. As for the magistrate himself, Prefect Bao was well pleased with his conduct after the one careless slip over the discovery of the first corpse, and he was allowed to keep his office.

The news of the judgement of this complicated case spread far and wide and enhanced the reputation of Prefect Bao. He then left for Chenzhou to oversee how the famine relief fund was progressing.

Let us turn now to the hero warrior, Zhan Zhao. When he parted from Bao Zheng at the Earth Dragon Crag after coming to his rescue several times, Zhan Zhao decided to go home to see his mother before any further heroic exploits. Luckily he had left her in the tender care of an old servant who was an honest and upright old man. Zhan Zhao carried out his filial duties punctiliously, making sure she was comfortable and happy. But one day she became ill and despite medical treatment died. He went into deep mourning for a hundred days before leaving the old servant to take care of the estate while he travelled about giving help to those in need.

One day he saw a crowd of refugees carrying their children and wailing out loud. He distributed silver among them and asked where they had come from.

"Better not ask, young man. It's too painful to relate," they told him. "We're from Chenzhou, fleeing from the famine there despite the fact that the son of Grand Tutor Pang has been ordered to dispense relief. Who would have imagined that he would spend the funds to build a luxury garden for himself and use it to despoil women. The prettiest ones become his concubines and the other women become servants. We are fleeing to another place to look for a better life." With this they continued on their way, weeping and wailing.

Zhan Zhao decided that as he had nothing particular to do, he might as well go to Chenzhou and have a look.

On his way he saw a woman weeping by a grave and wanted to find out more about her. But good manners prevented him from appearing too bold in accosting the woman. Instead, he found a piece of paper money and handed it to her suggesting she burn it as an offering to the dead.

"Why are you crying here all alone?" he asked, emboldened by her acceptance.

"Our family used to live well before," she replied. "Now I am left alone, how can I hold back my tears?"

"Has your whole family suffered?" he asked.

"If they were all dead, I would have no illusions," she continued. "But what is so distressing is I can neither live nor die."

Unable to understand her meaning, Zhan Zhao grew impatient

and asked that she tell him everything.

Because he was dressed in warrior's clothes she knew he must be of good character and related how her master, Tian Qiyuan, and her mistress had been persecuted and were in prison and that her husband had gone to the capital to seek justice and hadn't been heard of since.

Zhan Zhao felt very sorry for her. "Weep no more, auntie," he said. "Your master Tian is a close friend of mine." He gave her ten taels of silver and made his way to the garden of the dastardly son of the imperial tutor, Pang Yu.

CHAPTER 12

The Hero Changes the Sex-Arousing Potion. The Treacherous Marquis Pang Sets a Trap in the Soft Red Hall.

WHEN Zhan Zhao reached the imperial garden, he saw a sweep of newly whitewashed wall, behind which hall upon hall went off into the distance. He paced off an area from the wall and then rented a house nearby. At the second watch he changed into his black suit, blew out the lamp and remained still.

When all was quiet, he silently opened the door and sprang up to the roof of the house. He was carrying a rope with a steel claw, and knowing how far he needed to throw it to reach the wall of the garden, he was able to climb onto the top. There he lay prone and threw down a pebble on the other side to make sure there was no ditch or water or any other obstacle below. He then climbed down and jerking the claw and rope off the wall, put them into his bag. He walked on tiptoe, like a crane, towards a light coming from a building and saw the shadows of a man and woman drinking at the window. He heard the man say: "You may drink from this jar, darling, but not from that one, because that is a sex-arousing potion and if a woman drinks it, her sexual desires are aroused to fever pitch. The marquis has kidnapped a woman called Jade Goddess but she won't yield to him so I have made up a powder to mix with wine and when she drinks it, she won't be able to resist his advances. I've told him to pay me three hundred taels for it, even though it only costs ten taels to make up. How can I make my fortune otherwise?"

His wife sounded uneasy. "There's nothing wrong with trying to make your fortune but not at the expense of a woman's chastity."

The man laughed out loud.

Light appeared in the garden and a servant of the marquis arrived to escort the husband with the potion to his quarters.

The husband told the wife to lie low in the other room and left.

Zhan Zhao emerged from his hiding place and entered the room. He quickly changed over the wine from the jade bottle to the red jar, then slipped out again.

The wife was upset over her husband's knavery and she came back into the room and helped herself to some wine from the red jar. No sooner had she drunk it than she became flushed with desire, and when another servant of the marquis came with the three hundred taels of silver she would not let him leave. Fortunately her husband returned just in time and the highly embarrassed servant took to his heels.

His wife sat on the bed as if in a trance. He stared at her and with a start she came to and accused him of having designs on other people's wives yet neglecting her.

He took a gulp of wine from the jar and from the immediate symptoms he realised they had drunk the love potion. They quickly drank water to weaken the effects.

"Well, well," he said, "Buddha bless me. I nearly became a cuckold. But how did the wine get into that jar?."

His wife did not take the situation so lightly. "Due to your evil intentions, it nearly rebounded on us," she sobbed. "This proves that god's law is manifest and you can never escape retribution."

They decided to return home the following morning.

After switching the wine over, Zhan Zhao followed the husband and the servant to the Soft Red Hall where a maidservant was ordered to light the lantern and take the jade bottle to the Building of Beauty and Fragrance. He tiptoed to an incense-burning tripod and took a handful of ashes. He found a fly whisk behind a flower vase and stuck it behind his neck and then hid behind a portiere, where he could hear women talking.

"Because we were also kidnapped, we tried to resist him at first but we had no alternative and had to yield to his desires. Actually it's not too bad, we have delicious food and good wine..."

Another woman butted in: "You are worthless hussies, I would rather die than yield to him." She burst into tears.

The marquis, Pang Yu, entered and smilingly asked the women if they had managed to persuade his new acquisition to yield to him. "Never mind," he said, "if she drinks this cup of wine with me, I will let her go."

Jade Goddess snatched the cup and dashed it to the floor. Pang Yu became angry and told the other women to beat her up. Footsteps sounded outside and a maidservant announced that the governor had arrived with an urgent message.

"It must be urgent," thought Pang Yu, "for the governor to come so late at night." He left and as he started to descend the stairs, he felt something fluffy brushing his face and a cloud of dust hitting the back of his head. He stumbled and rolled down the staircase.

"Gracious me," exclaimed Pang Yu, "what on earth was that fluffy thing?"

The maids held up the lanterns and found that they were all covered in incense ash.

"Dreadful, dreadful!" he cried. "The fox fairy must have been angry with us."

They hurried on to the Soft Red Hall where Governor Jiang Wan was waiting in great excitement.

Zhan Zhao listened by the window, and heard the governor say: "Your humble servant was informed this morning that His Majesty has dispatched the great scholar of the Longtu Academy, Prefect Bao, to check the famine relief fund. He will be here in five days. I hope you are prepared."

"Prefect Bao is a protégé of my father," answered Pang Yu.

"He won't dare to stand up against me."

"My Lord, don't be so sure," answered the governor. "Prefect Bao is a man of high principle and impartiality. He has never been swayed by the powerful and influential. What is more, he has three imperial axes, sanctioned by His Majesty."

He stepped close to Pang Yu and whispered: "Do you imagine that he doesn't know what you have been up to?"

Though nervous, the marquis put on an air of bravado: "So what?"

"We have to be careful," rejoined the governor. "If he were dead, that would be the end of it."

The innuendo prompted the marquis to come up with the idea of finding someone who could assassinate the prefect.

"I have a bold fellow called Xiang Fu. He's skilled in leaping onto roofs and jumping over walls. I'll send him on two or three stations ahead to do the deed."

"Excellent," the governor sighed. "But be quick about it."

The would-be assassin was sent for. Zhan Zhao peeped in through the window. Sure enough, he was a man of powerful build and looked very impressive. It was a pity he had joined the wrong master.

When asked if he was prepared to kill someone, Xiang Fu replied: "I will go through fire and water, to say nothing of assassination."

"He seems an impudent toady," thought Zhan Zhao. "What a pity he looks so strong."

Xiang Fu was led away by the governor, after being sworn to secrecy by the marquis.

As they left, Xiang Fu's hat fell off several paces behind them and he went to retrieve it. The governor was mystified as to why it should fall off so far away. "It must have caught on the branch of a tree," replied Xiang Fu.

It happened again but when they looked round there was not a soul to be seen. The governor got into his sedan chair, Xiang Fu mounted his horse and they proceeded to the governor's office.

It was Zhan Zhao who had snatched the cap, testing the assassin's skills. The fact that he did not look more closely to see why his hat fell off twice convinced Zhan Zhao that he was not as vigilant or skilful as he had thought and he need not worry too much about him. He returned to his lodgings to plan his next move.

CHAPTER 13

Sleek Rat Helps an Old Man.
The Two Heroes Share the Spoils.

IT was very late when Zhan Zhao reached his lodgings. He took off his black suit and went to bed. The next day he went and kept watch at the governor's residence. Before the screen wall in front of a gate was tethered a black horse. Across the saddle was slung a bag of money. A groom, whip in hand, sat by the horse. Before long Xiang Fu emerged from the governor's residence, mounted the horse and galloped away. Zhan Zhao followed.

They reached a town called Anping and Xiang Fu went into a restaurant. He sat on the south side and Zhan Zhao sat on the north side, watching him. A handsome young warrior entered the room, and Zhan Zhao could not help putting his wine cup down in admiration. When he sat down, Xiang Fu hastened forward and bowed.

"Brother Bai," he said, "I haven't seen you for a long time."

"Yes, it's been ages," replied the young warrior. "What luck to meet you here."

Zhan Zhao was upset to see such a fine young man friendly with Xiang Fu.

The two men chatted, catching up on their news. The young warrior was called Bai Yutang, known as Sleek Rat, and was one of the five sworn brothers from Hollow Island. Unfortunately his elder brother had died. Xiang Fu mentioned that the brother had also been his benefactor. Sleek Rat's elder brother had helped him escape when he accidentally killed someone during a brawl. He was on his way to the capital when he met the wastrel marquis Pang Yu, and had been recruited by him. Xiang Fu had thought himself indeed fortunate to be in the employ of the marquis, even though it turned him into a worthless person.

As they continued talking, an old man dressed in rags came up the stairs. He rushed towards a stern-looking man sitting in the west corner, dropped to his knees and with tears running down his face, begged for merey. But the man coldly shook his head. Sleek Rat asked what all the fuss was about and the old man, seeing a well-dressed warrior, answered: "I borrowed some money from this landlord and he took my little daughter."

Sleek Rat angrily asked how much was owed and the landlord answered: "I lent him five taels of silver three years ago and now with interest he owes me thirty-five taels."

"That is not a lot of money," said Bai and he instructed his attendant to give the landlord the money in exchange for the IOU.

"From now on, the old man owes you nothing," he said, and went back to join Xiang Fu.

As the old man started to leave, Zhan Zhao caught hold of his sleeve and invited him to have a cup of wine with him and drew out information about the usurious landlord. He was called Miao and ran the Miao Family Fair. His son was a clerk in the governor's office and the landlord used his son's position to exploit his neighbours, lending money at exorbitant rates.

The other two men continued eating, drinking and chatting, but when Sleek Rat heard that Xiang Fu was in the service of Marquis Pang his face went red with anger. He called for his attendant to pay the bill and left without ceremony.

"That's more like it," thought Zhan Zhao. "As Prefect Bao isn't expected in Tianchang for several days, I might as well go to the Miao Family Fair and take a look." Although a native of the south, he was at home wherever he went, and whenever he came across any injustice, he could not let it pass — the true mark of a hero.

Later that night, he changed into his black clothes and got into the Miao family home. As usual his skills at leaping over roofs and walls came in useful. He saw a man in the reception room and tiptoed over to hear what he was saying. It was the landlord Miao speaking to his son, Hengyi.

"I made a little fortune today of thirty-five taels of silver." He told him about his encounter in the restaurant.

"And I've made three hundred taels without spending a penny," replied his son. He explained to his father: "After the governor sent Xiang Fu to Tianchang he suggested to the marquis that if the assassination plan did not work out, he should go in disguise to the mansion of the grand tutor and find out what Prefect Bao reported to the emperor. In the meantime all the gold and jewels he had acquired through milking the famine relief fund, and the women, including Jade Goddess, could be taken to the capital by boat. The governor gave me three hundred taels of silver to make the arrangements. But I thought why should the marquis get away with all the evil he has done. So I told the boatmen that they would be paid once they got to the capital and that they would not lose if the marquis refused to pay, because the cargo was worth more than the fare. So I've got three hundred taels of silver for nothing."

Listening outside, Zhan Zhao said to himself: "Truly, for every wicked one there are others more wicked than him."

He caught sight of a figure dashing across the other side of the courtyard and made out that it was the young warrior he had seen earlier at the restaurant. Zhan Zhao smiled to himself: "You have come to collect by night the silver you gave during the day."

He shinned up a post, hid under the eaves and continued his watch, wondering where the other man had gone.

Suddenly a maid came into the reception room screaming: "Master, our mistress has disappeared!"

The two men hurried out and Zhan Zhao sneaked into the room, where he saw six parcels of silver and a small packet on the table. "I'll take three and leave the rest for the young warrior which he can collect with interest."

Meanwhile, Sleek Rat followed the landlord's wife to the bathroom. As her maid went to get some towels, he seized the chance to capture the wife. He cruelly cut off her ears and then thrown the bound and gagged woman into a grain bin. He went into the reception room and took the rest of the silver. He had noticed Zhan Zhao in the courtyard earlier and appreciated his thoughtfulness in leaving him his due.

Father and son found the groaning woman and they realised they had been tricked and robbed of their ill-gotten gains.

CHAPTER 14

Bao Xing Tries the Wandering Fairy Pillow.
Brave Zhao Hu and Zhang Long Capture the Evil Marquis.

AFTER the case of "The Pig's Head" had been tried, Prefect Bao's servant, Bao Xing, had time on his hands and his thoughts turned to the confiscated Wandering Fairy Pillow. He told another servant to take care of his master while he went to his own room with the pillow, put it under his head and fell asleep.

He dreamt that two servants in black helped him mount a black horse with a black saddle which then took him to what looked like the court of Kaifeng Prefecture. Over the gate was a placard inscribed with the words: "Human and Ghost Palace". A judge from Hell walked towards him.

"How dare you pretend to be the upright prime minister and come here?" he demanded and then shouted in a loud voice: "Seize him!"

A warrior dressed in gold armour appeared and gave a bellowing roar.

Bao Xing woke up in a cold sweat.

"It seems everything is predestined," he mused, "and I am not entitled to use the pillow. Only the upright prime minister can sleep on it."

Unable to sleep again, he heard the fourth watch sound and went to Prefect Bao's bedroom, where he saw the servant asleep in the chair with the wick of the candle burning long and uncut. There was a note on the table. Bao Xing took it over to Prefect Bao who woke up and called for his assistant, Gongsun Ce, to attend on him. They read the note which said: "Be on your guard against assassins when you reach the town of Tianchang. Dispatch your police to arrest the villainous marquis, Pang Yu and rescue a young lady from the convent. She is called Jade Goddess."

No one could tell how the note got there but Prefect Bao immediately ordered the police to keep their eyes open on the routes mentioned in the note.

In particular, Gongsun Ce alerted the four warriors, Wang Chao, Ma Han, Zhang Long and Zhao Hu.

It was Zhan Zhao who had left the note. When he left the Miao family's property, he hurried to Three Star Town, where the prefect was staying, and left the note before going back.

Prefect Bao and his entourage travelled to Tianchang and took up residence. Strict precautions were taken to guard him. The whole area was brilliantly lit up and the four warriors patrolled the inner courts.

After the third watch, Zhao Hu discovered a figure hiding in a big elm tree. He called his companions and they watched as the man began leaping from branch to branch and then to the roof of the main room. He was about to climb the ridge of the building, when he gave a cry and rolled down to the ground with an arrow in his leg. He was tied up and taken to Prefect Bao and Gongsun Ce who were all smiles. After congratulating them, Bao ordered that the man be untied, much to everyone's protest. Gongsun Ce asked why a would-be assassin should be untied.

Prefect Bao answered: "I am in need of able men. Why should I not recruit such a brave warrior. He must have been ordered to kill me by a low-down character."

The assassin who, of course, was Xiang Fu, was helped to a chair and his wound attended to. Finding himself surrounded by such spirited men, he felt conscience-stricken and thought: "It's true Prefect Bao is of man of high integrity and recognises the worth of a hero."

He prostrated himself and said: "This worthless person has offended Your Excellency, the Imperial Commissioner. I deserve to be sentenced to death."

He then told the whole story of how he had been ordered by Pang Yu, the marquis, to assassinate him.

Prefect Bao smiled: "Owing to the great favour conferred on me by His Majesty, my reputation is spreading far and wide. I have courted many jealousies and slanders. When you are confronted with this decadent marquis, I hope you will serve as witness to this fact, in case out of fear of damaging the friendly relations with his father, the grand tutor, I suppress the truth."

He ordered Wang Chao to set him free in public and then secretly detain him again. Wang Chao showed him the arrow he had removed from the captive's leg. "It belongs to Southern Hero, Zhan Zhao," he said. "It must have been him who left the note."

The warriors were dispatched to arrest the marquis and to rescue Jade Goddess from the convent. On the way to the convent, the men saw a shabby sedan chair also going in the same direction. A man called out: "You're a bit late brother." It was Southern Hero, and in the sedan chair was Jade Goddess. Together they continued on their way to the convent, where the old woman, whom Zhan Zhao had found weeping by a grave, was waiting for her young mistress, Jade Goddess — the wife of his good friend Tian Qiyuan, who had been imprisoned by the dastardly marquis.

Zhan Zhao told the two women to seek refuge in the convent until matters were sorted out.

He then told his fellow warrior, Ma Han, to report back to Prefect Bao, saying: "Tell him it is not necessary for her to appear in court with the others, for she is a woman of virtue."

He clasped his hands respectfully and left while Ma Han and his party returned to Prefect Bao.

The other two warriors, Zhang Long and Zhao Hu, had been

dispatched to find the marquis. They saw a group of people on horseback approaching but they were too heavily disguised to make out who they really were, so while the others hid behind a tree, Zhao Hu flung himself down in front of the leading horse.

"He's been crushed to death," shouted Zhang Long emerging from behind the tree and took hold of the bridle of the marquis's horse.

His servants threatened Zhang Long saying he was preventing the passage of the son of the grand tutor, who was in disguise.

Hearing that it was the marquis, Zhao Hu sprang up from the ground, pulled him down and shackled him while the rest of his party fled. The marquis was marched off to the official residence.

CHAPTER 15

The Evil Marquis is Executed with the Dragon Axe.
Prefect Bao Meets the Real Mother of the Emperor.

TWO of the gallants escorted Marquis Pang Yu to the law court, where Prefect Bao, seeing him in chains, scolded them for their ill manners in shackling such an eminent personage.

When the police freed him, he began to kneel but Prefect Bao stopped him, saying: "Although we should not mix up personal feelings with official duties, I can't ignore the friendship between my patron, the grand tutor, and myself, his protégé. You and I were students together in the imperial examinations and have been friends for years. But because of these charges, you have to be confronted with your accusers. You must tell the truth and be sure not to cover anything up. Then we can discuss what to do next."

He ordered that the victims of the marquis and the kidnapped women be brought to the court to be questioned.

Pang Yu thought to himself: "As he looks kindly and pleasant, I may as well make a full confession and beg him to consider my father's position. Then he will have to acquit me."

"I confess to all the charges," he said. "What has been done, can't be undone and it's too late for regrets. I just hope you will give me a lenient sentence."

"Now that you've owned up to your crimes, I have another question to ask you," said Prefect Bao. "Who sent Xiang Fu here?"

Pang Yu's heart missed a beat and he replied: "He was sent here by Governor Jiang Wan. That's all I know."

Xiang Fu was brought to confront him. He looked well, unlike someone who had been kept in prison. The marquis had no choice but to admit that he had dispatched Xiang Fu to kill the prefect.

All the victims of the marquis were freed. Amidst a lot of crying and wailing, fathers claimed their daughters, brothers their sisters, husbands their wives and mothers-in-law their daughters-in-law. They stood on one side as Prefect Bao delivered his verdict.

"By rights you should be sent to the capital," he said to Pang Yu. "Tortures would be hard to avoid and if His Majesty should fly into a rage, your sentence would be severe and I would be unable to help you. It is better we settle the case here."

The still hopeful Pang Yu agreed.

Prefect Bao put on a serious expression, his eyes glaring and commanded: "Fetch the imperial implement of punishment!"

Four men carried in the dragon-headed axe and set it down in the centre of the court. Wang Chao yanked the yellow dragon-patterned cover off the brand-new axe shot with shining gold. Before the trembling marquis could utter a sound, Ma Han threw him to the floor and gagged him with a piece of wood. The four warriors removed his clothes and rolled him up in a straw mat which they bound with three circles of rope. The hefty Wang Chao gripped the handle of the axe and waited for Prefect Bao to call out: "Execute!"

With a snap Pang Yu's body was cut in half and his corpse was carried away.

Prefect Bao then ordered that Xiang Fu be brought before him.

"What crime have I committed?" he wailed, trembling like a leaf.

Lord Bao struck his gavel on the table and shouted: "How dare you come to assassinate me, the imperial commissioner and representative of the government!"

He too was stripped of his clothes, a piece of wood stuck in his mouth and rolled up in a mat. The dog-headed axe was brought in and he was also executed.

The dastardly governor, who had suggested to the marquis to have Bao assassinated hanged himself rather than be brought before the court.

"He has been let off lightly," said Prefect Bao when he heard the news.

He spoke to the former victims before they left, reminding the men of their duties to their families. Zhan Zhao's friend, Tian Qiyuan, was reunited with his wife Jade Goddess. The servant who had been arrested by the marquis when he had attempted to seek redress from higher authorities and whose wife Zhan Zhao had found weeping at the roadside, was reprimanded for not taking care of his elderly wife.

They kowtowed and left, convinced that Prefect Bao was a loyal and incorruptible official and feeling that their tribulations had been avenged.

The evil-doers' confessions and an account of the punishment inflicted on the criminals was dispatched to the emperor, including a request that the vacancy left by the disgraced governor be filled.

Soon a royal decree arrived congratulating Lord Bao on dealing with the case fairly and with justice.

Prefect Bao felt a little uneasy: "Though the emperor has shown great kindness," he mused, "that old scoundrel, Pang Ji, the grand tutor, is still there. He is bound to feel anger over his son's death and he must be scheming something by this conciliatory approach. Then when I reach the capital he will persecute me. Of that I am convinced even though I have devoted my life to the state."

He decided that he would go elsewhere and bring about some earthshaking event to rid the people of evil and thus prove his loyalty to the imperial government.

He began a new journey to an area east of Grass District Bridge. As he was being carried in his palanquin, creaking sounds were heard and the palanquin was hurriedly dropped to the ground. Bao Xing dismounted from his horse and examined the carrying poles, which he found were badly cracked. A horse was brought for the prefect but as he was about to mount, the horse reared. Luckily a servant was able to control it. Attempts to mount the horse again proved unsuccessful as it retreated, its nostrils flaring.

"I have ridden horses for many years," Prefect Bao said to himself. "Three times this horse has refused to be mounted. The first because it senses danger, the second it sees a wronged ghost and the third time perhaps it senses an assassin. There is something extremely fishy here."

The local bailiff was sent for. His name was Fan. He told the party that though the place was called Grass District Bridge, there was neither grass nor bridge; although there was a road, there was no town and no harbour.

"Is there any official residence here?" the prefect asked.

"How can there be, in such an out-of-the-way place?" answered the man.

Bao Xing thought he protested too much and was deeply suspicious.

Prefect Bao pointed with his whip at a building in the distance and asked what it was.

"It's the Monastery Flush with Heaven," the local answered. "It houses the palaces for Buddha, Lord Guan Yu and Goddess Queen Mother. Alongside stands the Hall of the Tutelary God. But as so few people come here there is only one priest to tend them."

Bao Xing rode on ahead just in case there were any crowds to disperse and to prepare the monastery for the distinguished party. He told the priest not to prepare refreshments and that after he had served the incense he should "leave our lord in peace".

After Prefect Bao burned the incense the priest took the hint and left. Bao Xing was told to bring in Bailiff Fan and warned him not to be so talkative when the prefect asked him questions but to answer straightforwardly and precisely.

When asked how many households there were in the area, Fan said: "From here to the south there is a highway, to the east of it is the Elm Forest; on the west the Yellow Earth Mound and to the north the Dilapidated Kiln. There are not more than twenty households altogether."

Prefect Bao told him to carry a long placard calling on anyone with complaints to come to the Monastery Flush with Heaven.

He went to Elm Forest first but when he asked the villagers there whether they had any complaints, he was showered with insults. "Going to law to complain is just an excuse for you to extort bribes from us. You are not fit to be the bailiff, that's the only grievance we have!"

He got the same reception when he went to the Yellow Earth Mound but when he reached the Dilapidated Kiln an old lady cried out: "I have a complaint, take me to the Monastery Flush with Heaven."

Fan only knew her as a relative of the eunuch Major-domo Qin Feng. What he did not know was that in reality she was Lady Li. After she had given birth to the emperor's son, the jealous imperial concubine Liu had substituted a dead cat for the baby and had made false accusations against Lady Li, who was ordered to commit suicide. The kind-hearted eunuch had managed to smuggle her out of the palace and taken her to safety in his own home. The bailiff's father had worked at the home of the eunuch, an honest and kind old man who took good care of Lady Li. But when the e-unuch also became a victim of palace intrigues and was killed, she lost her protector and had to leave the house. By then she had gone blind through crying over her lost baby. The bailiff's father found a dilapidated kiln and made a home for her there, not real-ising that she was the ill-starred mother of a future emperor. When he was on his death-bed the old man instructed his son, the present bailiff, to look after her. He told his son: "She was under the protection of Major-domo Qin Feng and must have a history and have seen better days."

Because he had been a good man, he had an obedient son and the bailiff Fan kept the promise he made to his father and looked after the blind old lady, treating her with respect.

Now she wanted to make a complaint. "What about?" asked Fan.

"I want to complain about a disobedient son of mine," she answered.

Fan thought she had gone senile. "How is it I have never heard of this son before?" he asked.

"My son cannot be tried by ordinary officials, only by an official of integrity," she answered. "I hear Prefect Bao is an honest and upright official and now he is here I must seize this opportunity before it is too late."

Fan held out a bamboo rod to lead her to the monastery. "Kneel when you get there, otherwise I will be flogged," prompted Fan.

When she got there, he pulled the rod to remind her to kneel but she ignored it and pulled it back instead and then said: "Please order your men to leave before I speak."

Prefect Bao complied and said: "Now tell me what is wrong."

The old lady could no longer contain herself and cried out: "Oh my dear Bao Zheng, what a miserable life I have had!"

Cold shivers went down Bao Xing's back at her audacity at calling him by his common name, and the prefect went pale.

"How dare she address His Excellency in such intimate terms?" Bao Xing wondered.

CHAPTER 16

The Faithful Scholar Pretends to Be the Wronged Consort's Son. Madam Bao Prays for Dew to Restore the Sight of the Emperor's Mother.

ALTHOUGH Prefect Bao felt his dignity was threatened by a poor woman addressing him as "dear Bao Zheng", he listened patiently as she told her sad history.

He gently asked for proof and she took out a worn and dirty package from her bosom. Bao Xing lifted his gown and told her to drop it in. Wrapped inside a yellow silk scarf was a gold ball inscribed with the characters "Crystal Jade Palace" and the name of Lady Li as the consort of the late emperor.

Prefect Bao got up from his seat and handed the package to Bao Xing, who quickly caught on and knelt down in front of her, placing the package on his head as a token of respect, before handing it back. He then led her to the seat of honour which the prefect had vacated.

"Please set your mind at ease, Your Highness," Prefect Bao assured her. "I will do all I can to repay the kindness of His Majesty. But to prevent malicious rumours, we must pretend, for the time being, that you are my mother."

She agreed.

Bao Xing arranged for a brand-new palanquin, two maids, fine clothes and jewellery for the emperor's mother and rewarded Fan the bailiff by assigning him the position of personal attendant to the old lady.

Bao Xing was then dispatched home to deliver a letter.

Prefect Bao's personal assistant, Gongsun Ce, was mystified by all the preparations and the secrecy but he did not ask any questions or mention anything to the four warriors.

Bao Xing reached the capital that very night and announced his return to Madam Bao, his master's wife. She had been in fear and trembling when she heard of Pang Yu's execution, worried that the grand tutor, his father, would have a grudge against her husband.

Bao Xing gave her the letter and she hastily tore it open. The letter instructed her to prepare a room for the empress dowager and to pretend she was her daughter-in-law.

She gave Bao Xing twenty taels of silver with instructions to make sure that her family servants worked hard.

Before Bao Xing returned to join his master, he went to see his friends to find out if the grand tutor had planned anything to revenge his son's death.

"He tried," they said, "but His Majesty was furious and made him read his son's confession. He then begged for mercy and His Majesty forgave him, but for the time being, he has to be on his guard."

In the family home, Madam Bao prepared rooms for her royal guest. The advance party announced the imminent arrival and she changed into formal dress. When the palanquin arrived in the courtyard, she removed the armrest from the chair and went down on her knees.

"May the undutiful daughter-in-law greet you here."

She helped the old lady into the Buddha Hall and served her tea and dismissed the servants. She knelt down once more and said: "The wife of your subject Bao Zheng wishes Your Royal Highness a long life." The old lady suggested she stick to mother-in-law to allay any suspicion. "We both have the same family name of Li," she said, "so I ought to treat you as my daughter."

The old lady wept as she related the injustices she had suffered. "It is because I missed my son that I became blind through crying so much," she said.

Madam Bao remembered the magic pot she had brought on her marriage and suggested that she pray that night for it to be filled with dew.

The old lady was touched by her concern, though she had little faith that it would cure her blindness. But she did not want to disappoint her and consented to the attempt.

That evening Madam Bao, holding the magic pot in her hands, burned incense and prayed to Heaven and Earth for the dew. The bottom of the pot became moist and soon dewdrops formed on the inside, gradually growing bigger and bigger until it flowed into the two holes. Overjoyed, she took the pot to the emperor's mother who dabbed her eyes with the dew. Instantly she felt a chill flowing into her lungs and a whiff of fragrance permeated between her eyebrows. She closed her eyes and felt calm and relaxed. When she opened her eyes again, the cloudiness had disappeared and they were like limpid autumn water, with the black pupils visible.

She pulled Madam Bao towards her and scrutinised her face for a moment.

"Your sincerity has healed me," she said, "and it speaks volumes for your filial piety."

The two women retired for the night and in the morning Bao Xing came back to report that Prefect Bao would be staying that night at the Monastery of the Great Chancellor and would return after he had seen the emperor.

CHAPTER 17

Homage Is Paid to Prefect Bao. The Emperor's Mother Prepares to Go to the Southern Green Palace.

AFTER recovering her sight the real empress dowager grew healthy and strong due to Madam Bao's care and nursing.

The next day, Prefect Bao was received by the emperor. Despite his wife's fears that the emperor would be angry over the execution of the marquis, he was received with great courtesy and was presented with a costume embroidered with five pythons, a belt studded with precious stones, a jade thumb ring and a pair of pouches decorated with coral beads. Prefect Bao knelt in gratitude and the courtiers treated him with even more respect, now that he had received the emperor's blessing.

Madam Bao, waiting impatiently at home, was relieved when her husband eventually arrived.

"I have to pay my respects first to the empress dowager," he said, and asked his wife to request an audience.

Madam Bao walked ahead of her husband and entered the empress dowager's apartment. "I beg to report that the great scholar of the Longtu Academy, Prefect of Kaifeng, your loyal subject, Bao Zheng, my husband, has returned from the palace."

"Come in, my son," returned the empress dowager. This was the first time since her blindness was cured that she was able to see the man who had rescued her from the Dilapidated Kiln. She saw a man with a square swarthy face and big ears, a slight moustache and bright eyes. He looked impressive and imposing and despite kneeling before her, he appeared to be taller than her. How fortunate her son, the Emperor Renzong, was to have such an able man to serve him.

The next morning, Bao Xing announced a visitor. "Major-domo Ning from the Southern Green Palace requests an interview with you."

Prefect Bao had never had much contact with palace eunuchs so he was reluctant to see him, but his wife persuaded him. "He serves the Princess Dai," she said, "and through him we can make arrangements for the empress dowager to see her." The reader will recall that when the wronged empress dowager's infant son was removed from her, the baby ended up being taken secretly to the Southern Green Palace and put in the care of Princess Dai and her husband, the loyal Eighth Prince. That infant was now the grown-up emperor.

After the formalities were over, Ning congratulated Prefect Bao over his handling of the marquis's case and how impressed Prince Liuhe — son of Princess Dai — had been. He in turn had told Princess Dai, who urged her son that he should cultivate the company of Prefect Bao and learn how to be an upright and wise prince and not disappoint the emperor.

The eunuch suggested that Prefect Bao use the opportunity of Princess Dai's birthday to meet them.

Prefect Bao debated for a while. "I've never associated myself with powerful nobles in the government, but the case of the empress dowager needs to be resolved, otherwise how can she ever be reunited with her son?"

Prefect Bao consented to send presents to Princess Dai, but as he was not a palace official, and therefore not allowed to see royalty, he would send "his mother" instead.

Bao Xing was told to prepare the birthday gifts and was again cautioned to use great secrecy, so Gongsun Ce and the four warriors were still in ignorance of the true identity of the old lady.

Eight kinds of presents were prepared, eight being an auspicious number. They included wine, candles, a peach-shaped cake and noodles, all symbolic of a long and healthy life.

Bao Xing escorted the presents to the Southern Green Palace, walking through the officials and people all waiting to present their gifts. As soon as he arrived he was escorted straight away into the palace where he was received by Prince Liuhe dressed in a gown embroidered with pythons, a belt set with jade and a gold coronet on his head, sitting on a chair surrounded by eunuchs. The prince told Bao Xing to convey his thanks to his master and his wish to see him very soon. A eunuch was told to give him fifty taels of silver for his trouble. On his way out, Bao Xing mused: "I've done rather well out of this; the presents only cost twenty taels."

Major-domo Ning followed him out of the palace and told him that the imperial consort, Princess Dai, was eager to meet Prefect Bao's "mother".

The next day, the empress dowager, dressed in the clothes of a first-ranking lady, was taken in a palanquin to the Southern Green Palace to meet the imperial concubine, Princess Dai.

CHAPTER 18

The Emperor Meets His Mother.
Prefect Bao Exposes the Conspirators.

WHEN they reached the Southern Green Palace they were met by
Major-domo Ning who escorted the old lady to meet Princess Dai.
The princess looked closely at the old woman, trying to remember
where she had seen her before and thinking how much she resembled the imperial concubine Li who had been ordered to commit
suicide. The two women took to each other immediately and the
princess insisted that she stay with her in the palace for a few
days.

"How old are you?" Princess Dai asked.

"Forty-two," she aswered.

"And your son?"

The old lady went red with embarrassment and quickly changed
the subject.

"How strange," thought Princess Dai, "she doesn't know how
old her son is. There is something very odd about this." The more
she looked at her, the more she reminded her of the imperial concubine Li, especially in her bearing and manners.

"We will share a room tonight and I'll question her more dis-
creetly," she decided.

This was what Li was hoping for and that evening as they prepared to go to bed, unable to restrain herself any longer, she

blurted out: "Don't you recognise me, sister?"

Princess Dai then knew she was the former imperial concubine Li and for the next few hours listened as she told her the whole sad story of how she had been framed by the imperial consort Liu who plotted with her chief eunuch Guo Huai and substituted a cat for her son. It was the palace maid Kou Zhu who sought the help of e- unuch Chen Lin who rescued the baby and took him to Princess Dai and her husband the Eighth Prince.

The maid, Kou Zhu, committed suicide after being tortured by Liu, who then accused her rival, Imperial Concubine Li of plot- ting against the emperor. Li was ordered to commit suicide but a- gain she was rescued when a young eunuch took her place and she was spirited away to Grass District Bridge where she spent twenty long years in misery and squalor.

Princess Dai was moved to tears and asked if she could produce any proof.

Li took out the gold ball which the old emperor had given her when he learned she was pregnant and the princess went down on her knees before her.

"How can I impart the truth to my son and reunite us?" she asked.

They decided on a plan: the princess would pretend to be ill and send Major-domo Ning to inform the emperor. "He will surely vis- it me," Princess Dai said, "and then I can reveal the whole story."

She also decided to tell Prince Liuhe.

The previous night the emperor, Renzong, dreamed an extraor- dinary dream. He saw a brightly coloured phoenix but not in full plumage. It screamed at him three times and he awoke, wondering what its significance was. In the morning, Guo Huai, the chief e- unuch of the empress dowager, hurried from the Palace of Kind- ness and Longevity to inform him that she was ill.

The emperor thought the dream must have some connection with the illness and hurried off to see her.

He walked softly into her bedroom and heard her groaning and muttering: "Kou Zhu, why are you haunting me?"

The emperor, greatly perturbed, sent for the court physician and on his way out of the royal chambers met Major-domo Ning who told him that Princess Dai was also ill.

The ruse was working exactly as planned. When he entered the Southern Green Palace, he was met by her son, Prince Liuhe, who took him to her room where he found her lying on the bed.

"Tell me," she asked, "what is of paramount importance in the world?"

"Filial piety," the emperor answered.

"So how can there be a son ignorant of whether his mother is dead or alive? Or a sovereign unaware of his mother's homelessness?"

The emperor was baffled and thought she must be delirious.

"Your subject knows the answer," she said. "But I am afraid you will not believe me."

She handed him a yellow box which held a jade seal wrapped in a scarf embroidered with dragons and written in the late emperor's hand the characters "Suppress the Dog Star" under the imperial seal.

A look of distress appeared on Major-domo Chen Lin's face as he recognised the objects and tears streamed down his face as the princess related how the eunuch Guo Huai had conspired with the imperial concubine Liu to become empress and frame the imperial concubine Li who was his real mother.

At this, an old lady appeared from behind the screen and gave him the gold ball which was identical to the one Imperial Consort Liu had. He fell on his knees before his mother, begged forgiveness for being such an unfilial son and asked how he could recompense her for all the misery she had suffered.

Li, the real empress dowager, suggested that an edict should be issued to proclaim her rightful position and the two chief eunuchs, Guo Huai and Chen Lin, should take it to the Kaifeng Prefecture. "There the scholar Bao Zheng will know what to do next," she said.

When Prefect Bao and his wife heard the news they were elated because it was exactly as they had planned and they waited for the edict to arrive.

Guo Huai took possession of the edict and walked ahead of Chen Lin because he regarded himself as the major-domo-in-chief and felt that he should personally read it out to Prefect Bao.

With great ceremony he opened it before the kneeling Prefect Bao and his four warriors and the rest of the assembled court.

"To comply with Heaven's mandate the emperor decrees: 'The eunuch Guo...'"

Seeing his own name written there he stopped, unable to go on and Chen Lin took it from him and continued reading: "'The eunuch Guo Huai schemed to overthrow the imperial government. He plotted against the empress dowager and caused the death not only of the palace maid Kou Zhu but also a young eunuch. After he admits his evil deeds he is to be tried by the Kaifeng Prefecture and if found guilty be put to death by gouging out his heart.'"

The four warriors took off Guo Huai's clothes and forced him down before the tribunal headed by Prefect Bao.

"Now confess to what you have done," he commanded.

CHAPTER 19

The Wicked Eunuch Is Sentenced to Death.
The Empress Dowager Returns to the Palace.

THE eunuch Guo Huai turned out to be a tough nut to crack. He repeatedly denied having any part in the conspiracy to depose the rightful mother of the royal heir to the throne.

"It wasn't my fault that the imperial concubine Li gave birth to a monster and made the late emperor so angry she was exiled to the deserted palace."

"Then why was the maid Kou Zhu ordered to strangle the baby and throw it into the water under the Gold Water Bridge?" demanded Chen Lin.

"You know as well as I do," retorted Guo Huai, "that if Empress Dowager Liu orders us to do her bidding, we have no choice."

At this Prefect Bao became furious. "Don't think you can intimidate me by mentioning the imperial consort's name. For that you will be flogged twenty strokes."

Guo Huai was thrown to the floor and flogged until his flesh was torn but still he did not confess but accused his fellow eunuch, Chen Lin, of causing the death of the palace maid.

"You are too tricky," Prefect Bao said and ordered that his fingers be put to the rack.

Guo Huai screamed like a pig but still would not admit his

crimes. He was returned to the prison cell while Prefect Bao retired to his office to decide on the next move.

He sent for Gongsun Ce. "This man, Guo Huai, still won't confess despite torture. Can you think of some device that will only hurt his skin and flesh but not damage his muscles and bones? Otherwise if he dies under torture without a confession the case cannot be solved satisfactorily."

Gongsun Ce went to his room and made a sketch. The instrument he drew looked like a large flat piece of iron studded with pearl-like buttons which were to be made red-hot. When a person was placed on it, it would only burn the fleshier parts of the body.

"I've called it 'Apricot Flower Raindrops'," smiled Gongsun Ce "because it leaves pink dots on the skin."

"It's a cruel instrument of punishment but has a gentle name," commented Prefect Bao. "What a clever man you are." He ordered blacksmiths to make it.

Three days went by. Guo Huai hoped that the empress dowager would learn of his fate and order his release, but then realised she was still ill. "I must grit my teeth and hold on," he thought. "Without a confession I can't be punished."

When he was brought into the courtroom again he still stubbornly stuck to his story which so enraged Prefect Bao that he was put on the red-hot "Apricot Flower Raindrops".

The heat seared his skin and gave off a smell of roast pork and after a while he became unconscious.

Gongsun Ce had anticipated this and ordered that Guo Huai be taken to the Temple of the Underworld God.

When the eunuch came to, he saw the jailer smiling with sympathy. "I'm so sorry, my lord," he said, "have some wine with this painkiller. It will help you."

Guo Huai drank the wine and medicine promising to reward the jailer when he was released.

As he drank several cups of wine, the jailer told him that Empress Dowager Liu was ill because the ghost of the palace maid

Kou Zhu would not leave her alone. "I'm sure, when she is better, she will order your release and even Prefect Bao dare not disobey," said the jailer.

Gradually Guo Huai became quite drunk and the jailer left.

After a while a chill descended on the cell and he shivered with the cold. A figure emerged from out of the gloom.

"Don't be afraid," said the apparition. "I'm the ghost of Kou Zhu. Empress Dowager Liu has admitted in the Palace of the King of Hell that you were the instigator in the conspiracy and she has been allowed back to the imperial palace with the promise that you and she will be able to live another twelve years. Please admit your part so that I can return to the human world as well."

The eunuch's hair stood on end as he saw the dishevelled hair and bloodstained face of the maid Kou Zhu.

"It is true," he said, "it was I who plotted with the midwife and substituted the cat for the crown prince."

The ghost sobbed and thanked him. "In a moment you will be escorted to the Palace of the King of Hell. If you tell them everything, I will be released from this limbo."

Another two spirits appeared holding tablets which said 'Demanding Souls'. "The King of Hell summons you to be confronted with the wronged ghost," they said and led him through a winding dark path. "Kneel," ordered the spirits.

He heard a voice in the dark saying: "Everything that you and the imperial consort Liu have done has been written down. By rights you should have been transformed into a beast but all is not lost. You have time to make a clean breast of all your evil deeds."

Guo Huai kowtowed and made a complete confession.

Suddenly the room was brightly lit and above him sat Prefect Bao flanked by his men. The scribe presented the confession as well as a record of what the eunuch had told the ghost in the cell. Confronted with the evidence, the eunuch had no option but to sign the confession.

It had all been a trick devised by the wily Gongsun Ce. He had recruited a prostitute to play the part of the ghost of the palace maid. She was rewarded with fifty taels of silver and returned to the brothel.

The next day Prefect Bao had an audience with the emperor and presented him with the signed confessions. The emperor confronted Empress Dowager Liu with them. She was so struck with terror that she died of fright. The emperor ordered that her body be taken to a side temple and she be interred with the ceremony befitting an ordinary imperial concubine rather than the more elaborate rites normally accorded to an empress. He decreed that the country should be made aware of her change of status, and the real empress dowager took her rightful place at court.

The eunuch Guo Huai was sentenced to death. A memorial temple was erected on the land surrounding the Palace of Kindness and Longevity for the tragic palace maid Kou Zhu and was named the Temple of the Faithful and Dauntless Maid. Another temple called the Temple of Two Champions was erected in memory of the loyal Qin Feng, who had taken the baby to the Southern Green Palace and placed it in the care of Princess Dai and her husband, the Eighth Prince, and to commemorate the young eunuch who committed suicide instead of the imperial consort Li.

Prefect Bao was promoted to the rank of prime minister. The title of secretary was given to Gongsun Ce and the four warriors were named guards of the sixth rank. They were to be permanently attached to the Kaifeng Prefecture. Chen Lin was appointed major-domo-in-chief, and Fan, the bailiff of Grass District Bridge, was made an official of the seventh rank. The Dilapidated Kiln was converted into a monastery for public worship, endowed with a thousand taels of silver and land. Fan was put in charge of the monastery where he would every year sacrifice to the gods in spring and autumn.

CHAPTER 20

The Loyal Official Is Possessed and Is on the Verge of Death.
The Hero Kills a Wicked Priest.

PRIME Minister Bao Zheng now worked even harder for his country, fearless of any officials who were influential but treacherous. The emperor trusted him to be impartial in all his decisions and he earned the admiration of all his colleagues in the imperial government.

One day Prime Minister Bao was holding court when an elderly couple was brought before him with a complaint.

The woman knelt down before him and said she had two daughters, the elder named Golden Fragrance and the younger Jade Fragrance. Golden Fragrance had suddenly disappeared the day before her young sister was married to the son of Zhao Guosheng. "I am a widow," she cried, "and depend on them to support me. Now Zhao Guosheng has accused me of marrying off the wrong daughter to his son."

Zhao Guosheng was next brought up before Bao and said that the elder daughter was so ugly he had chosen the younger one to be the bride of his son but then discovered that he had been tricked and he was now the father-in-law of the elder sister.

"Are you sure of your identification?" Prime Minister Bao asked.

"Of course I am sure," said Zhao Guosheng. "The younger one

is extremely pretty, that's why I wanted her as my daughter-in-law."

Prime Minister Bao retired to his study to think it over but when Bao Xing entered later with some tea he found his master shaking and trembling. He fell back in his chair exclaiming: "What an offensive smell of blood!" and lost consciousness.

Madam Bao sent for Gongsun Ce, who feeling his left pulse said it was normal but was puzzled when he felt his right pulse.

"He is not ill," he said, but was unable to say what was wrong with the unconscious prime minister. Despite the royal physician who was dispatched by the emperor and various others' ministrations, he remained as if in a deep sleep.

Five days went by and Gongsun Ce felt his pulse weakening. Bao Xing remembered that his master had suffered a similar illness when he had lodged with the monk Liao Ran, after he had been deprived of his post. That monk had cured him but had since taken to the road and was wandering about the country, his whereabouts unknown.

In the meantime, Southern Hero Zhan Zhao was drifting around like duckweed. After he intercepted the sedan chair and rescued Jade Goddess he heard the good news of the empress dowager being reinstated through the efforts of his lord Bao Zheng. He decided to go to the Kaifeng Prefecture.

He came to a place called Elm Forest Town and stopped for refreshment. A woman entered the restaurant. Though rather sallow and gaunt, she was lovely despite her homespun clothes. She was rather shy and hesitated before speaking to him.

"My husband is called Hu Cheng. We live in Three Treasure Village but because of the famine we have nothing to eat. Now my mother-in-law and husband are ill and I am forced to beg. Please help me."

Zhan Zhao took out half a silver ingot from his bag and placed it on the table before her. "Buy some medicine with this," he said.

"That is too much," she protested. "Just a few coins will do. If I took that much home, my husband and mother-in-law would be suspicious."

The waiter standing by promised he would vouch for how she had come by the silver, so she took the money and left.

A man at another table saw the scene and sneered. He was called Ji, a foxy bad lot.

"You shouldn't have given her that silver," he said. "She's only putting it on. Someone else gave her money and he was later blackmailed by her husband who insisted he had seduced her and the victim had to give him a hundred taels of silver. Now the husband will come and demand the same."

Zhan Zhao thought to himself: "If that is true, I'd better go to Three Treasure Village and find out for myself and make sure it doesn't happen again."

On the way he went to pray at the Monastery of the Apprehension of Truth and then changed into his black suit and continued on his way to the home of Hu Cheng. He heard an old woman mumbling and the voice of a man angrily shouting at his weeping wife.

"If she wasn't unfaithful, how could she have got so much silver?" the old lady asked.

"Don't waste your breath, Mother, she can go back to her family tomorrow."

Zhan Zhao could not help sighing. "She certainly knew what her husband would think."

He caught sight of a figure standing outside who bawled out: "Since you've taken my money and promised to be nice to me, come out. Otherwise return the silver to me."

Zhan Zhao grabbed hold of the man who turned out to be Ji.

He took him into the courtyard and shouted: "I am a god of the night; the day god has just informed me that there is a virtuous and filial woman here and because her husband and mother-in-law were ill, a very respectable gentleman gave her some money. But this evil-doer has designs on her and wanted to blackmail her. As the god of the night I cannot allow this evil deed to happen so I am going to take him with me into the wilderness so that a decent family can live in peace."

Zhan Zhao went to a remote place and killed Ji. Afterwards he walked along a winding path which took him to the back of the Monastery of the Apprehension of Truth. He jumped over the wall and landed as light as a feather on the inside where he noticed a light from the side courtyard.

"It's very late, so why is the light still on?" He went to see and saw two shadows on the window and heard voices. One was a young priest named Tan Yue and the other was a woman. She was saying: "Though we've let my elder sister take my place, I'm not sure whether he'll agree or not."

"Even if he doesn't our mother-in-law will deal with him, so don't worry about it," replied the priest. "Now let's enjoy the night together and have a good sleep."

Zhan Zhao was astonished. "This priest behaves ignominiously. It is forbidden for priests to have affairs." Then he heard the woman ask: "What designs does Grand Tutor Pang have on Bao's life?"

"The method used by my master is highly effective," replied the priest. "He has set up an altar in his garden. By now five days have passed. When the seventh comes it will bring about the result intended and he will be rewarded with a thousand taels of silver. I will steal it from him and we can escape to distant parts and become husband and wife."

Zhan Zhao quickly jumped down from the wall, packed his bags and left for Kaifeng. The stars were still shining in the sky when he reached the grand tutor's residence. He jumped over the wall and saw a tall altar in the garden, on which candles and incense were burning. An old priest with long straggly hair was practising sorcery. Zhan Zhao crept up behind him and drew his sword.

CHAPTER 21

Zhan Zhao Terrifies the Evil-Doer with a Human Head.
The Scholar Recovers and Brings the Bawd to Trial.

THE old priest, named Xing Ji, was in the middle of his black
magic when he caught a flash of cold steel which struck the bottle
on the altar. Verily, immorality can never win over probity and
the bottle broke in half. The priest kicked out but with one stroke
of his sword Zhan Zhao cut off his head. He found a wooden effigy on the altar standing in foul blood. He wrapped it in a piece of
cloth and tucked it in the front of his tunic.

At the same time, Grand Tutor Pang Ji was gleefully anticipating the death of Prefect Bao the next day. "My son's death will be
avenged even though Bao's body will show no suspicious marks."

Suddenly there was a loud bang: a large, hairy, bloodstained
head smashed through the window and Pang Ji realised that it must
be the doings of one of the able men from the Kaifeng Prefecture.
He ordered his men to search the garden but Zhan Zhao was already on his way to Kaifeng, taking the wooden effigy with him.
The worried Gongsun Ce and the four warriors were very pleased
to see him and asked how he had learned of the prefect's illness.

"It's a long story," he replied. "Look at this first and then you
will understand."

He took out the wooden effigy from his tunic and Gongsun Ce
could see that Prime Minister Bao's name and birth date had been

inscribed on it.

"It has been used for black magic," he exclaimed.

Zhan Zhao was about to tell them of his adventures when Bao Xing entered and in great excitement announced that Bao had regained consciousness and had begun to eat.

They all went to pay their respects to the prefect who thanked Zhan Zhao for breaking the black magic.

"You have rescued me so many times," said Bao. "I hope you will remain in my office and become my champion."

"I've been drifting around the country like duckweed," replied Zhan Zhao. "I had no idea that I would discover the cause of your illness in the Monastery of the Apprehension of Truth."

Prime Minister Bao and Gongsun Ce were puzzled and wanted to know more.

He told them what he had overheard between the little priest and the young woman. Gongsun Ce and the prefect now put two and two together and realised this had a bearing on the case of the widow and her two daughters.

"Prepare an impeachment to present to His Majesty," said the prime minister, "accusing Grand Tutor Pang of attempting to murder a courtier by means of sorcery. We have the proof of the dead priest and the wooden effigy."

Now that the prime minister was no longer at death's door, everyone felt happy and relaxed and celebrated with wine and good food and then retired for the night.

The next morning the court was in session and the two priests from the Monastery of the Apprehension of Truth, Widow Huang and her two daughters, Golden Fragrance and Jade Fragrance, and the father of the bridegroom, Zhao Guosheng, and his son were brought in. One of the priests, Tan Ming, was the first to face Lord Bao. He was not more than thirty years old and did not look like an evil-doer.

He bowed and said his master was Xing Ji who was always doing underhand things and refused to take his advice, which made him sick with worry. Then his brother Tan Yue, arrived at his monastery to seek his help. He was a profligate who spent his time with prostitutes and gambled until penniless. Unfortunately, Xing Ji persuaded him to become a priest as well and the two of them became more dissolute and their behaviour was not in keeping with what was expected from priests.

When Grand Tutor Pang sent for his master to perform his black arts, Tan Ming was left in charge of the monastery. Then his brother brought in a young woman and disguised her as a priest. "There was nothing I could do," the young priest said, "he is a stronger character than me."

Prime Minister Bao nodded. "As I thought, he is not an evil person."

When the young priest's brother, Tan Yue, was confronted with the facts he had to confess to his crimes. He had gone by Widow Huang's house and seen the two girls — one very ugly and the other beautiful. He fell in love with the beautiful one but she was already betrothed to the son of Zhao Guosheng and so they persuaded the ugly daughter to take her place since once she crossed over the threshold "the raw rice would become cooked" and it would be too late to do anything. In the meantime, Jade Fragrance eloped with Tan Yue who took her to the monastery.

"How much did you bribe Widow Huang with?" asked the prime minister.

"Three hundred taels of silver," was the reply.

"How can a young priest have so much money?" he asked.

"I stole it from my master, who made money by sorcery. If he wanted to harm somebody, he would make a wooden effigy and write his name and birth date on it and put it into a bottle filled with foul blood. Then he would mutter his black magic and in seven days, the victim would die. Because the grand tutor wanted revenge for the death of his son, he offered my master one thousand five hundred taels of silver. He was given an advance of five hundred, and the rest was to be paid when the deed was done."

"And so you were waiting to steal the one thousand taels of silver from your master and run away with Jade Fragrance to distant parts and get married?"

Tan Yue was taken aback. "How does he know what I told Jade Fragrance in secret?" he wondered, not realising that Zhan Zhao had told all.

The two young priests were removed from the court and Widow Huang and her two daughters brought in.

CHAPTER 22

The Grand Tutor Is Accused.
Southern Hero Is Promoted.

GOLDEN Fragrance was indeed very ugly, whereas her sister, Jade Fragrance, was exceedingly beautiful.

Aware that the false priest had confessed, Widow Huang admitted that she had been given three hundred taels of silver which she had hidden in a chest at home. The court awarded fifty taels of silver to the deceived father-in-law, Zhao Guosheng, to find another wife for his son. Jade Fragrance was sentenced to become a prostitute as she was so fond of enticing men. Golden Fragrance, because she was too ugly for marriage, was told to go to a nunnery, while the widow was to become a brothel madame because she was greedy for money and enjoyed pandering to the evil desires of others. Tan Ming, the young priest, was appointed abbot of the monastery and his brother, Tan Yue, exiled to the borderlands.

Faced with the confession, Grand Tutor Pang pleaded guilty but because he was the father of one of the emperor's concubines, he was treated leniently and his grant from the court was cancelled for three years. He also had to apologise to Prime Minister Bao.

Word of Zhan Zhao's heroic deeds reached the ears of the emperor and a few days after the case of the grand tutor was settled the emperor sent for Bao, wanting to know more.

"He is a hero who has saved me time and time again," answered the prime minister. "When I came from my native place to the capital to sit for the imperial examinations I stayed at the Golden Dragon Monastery and encountered a villainous monk. It was Zhan Zhao who came in the dead of night and rescued me. Then when I was in charge of administering the relief funds, I became the target of an assassin called Xiang Fu, and he rescued me again. And it was he, too, who has destroyed the black magic in the garden of Pang Ji."

"He must be very skilful with weapons," said the emperor.

"He has three skills. First, he's skilled in swordmanship, second, he can hit a target accurately every time with his pocket-size arrow, third, he can leap onto roofs of houses and jump over high walls."

The emperor clapped his hands with joy. "He seems to be the answer to my prayers. I've long been seeking for such a man as this. Bring him to the imperial court tomorrow and I will have a demonstration of his skills in the Prowess-Display Building."

When Zhan Zhao was brought to the vermilion terrace the emperor saw a man not more than thirty years old with an impressive bearing. He was asked to display his skills with the sword, which was handed to him with great ceremony by Gongsun Ce and the four warriors. Tucking in a little of his gown, he struck a pose then wielded the sword like a flashing silver light.

Slashing the air, hacking, chopping, curving, sweeping and stabbing, he won great applause from the onlookers.

"He really lives up to the title of 'Southern Hero'," they exclaimed.

When he finished the display, he kowtowed to the throne, his colour unchanged and breathing normally.

This pleased the emperor, who then asked him to demonstrate shooting his pocket-size arrows.

Prime Minister Bao boasted that Zhan Zhao was able to shoot off the tip of a burning incense stick in the dark but as it was still daylight he suggested that the emperor mark off three red dots on a piece of paper as targets instead.

The wily prime minister had the paper and brushes near at hand, so it only needed the emperor to paint the red dots. The target was then taken by a eunuch twenty paces away. Zhan Zhao once again kowtowed before the Prowess-Displaying Building and taking up the pose of a pointing tiger, took aim. Three times his bow went twang and three times his arrows found their targets.

"Your skill is unique," commended the emperor.

"His third skill is leaping," said the prime minister. "How about letting him jump onto the roof of the tall hall and Your Majesty can go upstairs to watch," he suggested.

As the party moved upstairs, the fourth brother gallant Zhao Hu gave the hero a cup of warm wine.

"It will pep you up," he said.

At the foot of the building, Zhan Zhao once again kowtowed towards the building and stalked a few paces like an egret before he crouched. Swish, like a swallow he landed on the roof.

Everyone cheered. Zhan Zhao, now in his stride, walked to the base of a pillar and grabbing it with his hands, his legs splitting in the air, he climbed up backwards. When he reached the top, he held on with his left arm and leg and stretched out his right leg and arm, as if he was a man looking out to sea. Suddenly his body gave a swerve and he scurried sideways like a crab along the purlins from east to west several times before coming to halt in the middle where he drew up his legs and swung backwards to the roof.

The emperor cried out: "Remarkable! He doesn't seem human at all. He's more like one of my royal cats."

From then on he was nicknamed "Royal Cat". This nickname was to attract many soldiers and heroes thenceforth, who rallied round the royal house of Song when it was threatened by rebellion.

The emperor promoted Zhan Zhao to royal guard of the fourth rank assigned to the Kaifeng Prefecture and the grateful Prime Minister Bao ordered a uniform denoting the higher rank of his loyal guard which made him look even more impressive.

Prime Minister Bao told Gongsun Ce to prepare a memorial to the throne to express Zhan Zhao's gratitude for his promotion and at the same time suggested that another imperial examination be set to find more men of Zhan Zhao's calibre. This suggestion was immediately put into effect and news of an imperial examination to recruit able and brave men was sent to every province in the country.

CHAPTER 23

An Imperial Candidate Loses His Wife and Son.
A Grandson Meets His Grandmother Because of a Tiger.

A poverty-stricken scholar in a distant village saw the imperial notice inviting candidates to sit for the examination in the capital. His name was Fan Zhongyu but he did not have the money to make the long journey and he became very despondent as his colleagues were busy making preparations to leave. It did not make him feel any more cheerful to hear them say that if he sat the examinations he would be sure to come first.

His wife told him to forget the idea as it had also been her wish to accompany him so that she could take their little son Jinge to see her mother whom she had not seen for many years. But because they were so poor, there was no chance they could realise their dreams.

The following morning his close friend named Liu, an upright old man, visited them and when he heard of their plight offered to find the travelling expenses for the family thus enabling Fan to sit for the examination and Mrs Fan with their little son to fulfill her filial duty towards her mother.

He returned the next day not only with one hundred taels of silver but also his black donkey, which he stated was too difficult for an old man like him to handle.

"I've borrowed the money from a good friend. He doesn't want interest. If he does, I'll answer for it. There's a bit extra because as the saying goes, 'Be thrifty at home but spend liberally while away.' If you fail the examination, you should stay in the capital and try again the following year."

The next day they left the old man to take care of their house and taking the black donkey with them they set off on their long journey to the city.

They reached the capital safely and the husband entered his name for the imperial examination. The chief examiner was Prime Minister Bao and therefore it was conducted fairly and impartially. Fan was grateful to his wife for insisting that they should not waste time by visiting her family first before he took the examination. But now without any distractions they could set off to Wanquan Mountain where the mother lived. He saddled the black donkey and hired a carriage. When they reached the mountain area, he sent the carriage back and they continued on foot towards his mother-in-law's house, unaware that they were on the wrong side of the mountain. They became very tired, so while his wife and son rested by a rock, he decided to go on alone but could not find his in-laws' house. Footsore and weary he returned to the rock only to find his wife and son had disappeared. Frantic he shouted himself hoarse but there was no sign of them. As he cried in despair a woodsman came along the path and told him that he had seen a distressed woman lying across the saddle of a ruthless marquis called Ge Dengyun who lived in Single Tiger Manor. This man made a habit of kidnapping other men's wives. The woodsman had not seen the little boy.

Fan went in the direction of the manor.

His little son, Jinge, had been caught by a fierce tiger but was rescued in time by the same woodsman who took him back to his cottage in Eight Treasure Village where his old mother tended the boy and helped him to recover from his frightening ordeal.

"You have survived a disaster, my little one," she said stroking his face. "It must mean that you will have a happy and easy life from now on."

She asked him his name and where he had come from.

"My father's name is Fan Zhongyu and I came from Huguang," he answered.

The old woman was startled: "Is your mother's name Jade Lotus?" she asked.

"Yes," he answered, at which the old woman flung her arms around him and burst into tears.

"I am your grandmother. Jade Lotus is my daughter and this is your uncle Bai Xiong."

The little boy related how they were on their way to visit them but had become lost. "I never thought my own uncle would rescue me from the tiger but what has become of my parents?" He began to cry.

CHAPTER 24

Fan the Scholar Becomes Insane.
A Drunk Loses His Identity.

THE next morning the uncle, Bai Xiong, tucking his axe into his belt and carrying his shoulder pole, went to the rock in the ravine and searched for his sister and brother-in-law. In the distance he saw a man coming towards him. His hair was dishevelled, his face covered with blood, and he was holding the skirt of his gown in his left hand and a vermilion slipper in his right. The man rushed up to him and began hitting him with the slipper.

"You've beaten me, you dog, do you want to kill me as well?" he bawled.

Bai Xiong, dodging the blows, wondered if this was his missing brother-in-law Fan Zhongyu, but was unable to get any sensible replies to his questions. He decided to go back home and bring the young boy to identify him.

The madman was truly his brother-in-law who had hastened to Single Tiger Manor to demand his wife back from the wicked marquis, Ge. The marquis accused him of murdering one of his servants and he ordered his other servants to flog him to death and then put his body into a trunk and dump it in the wilds.

On the way they met a group of messengers sent from the city to notify Fan that he had come first in the imperial examination. Frightened by superior numbers, the servants dropped the trunk and fled. When the messengers opened the trunk they found the scholar bereft of his senses. He set about them with his slipper and they ran away in fright.

When Bai Xiong returned with his nephew to the rock, Fan had disappeared. They proceeded to the city where the Fans had lodged only to learn that the scholar had come first in the examinations but no one knew his whereabouts.

The little boy was returned to his grandmother while Bai Xiong began searching over a wide area for his mad brother-in-law.

Near the mountain area of Wanquan there were two brothers in Drum Tower Street who kept a prosperous lumber mill. The elder was called Qu Shen and the younger was called Qu Liang. The older brother had a hairy face and was fond of drink. He had two nicknames — Qu the Whiskers or Qu the Yeast. Despite his weakness for alcohol he was a shrewd businessman and the two brothers ran their business as solidly as an iron pail.

One day, Qu Shen decided to go to the other side of the mountain where he heard a shipment of timber had arrived. Hoping to make a profit he took four hundred taels of silver, saddled his brown and white donkey and set off. When he got there he found the prices were too high, but as he was a convivial man, he stayed for a while to drink with his fellow merchants and had a merry time until he saw the sun sinking in the west and hurriedly started to make his way home before it got too dark.

He mounted his donkey and set off for Wanquan Mountain but this donkey was not only very stubborn but if it saw another donkey it would give chase. At first it refused to budge but then suddenly it pricked up its ears and bolted. Qu Shen held onto the reins and let him have his head when it suddenly stopped short and threw him onto the ground. Tied to an elm tree was the black donkey.

Qu Shen looked at its teeth. It was plump and sturdy, with a new saddle on its back. "I might as well swap my donkey for this one," he thought, transferred his money bags to the black donkey

and cantered away, congratulating himself on his good luck. Unfortunately a gale blew up and made further progress difficult. "I
shall have to find somewhere to put up for the night in case a high-
wayman steals my four hundred taels of silver," he said to himself.

He saw a light ahead, got off his donkey and led it up to the
house. He was just about to knock on the door when he heard
voices and a woman grumbling. "If you didn't spend all our money
on drink we wouldn't be hungry now. There's nothing for it, I
shall have to earn some money in any way I can."

"Don't talk rubbish," said the man. "I may be poor but I'm decent."

She scoffed: "Who has seen such a decent man as you around?"

Qu Shen thought: "She seems a right hussy." He knocked on the
door with his whip but there was no reply. He knocked again and
the woman answered.

"I'm a traveller," said Qu Shen. "As it is getting dark can you
put me up for the night? I can pay you."

The gate was opened and he entered the courtyard. The man
tied up the donkey and Qu Shen followed him into the room.

They introduced themselves. "My name is Qu Shen and I own
the Prosperous Lumber Mill."

The man introduced himself as Li Bao. This was the very servant who had been sent by Squire Li to accompany his daughter
when she married Prefect Bao but when the prefect was dismissed
from his post, the servant had made off with their silver and possessions. He soon squandered all the money on women and wine
and married the daughter of the innkeeper where he lodged. He
and his new wife then proceeded to spend the savings of his in-
laws, who died destitute and broken-hearted.

They sold off all the furnishings and property, leaving only the
three thatched rooms in which they now lived and where the unfortunate Qu Shen turned up.

Li Bao and his wife plied him with drink, making a great fuss of him until Qu Shen became fuddled with drink. Unable to sit up any longer he pushed his bag of money under his head and fell fast asleep.

"Now get a rope," said the wife.

"What for?" asked her husband.

"To strangle him, you idiot," she replied.

"Murder is not a joking matter," he replied and shook his head.

"You want a fortune but you are as timid as a rabbit," she scolded. "You're spineless. Do you mean me to be hungry as well as you?"

He brought the rope but she realised he was too timid to do the deed. She snatched it from him and gingerly passed one end of it round Qu Shen's neck and gave the other end of the rope to her husband. They tugged both ends while the woman placed her foot on Qu Shen's neck until his struggles ceased. The wicked woman then pulled the bag from under his head. There were eight packages altogether and she was overjoyed.

CHAPTER 25

Qu the Whiskers Behaves Like a Woman.
The Candidate's Wife Behaves Like a Man.

THE murderous couple hid the bags of silver inside their *kang* and
then proceeded to dispose of the body. Li's wife helped to lift the
heavy weight onto Li's back: they planned to dump Qu Shen behind a temple on the northern slope. As Li Bao staggered up the
hill he thought he saw a shadow. He took fright, threw the corpse
down and ran for dear life.

His wife scolded him, saying that what he saw as a figure was
only a young willow tree and now they had to dispose of the black
donkey by driving it away. Li Bao untied the donkey, his wife
gave it a hefty whack on its rump and it galloped off.

"Tomorrow," said his wife, "you must behave as normally as
possible. Go to the well and draw water as usual. When the corpse
is discovered you must go and look at it like the other people.
Then when things have calmed down, we can enjoy ourselves."

When somebody found the body of Qu Shen, the bailiff was
summoned. He saw the rope round his neck and was just about to
report the murder to the county magistrate when the "body" began
to stir and groan. Qu Shen opened his eyes and saw a curious group
of people including the bailiff staring at him.

"Oh dear," said Qu Shen in the falsetto tones of a woman, "why
are you staring at a woman like that?" and he covered his face

with his sleeve.

The onlookers burst into laughter but the bailiff told them to desist. "He's only just coming round and must be feeling giddy. I must question him as to who tried to murder him."

Qu Shen answered coyly: "I tried to commit suicide. No one tried to strangle me. My husband, son and I were on our way to visit my mother, but I was captured by a bully of a marquis who tried to seduce me, so I hanged myself rather than submit to his demands."

The bailiff was bewildered. A hairy-faced man speaking like a woman. There was something really odd going on.

He felt a blow on his head and turning round saw Fan the madman hitting him with a slipper.

"What a strange morning," he said to himself, "first I meet with a man who thinks he's a woman and now I'm being hit with slipper."

"Stop him," cried Qu Shen, "the man with the slipper is my husband."

At this everyone began laughing again at such an ugly man claiming to have a husband.

Two men then appeared leading a donkey, calling for the bailiff.

By this time the bailiff was getting annoyed with all the interruptions. "One thing after another," he shouted. "Now what's up with you two?"

One was the brother of Qu Shen, Qu Liang, and the other was Bai Xiong, the brother-in-law of the scholar. Bai Xiong had found the tethered brown and white donkey and thought it was his brother-in-law's and would lead him to the missing scholar. Qu Liang found Bai Xiong with their donkey and an argument began which ended up with them going off to court to settle the matter. Now Qu Liang saw his brother sitting in the road with a rope round his neck and demanded the reason.

His brother, showing no signs of recognising him, spoke in a woman's voice.

"This is terrible," protested Qu Liang, "what's wrong with you? We are respectable decent country folk. How can you face our friends like this?"

In reply Qu Shen turned to Bai Xiong and said: "You must be my brother. Oh woe is me!"

And then seeing the madman he cried out: "Here is your brother-in-law Fan Zhongyu. Stop him!"

The exasperated bailiff called for two carriages to take Qu Shen and Fan Zhongyu to court. To great hoots of laughter, Qu Shen minced along to the carriage like a woman with bound feet and insisted that the woodman, as his "brother", should sit beside him.

Qu Liang had no alternative but to sit in the carriage with the madman who continually hit him with the slipper all the way to the court building. The bailiff followed behind on the brown and white donkey, but just as they were about to set off the black donkey appeared on the scene and the brown and white donkey would have given chase if Qu Liang had not grabbed hold of its bit.

"I know his tricks," he said. "The instant he sees a mare he chases after her."

The donkey was being chased by a dark stumpy man who was no other than Zhao Hu, one of Prime Minister Bao's warriors. Because the scholar Fan Zhongyu was missing, Bao had ordered a search. On his way to the office he met the donkey running towards his palanquin. It then bent its forelegs and nodded three times to it. Others were puzzled but Prime Minister Bao understood and said: "If you have complaints to make, turn your head to the south and your tail to the north and I'll send someone to follow you."

The donkey turned its head to the south and its tail to the north. Prime Minister Bao then ordered Zhao Hu to follow it. The donkey galloped on ahead and Zhao Hu and his page found it hard to keep up. After a while the warrior sat on a rock gasping for breath. The donkey came back. "Aiya," gasped Zhao Hu, "if you really have complaints to make, either go slowly or let me ride you."

The donkey laid back its ears and Zhao Hu mounted him. Soon they reached the northern slope of Wanquan Mountain where the donkey stopped by the back wall of a temple. They heard somebody crying for help and Zhao Hu jumped over the wall and saw an open coffin where a good-looking woman was pummelling a priest under her.

"It is very improper for men and women to be locked together and fighting," he said.

"I've been murdered and robbed of four hundred taels of silver," shouted the woman. "This priest opened the coffin, what for, eh?"

"Let him go," said Zhao Hu, "and we'll find out."

The priest said that the temple belonged to the family of the marquis and the coffin held the body of the steward's mother. He had been told to bury it immediately but as the day was not auspicious for burial he had put it in the back courtyard. This morning he had heard a loud noise from the coffin and when he opened it out jumped a woman who started beating him.

Zhao Hu studied the appearance of the woman who spoke like a man with a rough country accent and said she had been murdered for her money.

It was too much for Zhao Hu, who decided to take them both to Prime Minister Bao to sort out.

He tied the priest with a sash from his waist and told the woman to follow him.

CHAPTER 26

Confusion and Embarrassment Fill the Prefect's Court.
A Man Is Confused with a Woman.

OUTSIDE the temple Zhao Hu proceeded to escort his captives to the prefecture. As they passed the southern slope of the mountain the woman from the coffin suddenly espied Li Bao and shouted: "That's the one who murdered me!"

She grabbed hold of the protesting Li Bao: "Where are the four hundred taels of silver you took after you strangled me?"

Li Bao protested: "I've never seen you before. How could I have robbed you of your silver?"

Zhao Hu had no alternative but to bind the still protesting Li Bao with the other end of the silk sash and marched them off to the Kaifeng Prefecture.

Prime Minister Bao called his court into session and Fan Zhongyu, being a scholar of distinction, was brought in first.

He was still shouting and hitting his escort with his slipper until one of the policemen managed to wrest it from him. Gongsun Ce, seeing him raving like a madman, suggested to Prime Minister Bao that he should be treated first and cured before he was questioned.

Next the woodcutter Bai Xiong was brought before the court. He told how he had rescued his nephew from the tiger and was searching for his brother-in-law when he found the donkey which he thought was Fan's. Unfortunately he was set upon by Qu Liang who accused him of doing away with his brother Qu Shen and taking his silver. When they met Qu Shen at the bailiffs, he spoke in a woman's voice and referred to the woodcutter as his brother.

"What is your brother-in-law's name?" asked Prime Minister Bao.

"His name is Fan Zhongyu," replied Bai Xiong.

Prime Minister Bao nodded and questioned all the protagonists in turn, including Qu Shen who still thought he was Fan Zhongyu's wife and coyly swayed this way and that in court until everyone started laughing.

"I'm the wife of Fan Zhongyu," Qu Shen lisped. "A tiger snatched my child away and then I was kidnapped by a man who carried me to his home where I hanged myself rather than be seduced. When I opened my eyes I found so many people staring at me because I had changed into a man!"

Prime Minister Bao was nonplussed and cleared them from the court while he pondered.

The bold Zhao Hu returned with the black donkey, the priest and Mrs Fan, the scholar's wife.

The priest, dropping to his knees, related how he had been ordered to bury a coffin from the marquis's mansion but because grave-digging was taboo that day he had put the coffin in the backyard.

"Don't talk rubbish," shouted Prime Minister Bao. "There is no season for grave-digging. Slap his face!"

The priest then hurriedly confessed that because the coffin came from the marquis's mansion, he thought it must contain valuables which he hoped to ransack, but when he opened it a woman jumped out and speaking in a coarse country dialect started to beat him up. He was so terrified that he yelled for help and a man jumped over the wall, tied him up and brought him to court.

The scholar's wife, Mrs Fan, was then called but she insisted her name was Qu Shen, the timber merchant who had been murdered by Li Bao who took the four hundred taels of silver. As she was gasping for air, a streak of light filtered into the coffin as the priest prised open the lid and she started to beat him up. As Zhao Hu was taking them to the prefecture she saw Li Bao her murderer and he was also brought in.

Bai Xiong recognised the woman as his sister but she still insisted that Qu Liang was her elder brother.

"Since when have I an elder brother looking like this?" Qu Liang wondered.

Prime Minister Bao realised that the male and female souls had entered the wrong forms and temporarily dismissed them from the court before calling in Li Bao whom he recognised as the disloyal servant who had deserted him when he was in trouble, taking all his goods and luggage.

Li Bao seeing Prime Minister Bao in his official garments regretted his past mistakes and said he hoped he would be executed as soon as possible. He was ordered to sign the confession; the silver was to be confiscated and Mrs Li Bao to be arrested.

Prime Minister Bao then turned to investigating the marquis and sent for his steward to find out how the scholar's wife came to be in the coffin. At first the steward said it was his mother but after a flogging he could not give any information about his mother, which incensed the prefect even more.

"Who can't remember his mother? It proves you've never thought about her and have not carried out your filial duties. For that you will be flogged again."

The wicked servant then confessed that the marquis, his master, had seen a woman crying by a rock and found her so attractive he had her carried off to his mansion. They had not expected her husband to come looking for her and had tricked him by saying he had killed one of the servants; he was flogged and his body taken away in a trunk which his servants had dropped in their fright when they saw the messengers looking for the scholar. In the meantime the wife had hanged herself and they had put her body in a coffin and taken it to the priest with the story that it was the steward's mother.

The steward was ordered to sign the confession and sent to prison.

After his meal, Prime Minister Bao pondered over this confusing case but could think of no solution, muttering all the while: "Embodied in the wrong forms. What shall I do?"

His page Bao Xing could restrain himself no longer and suggested: "I think you should inquire in the Human and Ghost Palace."

"Where is it?" asked Prime Minister Bao.

"In the nether world," Bao Xing replied.

"Fool. What rubbish you talk!" his master retorted.

CHAPTER 27

The Prefect Resorts to the Wandering Fairy Pillow and the Antique Mirror. The Victims Regain Their Lost Identities.

"THE nether world is not rubbish for I have been there," said Bao Xing.

He told his master how, when they had confiscated the Wandering Fairy Pillow from a murderer, he had secretly tried sleeping on it and in his dreams entered the Human and Ghost Palace. But because he had tried to pass himself off as a prime minister he had been driven back by the ghosts.

The title "prime minister" reminded Prime Minister Bao of the times he had been addressed in that way when he tried the case of the Black Pot and the wronged servant girl Kou Zhu and this was a sign that he should use the pillow.

Bao Xing brought him what looked like a block of rotten wood inscribed with illegible characters which resembled tadpoles. He looked at it and nodded and Bao Xing took it into the inner room and put it on the bed. Prime Minister Bao then lay down and his servant left him.

As soon as he laid his head on the pillow he found himself standing on a vermilion terrace and below him were two men in black leading a black horse with a black saddle.

"Mount it please, Prime Minister," they said.

He complied and as soon as he took the reins the horse galloped so fast that the wind whistled past his ears. The scenery looked sombre and dark. They reached the gate of a city which was tightly shut. The horse did not stop and he thought they were going to crash into it but it went through it easily and reached a spacious office with another vermilion painted terrace where it halted. Two judges in red and black greeted him. When he alighted from the horse he saw a tablet inscribed with "Human and Ghost Palace" over a door and in the room a black table and chairs were arranged, so he took a seat.

The judge in red handed him a book saying: "You are here because of two souls embodied in the wrong forms."

When the prime minister opened the book the first few pages were blank but the judge in black turned over a few pages and he saw written in neat characters: "If you want to clear up the matter, use the antique mirror you found in the well. Let a drop of blood from the tip of the middle finger of each of the two fall on the mirror, then you shall tell one from the other." He looked up to question the judges but they had disappeared with the book.

He woke up and called for Bao Xing who brought him a cup of tea and said the third watch was sounding.

Secretary Gongsun Ce was announced who told him that he had cured the scholar Fan Zhongyu of his madness by giving him a decoction of five woods.

"I filled a bath with water in which mulberry, elm, peach, locust and willow wood had been boiled and put him in it. Afterwards I covered him with a quilt and he perspired, which got rid of all his accumulated phlegm and thinned his blood. He is now recovering."

"You really are skillful in curing diseases," said Prime Minister Bao in admiration.

He then took the antique mirror and called the court into session. Mrs Fan, the scholar's wife, and Qu Shen, the timber merchant, were brought in. He told them to bite the tip of their middle fingers and let a drop of blood fall on the mirror. When the blood fell on the mirror, the blood was seen to disperse and turn into a hazy vapour which sent out rays of light so bright as to dazzle the eyes and chill the hearts. Prime Minister Bao ordered the man and woman to look into the mirror. They saw a woman hanging herself and a man gasping for breath struggling for life. They fainted and the light in the mirror faded. Qu Shen stirred and then opened his eyes bawling out in his own voice: "Li Bao, damn you! Strangling me was a mere trifle but stealing my four hundred taels of silver is no joking matter!"

With that he looked at himself and felt his chin and said happily: "Yes, that's more like it. It's really me now." Then he kowtowed to Prime Minister Bao and asked him to help him retrieve his stolen silver.

Mrs Fan recovered from her faint, highly embarrassed. She was escorted to the women's quarters.

The next day Gongsun Ce brought in the weak but recovered scholar and the prime minister promised that when he wrote up his findings for the emperor his position as Number One Scholar would be verified. The happy man was reunited with his wife and son and together with his brother-in-law Bai Xiong returned to Eight Treasure Village to await his promotion.

Prime Minister Bao then turned to clearing up the other cases. The marquis who had tried to seduce Mrs Fan was executed with the tiger-shaped axe. The rascally Li Bao was executed with the dog-headed axe, as was the marquis's steward. Li Bao's wife was hanged and the priest who had tried to rob the dead was exiled to a bleak and arid place. The two brothers were given back their silver but Qu Shen had to give up his brown and white donkey for trying to exchange it for the black one. The black donkey won merit for making a complaint and was lodged and fed in the local government stables.

Prime Minister Bao then wrote out a memorial describing all the cases and his judgement which delighted Emperor Renzong who praised him for his impartiality in removing the scourge from the people. The gallant Zhan Zhao was granted two months' leave to return home and sacrifice to his ancestors.

Truly, the probity of the emperor and the loyalty of his courtiers were a sign of peace.

After being given a grand send-off by Gongsun Ce and the other gallant warriors, Zhan Zhao changed into his garments of a warrior and headed for his home in Gallant Meeting Village.

When he got to his house, he knocked on the door and heard his old servant grumbling. "No one has knocked on the door for a long time. We don't owe anything to anyone and mind our own business. So who is knocking now?"

When he eventually opened the door and saw his young master he berated him for neglecting his home and family affairs and when he saw Zhan Zhao's page and horses, he complained: "Oh goodness! How much is all this going to cost?"

Zhan Zhao did not argue with his faithful servant, who continued complaining about all the responsibilities put upon him but then seeing the young page, ordered him to get the rooms ready while he prepared tea for his master. At first he didn't believe that Zhan Zhao had been promoted military officer of the fourth rank until he saw his grand new uniform. "Now that you have such a high rank," he said, "you should show more concern for continuing the family line and get married."

Zhan Zhao agreed, saying that when he was in Hangzhou a friend had introduced him to a family with a daughter and he would go in a couple of days and get married.

The next two days were spent in celebrating his new position with friends and neighbours and making sacrifices at the family grave wearing his new uniform. Men and women, old and young gathered round to admire him and addressed him as lord, much to his old servant's pride and joy. But Zhan Zhao soon got bored and felt the urge to travel again, so he left his old servant to take care of the village and set off for Hangzhou.

CHAPTER 28

A Promise Is Made and a Kind Deed Performed in the Bower.
Friendship Is Established in the Teahouse.

ZHAN Zhao had no intention of getting married but went to Hangzhou to visit the sights. He left his horse and page in the Five Willow Restaurant close to the West Lake and strolled to the bower on the Broken Bridge. He felt relaxed and happy. Suddenly an old man on the bank picked up the skirt of his gown and flung himself into the water.

Zhan Zhao could not swim and rubbed his hands and stamped his feet in consternation. A small fishing skiff skimmed the water like an arrow and a young man slid into the water and brought the old man to the bank where he held him upside down by the ankles for the water to trickle out of his lungs. Zhan Zhao went down from the bower and saw a young man about twenty years old, handsome, well built, with a distinguished air.

"Wake up old man," the fisherman said gently. The old man groaned and gradually came to. His hair was white and he was gaunt. He scolded the man for saving him. "Why didn't you let me die, you meddlesome person?"

Instead of being angry, the young man smiled and said: "Even mole crickets and ants prefer life to death, to say nothing of human beings. If you have grievances, pour them out and if after that you still want to die, I'll put you back in the water."

"My name is Zhou Feng. I used to own a teahouse but one day I found a man dying outside during a heavy fall of snow. I called some assistants who carried him in where I covered him with warm quilts and fed him ginger tea until he recovered. His name was Zheng Xin and he was destitute, with no family. I felt sorry for him and nursed him. He was able to write and keep accounts, so he helped me with the business and was very diligent. I married my daughter to him, but she died and he then married the daughter of the Wang family and since then they have taken over my teahouse and even changed the name from the House of Zhou to the House of Zheng and have cheated me out of my rights. They bribed the magistrate when I complained to the court and I was given twenty blows and expelled from the county. So why should I want to go on living? I might as well take my life and lodge a complaint in the nether world."

"You're wrong, uncle," replied the young fisherman. "Rich men can bribe the spirits of the nether world as well. Why don't you open up a new teahouse and compete with Zheng Xin?"

The old man scowled and retorted: "Better throw me back into the water. I have no clothes to wear and no food to eat so where can I get money to open a new teahouse?"

The young fisherman offered to lend him the money and Zhan Zhao, who had listened in to the conversation, said to himself: "He may talk big but he is righteous and generous and even if he can't find the money I will vouch for him." He stepped forward and made the offer. They agreed to meet the next day in the bower of the Broken Bridge. The young fisherman jumped into his boat and rowed across the lake and Zhan Zhao made the old man promise to keep the next day's appointment.

Zhan Zhao then found lodgings before making his way to the Zheng Family Building. Half of it was now called "The Prosperous Shop". A man in a richly patterned gown, wearing a hat shaped like the slope of a roof, sat in a bamboo chair behind the counter. He was thin and weak-looking with a mouth like a bird's beak, his cheeks like a monkey, his eyes like two slits and ears pricked up like a dog. He stood up and clasped his hands in greeting as Zhan Zhao entered. "If you want tea, lord, there are nice and spacious rooms upstairs."

He went upstairs where there was a row of commodious rooms. A waiter set before him a tray containing four small dishes of choice fruit and four dishes of dainties, covered with a gauze cloth.

"Would you like tea or wine, my lord, or are you waiting for a worthy friend of yours?"

"A cup of tea."

As the waiter handed him a list of teas, he asked his name. "This humble person is really Number Three or Number Four, I am not sure, but you may call me Seven or Eight," answered the obsequious waiter.

"It's bad if I call you less or more than those numbers, so let's compromise; I'll call you Number Six," replied Zhan Zhao.

"Just right. The middle," replied the waiter.

"What is your master called?"

"His name is Zheng."

"I heard the building was owned by a man called Zhou," said Zhan Zhao.

"It belonged to the Zhous before but it was handed over to the Zhengs."

"And the two families were allied through marriage?"

"The wife died and he remarried."

"To the daughter of the Wangs," prompted Zhan Zhao, "and probably she wasn't good enough. That's why the father-in-law and son-in-law have appeared in court. Where does your master live?"

The waiter gave him a quizzical look and told him the family lived in the five rooms behind the five tearooms. He wondered whether Zhan Zhao was an ordinary customer or an official in disguise and added that only the master and his wife and a maidservant lived there.

"I noticed a man sitting in a bamboo chair downstairs. His face glowed. He'll make a fortune as sure as fate. He must be your master," Zhan Zhao said. He then ordered the best tea plucked before Grain Rain.

Another customer entered the tearoom, a handsome young warrior in a bright uniform. He sat at a table opposite Zhan Zhao and the waiter greeted him as if he was a regular customer.

"This is the first time I've been here," retorted the young man.

The questions and answers between the waiter and the young man took on the same pattern as between Zhan Zhao even to settling on the waiter being called Number Six, the same questions regarding the ownership of the teahouse and ending up with the young man ordering the same 'best tea plucked before Grain Rain'.

"I saw your master's face glowing, when I came in," said the young man, "he'll make a fortune as sure as fate."

Taken aback, the waiter gave Zhan Zhao a black look and scurried downstairs.

CHAPTER 29

Silver Is Stolen from the Teahouse.
Southern Hero Keeps His Rendezvous on Broken Bridge.

ZHAN Zhao was almost sure that the young man dressed as a warrior was the fisherman who had saved the old man at the lake.

A teacup in hand, he was suddenly aroused from his thoughts by the young man who stood before him, clasping his hands in respect. "Greetings, brother," he said.

Zhan Zhao invited him to sit. The waiter thought it was no wonder that they had asked the same questions, they were two of a kind — and what a waste of the second set of eight dishes.

The young man ordered two measures of the best liquor and anything that was tasty to eat.

The two men then introduced themselves.

"So you are the famous Zhan Zhao of the imperial guard, fourth rank, with the name 'Royal Cat'," said the young man and then said his name was Ding Zhaohui from Jasmine Village in Songjiang Prefecture.

It was the turn of Zhan Zhao to be surprised. "You are the younger brother of the twin heroes. I have long wished to meet you both. What luck to meet you here today. As to my promotion to the imperial guard, I find it prevents me from doing what I like best and that is travel around enjoying the beauties of nature. Now I'm tied down by officialdom. If it wasn't for the high regard I have for Prime Minister Bao I would have resigned long ago."

When Zhan Zhao asked why Ding had dressed up as a fisherman he said he had been bidden by his mother to burn incense at the Concealed Spirit Monastery but when he saw the famous mountains and springs he wanted to act the part of a fisherman just for fun and by coincidence had saved the old man.

A young boy entered with a message for Ding and he left, reminding Zhan Zhao of their appointment in the bower of the Broken Bridge the next day.

Zhan Zhao went to his inn and rested until the second watch. Then taking his sword he slipped out and found his way to the Zheng Family Building where he hid under the eaves. He saw the shadow of a woman at the window and heard the clink of cups and chopsticks.

"Have you called your master?" he heard the woman ask.

"He's weighing silver on the counter and will come when he's finished," replied the maidservant.

The impatient woman sent the maidservant down to get her husband who came up the stairs and placing eight packages of silver behind a hidden panel in the wall grumbled: "I'm busy working but Madam bids me to come. What is it that's so urgent?"

It was the owner of the teahouse Zheng, whom Zhan Zhao had seen sitting in the bamboo chair behind the counter earlier that day.

"I've just remembered something," said the woman. "It's that old nuisance. Although he's been expelled from the county he can still make trouble at the prefecture or even the capital. We must do something about it."

The husband sighed. "He has been so kind to me in the past. What we've done to him is very sad. I've betrayed my dead wife."

"He still has a conscience," thought Zhan Zhao.

There was a clatter of chopsticks and a banging of a wine cup as the woman burst out crying: "Since you miss your late wife, you shouldn't have let her die and married me!"

The husband begged her forgiveness and promised to dispose of the old man the next day.

He pleaded and cajoled over and over again, anything to stop her wailing.

If a woman knows her place, she will be counted among the virtuous women. But women like Mrs Zheng had three secret weapons: seduction, provocation and intimidation. When she sees her husband she treats him respectfully and amiably and if he says something that is to her satisfaction, she will agree it is excellent. If he says something is bad, she will also agree and get him in a good mood, then she begins hinting what he should have done. If he knows his own mind, he will cut her short. So she realises that ploy will not work and she tries another tactic.

If he hasn't a mind of his own, he will become putty in her hands and thus she can run wild and if she doesn't get her own way will bang her bowl and chopsticks and make a scene and he exhausts himself trying to please her and like a cringing dog will do anything for peace of mind. And this was what Mr Zheng had become even before his wife had tried the third tactic of intimidation.

He sent the maidservant downstairs to heat up some wine for his wife. After a few minutes the maid came up wild-eyed and frightened saying there was a ball of fire in the kitchen.

Mrs Zheng thought it might be a sign of wealth which the old man had secretly hidden. The couple decided to go downstairs and look.

Just as the watching Zhan Zhao was about to enter the room to take the silver, he saw a light flickering and his new friend Ding come making straight for the secret panel and removing not eight packages but nine.

Footsteps sounded on the stairs and Zhan Zhao was worried that Ding would not get out in time. But suddenly the light went out and the room was in complete darkness and when the couple returned the room was empty.

Zhan Zhao jumped down from the building, returned to the inn and soon fell fast asleep.

When the red sun rose in the east he got up and after breakfast strolled to the Broken Bridge where he found the old man Zhou and in the distance Ding Zhaohui with two attendants who on coming up gave the old man a bundle and an offer of one of the attendants to help him set up a rival teahouse. Zhan Zhao watched closely as the old man untied the bundle.

CHAPTER 30

A Man in Need Is Saved.
Southern Hero Accepts an Invitation.

WHEN the bundle was opened, Zhan Zhao noticed that the silver from the nine packages had been re-wrapped into eight larger and heavier packages.

"If anyone asks where you got the silver," said Ding Zhaohui, "tell them the son of the garrison commander at the Xiongguan Pass gave it to you."

"And if anyone asks who is the sponsor," said Zhan Zhao, "tell them it is Zhan Zhao from the Gallant Meeting Village."

The old man was full of gratitude but the generous-hearted Ding said that the only interest he wanted on the silver was a cup of fragrant tea if ever he visited the teahouse.

Ding Zhaohui then invited Zhan Zhao to visit his manor house and twin brother and as "Royal Cat" still had some leave left he readily consented.

They went by boat to Ding's family home, enjoying the beautiful scenery on the way. Zhan Zhao asked his new friend how he was able to give so much silver to the old man and not save any for himself if he was going to burn incense for his mother.

"I can borrow more, if I need it," was the answer.

Zhan Zhao laughed and said: "Well, you can always blow out the lamp, if you can't borrow any more."

He then told the astonished Ding how he had seen him enter the Zheng Family Building the night before.

When they disembarked they walked up an even path flanked by shrubs and bushes. In the middle of the path was a line of trees and under every tree stood a man of powerful build with big eyes beneath bushy eyebrows. Instead of a hat, they wore a brim of reeds with their hair tied in a knot on top of their heads. The veins stood out like cords on their bare crossed arms. Some of them were barefooted; others wore straw sandals.

Ding explained that there were more than five hundred fishing boats in the river and the fishermen often fought and wounded people. The line of trees was a demarcation line which separated the warring boatmen and the twins were in charge of one side of the cove. A path laid with blue fish-like scales led up to the gate of the manor house and a man flanked by his page-boys and attendants stood at the top of the stairs waiting for them. It was the older twin called Ding Zhaolan and they were as alike as two peas.

As children they had often played tricks on their elders by pretending to be each other and Zhan Zhao would have found it extremely difficult to tell the difference between the two even when they stood side by side.

As he entered the manor, he took off his sword as a mark of respect not only because it was the first time he had been there but also to show respect for their mother, who sent a message that she would see him when he had rested. To while away the time while they waited he was asked to relate his adventures when he rescued Prime Minister Bao from the ferocious monk in the Gold Dragon Monastery, and at Earth Dragon Crag, how he captured the assassin and how he destroyed the black magic in Grand Tutor Pang's garden.

To their exclamations of admiration he said modestly: "Those are deeds which we gallants should do as part of our duty and therefore not worth mentioning."

"But you have also performed your skills before the emperor," remarked Ding, "who named you 'Royal Cat'."

"It was all done for Prime Minister Bao's sake," said Zhan Zhao, "but I really feel quite weighed down by all the honours bestowed on me."

Ding asked to see the famous sword that Zhan Zhao had used in front of the emperor and to demonstrate his prowess with it on the Moon Platform. Afterwards, Ding Zhaohui remarked: "Your skill is not bad, only the sword appears a little heavy. I have one that will suit you well."

A page-boy brought in the sword and Zhan Zhao was asked to try it out.

As Zhan Zhao flourished and sliced the air with the sword on the Moon Platform, Ding asked if it wasn't a great strain and the vexed Zhan Zhao replied that it was much lighter than his own.

"Don't be so boastful," rejoined Ding, "making rude remarks about the sword is the same as slighting its owner. You cannot afford to displease its owner."

Zhan Zhao was annoyed and retorted: "I'm not afraid of anybody and will answer for my actions. To whom does the sword belong?"

"It belongs to my cousin," said Ding.

Just then a maid announced that the matriarch was coming.

Zhan Zhao stood up, straightened his clothes and bowed. Lady Ding modestly returned the courtesies as if he was her nephew. She scrutinised him closely, seeing him much more clearly than when she had peered at him earlier from behind a screen. She saw a handsome man, and referring to him as "her nephew" had been a ruse devised by her son. If she approved of Zhan Zhao as a prospective husband for her niece, she was to use that term; if she had not approved she would have referred to him as "distinguished guest".

Ding sneaked out of the room to inform his cousin of what had taken place.

CHAPTER 31

Southern Hero Crosses Swords with His Intended.
Sky Rat Apologises for Poaching.

DING crossed the courtyard and entered the quarters of his cousin, Moon Flower.

She was sewing quietly because of the guest in the drawing room.

"Who told you of our guest?" he asked.

"The page who took my sword told me," she answered.

"His name is Zhan Zhao, otherwise known as Southern Hero. He's very good-looking and a skilful swordsman but when I told him that you owned the sword he had been trying out, he said a mere slip of a girl could not possibly have the necessary skills."

Moon Flower flushed with anger and flung down her needlework.

"Good," thought Ding, "I've made her angry." He added aloud: "I asked him, 'Don't you believe a general's family can produce a heroine?' Why don't you show him how good you are?"

"I'll be there in a minute," she said in a fit of pique.

Zhan Zhao's first glimpse of his friend's cousin when she entered the drawing room was a good-looking young woman with a face of thunder.

Ding said: "She's angry with you because you criticised her sword and now she wants to challenge you."

The matriarch settled herself down in an armchair and the twin brothers stood behind her as the two contestants prepared themselves.

Moon Flower took off her topcoat and exposed a red embroidered jacket and a white silk pleated skirt. The milk-white bandanna round her head made her look lovelier than before. Zhan Zhao reluctantly tucked up his gown and sleeves and they began. For the first few rounds the contest was even because Zhan Zhao just parried her moves in deference to her sex. But finding her so adept, he became more serious until a small object fell to the ground and as he bent down to look, the girl made a sweep of her sword like the wind blowing off dead tree leaves, and sliced off the bandanna round his head. He jumped out of the circle crying: "I surrender, I surrender!"

One of the twins picked up the small object that Moon Flower had dropped. It was an earring, and the twin said: "It was my cousin who was defeated." As she retired to her own rooms Zhan Zhao, replacing the bandanna round his head, commented: "Your worthy cousin is very good."

Lady Ding then drew Zhan Zhao aside and said: "Moon Flower is my niece and when her parents died, I took her as my own daughter. I've heard of your good reputation and want to arrange a marriage between you two and so ally our two families. I did not imagine that one day you would honour us with a visit to our humble family. There must be an invisible red thread round your ankle that has led you here to ensure a happy union."

"As you had no marriage broker to inspect the prospective bride for you, we arranged this sword contest so you could test her."

Zhan Zhao consented to the betrothal, realising that it must have been destined, and gave his sword in exchange for her sword as a betrothal gift.

Ding then took the sword and the earring to his cousin's quarters and told her of his mother's decision. He put down the sword and left smiling. Moon Flower realised she had been betrothed to

Zhan Zhao and did not speak.

Three days went by and Zhan Zhao decided to go on his way but the twins insisted that he stay a little longer by promising to give him a dinner party first on the Terrace Overlooking the Sea which was a short distance away from the manor house along a winding path to the ridge of a mountain. In the distance was a huge stretch of water with boats plying to and fro. It was a pleasant relaxing view and the three men sat enjoying the wine and food. Later a fisherman came and whispered to the older of the twins who said: "Tell the chief to handle the matter."

After a while another fisherman entered and the twin number two said loudly: "Bring him here and let me see him."

Zhan Zhao asked what the trouble was and the twins explained that there were five blood brothers, and they were responsible for the southern side of the river. The oldest was known as Sky Rat because he could swarm up tall posts. The second was known as Earth Rat because of his tunnelling expertise. The third was named Mountain Rat because he could worm his way through the eighteen tunnels of a mountain. The fourth, although slightly built, was known as Water Rat because he could swim under water and find objects. The fifth although very handsome was rather cruel and unfriendly but he fought injustice and he was called Sleek Rat.

"I know him and have been looking for him," exclaimed Zhan Zhao and related how he had met Sleek Rat during the happenings in the Miao Family Fair.

A fisherman then came complaining that during a fight with the poachers they had cut off four fingers of his hand. "Only my thumb is left. They're no friends of ours," he cried.

The three men boarded boats with an armed escort to investigate where the poaching of fish was taking place in Reed Catkins Cove. When they got there they saw a fierce-looking man with a seven-pronged trident in hand standing on a boat and ready to fight.

"Why don't you stick to the line of demarcation," Ding the eldest of the twins shouted. "You have trespassed over the Reed Catkins Cove and injured one of our fishermen."

"I don't recognise the demarcation line," bawled the man with the trident. "There's more fish on your side and we're willing to fight."

Finding him unreasonable, Ding asked his name. "I'm called Deng Biao, the Water-Splitting Animal," he said. "This fleet of boats is in my charge." He was about to aim his trident when he suddenly fell into the water and was captured.

It was Ding, the younger of the twins, who had felled him with an iron ball with a device he had invented when he was a boy. It was a piece of bamboo with a groove in which he could fit a ball the size of a walnut, made from yellow wax and iron pellets and fire it from quite a distance. The power of the shot was enough to fell the big, strong Water-Splitting Animal into the water.

As they questioned him about the whereabouts of his master they heard a man shouting across the water and saw a small boat flying towards them. "Brothers, don't be angry. I'll pay for any damages."

It was Sky Rat glowing with health and with a long sleek beard.

The twins clasped their hands in greeting and after mutual apologies were made, compensation was arranged for the loss of fish and damaged nets on the two sides. Sky Rat decided that Water-Splitting Animal should be delivered to the county office to be punished.

The two parties exchanged friendly remarks and left for their respective homes.

CHAPTER 32

An Old Servant Is Rescued.
A Poor Scholar Meets a Ragged Eccentric.

THE fisherman who had lost four fingers in the fight was given ten taels of silver as compensation, and Zhan Zhao decided it was time for him to leave the Ding brothers.

"I hear that Sleek Rat has gone to the capital to look for me," he told them. Reluctantly they had to let him go, so he paid his respects to Lady Ding and left.

He hoped to reach his destination that very night but as he hurried through an elm forest he heard someone shouting: "Help! Help! Someone is trying to rob me!" He found an old man running towards him being chased by another man. He told the man to hide behind a tree and as the pursuer came running by, Zhan Zhao stuck out his foot and tripped him up. Untying the sash round his waist he tied him up and propped him against a tree. The old man was on his way home to Elm Tree Village when the man had tried to rob him.

Zhan Zhao said to the mugger: "It's lucky you met me rather than someone less kind-hearted. I won't kill you but I'll leave you here for somebody else to untie you."

Elm Tree Village was on his way so he accompanied the old man to his house and then carried on to his own home in Gallant Meeting Village.

The old man was a servant of a twenty-two-year-old man named Yan Shenmin who lived with his widowed mother. Her husband had been a magistrate of integrity and honesty, but because he had never taken bribes he had left his family destitute when he died. Shenmin wanted to become a magistrate like his father and was a studious and well-read young man, but could not afford to go to the capital to take the imperial examination. His mother suggested he visit his wealthy aunt and at the same time conclude a marriage with her daughter, his cousin, but the son was reluctant to get in touch with them now that they themselves were in such straitened circumstances, let alone marry his cousin unless he was able to take the examination and gain a post. When the old servant came back with money they were borrowing from a friend, the mother was overjoyed and said he could now get in touch with his aunt. The servant was too tired to mention his ordeal or the meeting with Zhan Zhao and went straight to bed.

The next morning, as Shenmin got ready to leave, the old man related his adventures of the day before and insisted that he should accompany him to the capital to keep him safe. But luckily a young boy named Yumo arrived from the friend who had lent the money with instructions to wait on the young scholar. The old servant was left behind to look after the mother and the two, scholar and boy, set off.

Yumo was only fourteen but very clever and worldly-wise. As a very young child he had travelled throughout the country with his father, who was a trader and therefore was just the person to help the naive young scholar, who after only walking a few *li* complained of pains in his legs.

Yumo suggested that he should walk as if he was enjoying the scenery. "When you see a rock or a tree, take it as a foil to a beautiful scene." he said. "That way you will forget your tiredness and walk a longer distance."

In the evening they looked for an inn to stay the night. Yumo cleverly haggled and bargained with the waiters who tried to inveigle them into taking the most expensive rooms, but Yumo was wise to their ploys and eventually managed to get a simple room. He also refused the expensive menu and asked for fried leftovers. The waiter was then convinced that they did not have a lot of money to spend and left them in peace.

As they waited for the meal, they heard someone shouting: "How dare you look down on me? I am still a customer even if I only buy a small dish. Insult me again and I'll set fire to your wretched inn!"

"Good," thought Yumo, "he's our kind of man."

The innkeeper said all the rooms had been taken but the angry man shouted: "Rubbish. How dare you belittle a member of the educated class? Since when should people like us be lorded over by the likes of you?"

At that, Shenmin could not help but go out and invite the man to share his room.

Yumo was not at all happy. "Too bad," he thought, "my master will be taken in."

He hastened out but saw his master and the man had already come in and were sitting down in their room.

CHAPTER 33

The Worthy Scholar Meets a Mysterious Guest.
The Young Page Succumbs to a Confidence Trick.

THE man sitting opposite Yan Shenmin wore a ragged blue gown, worn-out shoes and a tattered headdress and looked more like a beggar than a scholar.

The innkeeper came in apologising profusely but the man answered with a wave of his hand: "The worthy won't hold a grudge against the lowly. I forgive you."

He said his name was Jin, which means gold, and Yumo thought: "Only people like my master deserve the name Jin, not this lowly man who doesn't even deserve the name of Yin (silver)."

Jin called over the waiter and asked what was on the menu.

"The first-class menu costs eight taels of silver, the middle menu costs six taels and the lower..."

"Who wants the lower-class menu?" bawled Jin. "What's on the first-class menu?"

"A dozen bowls of chicken, duck, fish, meat, sharks' fin and sea cucumbers."

"What about live carp?"

"The live carp is very large and costs one tael and ten grams of silver," answered the waiter.

"Since that is what I want to eat, I'll spare no expense," answered Jin. "The carp must weigh more than a kilo, otherwise it isn't carp. It has to be a live one with a red tail which shows it is fresh. And bring some vintage wine. It must be golden-red in colour and fragrant."

Two candles were lit and the waiter, happy now that he was serving lavish spenders, bustled in with a wooden tub which held a huge live carp.

"Kill it right here, in case you exchange it for another," said Jin "and boil it in fresh water with 'tiptop'." He explained to the puzzled waiter that 'tiptop' meant only the tender tips of fresh bamboo.

Yan and Jin drank and chatted and soon the fish was ready. Taking up his chopsticks Jin cut across the back of the fish and dipping a morsel in a saucer of ginger and vinegar helped it down with a cup of wine.

"Don't stand on ceremony, brother Yan," said Jin as he tucked into the fish and dunked his bread into the sauce.

After they finished, Jin told the waiter to give the leftovers to Yumo and the two men left the table.

There was much food left over and some of the dishes were not even touched. It made Yumo's heart ache to feel he could not take the food with him to eat on their journey. He went to bed with a heavy heart after the two had retired to sleep.

In the morning as he prepared water for his young master, Jin lay on the bed, stretched his legs and exposed his feet poking through worn-out socks. He recited a poem: "Who can explain the deep dream? I know what to do with my life. Spring puts me to bed in the thatched hut; the sun outside the window is late."

He then got out of bed saying that daylight had come before he was aware of it.

He refused water to wash, saying he was afraid of water and told the waiter to bring the bill.

"Good," thought Yumo, "he's going to pay." It came to over thirteen taels of silver.

"That's not bad," said Jin, "add another two taels for the waiters and the cooks as a tip."

He called out: "Brother Yan, I'm off. See you in the capital," and then shuffled away without paying the bill.

In a huff, Yumo paid the bill but could not help asking his master why he tolerated such a man as Jin.

"Because he is a good scholar," Yan Shenmin replied.

"I am more familiar with the ways of the world than you," replied Yumo. "You have never been out of your home and don't know the kinds of people you will encounter. Some will coax you into treating them to a meal, others will cheat you out of your belongings. Now you regard Mr Jin as a scholar and a gentleman. To me he is nothing but a confidence trickster."

Yan was not to be moved and scolded his young page.

When evening came they found another lodging and as they settled in, the waiter told them that a certain Mr Jin was coming to call on them.

"This is too much," thought Yumo. "I must do something about it."

He said to Jin: "My master hasn't eaten yet. Why not share the same table?"

"Excellent, excellent," said Jin.

Yumo then called the waiter and asked: "What dishes do you have?"

The waiter replied: "We have three menus. Grade A costs eight taels, Grade B six taels and Grade C..."

Yumo interrupted: "We'll order Grade A, no doubt it includes chicken, duck, fish, meat, shark's fins and sea cucumbers and do you also keep live carp? Spare no expense," continued Yumo. "The carp must weigh more than a kilo, otherwise it isn't carp and it must have a red tail to indicate it's fresh. As for wine we want the vintage stuff — the golden-red with a fragrant bouquet."

When the carp was brought in, Yumo went through the same sequence as Jin had done in the previous inn, including demanding 'tiptop' — the tender tips of bamboo.

He then waited on the two men, repeating the same words that Jin had said to Yan Shenmin, at the last meal. Jin gave him a suspicious look but carried on eating.

After they finished the meal they retired for the night and in the morning Yumo recited the same poem as Jin had recited the morning before.

"No need to get water for you," said Yumo, "I'll tell the waiter to make out the bill."

It came to over fourteen taels, but before Yumo could arrange for Jin to pay it, he had disappeared.

"For shame," said Yumo to himself, "he's done it again," and laughed at the way his trick had rebounded on him.

CHAPTER 34

The Young Scholar Forms an Alliance with the Hero.
He Is Despised by His Wealthy Relatives.

THEY did not have enough money to pay for the meal, so the scholar ordered his page to pawn some of his clothes.

"Just two days after leaving home, we have to visit a pawn-shop," grumbled Yumo. "What shall we do when we have no more clothes to pawn?"

Yan Shenmin turned a deaf ear.

"That Mr Jin sponged off us and didn't even touch the dishes and left most of that expensive wine. He has made a fool of you. I really don't understand it."

His master answered: "It is because he is an easy-going scholar who pays no heed to material matters."

They found a very cheap inn to stay for the night and when the waiter announced: "There is a Mr Jin come to see you," Yumo thought: "He can't order anything expensive in this cheap place. Good."

"What a coincidence," said Jin. "It must be fate that we keep bumping into each other. Let us become sworn brothers."

Yumo thought: "There he goes again," and said out loud: "You want to become a sworn brother of my master? I'm afraid this small inn can't prepare any sacrificial offerings. Let's do it another time."

"That's no matter," replied Jin. "Next door is the Grand Harmony Hotel. They have everything we want. We'll order from there."

Yumo stamped his foot in rage. "What bad luck that we've taken on such a leech," he fumed inwardly.

The usual food was ordered: fresh carp with "tiptop", and vintage wine. The two "brothers" chatted and drank while Yumo worried about how they were going to foot the bill the next day.

Soon the sacrificial offerings were ready and as Yan was two years older than Jin he was the first to burn the incense and as the eldest he would also have to treat Jin to dinner.

After they finished Yumo decided he might as well be hung for a sheep as a lamb and he and the waiter tucked in and finished the dishes and wine before he turned in.

The next morning as Yan Shenmin was washing, Yumo admonished him about becoming a sworn brother of a total stranger who might sully his reputation.

Yan again scolded him, saying that Jin was different and spoke in the style of a gallant gentleman and they would support each other through thick and thin.

When Jin appeared he asked as usual for the bill and suggested adding an extra two taels as a tip but then he astonished Yumo by turning to Yan Shenmin and instead of passing on the bill said: "Surely you are not going to visit your relations in those clothes? Won't they look down on you?"

Yan sighed: "I don't really want to go, as I haven't seen my aunt and uncle for many years. I'm only doing it to please my mother."

"Well, take care," rejoined Jin.

"He's become quite a different person, since they've become sworn brothers," thought Yumo.

A tall man dressed in a black tunic with a leather belt round his waist and wearing home-made shoes entered the room and kowtowed to Jin. "Our old master has sent me and wants you to have this four hundred taels of silver as travelling expenses."

"I don't need so much money!" protested Jin. "I'll just take two hundred taels and you can take the rest back and thank him."

Seeing he had come by horseback, Jin took the pawn ticket from Yan Shenmin and told the messenger to redeem his clothes.

The young scholar and his page were baffled how Jin knew they had pawned their clothes. Yumo decided that perhaps Jin was a kind person after all and that his master had a gift for choosing the right kind of man to be his friend.

The man was ordered to bring the clothes to the Grand Harmony Hotel where they would be waiting. Jin handed over the rest of the silver to Yan, bowed and left, saying he would meet him in the capital.

The now happy and relieved Yumo packed their luggage and they proceeded to Xiangfu County where Yan's aunt and uncle lived.

Yan's uncle, Liu Hong, was a wealthy farmer but obstinate and avaricious. He and Yan's father were brothers-in-law and because the latter was a magistrate and therefore of higher social standing, had engaged his daughter, Gold Cicada, to his nephew. When the magistrate died, he regretted the engagement. Then his wife died; he married again and put the engagement of his daughter to his former in-laws out of his mind. The second Mrs Liu was a ruthless woman who decided to marry off her step-daughter to her nephew and thus keep the property and money in the family. So she directed her nephew, who was ugly and uncouth, to curry favour in her husband's eyes.

It gave the old squire a shock when a servant announced that his former wife's nephew had arrived to pay him a visit.

At first he told the servant to say he was not in and then stopped and asked: "What does he look like?"

"He's well-dressed, riding a noble horse, accompanied by a page-boy," the servant answered.

"He must have come into a fortune," thought the squire, "so

he's come to marry my daughter."

He went out to greet him and sure enough saw a handsome young man, dressed in good clothes, accompanied by a page-boy leading a big white horse. They bowed and tea was served.

Yan explained to his uncle that he was on his way to take the imperial examinations and if a friend had not lent him the money for the journey, it would have been impossible otherwise as they were in straitened circumstances. He gave him the letter his mother had written. At this the squire looked happy no longer, pulled a long face and bade his servant to put his nephew in the Quiet Study, saying his wife was not well enough to receive him. In the meantime he would decide what to do with this unwelcome visitor.

It was fortunate that Jin had provided Yan with new clothes and a good horse before he visited his uncle, otherwise he would not have been received in the first place.

CHAPTER 35

The Engagement Is Broken Off.
A Poetry Competition Takes Place Between Two Rivals.

WITH a woebegone face, Liu Hong took the letter from his former sister-in-law to his wife and told her of Yan's visit.

"Look at this letter from my former sister-in-law. It asks us to let her son stay at our home to read and prepare for next year's imperial examination. How much is that going to cost us? What is more, if he passes, how many guests will we have to invite to celebrate? And if he fails, I shall have to conclude the marriage between him and my daughter and they will go back to his home with the dowry and I will lose not only my daughter but also my money! I would like to break off the engagement and find a wealthy son-in-law. Then my daughter won't have to live in poverty."

Now that she saw he wanted to get out of the old arrangement, his wife suggested that they leave him alone in the Quiet Study and ignore him for a few days. He would then take the hint and go.

But they were overheard by Gold Cicada's nurse who told the girl what her parents were plotting. "You had better do something quickly," she urged, "but whatever you decide must not ruin your reputation or prospects."

The old nurse suggested that Gold Cicada write a note to Yan, not as her prospective husband but as a brother, and suggest meeting him in the inner study late at night. "Give him some money and tell him to go away. After he passes the imperial examinations and becomes an official, he can marry you."

Gold Cicada told Scarlet, her personal maid, to deliver a message and money to Yan arranging to meet him.

Gold Cicada's nurse and maid loved their young mistress and wanted to do what was right for the engaged couple, but the stepmother's nephew, Feng, was eager to pursue his selfish ends.

He was desperate to marry his aunt's stepdaughter and tried in all manner of ways to ingratiate himself with the squire, who had taken an active dislike to this ill-mannered and uneducated fellow.

There is a belief that eyebrows and eyes give expression to love. Although the eyes are an organ of sight, the brows appear to have no use, but if there were an empty space where the eyebrows should be, it would make the face look very peculiar indeed. Suppose there was a dialogue between the mouth and nose. "Hello nose, what can you do?" asks the mouth and the nose retorts: "But for my ability to smell, you could never tell fragrance from stench," and then the nose asks the eyes: "Why should you be above me?" The eyes answer: "If we couldn't see, you could never tell the good from the bad." Then the eyes ask the brows: "Why should you occupy a place higher than ours?" The eyebrows admit they can do nothing. "We would be quite willing to move to below the eyes, but what would the face look like then?"

The eyebrows of Feng can be cited as an example: after this oaf saw Gold Cicada, his eyebrows seemed to be anywhere but where they belonged, as his lust for the girl grew by the day.

Knowing from his aunt that the squire was now not happy with the proposed marriage to a penniless scholar, he decided to see Yan for himself and find fault with him. But when he entered the Quiet Study, he found instead a handsome young man, elegantly dressed and well-spoken. The contrast between the two men was so strong that even Squire Liu Hong could see the difference.

"Yan is by far the better of the two," he thought. "If only he wasn't so poor." Embarrassed, he left the two men to their own devices.

Feng felt awkward, deeply regretting that his parents had not made more efforts to cultivate his mind when he was young.

"How old are you?" he asked Yan.

"A score and two," was the reply.

Feng did not understand the word 'score' and Yan wrote it down.

"Oh, it means twenty. I am a score too."

"So Brother Feng is twenty years of age?" said Yan.

"Ache? No, I have no aches." Feng replied.

Yan laughed: "I said 'age' not 'ache'."

Feng was aware he had been caught out and said: "Don't speak to me in such a literary style."

"What do you do at home then?" asked Yan.

Feng told him that he had a tutor who taught him poetry but he found it very difficult to write more than two lines that rhymed.

So the two men spent some time composing poetry in which Yan showed his superiority in rhyming couplets and literary allusions.

Feng then noticed the fan that Yan held in his hand and admired his handwriting and begged that they exchange fans and he write something on his. Reluctantly Yan consented. Feng left very peeved that he had come off badly in the poetry contest; he was determined to get his own back on the young scholar.

CHAPTER 36

A Maid Is Murdered in the Garden.
A Black-Hearted Servant Attempts to Rob the Dead.

THE disgruntled Feng was going through the garden when he saw
Scarlet, the maid, approaching. Suspicious, he asked her what
was she doing.

"I went to pick some flowers for my mistress," she answered,
'but they are not open yet. Why are you questioning me? This garden belongs to the Liu family, not the Fengs."

He hastened back to the Quiet Study where he saw Yan unfold-
ing a note which he quickly placed between the pages of the book
as he entered the room.

"Would you lend me some easy books on poetry?" he asked.

While Yan went to a shelf, Feng surreptitiously removed the
note from the volume and hid it in his sleeve.

Afterwards he read the note, which asked Yan to meet Gold Cicada by the inner side gate during the second watch.

Feng thought: "If they meet tonight, she will promise to marry
him without fail and all my efforts will come to nothing." He decided to take Yan's place. He thought he could force her to agree
to marry him instead by showing her that he held the compromis-
ing note.

The modest Gold Cicada, however, decided it would be improper conduct for her to meet Yan and sent her maid Scarlet instead,

with money and clothes.

When the maid went to the inner side gate she discovered Feng waiting. She was about to scream for help when he grabbed her throat and strangled her. He hurried off with the silver and clothes, leaving the note and Yan's fan lying beside her body.

A watchman going on his rounds discovered the body and reported to the squire, who found the fan and note. His wife persuaded him to lodge a complaint at the magistrate's court accusing the young scholar of murder. Yan was arrested and the magistrate called his court into session where the squire demanded the death penalty. The magistrate saw a rather timorous young man standing before him who did not look like a murderer. But nevertheless he asked him: "Yan Shenmin, why did you murder the maid?"

"Because she refused to do my bidding and was rude to me," Yan answered. "In a fit of anger I chased her to the inner side gate and strangled her. I hope Your Lordship will speedily wind up the case." He kowtowed.

The magistrate wondered why he had owned up so quickly and whether there were some facts he wished to hide. He ordered him to be taken to the cells while he thought it over.

In reality, Yan did not want his future wife's reputation to be sullied and had therefore confessed to the murder. It was his fault that he had lost her note and he believed it was the honourable thing to do.

Yumo, his page, was opposed to his master's move, unaware of the noble intentions. He bribed the jailer to make sure his master was well looked after, at the same time crying out: "You should not have taken the blame."

Yan only smiled and did not seem to care, which made Yumo even more puzzled.

In the meantime, although Liu Hong was relieved at Yan's confession, his daughter, Gold Cicada, became despondent and felt it was all her fault. "I may as well repay his sacrifice with my death," she told herself and bade her nurse to go and make some tea. When she returned she found her young mistress had hanged herself with a silk handkerchief.

Mrs. Liu blamed her husband for the whole sorry situation but she was more worried about the ensuing scandal and the damage to their reputation.

They decided to pretend that Gold Cicada had been taken ill and then after a few days tell everyone she had died. She was placed in a coffin, surrounded by her favourite clothes and trinkets. The servants were bribed and the gates kept locked against inquisitive neighbours. But one servant, named Niu the Donkey, described to his wife the valuable articles that had been placed in the coffin, and she was greedy to possess them. "What a pity to leave such valuables in a coffin to be buried for ever. Sneak in tonight and get them for me," she said.

At the second watch Niu the Donkey took his axe and, jumping over the Liu family's wall, made his way to the hall where the coffin lay.

CHAPTER 37

Gold Cicada Is Brought Back to Life and Niu the Donkey Is Put to the Sword. The Gallant Sleek Rat Hands Out More Silver.

WHEN Niu the Donkey jumped down from the wall he fancied there were human figures in the garden but it was only the moonlight flickering through the branches of the trees as they swayed in the breeze.

Nervously he entered the hall and trembled at the thought of seeing a dead body, but the thought of the valuables in the coffin overrode his fears. He got down on his knees, praying: "I am a poor man, I'll just borrow those hairpins, rings and clothes for the time being and when I am rich I will burn paper ingots for you."

He took his axe, levered off the lid and gently placed it crosswise across the coffin. Just as he put his hand in he heard a sigh and saw Gold Cicada move.

"Thank you," she gasped and sank back exhausted.

Niu the Donkey trembled but then thought: "She may not be dead but she is very weak. I'll throttle her and take the valuables. No one will be any the wiser."

Something hit his hand painfully. He looked round and saw a man in black charge at him and fell him with a kick.

Pinning him down, the man in black demanded: "Who is in the coffin?"

"It's my young mistress," Niu the Donkey babbled. "She hanged herself yesterday because her betrothed Yan Shenming confessed to a murder. Spare me, I beg you."

"I could spare you for being greedy for gain but not for the murder you intended. You deserve to die."

With a flash of his sword, Niu the Donkey was done for.

The man in black was Sleek Rat, otherwise known as Jin, who had befriended the young scholar. Sleek Rat had gone on ahead to find out what sort of man was the squire whom his friend regarded as uncle. He then learned that Yan was in prison and had come to the squire's house at the dead of night to find out why. That was when he discovered Niu the Donkey. Now he knew what to do. He called out in a loud voice: "Your young lady has come back to life. Help, quick!"

He kicked down the side gate, thus alerting the watchmen who came running into the hall and saw Gold Cicada sitting up in the coffin and the body of Niu the Donkey lying beside it. Sleek Rat jumped over the roof and made his way to the squire's quarters.

Everyone went wild with joy to see the young mistress alive and well. She was carried into her room where she rapidly regained her strength with ginger soup. Her father reported the death of another servant in the family to the bailiff, who said sarcastically: "The case of the strangled maid is still unsolved and now another servant has been killed. What jolly goings-on take place in your household."

To save any awkwardness, Liu Hong decided to give the bailiff some silver and went into his private room where he kept his money. He was surprised to see the treasure chest open and the lock on the floor. Ten packets of silver were gone. With tears streaming down his face he called for his wife, who berated him saying: "Why are you crying over the death of Niu the Donkey? You should be happy now your daughter is alive."

"I'm not crying over the coffin robber's death," he retorted. "Ten packets of silver have disappeared. I have to go and report it."

His wife, a highly intelligent woman, said: "Two murders have taken place in our household. If you tell the magistrate about our silver, he will think we have plenty of money and we will have to spend another ten packets of silver before the cases are solved. You may as well accept the loss of the money."

Liu Hong had to agree with the sensible advice although his heart felt heavy at the loss of his silver.

Yan in the meantime was still in prison and nothing had been done about his case. The money that Yumo had bribed the prison guards with had gone and they were demanding more, otherwise their prisoner would be ill-treated. As Yumo wept and begged for more time, Sleek Rat suddenly appeared dressed in a warrior headdress, pale blue embroidered gown and official boots. He looked very impressive and Yumo saw a slight resemblance to Mr Jin.

"Yumo," the man said, "I didn't expect to see you here. It must have been quite an ordeal for you."

Hearing his voice, Yumo could not hold back his tears and bowed to him. "It is you, Mr Jin." To himself he said: "His accent has changed too."

"Where is your master?" Sleek Rat asked.

CHAPTER 38

Yumo Pleads for His Master.
Sleek Rat Risks His Life to Save His Friend.

SLEEK Rat was shocked at his friend's unkempt appearance when he visited his cell. He took his hands and asked: "How have you been wronged, brother?"

"I'm ashamed for you to see me in this condition," Yan replied bravely.

"We are sworn brothers and you must not hide the truth from me," said Sleek Rat.

"It was all my fault," Yan said, and then related the story of his impeachment and arrest, ending with: "If I had not pleaded guilty, I would have implicated the girl and her honour."

"That is very manly of you," commended Sleek Rat. "It's a pity you don't worry about your old mother as well."

Tears streamed down Yan's face and his heart ached. "It must be fate; I can't escape retribution for the evil I have done in a previous existence. When I am dead please take care of her. Then when I am in the nether world, I shall be at peace." Yumo also began crying.

"Don't be so morbid, brother, there is an alternative. I hear that Prime Minister Bao tries cases like a god. You should appeal to him."

Yan refused, saying that as he had pleaded guilty it was useless to appeal to highter authority.

As persuasion did not convince his friend, Sleek Rat gave the warders some silver to take good care of him and asked Yan's permission to borrow Yumo for a few days.

When they were a distance from the prison, Yumo asked: "Are you sending me to the Kaifeng Prefecture to personally appeal for my master?"

"Remarkable boy," said Sleek Rat, "young as you are, you are very clever. Do you dare?"

"If I didn't, I wouldn't ask you about it," retorted Yumo.

Sleek Rat laughed. "Go to Kaifeng tomorrow and I'll do something on the sly and we'll get your master free."

They went their separate ways.

That night a very strange event took place in the office of the Kaifeng Prefecture. Prime Minister Bao usually attended the imperial court at the fifth watch each morning and as usual his page Bao Xing and servant Li Cai had his clothes ready for him to wear. When they entered his room they uttered a cry of dismay. On the table in front of the curtained bed lay a sword and beneath it a note which said: "Yan Shenmin is innocent." Lord Bao was puzzled and decided to investigate it after his audience at the imperial court.

Yumo was standing among the crowds when the palanquin carrying the prime minister with his escort of guards and servants came into view. They came to a sudden stop as Yumo threw himself down shouting for justice. He was grabbed by the warrior Wang Chao who later marched him into court where Prime Minister Bao, looking as black as thunder, said:

"What's your name, boy? Speak."

"I'm Yumo from Wujin County," said the page falling on his knees. "I accompanied my master to visit his relative..."

"What is your master's name?" demanded Lord Bao.

"Yan Shenmin," was the reply.

"So there is such a person," thought the prime minister.

He then questioned Yumo further who told him the whole story of why he was seeking justice for his master. His uncle, Liu Hong, had not been very welcoming and isolated them in a separate study in the garden. "He has not treated my master as a relative, fed us badly and we have not even met his second wife. The only kindness we have received in that house has been from Gold Cicada's nurse who warned us that something nasty might happen. Now he has admitted to a murder which I am sure he did not commit. I never stirred from his side."

Yumo was taken away and the uncle and the nurse were sent for.

"What is Yan to you?" Lord Bao asked Liu Hong.

"He is the nephew of my first wife who came here to study to sit for next year's imperial examinations."

"And is your daughter engaged to be married to him?"

Liu Hong was bemused. "No wonder they say Prime Minister Bao tries cases like a god. He seems to know a lot about us," he said to himself.

Under further questioning, Liu accused his nephew of the maid's murder, which incensed the prime minister, who banged his gavel on the table and shouted: "How can you conclude that Yan is a murderer on the say-so of a servant, without investigating first? It's obvious to me you despise the poor and favour the rich. You throttled the maid in order to incriminate an innocent person."

Liu Hong kowtowed and described how he had found the fan inscribed with Yan's name by the body and thought that was conclusive enough.

Prime Minister Bao could not but agree. He waved the squire away and sent for the nurse.

She admitted to hearing Liu Hong and his wife conspiring to get rid of Yan and had told her young mistress who sent him some silver by her maid. "Who would have thought that the young master would strangle the maid and take the silver? When Master Liu

Hong found the fan he took him to the local authorities and my young mistress hanged herself, but luckily she revived."

"That pure young maid has been betrayed by the ungrateful Yan," thought Prime Minister Bao, 'just for a handful of silver. But I can't understand how a sword and a note saying he is innocent should mysteriously have been left in my bedroom, and then there's the boy Yumo appealing on his master's behalf. This is really a complicated case."

He ordered Yumo to be brought back into court. Hoping to intimidate him, he shouted angrily, threatening a slapping. "You said your master never left his study. How then was his fan left outside the inner side gate?"

CHAPTER 39

One Nephew Is Executed, the Other Is Acquitted.
A Warrior Is Taken by Surprise and a Duel Takes Place.

YUMO recounted how his master and the nephew of the squire's wife had spent an evening writing poetry and then exchanged fans. "That wretched fan is not my master's but belongs to the nephew Feng," he said firmly.

Lord Bao laughed out loud. He now knew the whole truth of the case and issued a warrant for the arrest of Feng.

He ordered Yan to be brought before him, saying to himself: "One is ready to pay with his life; the other requites his kindness with her death."

"Raise your head, Yan Shenmin," he said, as the scholar knelt before him. "What time did you go out of the study and reach the inner side gate? What time did you strangle the maid?"

The scholar remained silent.

Yumo cried out: "Tell the truth, master. Think of your poor mother!"

Yan burst into tears and kowtowed, saying: "The offender deserves to die ten thousand deaths. Spare me, I beseech you, Your Excellency. I did not have time to read the note Gold Cicada wrote because Feng came to borrow some books. When he left, the note had gone."

The mystery was now cleared up and Feng was brought in. The

prime minister saw a man with ears like a rabbit and cheeks like a bird, sneaky eyebrows and beady eyes. "He must be a bad lot," he thought.

"I have nothing to confess," Feng said, but at the sight of the implements of torture he quickly made a full confession.

Four of Bao's loyal warriors carried in the dog-headed axe and he was executed on the spot and Liu Hong was brought in.

"Old dog!" said the prime minister. "Your nephew has been wronged, your daughter tried to hang herself, her maid murdered, Niu the Donkey killed and Feng executed — all this due to your prejudice against the poor and favouring the rich. Tell me why I shouldn't mete out the same punishment to you as your nephew?"

"Spare me, Your Excellency, and allow me to atone for my faults."

"You have a chance to atone if you allow Yan to continue his studies and treat him well. Whether he passes the examinations or not, you must conclude the marriage between him and your daughter. If any accident happens to him, I'll have you executed. Is that clear?"

"I will, I will," gasped Liu Hong.

Then Yan Shenmin was brought before the prime minister.

"When you study you have to stick to the major principles and not get sidetracked by minor details. You are not a man of integrity, but a pedant. From now on you must mend your ways, study hard and hand in your written work regularly, which I will read and correct. Any progress you make will meet Yumo's expectations of you. Treat him kindly."

The case was settled and Prime Minister Bao retired to his study to receive Zhan Zhao, who had just returned after visiting his village and telling his old servant of his engagement to Moon Flower. This had pleased the old man immensely and he did not make a fuss when Zhan Zhao left for Kaifeng. He paid his respects to Prime Minister Bao and mentioned his encounter with Sleek Rat.

They realised that the mysterious sword and note left in the prime minister's bedroom were Sleek Rat's doing.

There was great rejoicing when Zhan Zhao met his brothers-in-arms and Gongsun Ce. He told them of how he had become allied with the Dings by marriage by crossing swords with Moon Flower, his betrothed, and also that Sleek Rat had boasted of wanting a duel with the Royal Cat as Zhan Zhao was known.

"What is Sleek Rat like?" asked Ma Han.

"His real name is Bai Yutang. He is one of the five gallants," replied Zhan Zhao.

He told them of the battles with rival fishermen on Hollow Island and the nicknames of their leaders — the Five Rats.

"Think about it," said Gongsun Ce, "because you're known as the Royal Cat and cats catch rats. He's annoyed with you because of your name."

"But the title was conferred on me by His Majesty," protested Zhan Zhao. "If he's coming only for that, I'll give up the title."

Another warrior, Zhao Hu, slightly tipsy with wine, said: "You are usually more courageous than us. Why lose heart today, brother? The title was given you by the emperor: how can you give it up? If this Sleek Rat comes here I'll knock him down as easily as I down this cup of wine."

No sooner had he spoken than something flew in from outside and smashed the cup in his hand.

Zhan Zhao blew out the lamp, took his sword and jumped out of the window. In the dark he made out a man in black, nimble in his movements just like the man he had met in the Miao Family Fair. No sound was made as Zhan Zhao parried the man's sword until finally, losing patience, he raised his sword to make a movement like a crane singing in the air and broke the other's sword in two. His sword broken, the man leaped onto the top of the wall where Zhan Zhao gave chase. He caught a streak of light and before the words "Dear me" were out of his mouth, his bandanna was knocked off his head. His adversary had good sight and could see in the dark and had Zhan Zhao not been so nimble he would have been hit on the head. He ducked and when he looked up the man had disappeared.

The grounds were searched but there was no sign of the man and the warriors with Gongsun Ce retired to the hall to decide what their next movements would be.

CHAPTER 40

Three Heroes Set out to Find Their Missing Brother.
Five Gallants Are Mustered to Steal Dirty Money.

AFTER two months of hearing nothing since Sleek Rat had left his home on Hollow Island, his brothers began to worry.

The four of them, Sky Rat, Earth Rat, Mountain Rat and River Rat, were sitting in the drawing room recalling how happy they were when Sleek Rat completed the circle. Sky Rat muttered: "Fifth Brother has a child's disposition. He's too fond of parading his skills and is determined to measure his prowess against one called Royal Cat."

River Rat added: "He is too ambitious and arrogant. I gave him a piece of my mind last time and as it's my fault he left in a huff, I should go and look for him."

"You can't do that," said Sky Rat. "If Sleek Rat wins, he'll come back satisfied, but if he loses against Royal Cat your being there will only remind him of what you said."

Sky Rat mused over who would be most suitable to send. Mountain Rat was far too rough and might cause trouble. After much discussion they decided that three of them would go to Kaifeng, leaving Sky Rat to hold the fort.

Just then a message arrived saying that a squire Liu was coming to see them. He was a disciple of the Gold Head Giant Gan Bao and he was also known as Fair-Complexioned Judge.

Although not tall he dressed in bright colours and had a fierce look on his fair face, with bulging eyes. He had come to seek Sky Rat's help after hearing what a chivalrous man he was.

"In our prefecture," he began, "we have a governor named Sun Zhen who is the grandson-in-law of Grand Tutor Pang Ji. He is lecherous and avaricious, feeding on the flesh and blood of the people. In order to celebrate the grand tutor's birthday, he is preparing eight pots of miniature pine trees, under which are hidden a thousand taels of gold, which he will present to him. We are suffering from a severe drought and I want to intercept this present and buy rice to relieve the distress of the victims. I can't do it on my own and want you to help me."

Sky Rat was still too preoccupied with the missing Sleek Rat and told the squire not to waste his time in enlisting his help and suggested he try someone else.

The embarrassed Fair-Complexioned Judge became a bright red-faced judge and bowing, left.

As he went through the gate he saw three men approaching. They were Earth Rat, Mountain Rat and River Rat.

"Don't be annoyed," said River Rat. "Our elder brother didn't mean to rebuff you but he has other things on his mind." He was persuaded to go to their quarters, where Liu explained his predicament and plans of stopping the evil governor by slipping him knockout drops and soul-draining incense and thus retrieve the gold.

The three "Rats" decided to kill two birds with one stone helping Liu and also looking for their missing brother who was still in Kaifeng.

Despite losing the first round with Zhan Zhao, Sleek Rat was eager to seek fame and fortune by having another opportunity to fight him. Thinking back to the time he removed the silver from the Miao Family residence, he realised, despite it being night, that his fellow conspirator had been this very man, but he had set his heart on beating the Royal Cat and threw all caution to the winds.

In the royal garden around Longevity Hill lived a major-domo named Guo An, who was the nephew of the disgraced and executed major-domo-in-chief, Guo Huai. He had never accepted the justice of the sentence but nourished a deep hatred against Guo Huai's successor, the loyal Chen Lin.

"When my uncle made an attempt on the life of the crown prince, it was Chen Lin who rescued the prince and had my uncle executed. Now he is the major-domo-in-chief and I am his underling. Who is to know whether he will mete out the same punishment to me? I must think of a way to kill him and also avenge my uncle."

One evening, his little eunuch, He Changxi, brought him his tea, saying: "The Plucked Before Grain Rain tea is not so fragrant, so your slave has managed to cadge some excellent Dragon Well tea from my friends working in the major-domo-in-chief's office."

"Fine," replied Guo An, "but I prefer you don't go there too often; they are a lot of blackguards and they may do you harm."

"There's more to that than meets the eye," thought Changxi. "Is he hoping to settle old scores with the major-domo-in-chief?" He said out loud: "I go there to find out what is going on and just hang around."

"What have you heard?" asked Guo An.

"Only that the major-domo-in-chief is getting rather old and weak and works too hard. His Majesty sent some ginseng in medicinal wine to make him better."

Guo An ground his teeth in rage. "To make him better! If only I could arrange his death quickly and thus vent my hatred for him!"

CHAPTER 41

A Poem Is Written to Praise a Faithful Maid.
The Kaifeng Prefecture Investigates Another Case.

THE young eunuch's heart missed a beat as he saw his master's face so full of hate.

"The major-domo-in-chief has a heart of gold and has always been kind to you," he said.

"You are too young to understand," Guo An replied. "Chen Lin framed my uncle and I have harboured thoughts of revenge for a long time. Now he is taking this ginseng with wine, and it gives me the chance at last."

"How come?" He Changxi asked.

"Help me in my plan," Guo An said, "and I will adopt you as my son."

Changxi felt he had been pushed into a corner. "If I refuse he'll find someone else and he'll have a grudge against me." He hastily knelt down and said: "Father."

"Good boy," said Guo An, "I'll make sure you get promoted."

He then told the young boy how he had a family prescription which, if taken with ginseng, worked as a poison, for it was one of eight contradictions in herbal medicine — and no trace would be found. He took a silver pot inlaid with gold from the curio stand. At the bottom of the pot were two holes and a separate cylinder.

"It is called Centre-Shifting Pot," he said, and demonstrated by pouring water in one side and tea in the other. By pressing a finger on one or the other hole he was able to pour either water or tea.

"I will write an invitation to the major-domo-in-chief to come and drink tea with me and enjoy the new moon tomorrow. When he comes, take the wine pot and be sure to remember which of the two holes you must cover."

The eunuch left with the invitation and as he went round the rockery in the garden a man sprang from under the shade of the willows, his sword glistening in his hand.

"Cry out and I'll kill you," he said.

Changxi was tied up and placed under the willow tree.

"If you are given up to the Supreme Court tomorrow, tell them the truth. If you don't I'll come in the evening and cut your head off."

The man then went to Guo An's room and with one sweep of his sword decapitated the major-domo. When his body was discovered by eunuchs patrolling the grounds they searched and discovered Changxi still trussed up. He refused to say anything until he was taken before the court. The major-domo-in-chief, Chen Lin, said he would report to the emperor the next morning.

At the fifth watch the following day, the emperor received Chen Lin who told him of Guo An's death. The emperor was dismayed. "How can a man come into the royal garden and commit such violence?" he exclaimed. "What daring!"

As it was the fifteenth day of the lunar month the emperor decided to burn incense at the Temple of the Faithful and Dauntless Maid erected in memory of Kou Zhu who had died saving his life. As he gazed at the statue of the palace maid and burned incense he could not help but shed tears. Looking up he noticed a banner inscribed with a poem which read:

Having faithfully defended the sovereign,
She was piteously flogged to death.

Her loyalty earned her good reputation
As well as a burner of incense.

"Who wrote that poem?" demanded the emperor.

Chen Lin was unable to answer and fell on his knees.

Emperor Renzong realised that it must have been written by the same man who had killed Guo An, so he ordered Chen Lin to summon Prime Minister Bao.

When Bao was informed he could only think it must be the workings of Sleek Rat, as the whole incident was too much like the disturbance he had created in Kaifeng Prefecture.

He assured the emperor he would get to the bottom of it and returned to his office.

The young eunuch was brought before him and told him how Guo An had planned to poison the major-domo-in-chief with the Centre-Shifting Pot. He gave a detailed description of the man who had tied him up.

When the emperor was told he was very pleased. "He must be a good man because he punished the evil-doers. When you catch him, I would like to meet this brave man."

The prime minister's warriors set about searching for Sleek Rat. Zhao Hu, however, remembered the time he had disguised himself as a beggar and solved a previous mystery, so he dressed himself in rags again and, to the amusement and derision of everyone, set off to look for Sleek Rat.

CHAPTER 42

A Felon Is Caught by Mistake.
Dirty Money Arouses Suspicion.

ZHAO Hu, dressed in his beggar's clothes, ran for two or three *li* before getting away from the jeering onlookers. Now he was alone his bravado left him and he shivered as the cold wind blew through his rags. He clutched his jacket tighter, hunched up his shoulders and jogged along until the setting of the sun took away what warmth there was in the air. Zhao Hu thought what a fool he had been not to have worn his tattered padded coat.

He saw another man in rags throw an armful of dried grass into the hollow trunk of a willow tree and then jump in.

"When you're well-fed and warmly-clad you forget about being cold and hungry," he thought, "and that man in the tree-trunk is much better off than me, a guard of the sixth rank."

A second man appeared carrying an armful of dried grass and like the first threw it into the hollow trunk.

"Aiya!" the man inside the trunk cried. "You've thrown the grass all over my head."

"It can't be helped," the second man replied, "move over and make room for me. We'll be company for each other and I'll tell you something interesting."

Zhao Hu decided to join them and as he neared the trunk he heard the second man say: "We are nice and comfortable with the dried grass to keep us warm, not like someone else who won't get a wink of sleep tonight."

"That must be me," Zhao Hu thought, but the second man continued: "The prime minister has a warm bed and quilts but he can't sleep."

"How so?" asked the first man.

"Because some stranger wrote a poem in the imperial Temple of the Faithful and Dauntless Maid and killed a eunuch and the Kaifeng Prefecture has been ordered to investigate and so far has found nothing."

"I know something about that," said the first man, "but I'm too scared to go to the Kaifeng Prefecture."

"Tell it to me," said the second man, "and I'll help you."

"Well, a handsome young man with a band of attendants booked all the rooms at the Jisheng Hotel and said they were waiting for their friends. His name is Sun and he has connections with the imperial palace and is wallowing in money."

Zhao Hu was excited at hearing the name Sun. Wasn't he the grandson-in-law of Grand Tutor Pang Ji? Lord Bao must hear of this, and he raced back to the prefecture to report what he had heard.

Prime Minister Bao dispatched his guards to the hotel and the man Sun was brought before him, with two sealed letters he was carrying. Bao read the letters and realised a blunder had been made, because this Sun was only the servant of the grandson-in-law, escorting his birthday gifts for Grand Tutor Pang.

"What are the birthday gifts?" the prime minister asked.

"Eight pots of miniature pine trees. I am waiting for my friend who is in charge of the gifts. I am in the advance party and was waiting for him to arrive at the Jisheng Hotel."

Prime Minister Bao was not satisfied because the letters had mentioned something else, and after further interrogation the hapless Sun was forced to confess that the miniature trees concealed ten thousand taels of gold. "We never dreamed Your Excellency would have such sharp eyes."

Sun was taken to the cells and Prime Minister Bao conferred with his assistant Gongsun Ce who prepared a report to send with the letters to the emperor. Because it was not in his jurisdiction to try Sun, the case was referred to Judge Wen in charge of the Supreme Court who ordered the interception of the birthday presents for safe-keeping. When the pots were brought into the court no gold was found in them except an ivory slip in the last pot which had "Dirty Money" written on one side and "Seized on Purpose" on the other. The judge realised something was very wrong and questioned the man in charge, a man named Song.

"We met four men with their attendants," Song recounted. "They said they were guards of the sixth rank from Kaifeng. We began drinking and they must have taken the gold."

The mystery deepened when it was discovered that the prime minister's four guards had not left his side and someone else must have passed themselves off as his guards.

The emperor, advised of the facts, ordered Prime Minister Bao to investigate and dismissed the grandson-in-law of the grand tutor from his post. The two men who had accompanied the gifts were released.

Much to Prime Minister Bao's annoyance, the emperor pardoned Grand Tutor Pang and his son-in-law Sun Rong. The unsatisfactory outcome of the case riled Lord Bao. Zhao Hu was pleased at his part in exposing the secret of the miniature pines even though the wrong men had been seized.

Grand Tutor Pang Ji was furious and sulked in his room, telling his son-in-law to receive the birthday guests on his behalf.

"Black Bao really is my enemy," he sighed. "My birthday should be a happy day for me but the gold is lost and my grandson-in-law dismissed from his post. How is Bao able to ferret out all my business?"

His page-boy announced that his two concubines were outside waiting to wish him a happy birthday. When he saw his favourites

enter, dressed in their finery and looking so attractive and charm-
ing, he forgot his unhappiness and his face wreathed in smiles.

"It's taken us ages to find you," Rose and Cherry pouted, "and
we have to get our breath back before we kowtow to you."

The two coquettes sat on his lap, giggling and behaving in a
manner no respectable woman of virtue would tolerate until they
were disturbed by the page-boy coughing loudly to herald his approach.

CHAPTER 43

The Grand Tutor Is Forced to Take Foul Remedies at His
Feast. He Kills His Favourite Concubines.

THE page-boy entered the room carrying an invitation from the
twelve scribes and secretaries of Pang Ji's mansion to receive their
congratulations and their birthday gifts.

He sent Rose and Cherry out of the room, promising to resume
their playful activities after he had received his presents from the
staff.

The grand tutor sat in the middle as they presented paintings,
couplets and fans, presents that any scholar would give. Wine cups
and titbits were placed on the table and soon they were all merrily
drinking and playing the finger-guessing game, in which the loser
had to gulp down his cup of wine in one go. A servant announced
that Pang Ji's son-in-law had sent a rare globefish. "The globefish
is the most delicious of all fishes," they cried, their mouths watering with anticipation.

The now happy Pang Ji ordered it to be cooked and served immediately.

To the accompaniment of clinking wine cups and clattering of
chopsticks the fish was polished off in no time.

No sooner had they finished, than one by one the merrymakers
collapsed, poisoned by the fish which, if not prepared properly, is
highly toxic.

As they began to groan and writhe in agony one of the men suddenly remembered a remedy.

"We need molten gold or powdered liquorice root which has been put in a bamboo tube and soaked in a cesspool for several months, but as there isn't time, excrement will do."

Pang Ji lost no time in bidding his guards to collect excrement from the cesspit. They grabbed an emerald vase engraved with dragons and a white jade bowl in the shape of a lotus leaf from the curio stand and rushed to collect a mixture of excrement and urine, using the jade bowl as a ladle and pouring the smelly mess into the emerald vase.

Holding their noses and breath they rushed it to the grand tutor who took a small jade cup and drank a few mouthfuls. Each of his staff partook of the stinking mixture, vomiting and passing out in turn. The stench from their mouths and in the room was so bad that the grand tutor, in order to save face in front of his guests, suggested they adjourn to the Open Peony Hall where they were given cups of fragrant tea and gradually recovered. Soon the lamps and candles were lit and they began drinking and eating again until the now drunken Pang Ji suddenly remembered that his two concubines were waiting for him.

"Those mistresses of mine must be getting impatient," he said to himself. "I won't announce my arrival, I'll surprise them."

As he crossed over a small bridge he thought he saw someone moving and he became suspicious. When he came to the half-open door he heard a man's voice.

"It's been a rare chance for us but our wish has been fulfilled today."

"Let's seize this opportunity while that wicked old rogue is celebrating and go upstairs and enjoy ourselves," they giggled.

The furious Pang Ji rushed upstairs where he saw the shadows of two people asleep in the bed. He drew out his sword and chopped off their heads, only to discover too late that they were Rose and Cherry, who had tired of waiting for him and had drunk themselves into a silly state. Rose had then pretended to be him.

Pang Ji was too befuddled with drink to wonder how they came to be asleep so soon after he had heard a man's voice downstairs and as he was naturally an evil and ruthless man, he automatically thought the worst. Very annoyed, he had Rose and Cherry put into coffins and sent for his favourite protégé named Liao to consult him.

Liao was a toady and suggested that it was most likely someone from the Kaifeng Prefecture who had engineered the whole scene, mimicking the voices of a man and woman. He suggested that the grand tutor send a petition to the emperor accusing the prefecture of causing the death of the two women. "Black Bao is bound to be relieved of his post."

The two men retired to the office, dashed off a petition and added another five names to make it a collective accusation. Afterwards Pang Ji sent a page-boy to get some tea.

As he returned with the tea he saw a man with a sword resting on his arm calmly squatting on the ground. Frightened out of his wits, he threw down the tea and ran into the study. Everyone rushed to the spot but they saw instead the cook trussed up and gagged, with his butcher's knife stuck in his belt. When he was set free he told them that a handsome young man of about twenty, dressed in black, surprised him in the kitchen and bound and gagged him and then for some unexplained reason stuck the knife in his belt.

"That must be the same man who mimicked the voices of a man and woman in the Crystal Building," said Pang Ji, but though his guards searched high and low not a shadow of the intruder could be found.

Liao suggested that they hurry back to the study to make sure the petition which they had left on the table had not been altered. He studied it carefully but found nothing had been changed and it was put in a box ready to present to the emperor after breakfast.

The emperor frowned when he read the impeachment, knowing

the bad blood between the grand tutor and his prime minister but he was obliged to read it. As he turned over the pages a slip of paper fell out.

CHAPTER 44

A Hero Rescues a Girl in the Monastery of the Goddess of Flowers. The Unknown Warriors Reveal Their True Names.

THE memo had been secretly placed between the pages of the petition while the two men had been lured into the garden. It read: "Nonsense, nonsense these are false charges. Old Pang is framing Old Bao."

"This memo is written by the same man who wrote on the wall of the Temple of the Faithful and Dauntless Maid," said the emperor to himself. "He has fought injustice time and time again but why does he hide and not make an appearance? I must chase up Bao Zheng to find out."

He threw the petition and memo on the floor and turned the two men over to the Supreme Court to be tried. Pang Ji's stipend was cancelled for three years and the other signatories on the petition lost one year's stipend.

The emperor also gave a set time for Bao to arrest the man who had inscribed the poem on the wall and killed the eunuch. The prime minister sent out his four warriors to find him but winter came and went, then the Spring Festival and the Lantern Festival but still they could find no sign of the secretive hero.

One day two of the warriors, Wang Chao and Ma Han, decided to search again and changing into plain clothes set off. Outside the city they saw crowds holding incense and flowers. They were go-

ing to the Monastery of the Goddess of Flowers which had opened
its doors, and the two men followed them. At the back of the
monastery sat a very haughty young man of about thirty. He was
Yan Qi, the nephew of the late Marquis Ge who had been executed. Yan was a bully and called himself Giant of Flowers because
he was fond of frequenting brothels. He had learnt how to box and
wrestle and challenged others to fight him. Because nobody ever
did, he became even more arrogant.

The two warriors noticed a young girl being hustled by a gang of
thugs and an old woman shouting to leave her alone.

One of the thugs said she was a maidservant to his young master
and had stolen some of his property and threatened the old woman
with the law.

As the thugs tried to drag the screaming girl away, a man
dressed as an officer, with a deep voice and purple complexion,
blocked their way and demanded to know what the furore was.
"Let the old woman be heard," he ordered.

One of the thugs told him to mind his own business and raised
his fist to beat the old woman off, when his arm suddenly swung
helplessly by his side.

"Don't be afraid," said the warrior to the old woman, "have
your say now."

"This young girl is a neighbour of mine," she sobbed, "whom I
accompanied to burn incense, when she was snatched by these
men. Please help me, sir."

After seeing what had happened to their friend's arm, the other
thugs were not so brave. They sneaked away and reported everything to the Giant of Flowers, who stormed off to challenge the
officer who had dared to interfere. He was a little taken aback
when he saw the young warrior who politely greeted him with a
bow and said: "I hope the worthy gentleman will show a little
compassion and let them go."

Yan Qi, seeing how polite and amiable he seemed, thought it
would be easy to intimidate him, never dreaming that he would be

like an egg striking a cobblestone.

"Dirty dog! Who told you to interfere?" and he lashed out with his foot at the still bowing warrior's face.

The officer raised his hand and gave it a slight brush saying: "Don't be so rude young man!"

Yan Qi fell to the ground with a howl of pain.

His thugs rushed forward, hoping by sheer numbers to subdue the warrior but his rapid whirling fists sent them tumbling to the ground.

Another man with a staff in his hand tried to strike the warrior who dodged the blow which hit Yan Qi instead. He fell back with his brains dashed out.

"Seize the officer, he has killed our master!" cried the thugs. To the admiration of the onlookers, the officer gave himself up without a struggle.

Wang Chao and Ma Han, who had observed the whole incident, then demanded that the man with the staff should also be arrested as he was the man who had actually killed Yan Qi. After a struggle they helped the policeman to tie him up.

"All this trouble for nothing," said the officer. "I haven't helped the old woman or the girl." The two warriors promised him that they would rescue the young girl who left with the police escort. They reunited the old woman with the young girl and then arranged for the accused men to be taken to the Kaifeng Prefecture to be tried. They described the young officer to their fellow warrior Zhan Zhao, who recognised him as Sky Rat from Hollow Island and greeted him with great delight.

"How do you know my name?" Sky Rat asked.

"I saw you during the trouble over the fishing rights at Hollow Island," said Zhan Zhao, "and have longed to renew our acquaintance."

Sky Rat found the "Royal Cat" or Southern Hero a broadminded and generous man and not like the kind of man his brother Sleek Rat had described.

Sky Rat was taken to the assembly hall where some of the other warriors and Gongsun Ce were waiting to greet him as an honoured guest and not a felon on a charge of murder.

Wang and Ma assured Sky Rat that they would come forward as witnesses to what really happened at the Monastery of the Goddess of Flowers when Prime Minister Bao came to try the case.

CHAPTER 45

Sky Rat Is Freed and Finds Sleek Rat.
Warriors and Gallants Fight in the Kaifeng Prefecture.

SKY Rat insisted he be brought into court in chains as befitted a
man charged with murder, but Prime Minister Bao ordered the
chains to be taken off and addressed him as "champion".

"I've heard of your gallantry at the Monastery of the Goddess of
Flowers. You are a man who fights injustice and protects the
weak. Yan Qi is dead and the man who killed him with his stick
will pay with his life. The two men were evil and deserved to
die."

Sky Rat, stealing a glance at the prime minister, could not help
but be impressed by his serious and awe-inspiring demeanour and
when he was asked why he had come to the capital, he blushed as
he said he was looking for his brother Sleek Rat. "In the early
winter of last year, our other three sworn brothers were sent to
look for him but as I have heard no news I came as well."

"That fifth brother of yours has done some extraordinary things
in the capital. Even the emperor knows of his chivalrous deeds and
has ordered me to find him."

Sky Rat promised to bring him to court and clasping his hands in
salute departed.

His attendant had found them lodgings but Sky Rat, in a depressed state, said:

"This brother of mine is really running wild. Who would have thought that he would challenge Southern Hero, then intrude into the royal gardens, write a poem on the wall and kill the eunuch major-domo. Not satisfied with that he inserted a memo in a petition to the emperor and stole gold. I've promised to see the prime minister in three days with an answer, but I just don't know where to start."

His attendant then told him that the brothers were staying in the Literary Splendour Building in the back of the garden of Grand Tutor Pang.

Relieved, Sky Rat finished his meal quickly, put on his black suit and left for the Literary Splendour Building where he saw Bai Yutang — Sleek Rat — sitting alone. The others had already left for the Kaifeng Prefecture dressed in their black suits.

Sky Rat was alarmed: "How can I show my face there again if anything happens?"

The two brothers waited until the third watch had passed but still there was no sign of them.

The wily Gongsun Ce had anticipated that attempts would be made to rescue Sky Rat and had warned the warriors to keep alert and patrol the grounds. They armed themselves in preparation.

The three "Rat" brothers in the meantime had found their way into the grounds and when they saw how carefully guarded the prefecture was, hid on the roof of the house. Bao Xing passing through the garden caught sight of them and raised the alarm.

The five warriors raced into the grounds with their weapons. Zhan Zhao aimed one of his pocket-arrows at one of the brothers and hit him. He fell to the ground where he was quickly tied up. Zhan Zhao then noticed another man on the roof and was about to shoot again when a stream of cold light came towards him and he ducked. Ma Han standing behind him was hit in the shoulder by an arrow. Zhan Zhao jumped onto the roof to give chase and a sword fight took place between the two men but a three-edged object was sent whizzing toward him and trying to dodge it, he lost his balance and the other man disappeared.

The captive was taken before Prime Minister Bao and told him he was called Xu Qing, otherwise known as Mountain Rat, and he was willing to die.

"So you are the third brother," said Bao, and ordered him be untied and seated. Xu bent down and removed the arrow from his foot, remarking: "This is not as lethal as my brother's. His is poisoned and the victim loses consciousness in no time."

When he heard Ma Han had been hit he said that his second brother had the antidote but it must be given within twenty-four hours.

Bao questioned him about his brother Sleek Rat and he admitted he had done all the things he had been accused of except for the stolen gold. "We took that," he said, "by pretending we were your warriors."

The confession was greeted with approval with a thumbs up sign.

A policeman entered the court announcing the arrival of Champion Lu Fang — Sky Rat.

CHAPTER 46

River Rat Acquires the Antidote by a Ruse.
Prime Minister Bao's Nephew Appears on the Scene.

SKY Rat was waiting at the Literary Splendour Building and the brothers were surprised to see him safe and well. They told him of the fight at the Kaifeng Prefecture and the capture of Xu Qing — Mountain Rat — and Sky Rat wrung his hands in despair. "Every mistake we have made is because of Fifth Brother — Sleek Rat. If only we could persuade him to give up this idea of trying to better Zhan Zhao — the Royal Cat — in a contest."

"If Fifth Brother wins," rejoined River Rat, "it would reflect glory on us as well."

Sleek Rat glared angrily when his older brother, Sky Rat, suggested he give himself up.

"Why should I?" he shouted. "I have sworn to find Southern Hero and make him give in to me. Otherwise I won't rest."

"Why do you hate him so?" Sky Rat protested.

"I don't hate him, only the two characters he goes by, 'Royal Cat'. It will eclipse us Five Rats. If you can persuade Lord Bao to ask the emperor to revoke the title, then I will surrender and plead guilty."

"How can I ask him for such a favour when I am already indebted for his patronage?"

Sleek Rat sneered: "Ah, so it turns out my eldest brother has been patronised by the prime minister. Well, turn me in and get your reward."

Sky Rat, reduced to silence, went out of the building and paced to and fro in the grounds. "I have four sworn brothers. I never dreamed that Fifth Brother would turn against me."

The divided loyalty between Sleek Rat and the prime minister was too much for him to bear and he decided to hang himself. He untied the sash from his waist and flung it over the bough of a tree but it slowly slid off. "Even the sash is making fun of me," he said to himself, just as Fourth Brother, Jiang Ping — River Rat — jumped down.

"Don't take on so," he said. "Fifth Brother is not bad but he is stubborn and won't be convinced by our arguments. We have to think of another way to make him give up this idea of his. Let's go to Kaifeng to apologise for our fighting and also find out what has happened to Xu Qing — Mountain Rat."

Southern Hero welcomed the two brothers warmly and took them in to Prime Minister Bao who asked them to get the antidote from Earth Rat for the poisoned Ma Han. But River Rat thought he would be unwilling to let it out of his possession.

"I will have to trick him into giving it to me," he said.

He made his way to the Literary Splendour Building, jumping over the roofs of houses as a shortcut, causing much admiration for his prowess. He carried a letter signed by their elder brother telling him that it was Mountain Rat who had been poisoned by the arrow and also instructing Earth Rat to hold Sleek Rat prisoner.

River Rat quickly mixed the antidote with water and poured it down Ma Han's throat. Soon he recovered consciousness and vomited a quantity of poisoned water.

When Earth Rat discovered how he had been duped he was furious and told Sleek Rat about the plans to capture him. "You are my sworn brother," he said, "I won't help them to catch you but neither can I condone what you have done." He rose and left.

When the other brothers returned to the Literary Splendour

Building Sleek Rat and Earth Rat had disappeared and so they joined the five warriors of the Kaifeng Prefecture patrolling the grounds in shifts.

One day when Prime Minister Bao was at the imperial palace, Zhao Hu had time on his hands and decided to visit the Monastery of the Goddess of Flowers, disguised as a merchant. Feeling hungry he walked into a tavern and taking a seat ordered some wine. He was just about to drink when he noticed an old peasant with a woebegone look staring at him.

Zhao Hu, feeling sorry for the old man, offered to share his food and drink but as he ate he shed tears and Zhao was displeased. "That's not sensible of you, old man," he said. "You said you were hungry. I give you food and now you're crying."

"I'm crying because I am so worried," he answered. "My name is Zhao Qing. I was a clerk of the County Office here. The nephew of Prime Minister Bao has come to burn incense but came by a roundabout route to see the sights and also to extort as much money as he can from the local prefectures and counties he passes through. I was ordered to prepare food and wine and entertain him but he complained the lodging was not good enough and he wanted three hundred taels of silver. My master is an honest man and can't afford to pay that much, so instead the nephew accused me of trying to extort the money and I have been beaten and dismissed from my job. I have pawned all my clothes, have nowhere to go and am starving."

Zhao Hu could not help but feel hatred for Prime Minister Bao's nephew and was determined to find and seize him.

"Since you have been unjustly treated," he told the old man, "why don't you appeal to a higher authority?"

CHAPTER 47

The Indictment Is Delivered to the Wrong Official. The Case
Is Brought to an End and the Guilty Found Innocent.

ZHAO Hu thought: "Our prime minister has dedicated his life to
the service of the country. He doesn't know about this nephew of
his. Why not bring this old man to the Kaifeng Prefecture and see
if the prime minister will deal with the case fairly?"

He persuaded the old man to appeal to the Kaifeng Prefecture,
saying: "Whether the evil-doer is a relation or not, he will handle
the case with complete impartiality, without fear or favour."

He suggested that the old man intercept the prime minister's
palanquin and submit his indictment, when Lord Bao came
through the city in the next few days. He gave the old man half an
ingot of silver and made his way home. He was a little worried
about involving the prime minister with his nephew and decided
not to tell anyone else — which turned out to be mistake.

He waited several days for the old man to come and shout his
grievances but there was no sign of him. "Perhaps he fooled me
out of my food, and I've spent that half ingot of silver for nothing," he pondered.

What Zhao Hu did not realise was that the old man had intercepted the wrong palanquin and had given his indictment to the
evil grand tutor, who gleefully conspired with his son-in-law Sun
and his lackey Liao to get Prime Minister Bao removed from office

by means of an impeachment to the emperor. They sent documents to other prefectures and counties to find out how much money had been extorted by Bao's nephew.

The following day, Grand Tutor Pang Ji submitted the indictment to the emperor who in great displeasure summoned his prime minister before him.

"How many nephews do you have?" he asked.

"I have three," replied Lord Bao. "The eldest and second are farmers. The third is a student called Shirong."

"Have you ever seen him?" the emperor asked.

"Since I held office in the capital, I have not returned home and have only seen the eldest," answered Bao.

The emperor nodded and told Major-domo-in-chief Chen Lin to hand the indictment to him. Bao hurriedly knelt on the ground and said: "The depraved nephew of your subject should be arrested at once. I must be severely punished for not bringing him up properly." He prostrated himself before the throne.

The emperor had faith in his prime minister and said: "Since you have worked night and day for the government, how can you know what is going on in your hometown? We will wait until your nephew is brought here."

It only took a day after the royal decree was issued for the nephew to be escorted to the capital. On the way they were intercepted by Bao Xing who asked to have a word with the prisoner.

They had a private talk in a nearby tavern and then the prime minister's faithful attendant went on his way, watched by curious onlookers who guessed he had been interceding with the officer on behalf of the offender.

The grand tutor persuaded the emperor that the case should be tried by three judiciary bodies, the Supreme Court, the Garrison Headquarters and the Censorate, because he was not sure he could rely on the Chief Justice Wen Yanbo to do his bidding, whereas the garrison was under the charge of his son-in-law, Sun Rong, and the censorate under his protégé, Liao.

The court was called into session and Bao Shirong was brought before the three men and questioned. He did as Bao Xing had instructed him and admitted all the charges. "I did not have enough money and decided to borrow from those districts and counties. Who was to know they would offer it all as a present? I didn't deliberately extort money from them and I spent it as soon as I got it."

A bodyguard entered with a note from the grand tutor to his son-in-law. It gave the amount of silver extorted from the local authorities as well as instructions that Sun Rong must contrive to impeach Prime Minister Bao for it. When the chief justice read the note he put it in his sleeve and castigated the two men for contempt of court in bringing a message without the correct judicial procedures.

"Your father-in-law is a little reckless," remarked Wen. "Sending a man with a note to this court is audacious."

Sun Rong was forced to agree and did not dare to ask for the return of the note, while Liao felt inhibited when he questioned Bao Shirong about what the prime minister's attendant had told him when he was on his way to the city.

"He only told me not to shirk the responsibility and make a full confession and beg you to shelter me," the young man said.

Liao sent for Bao Xing to be questioned but really to vent his spite. "Dirty dog!" he snarled. "You're impudent enough to have waylaid the felon and prepared him for the trial."

"I have done nothing but wait on my master's instructions," replied Bao Xing.

Liao ordered that he be given twenty strokes of the cane.

He was questioned again but he refused to speak despite the flogging.

The rack was brought in and Bao Xing asked that the accused confront him, at which the chief justice, unable to contain himself any longer, ordered that Shirong be brought back into court. He looked closely at Bao Xing and then said: "He looks similar, only this one is fair and plump while the other one was a little darker and thinner."

In the meantime Prime Minister Bao had been overwhelmed with shame and anger at the thought that his eldest brother had not brought up this son properly and worried because his nephew and faithful attendant had been summoned before the chief justice. It was a lucky coincidence that in the middle of his deep despair, his three nephews should decide to visit him and when he saw the youngest nephew, a well-mannered and pleasing young man, he realised that the man charged with extortion was an impostor.

He immediately dispatched his three nephews with his assistant Gongsun Ce to appear at the court and confront the impersonator. He turned out to be a servant of the family who had been dismissed for dishonesty.

The chief justice announced he was preparing a document for the emperor to make his decision and dismissed the three men, who returned to their uncle's residence and celebrated together with the warriors to await the emperor's edict.

"When you see the emperor," said Sky Rat, "please tell him that we will leave no stone unturned to find our brother Sleek Rat."

CHAPTER 48

The Trickster Is Found Out and the Extortionist Is Executed.
Treacherous Officials Are Demoted While the Gallants Are Received in Court.

WHILE there was a great family reunion and celebration in the prime minister's residence, Chief Justice Wen was preparing his report to the emperor. He also enclosed Pang Ji's note. When the emperor read the two he was both delighted and vexed. Delighted that his prime minister's family lived up to the good reputation of a scholar family and vexed at Pang Ji's unscrupulous attempts to slander Bao. He felt he could no longer protect his grand tutor and turned over the file and the offenders to the Kaifeng Prefecture.

Bao first questioned the old clerk who had first brought the matter to the attention of Zhao Hu and the whole story of extortion and the people involved were exposed and the guilty punished. Bao then sent men to Pang Ji's mansion to find the man who looked like the false Bao Xing. They saw two men approaching, supporting each other in a drunken embrace. "So you're thought to be Bao Xing's brother," giggled one of them.

"Drinking has loosened your tongue," said the other, "be careful in case we're overheard." They were Pang Ji's accountants.

The police immediately took them to Prime Minister Bao for questioning. The false nephew was brought in and identified one of the men as the one who had pretended to be the prime minister's attendant. After a flogging he confessed how Pang Ji, his son-in-law and Liao had told him to disguise himself as Bao Xing.

The prime minister described the whole story in a memorial to the emperor in which he suggested that the false nephew should be executed and what kind of punishment should be meted out to the grand tutor, his son-in-law and Liao.

The emperor decreed that because Pang Ji was an imperial relation, he should have a lenient sentence keeping his title and stipend but relieved of all political power. The other two were to be demoted three grades.

The false Bao Xing and nephew were executed by the dog-headed axe and the old man who had first brought the matter up was rewarded with ten taels of silver.

As it was Prime Minister Bao's birthday, the emperor and the empress dowager showed their great esteem for their loyal minister by giving many valuable gifts but he refused the presents from other friends and officials in case they were regarded as bribes. After the birthday celebrations were over, the three nephews returned to their hometown with their uncle's request that the younger one should return and prepare for the imperial examinations.

When Bao next saw the emperor he told him the story of the Five Rats and their invasion of the prefecture to rescue their brother. Out of deference to the omniscient power of the emperor, Sky Rat was referred to as Mast Rat, as no one could be called a name higher than the emperor himself.

The exploits of the Rat brothers pleased the emperor, who said: "Judging by the nicknames they must be highly skilled."

"Yes sir," replied Bao, "but only three are in the office of your subject."

"Bring them here tomorrow. I'd like to try them in person," said the emperor.

The prime minister knew the emperor really wanted to see their skills and was using the trial as a pretext. When he returned to the prefecture he cautioned the brothers on how they should behave.

The next day they were taken to the palace garden. Bao Xing advised them not to make excuses about their maverick brother Sleek Rat and leave the rest to the prime minister.

Prime Minister Bao, with an ivory tablet in hand on which was a memorial written with the names of the gallants, knelt down on the vermilion terrace as Major-domo-in-chief Chen Lin announced: "The imperial decree summons Lu Fang, Xu Qing and Jiang Ping."

Trembling in awe the three Rat brothers knelt down.

"Why have you surrendered to the Kaifeng Prefecture?" asked the emperor.

Lu Fang bowed low again and said: "Because our brother Sleek Rat is young and ignorant, he has committed monstrous crimes and I blame myself for his shortcomings."

The emperor was impressed with his humility and then noticed the yellow banner on the flagpole flapping in the wind. This reminded him of his pseudonym and he asked: "Why are you called Mast Rat?"

"Once the halyard broke and I climbed up the mast and knotted the two ends together. That's why I was given the name."

"Look," said the emperor, "the streamer on the flagpole is stuck. Climb up and untangle it."

Lu Fang bowed and turning up his sleeves jumped up the stone pedestal. He swarmed up the flagpole like a monkey and undid the streamer, then undid another which was caught up in the pulley. To the astonishment of the court, he suddenly stretched out one leg, and with the other coiled round the flagpole extended his arms parallel with the banners, striking the pose of one dispelling clouds to see the moon. He coiled one arm round the mast and greased down it to alight on the pedestal to loud applause. "You really are worthy of your nickname," commended the emperor.

In the absence of the Second Brother, the emperor called on Xu Qing, the Third Brother, dubbed Mountain Rat, to display his skills. Already his looks — swarthy, bright-eyed, rough-and-ready — impressed the court.

CHAPTER 49

The Three Rat Brothers Become Officers.
Two Ravens Croak Their Grievances.

THE emperor was intrigued at such a rough looking fellow and asked him why he was nicknamed Mountain Rat.

"Because I..."

Jiang Ping gave him a tug and whispered: "Say 'the offender'!"

"I the offender have run through eighteen tunnels at a stretch in Hollow Island and earned the nickname of Mountain Rat," he replied.

"There are tunnels in Longevity Hill. Can you pass through them?" asked the emperor.

Xu Qing was taken to the foot of the hill where he slipped in and disappeared and before anyone could drink two cups of tea he emerged at the top of the southern hill far away in the distance. He disappeared again and finally emerged covered in dust and mud.

"You are also worthy of your reputation," commended the emperor.

The fourth on the list was River Rat, Jiang Ping, a short weak-looking puny individual. His looks made the emperor wonder how he could have earned his title.

"The offender can swim under water and see everything and stay in it for a full month," River Rat answered.

The emperor could not believe such a sickly-looking man was a good swimmer and commanded his Major-domo-in-chief Chen Lin to bring the gold toad. In a gold-painted bucket sat a three-legged toad, three inches broad and five inches long. Its eyes were like amber encircled with gold rims, a big red mouth, emerald green back studded with golden dots and a snow-white belly. It was a divine rare treasure.

Jiang Ping was taken onto a small boat accompanied by a eunuch with the toad. The emperor and the rest of the company followed on a royal barge.

Chen Lin was worried that Jiang Ping would fail in the task of retrieving the toad from the lake and whispered to tell him beforehand to save him from punishment.

Jiang Ping smiled and reassured him.

The young eunuch tipped the toad into the lake and with a flash of its three legs it vanished from sight. Only then did Jiang Ping glide into the water and disappear without leaving a ripple in the water.

The onlookers scanned the surface of the water for a long time but there was no sign of Jiang Ping. The emperor thought he had drowned rather than admit he could not find the toad but gradually bubbles appeared under the barge expanding until they formed a big ring and Jiang Ping emerged kneeling on the surface of the water holding a croaking toad in his cupped hands.

The delighted emperor exclaimed: "He really is worthy of the name River Rat!"

Just as Prime Minister Bao intended, the emperor promoted the three Rats to guards of the sixth rank to serve in the Kaifeng Prefecture with the order that they were to find the other two Rats, Bai Yutang and Han Zhang, as soon as possible.

The other guards and Gongsun Ce congratulated their new brothers-in-arms, except Zhao Hu who was a little peeved. "We worked hard before we became guards while those three haven't so much as flourished a sword or a spear. That Jiang Ping looks like a skeleton and if it wasn't for his tendons keeping his bones together, he would fall apart. What's more, he's conceited. How can the two of us work together?"

A month went by and Prime Minister Bao was returning from the imperial court when he saw two ravens flying around his palanquin croaking. A monk appeared before him holding an indictment above his head.

The monk was called Fa Ming and he was appealing on behalf of another monk called Fa Cong. Bao thought it was too trivial and waved the monk away but the two ravens reappeared and began croaking incessantly. He ordered two policemen, Huang and Jiang, to follow the ravens and find out where they went.

The ravens flew out of the prefecture and led the policemen to the outskirts of the city. Tired out the men sat down to recover their breath. The ravens croaked in a tree over their heads and then took wing again. When they reached a village called Baoshan, they vanished and two men in black, one big and one small, stood in their place. The big man hurried off, with the small hurrying behind when the latter stumbled and fell. A shoe came off and disclosed the bound foot of a woman.

Huang shouted: "Why are you kidnapping this woman?" and tried to grab hold of him only to be felled to the ground.

Jiang thought it highly suspicious that the woman should be disguised as a man and also tried to intercept the man but retreated when the man flourished a large fist in his face and knocked him down.

The man then shouted at the woman to run on ahead and get help from the manor. Soon servants with clubs and iron bars appeared and tied the two policemen up and took them to the manor. The squire of the manor emerged and stood back in astonishment when he saw the two men.

CHAPTER 50

Earth Rat Goes to the Rescue.
Sleek Rat Steals Three Treasures.

THE squire was an old acquaintance of Jiang and quickly untied him and made a fuss of him. His name was Lin and the two men had been friends when both were penniless. When Lin came into some money they parted ways and Jiang served as an officer in the Kaifeng Prefecture. Lin had heard that his former friend had become a police chief and intended to renew their friendship. Lin was not an honest man. Jiang, in contrast, was upright, had been impressed by his master, Prime Minister Bao, admired the chivalry of his warriors and wanted to emulate them.

Lin made a fuss of him and apologised for the behaviour of the big man who was his steward.

Jiang accepted his regrets, clasped his hands and made to go but Lin stopped him and told his page to bring four packets of silver to give him.

"Are you trying to bribe me?" asked Jiang and pushed the silver away. Lin pulled a long face and tried threats and blandishments but his former friend remained firm and demanded to be allowed to leave. Frustrated in his plans, Lin ordered his steward to suspend the two policemen from a beam and whip them. But Jiang refused to be intimidated and by shouting abuse at the steward managed to take all the blows on himself and save Huang, who was the weaker of the two. The beating eventually stopped when the steward went to have his evening meal.

A few minutes went by and the two policemen heard the sound of a man weeping from the inner room.

"Who are you?" called Jiang.

"I am an old man named Dou," the voice said. "Squire Lin wanted to kidnap my daughter. The champion Han Zhang came to our rescue and gave us five taels of silver, but we lost our way and the squire caught us and locked me up in here. I don't know whether my daughter is still alive or not."

The two policemen were overjoyed at hearing the name Han Zhang and while they discussed how to escape and find him, they heard the door open and a man in black entered, flashing a small light. It was, of course, Han Zhang. He set the men down and released the old man.

"Hide while I go and get Lin and try to find the old man's daughter," he instructed. The three men hid under an upside-down cattle trough while Han Zhang climbed over the roofs until he found some rooms with the light on. He laid down under the eaves to listen.

"You are very kind, my lady. You chant scriptures and burn incense every day for the well-being of the squire."

"That is my greatest wish," sighed the lady. "But he will not change his ways. He's snatched another young girl today and has locked her up in that room."

Han Zhang was cheered. "Good, she hasn't lost her chastity yet," he mused.

The dame continued: "It's much worse than that. The squire is having an affair with the tinsmith's wife. The tinsmith has just recovered from an illness and the squire suggested that she use his recovery as an excuse to go to the Precious Pearl Monastery and burn incense to give thanks and to go to the backyard, take off her dress and return home. At midnight a man came knocking at their door shouting he was returning her dress. When her husband went out, his head was cut off. The tinsmith's wife then lodged a complaint at the county court saying her dress had been stolen in the monastery and that her husband had been murdered. The magistrate ordered the arrest of the monk and when the police went to the backyard of the monastery they found the head of the tinsmith wrapped in his wife's dress. They arrested the monk Fa Cong but his novice monk Fa Ming appealed to the Kaifeng Prefecture. The squire, hearing about it, told the tinsmith's wife to dress up as a man and hide here in his manor where they plan to get married immediately."

Han Zhang made his way to the room where the tinsmith's wife was hiding and heard Squire Lin and her discussing what to do next, now that the two policemen knew of her disguise.

"I've told my man to finish them off at the third watch," he told her.

"Villain!" said Han Zhang and burst into the room. Squire Lin, seeing a hefty man dressed in black flourishing a sword, begged for his life, but the two were bound and gagged and Han went to get the others. He crossed the path of the squire's steward who was on his way to kill the two policemen but Han Zhang wielded his sword and a fight took place between the two men. The steward was very agile and quick and Han Zhang was beginning to lose ground when a flying stone hit the steward on the neck and sent him sprawling to the ground. It was Jiang who had come to the rescue.

The old man's daughter was released and reunited with her father and the prisoners taken to the Kaifeng Prefecture to be tried. Jiang tried to persuade Han Zhang to come with him and tell the prime minister about the conversation that he had overheard between the two women but he vanished in a twinkling of an eye.

The two monks were brought before the court and when they were asked to explain the mystery of the two ravens, they remembered that they had rescued them as fledglings when they fell from their nests and they took care of them until they could fly.

The two policemen described the role Han Zhang had played in their rescue and in bringing the culprits to justice and their attempts to persuade him to come with them. But Bao realised that until Bai Yutang — Sleek Rat — was apprehended, his brother would stay away.

Bao Xing was in the courtyard when he heard something drop to the ground. It was a letter which read: "I have come specially to borrow the three treasures to take to Hollow Island. Should Royal Cat follow me there, he will never escape." The three treasures were the mirror, the wonder-working basin and the Wandering Fairy Pillow.

CHAPTER 51

Two Gallants Are Trapped .
Three Evil-Doers Get Their Just Deserts .

THE Rat brothers were ashamed of their errant brother, Sleek Rat, and had decidedly lost face in front of the prime minister.

"Fifth Brother is too wilful and has gone too far," Lu Fang — Sky Rat — said. "We must go after him."

After much discussion it was decided that they should first find Han Zhang — Earth Rat — before going to Hollow Island and trapping Sleek Rat. Lu Fang should remain behind while River Rat — Jiang Ping — and the warriors Zhao Hu and Zhang Long should first go to the Emerald Cloud Peak where Earth Rat's mother was buried, because River Rat was sure he would be there tidying up the grave.

The journey was not without some squabbling between Zhao Hu and Jiang Ping, and Zhang Long often had to mediate.

One day as they sat down for lunch, Zhao Hu suggested that each pay for his own lunch but when the time came to settle the bill, Jiang Ping had already paid for all three and continued to do so until they reached their destination. This made Zhao Hu even more peeved.

When they reached the Emerald Cloud Peak, Han Zhang had not yet arrived and they decided to put up at the God Blessing Temple to await his arrival.

The monks were vegetarian and Zhao Hu was fond of meat so he decided to prepare his own meals and sent his servant to buy provisions. But he returned empty-handed and had to face an angry and hungry Zhao Hu.

"Your humble servant has something important to tell you," he said, backing a few paces.

"It had better be," raved Zhao Hu, "else I shall beat you!"

"When I was going down the mountain," quavered the servant, "I saw a man trying to hang himself. Should I have gone to his rescue or not?"

"Of course," said Zhao Hu.

"I've brought him here. He's the servant of Prime Minister Bao's nephew! They were on their way to Kaifeng when a tiger suddenly rushed out of the pine wood and carried the nephew off on his back."

Zhang Long, who was listening to the account, thought it very strange a tiger did not hold him in his mouth but on his back instead.

They questioned the nephew's servant who was called Wang. "The young master wanted to enjoy the moon and went into the woods," he said, "when out came a fierce tiger and carried him away. I have searched in vain so decided to take my life," he added tearfully.

The two warriors decided to find the tiger and remove the scourge from the area.

They descended the mountain and entered the woods, Zhao Hu shouting: "Where's the tiger? Where's the tiger?" and flourishing his sword this way and that. Suddenly they saw two men jump down from a tree and start running away in terror. Zhang and Zhao gave chase. The men ran into a dilapidated building and disappeared. There were no doors or windows and Zhao Hu wondered if they were ghosts. He trod on something hard and found a big iron ring in the floor which gave a hollow sound when he stamped on it. Despite Zhang's entreaties to be careful he lifted the ring and saw some steps leading down. The stairs were so steep that the investigators tumbled and were quickly tied up by the two men waiting for them in the dark.

When the two warriors did not return, Wang, the nephew's servant, began to get worried and told the whole story to Jiang Ping who armed himself with his three-edged weapon and went down the mountain to a village. At the doorway of one of the houses he saw two shadows and hid behind a tree. A man came out of the house and the two told him they had captured two guards from the Kaifeng Prefecture and did not know what to do.

"Aiya!" said the man. "You can never set them free now. You had better finish them off and then we'll leave for distant parts."

Jiang followed the two men as they hurried back to the dilapidated house. He managed to overpower the two men and release the warriors and then they went to the third man's house.

"Have you finished them off?" asked a voice behind the door.

"Yes, we have," Zhao Hu replied and grabbed him. They searched the room but there was no one else. The men were marched off to the local magistrate to be questioned. The latter was in the middle of trying the case of a man called Fang who had been accused of stealing a gold bracelet from the local squire. He adjourned the hearing to receive Prime Minister Bao's three warriors.

"A fine magistrate you are!" said Zhao Hu. "You allow a tiger to harm the nephew of Prime Minister Bao. I don't think you'll be long in this post."

When the magistrate was told of the whole story he ordered the offenders to be brought before him.

The first man admitted he had captured the young man and taken him to his sister's home because it was their brother who had been executed by the dog-headed axe for impersonating the prime minister's nephew. "I meant to kill him in revenge for my brother's death. But my sister let him go and then hanged herself and my little nephew also died."

CHAPTER 52

A Young Man Accepts an Offer of Marriage.
Dame Ning Delivers an Important Letter.

EVERYONE felt sorry for the sister who had hanged herself and when they asked her brother how her little son had died, he said he had kicked him in a rage and left his body on the hillside. The three men had made a living by waylaying travellers and robbing them. They were sent to prison until the whereabouts of young Bao, the prime minister's nephew, were discovered.

Young Bao was a good-looking youth but not very strong. He had found refuge in the home of an impoverished scholar called Fang and his only daughter and had fallen ill. On his way to get some medicine, Master Fang had found a gold bracelet and then been accused by the owner of stealing it and was arrested. It was his case that had suddenly come to a halt when the warriors burst in on the examining magistrate to find the nephew.

A neighbour of Master Fang was an old woman known for her sharp tongue but with a heart of gold. She was called Dame Ning and at the daughter's request visited her father.

He informed the old lady that they were sheltering a young scholar and in order not to compromise his daughter's honour, Dame Ning should try and persuade him to get engaged to his daughter. "A single boy and girl living under one roof with no other man or servants will get the neighbours gossiping. If they are engaged he will be able to help and manage the house and stop any idle talk."

"Set your mind at ease," Dame Ning assured him. "My glib tongue will soon win him over."

At first the young people were reluctant especially Young Bao who thought he should get the consent of his parents first. "Don't shilly-shally," she said, "the young lady is both decorous and pretty as a picture. Moreover she is virtuous as well as good at poetry and singing and very skilled in needlework. She is a very good match." The old lady finally won him over.

"Now," said Dame Ning, "as the future son-in-law you have to think of a way to get your father-in-law out of jail."

"I'm too feeble to go to see the magistrate. You can take a letter for me but you must insist you go through the central gate as befits a person of rank."

Dame Ning was a wordly-wise woman and realising the young man was no ordinary individual took the letter to Miss Fang who read it and was highly delighted to find the young man was the nephew of the prime minister and thought highly of her father's choice of a son-in-law.

Dame Ning had to cajole and promise a bribe to the guards at the gate of the yamen but eventually managed to pass through the central gate and placing the letter on top of her head strode up towards the seated magistrate. He was delighted at receiving news of the whereabouts of the nephew and quickly ordered a sedan chair for Dame Ning to ride back in triumph to bring him to the yamen.

CHAPTER 53

The Gallant Returns to Emerald Cloud Peak
Southern Hero Zhan Zhao Reconnoitres Hollow Island.

THE sedan chair was accompanied by Young Bao's servant and
four policemen while the magistrate resumed the court hearing and
threw out the false charge against Master Fang. The squire who
had accused him of stealing was given ten slaps on the face and
sent packing.

Master Fang was delighted to be treated with such favour now
he was becoming allied by marriage with a noble young man and
they waited with eagerness for his arrival.

There were great celebrations when he finally arrived and the
magistrate gave a banquet at which Jiang Ping, Zhang Long and
Zhao Hu were among the guests.

The magistrate was happy that the dreadful incident in his county had been cleared up and hoped that a good word would be put in
with the prime minister. "All the offenders are in prison," he
said, "and the only other matter is to find the body of the child."

The three warriors then took their leave to return to Emerald
Cloud Peak to find Earth Rat and when they had found him they
would accompany the prime minister's nephew to the city.

When they arrived at the God Blessing Temple the monks told
them Earth Rat had been and gone again after making sacrifices to
his mother.

"Did he say where he was going?" asked Jiang Ping.

"He is wandering all over the country aimlessly," replied the monk.

Jiang Ping heaved a sigh. "This fifth brother of ours is responsible for second brother's wanderings."

They bowed in front of the newly swept grave of Earth Rat's mother and decided to leave for the magistrate's court the next day to escort the prime minister's nephew and the three prisoners to the Kaifeng Prefecture. They did not know that the man they were seeking was hiding from them in the monastery. Prime Minister Bao greeted his nephew with great joy. After learning of his betrothal to Master Fang's daughter, he ordered gifts to be sent and the bride-to-be to live with her future mother-in-law to wait until the nephew had taken the civil service examination. Dame Ning was rewarded with a hundred *mu* of farmland, a hundred taels of silver and four bolts of satin.

The three men who had kidnapped the prime minister's nephew were executed with the dog-headed axe.

Everything had been settled satisfactorily except finding the two missing "Rats". Southern Hero, Zhan Zhao, decided to go to Hollow Island where Sleek Rat had taken refuge without telling the others. Jiang Ping was worried. "He doesn't realise how crafty my brother is. He should have waited until we found Earth Rat and together we could have apprehended Sleek Rat and brought him to Kaifeng," he told Gongsun Ce and the others.

Zhan Zhao made his way to Songjiang County where Hollow Island was situated and had an interview with the governor. He turned out to be his old friend Tian Qiyuan whose wife Jade Goddess he had rescued from the dastardly Marquis Pang Yu. The governor was eager to repay Zhan Zhao by helping him find Sleek Rat. "He is a remarkable man and is living in the mountains where it is very hard to get to," he said and offered a guide named Yu Biao, a tall man of about fifty. They took a boat and set off for the Lu Family Village where the guide turned for home. Zhan

Zhao came to a high wall and knocked at the gate calling out: "My name is Zhan and I have come to see your fifth squire."

"Oh you're Southern Hero, known as the 'Royal Cat'. Our lord has been waiting for you. I'll go and announce you," said the doorman.

Zhan Zhao kicked his heels for a long time but no one came. In a rage he shouted and banged at the door again. Another man came and grumbled: "Why are you shouting so loud? You have no manners at all. If you are so uncouth to come in unannounced then you certainly are a brave fellow," and he went away.

Zhan Zhao, now really angry, decided that it was all Sleek Rat's doing to provoke him into losing his patience — and promptly fell into the very trap which he realised was set for him.

He swung himself up to the top of the wall and jumped down. Wandering around he noticed a door inscribed with the vermilion characters "Big Gate" and a lantern with greetings written on it.

"Bai must be here," he thought and tiptoed in. Behind the screen he found a second gate and then another screen. The second gate was higher than the first and going up the steps he entered a house. In the centre there were five rooms, dark with no light, but there was a faint glimmer of light coming from the east side gate and the steps here were higher than those in front of the second gate.

"This house is terraced like a mountain," he thought. Mounting these steps there was another set of five rooms but this time brilliantly illuminated. The architecture was unfamiliar to Zhan Zhao and he went around looking here and there until one door opened out into a room where there was a table flanked by two chairs. A man dressed in a pine green embroidered gown entered.

"It must be Bai the Fifth. He won't face me but goes hiding inside the room," thought Zhan Zhao and followed him.

"Greetings, fifth brother," he said. There was no response and when Zhan Zhao went closer he saw it was a dummy.

"I've been tricked!" he exclaimed.

CHAPTER 54

Southern Hero Is Imprisoned in the Sky Reaching Cave.
He Undertakes to Find the Three Purloined Treasures.

ZHAN Zhao stepped back and trod on a spring-lock hidden in the floor. A board tilted up and he fell through. The banging of gongs sounded and voices shouted: "Got you, Got you!"

He fell into a sack made out of strips of leather which was tied tight at the mouth and he could not struggle free. The sack was lowered down to jeering remarks from Sleek Rat's vassals.

"As our squire is busy drinking with a guest, we had better not disturb him just now. We'll put him in the Sky Reaching Cave," said one of the men.

He was bundled to an entrance cut out of rock. One of the men tugged at a big brass ring which opened a space big enough for Zhan Zhao to be pushed in. The stone entrance was then pulled shut, leaving it impossible for anyone to get out.

The inside of the cave was cold and so smooth that there was no way to get a hold and climb up to a slit at the top. Through the slit could be seen a narrow strip of sky which was why it was named Sky Reaching Cave. He was able to decipher some red characters written on a white background: "Subject the Cat to Annoyance".

"Aiya," Zhan Zhao sighed. "I'm not worthy of the title of imperial guard of the fourth rank for allowing myself to be tricked."

He heard someone groan and shouted out: "Who's there?"

"The humble person is named Guo," said a man's voice. "My daughter and I were on our way to meet her future husband when we were kidnapped by the chieftain Hu who demanded she marry the Fifth Squire instead. He then imprisoned me here."

Zhan Zhao was furious at this sinister side of Sleek Rat. "Bah! The so-called good deeds you have done were worthy of a champion, but this shows you are really a bandit! I swear I'll fight you to the finish!" he said to himself.

The fourth watch was struck and they heard voices shouting: "Fetch the assassin. The squire is calling for him!" The stone entrance opened and Zhan Zhao strode out demanding to see Sleek Rat. He entered a brightly-lit hall where a banquet was taking place. At the head of the table sat a man with a thin beard, the fair-complexioned Judge Liu Qing. Sleek Rat sat next to him and continued talking, ignoring the visitor.

Zhan Zhao shouted: "Bai Yutang. Now you've captured me, what do you intend to do?"

Only then did Sleek Rat pretend to notice him and said in feigned surprise: "It's you, Brother Zhan! My vassals only told me they had captured an assassin." He arose from the table and untied him, apologising profusely. He turned to Judge Liu, saying: "This is the Royal Cat, the Southern Hero, imperial guard of the fourth rank."

Zhan Zhao sneered: "You are a robber and a knave and know nothing about law and discipline. So what right do you have to call me an assassin? The tragedy is I have to die by a dirty trick at the hands of a mountain bandit."

Bai just giggled. "I am a righteous gallant and have never waylaid or robbed families."

Zhan Zhao contradicted him, asking why he had kidnapped an old man and his daughter to force her to marry him.

Sleek Rat, surprised, denied all knowledge but when the old man was brought before him and told him the same story he sent for the man Hu Lie who admitted taking the girl in order to please him. Hu Lie and his brother Hu Qi had been recommended to Sleek Rat by Judge Liu, and they thought that as Sleek Rat was unmarried they would ingratiate themselves with their new master by kidnapping a pretty young wife for him. Unfortunately for him, Hu Lie had not heard of Bai's cruelty. Sleek Rat stepped forward and lashed out with his foot, knocking him down and then gave him a cut on the shoulder with his sword before telling his men to take him to the Songjiang Prefecture.

Sleek Rat then restored the girl to her father and gave him twenty taels of silver as compensation before sending them on their way with an escort, He Shou.

"Brother Zhan," said Sleek Rat. "If you hadn't been imprisoned in the cave I would never have known about Hu Lie's behaviour. He all but sullied my reputation. Now that is over and done with, I know why you are here. You have come by order of the prime minister to take me back to the capital. I will set you a task instead. If you can find the three treasures I stole from Lord Bao, I will go with you. If not you must never come to Hollow Island again."

Zhan Zhao agreed to the terms and Sleek Rat gave him ten days to find the treasures, but Zhan Zhao said he would recover them in three days. He was then put back in the Sky Reaching Cave again.

Meanwhile the old man Guo and his daughter were in a boat that took them to their destination when they heard someone shout the boat to stop on the orders of Sleek Rat.

The escort He Shou was suspicious. "Why should my master change his mind? He will have let down the judge not to mention Zhan Zhao. Even I will look down on him."

A skiff came skimming up to the boat and a man jumped over. It was Hu Qi, the brother of Hu Lie. He held a sharp blade and threatened to avenge his brother on the old man and his daughter. A struggle took place between He Shou and Hu Qi in which the escort was knocked into the water. Hu Qi advanced upon the frightened screaming pair with his blade raised but just then another skiff drew up with a group of men. One of them shouted: "You lout! Are you ignorant of the rules? In Red Catkins Cove no one is allowed to harm others."

The caller jumped for the boat but fell in the water as he dodged Hu Qi's sword. Another three men got on board wielding their weapons and the man in the water was able to grab Hu Qi's ankles and drag him into the water and held him down before overpowering him. The skiff belonged to the Ding family and their men were doing their usual duties of patrolling the lake when they rescued the old man and his daughter. They were taken to the residence of the Ding brothers who put the young girl into the care of their cousin, Moon Flower, and questioned the old man.

A maidservant entered and said that their mother, Lady Ding, wanted to see them urgently.

CHAPTER 55

Ding the Elder Is Shut in the Spiral Study.
Ding the Younger Ascends the Earthworm Cliff.

THEIR sister, Moon Flower, had discovered that the girl had been rescued by her betrothed, Zhan Zhao, and immediately informed her mother. The mother was very angry to learn that her future son-in-law had been captured and ordered the twins to rescue him.

The twins chose four men to escort the old man and his daughter to their destination and then the firstborn of the twins, Zhaolan, decided to go to Hollow Island under the pretext of returning their captive Hu Qi to Sleek Rat.

News of the fight and the capture of his servant had already reached him and he quickly put two and two together and saw through the brother's ruse, but nevertheless he went to greet Zhaolan as he disembarked from the boat and took him to the reception hall where he was introduced to the fair-complexioned judge Liu Qing.

Later at dinner, Sleek Rat boasted how he had left the note and sword in the prime minister's office, inscribed the poem on the wall of the Temple of the Faithful and Dauntless Maid, killed the wicked eunuch by Longevity Hill, how he had misled Grand Tutor Pang into killing his two concubines and ended with the stealing of the three treasures.

"I never thought Royal Cat would willingly walk into my trap," he continued, "but as he is a chivalrous man, I am treating him politely and then he spurns my friendship, so I have him..."

Ding Zhaolan involuntarily exclaimed: "You have landed in a real mess, brother. Don't you know he is an officer appointed by the imperial government? If he dies you will become a rebel and they won't take it lying down."

"And neither will the Ding twins," Bai said smilingly. "Don't worry, he is being well-treated and in a few days, I will hand him over to you."

Ding Zhaolan was kept in the Spiral Study all day, unable to leave. Towards evening an old man entered with a boy of about nine years. The boy bowed and said: "Uncle Ding, I am Sky Rat's son. I have come on the express orders of my mother so that you will know we are genuine. She has learnt of Royal Cat's imprisonment but has not seen Sleek Rat to find out why because he never consults her on any matters about Hollow Island. She is now very worried about his wilful ways and wants you to write a letter to your brother, Zhaohui, so that you two and my father, Sky Rat, can together stop Squire Bai from doing any more harm." Ding Zhaolan promised to write the letter to his brother and the young boy and the old man left.

The younger twin had been waiting impatiently for news of his brother's attempts to rescue their prospective brother-in-law from Sleek Rat's clutches but when he heard that his brother was staying for a few days as his guest, he became suspicious and even more so when he received the letter.

He was wondering what steps to take when he was told that Sky Rat, Mountain Rat and River Rat were waiting to see him. Ding Zhaohui gave them the latest news of their brother's pranks and they discussed what the next moves should be.

Jiang Ping, River Rat, suggested they should go without him, as he would only antagonise his brother Sleek Rat. It was decided that as the younger twin was more agile than the others he would find his way to Earthworm Cliff where a guide would lead him to the Sky Reaching Cave and rescue Zhan Zhao. Then the two of them would retrieve the three treasures. Sky Rat and Mountain Rat would wait in the Western Bamboo Grove for them and together they would capture Sleek Rat.

Ding Zhaohui made his way to Earthworm Cliff where he was to meet the guide. As he waited he was surprised to see a vast expanse of green water rippling in the moonlight. "I could have made my way by boat and not bothered climbing the cliff," he thought. But when the guide arrived he told the twin that the stretch of water was really made of stone. It was called Blue Stone Pool, and had been built by the Rat brothers to confuse strangers.

The younger Ding and the guide walked down the mountain and, sure enough, the pool was even and smooth and could be walked upon. The guide said he could go no further and told Zhaohui to walk across. That would take him to the Five Gallants Hall. Zhaohui crossed over, saw a light ahead and hid behind a tree, thinking they might be watchmen. He heard one of the men say: "Just my luck to be told by the Fifth Squire to watch over that man Zhan Zhao in the Sky Reaching Cave. My relief is too drunk to move and I can't carry on any longer."

The other man replied: "I don't know what has come over the Fifth Squire. He's changed. At the moment he won't let Ding the Elder go and the two of them together with Judge Liu drink all the time. Liu wants nothing but to see those three treasures so I have been ordered to go to the Interlocked Cave to bring them. I am afraid things won't change until Lu Fang, our eldest squire, returns."

Sighing, they took up their lanterns and departed.

CHAPTER 56

Zhan Zhao Escapes from the Cave. The Three Treasures Are Recovered and Sleek Rat Takes Flight.

ONE of the two men was called Yao, or the Swaying Mountain, and the other was Fei, or Crawling Snake. When Yao went off Ding Zhaohui leapt out from behind the tree and grabbed Fei by the neck.

"Do you know me?" he snarled.

"Ding the Second Squire," Fei replied.

"Where is the Sky Reaching Cave?" Zhaohui demanded.

When Fei told him, he was stripped and tied to a tree with his own sash, while the twin draped the clothes over his shoulders.

"Wait here till day breaks and somebody will come to your rescue," he said.

Fei murmured to himself: "What a sorry spectacle I'm making of myself! I must look like a monster kissing the tree."

As Zhaohui neared the Sky Reaching Cave he heard the drunken voice of a man singing.

"My name is Fei," he shouted. "I've been dispatched by the Fifth Squire to collect Zhan Zhao because he heard he is making a fuss about his food and has smashed all the crockery."

"Splendid," replied the drunken guard, "I dare not open the stone entrance, but be careful. He's dangerous and I'm too drunk to go near him."

Ding Zhaohui pulled the brass ring in the rock and a door opened. "Lord Zhan," he called, "our squire is waiting."

Zhan Zhao emerged, saying: "If he wants to play another trick on me, I'm ready!"

"Don't you recognise me, brother-in-law?" asked Zhaohui.

Zhan the Royal Cat was overjoyed and the two men made their way to the Eastern Bamboo Grove by the Five Gallants Hall where they overheard Sleek Rat, Bai Yutang, telling his servant Fu to go to the Interlocked Cave and bring the three treasures.

On his way back Fu felt someone pulling his jacket but it was only brambles which had caught it. He put down his lantern and the bundle containing the three treasures to disentangle himself and when he turned round, the lantern and bundle had vanished. A man held his shoulder. "Set your mind at ease, boy," said Zhan Zhao. "I won't hurt you but you have to take a little rest here," and he tied his hands behind his back.

"How can I rest this way?" the boy protested.

"Better lie down on your face, then," replied Zhan Zhao and placed a rock on his back, saying: "This will keep you from catching cold."

"Aiya," replied the boy, "it's too heavy and I don't feel cold."

"Let me see if you can move or not. If it's too light I can cover you with another."

"I enjoy this one," the boy said hurriedly. "Put another rock on me and I'll be no more."

Zhan Zhao went to pick up the bundle but it had gone. He saw a shadow passing by and heard someone laughing. It was Mountain Rat.

"I was afraid the treasures would be lost so I came especially to give you a hand." He took the bundle from under a rock. "I know all the secret places under rocks and stones in Hollow Island," he said.

When they reached the Five Gallants Hall they saw a table covered with wine and dishes. At the head was the elder twin, Ding

Zhaolan, with Liu Qing, the fair-complexioned judge, on one side of him and on the other Sleek Rat, Bai Yutang, with Zhan Zhao's sword hanging from his left side.

Bai looked a little tipsy and was boasting again: "Let me tell you, brothers. I'll make Zhan Zhao give in to me or get him dismissed from his post and even get Prime Minister Bao punished. Only then will I be satisfied, and how will my brothers face me then and what will they have to say to the Kaifeng Prefecture?"

Ding Zhaolan did not speak but Liu Qing complimented him. Mountain Rat, unable to contain his anger any longer, broke into the hall holding a sword in his hand.

"Take the first blow, little brother," he shouted.

Sleek Rat went to draw his sword only to find that Ding Zhaolan had removed it from his belt so he quickly raised a chair to ward off the blow. It shattered the chair.

"Stay, Xu Qing," he called. "I have something to tell you. I know what you have come for but I have vowed that if Zhan Zhao finds the three treasures within a certain time I will go back with him to Kaifeng voluntarily. The time isn't up yet. He'll never be able to find them on his own. That's why he is relying on you to help him. Let's see how Zhan Zhao can face me or return to Kaifeng."

Mountain Rat burst into laughter and called Zhan Zhao to enter with the bundle. "I've managed to get the treasures within three days," he said.

Sky Rat and the younger twin brother came in behind Zhan Zhao. Sleek Rat, faced with defeat, picked up the broken chair, struck at Mountain Rat and rushed out of the hall, pursued by the latter.

As he ran towards the mountains he left items of clothing to put Mountain Rat off the scent and made his getaway.

Judge Liu Qing was a silent observer of the fracas in the hall. He was in a quandary. "If I sneak away, I'll let down my friend," he thought. "If I fight Xu Qing, I'm bound to lose. I had better

put on a bold front and stand up for my friend." He took a leg off
the table and called out: "You have made a solemn alliance with
Bai Yutang as a blood-brother and now you are persecuting him."
He swung the table leg towards Sky Rat who felled him with a kick
in the ankle and ordered him to be tied up. Judge Liu's famous fair
complexion turned crimson with shame.

"It wouldn't be a gallant thing to hurt you," Sky Rat said, "but
I am offended at your meddling between us and our fifth brother."
He ordered him to be released and the judge sheepishly sidled
away.

Sky Rat, Zhan Zhao and the twins then began to search the
bamboo groves for Sleek Rat. There they met the empty-handed
Mountain Rat who told them their erring brother had made his
way to the Single Dragon Bridge over the river. This bridge con-
sisted of a single iron chain extended between two posts.

"What River Rat predicted has come true," said Zhaohui, and
repeated what he had been told. "Sleek Rat is not stupid and will
likely as not surrender himself to Kaifeng so that the rest of us will
lose face."

"All our efforts seem to have gone for nothing," Lu Fang and
Zhan Zhao said. "How can we face Prime Minister Bao?"

They decided to take the three treasures back and hoped that
that would somewhat save their face.

Sleek Rat in the meantime had reached the Single Dragon
Bridge only to find it broken and he was unable to get across the
river. He saw a small fishing boat and tried to bribe the fisherman
with double the fare to get him over and to safety.

CHAPTER 57

Sleek Rat Is Captured Under the Single Dragon Bridge.
The Prime Minister Asks to See Him.

THE fisherman demanded the fare in advance but Sleek Rat jumped onto the boat and said he would pay when he reached the other side. In his hurry to escape he had not brought any money, but the fisherman was adamant and rowed to the centre of the lake where he stopped. "Promises are no guarantee," he said. "Pay up now or get off!"

Sleek Rat had no alternative but to take off his gown and offer it as payment. "Pawn this and you will get more than your fare."

As they were arguing, another boat darted towards them and the fisherman joined his friend and abandoned Sleek Rat alone in the boat. The money they would get for the gown would pay for a long drinking session.

Sleek Rat had given his gown away for nothing and as he was unfamiliar with punting a boat only succeeded in going round in circles.

"I wish I had practised sculling a boat instead of balancing across the Single Dragon Bridge," he muttered. Suddenly Jiang Ping, River Rat, emerged from the cabin saying: "There's not a man who is able to do everything, so why blame yourself? You should have learnt how to row a boat instead of wasting your energies on balancing across the bridge. Now look where it has got you?"

Sleek Rat angrily swung the pole at him but River Rat dropped
into the water and disappeared. Sleek Rat fixed his eyes on the
water and tried to move the boat. But River Rat tipped the side of
the boat and he fell into the water where he took in several mouthfuls of water before River Rat decided he was chastened enough
and was able to grab his hair and bring him to the bank. He was
tied to a pole like a slaughtered animal and carried to Jasmine Village. The other Rat brothers, Zhan Zhao and the Ding twins were
there, beginning to be anxious, wondering where River Rat had
got to.

They were about to have their meal when River Rat arrived
with the trussed Sleek Rat. He was quickly released and after
vomiting more water sat up swearing he would never be friends
with River Rat again.

Zhan Zhao tried to pacify him, saying it was all his fault, and
the Ding brothers helped him up and told him a luxurious bath was
waiting for him. Slightly mollified, Sleek Rat was taken to the
bathroom where he soaked himself in sweet-smelling water and
powdered himself in fragrant talcum powder. He then dressed
himself in the clothes that had been placed on the bed for him. A
muslin vest, underclothes, light blue trousers, boots, stockings,
green embroidered gown and pale blue jacket, silk sash and red
embroidered kerchief — clothes suited for a warrior.

He was grateful to the Ding brothers but still had a grudge a-
gainst River Rat.

Afterwards hunger forced him to swallow his pride and he ate
and drank while the others tried to persuade him to go with them
to Kaifeng. He shook his head.

"You are too wilful," protested River Rat. "You have broken
your promise to Zhan Zhao and let your brothers down. Where is
your loyalty?"

"Coward!" Sleek Rat thundered. "I'll fight you to the death!"

"I won't retaliate," said River Rat. "Even if you kill me you'll pay with your life. It just shows how little you know of the real world. All the feats you have boasted of took place in the dead of night. Leaping about onto roofs and jumping over walls to escape is not a clever thing to do. You haven't seen much of the world if you have never been to court and seen the emperor ascend the throne in broad daylight and the solemn ceremonies that accompany it. First the golden chimes are beaten, then the gates on both sides are opened. Out of them file armed guards who stand on either side like gods. Following them are the military and civil officials, who stand on the east and west sides according to their rank. Under the vermilion terrace are the imperial guards. Then three cracks of whips are heard and the main palace gate is opened and in come the eunuchs two by two, holding bronze braziers, heralding the sedan chair borne by eight eunuchs carrying the emperor, followed by two eunuchs holding long-handled fans embroidered with the sun and the moon. Silence reigns everywhere. The scene makes your hair stand on end. Even when the prime minister holds court there is an awe-inspiring scene. He comes in with his sergeants and constables carrying instruments of torture which send cold shivers down the onlooker's back and then the warriors enter carrying the imperial axes. His presence alone showing probity and faithfulness to the state and people is enough to impress even you. But all the things you did were done during the night when everyone was asleep. So you could kill, steal and run off at your pleasure. I defy you to do the same in daylight! That's why you do not dare go to Kaifeng!"

River Rat's tirade put Sleek Rat on the spot. "What kind of man do you take me for?" he said. "Nothing will stop me going to Kaifeng!"

River Rat smiled. "Promise you won't find more excuses or escape, and when we get to Kaifeng, remember that what you did in the imperial garden is not an ordinary crime, so be careful when you see Prime Minister Bao and be prepared to take the consequences."

The elder Ding poured the two men a cup of wine each and they drank to each other, friends once more. Even Zhan Zhao, who had been Sleek Rat's adversary, drank a cup with him, saying what an honourable man he was in giving himself up. The rest of the evening was spent in pleasantries and much eating and drinking.

Before leaving, Zhan Zhao paid his respects to his future mother-in-law and the five gallant men then left for Kaifeng, where Sleek Rat was at last introduced to the four warriors who were impressed by his youth and handsome looks.

The three treasures were returned to Prime Minister Bao and Zhan Zhao related all the adventures that had taken place in his efforts to retrieve them and pleaded with him to stand up for Sleek Rat before the throne. Prime Minister Bao was curious to meet this wilful young hero and asked to see him. Sleek Rat was about to go when River Rat stopped him.

"You are not a relative or a friend of his but a man accused of crimes. Going there would be a breach of the law."

CHAPTER 58

Sleek Rat Is Promoted to Royal Guard.
A Child Presumed Dead Is Rescued.

SLEEK Rat donned the clothes and shackles of a criminal to show his humility when he came before Prime Minister Bao. He was accompanied by Sky Rat, the eldest of the Rat brothers, and four of the warriors. Sleek Rat shuffled forward on his knees and said in a low voice: "The offender Bai Yutang has broken the law. He begs Your Excellency for mercy." He prostrated himself before Lord Bao.

The prime minister ordered him to be unshackled and promised he would put in a good word with the emperor when Sleek Rat confessed to all he had done.

"His Majesty is looking for good men and I'm sure it will be to your advantage."

Sky Rat hurried forward and said: "If His Majesty should forgive him, it would be very fortunate for all of us. If he is punished we are also ready to atone for his crimes."

The prime minister was impressed by the loyalty shown and reassured him.

The next day Prime Minister Bao presented the petition asking for the emperor's pardon. The ruler was delighted that at last Sleek Rat would appear before him. He liked what he saw and decreed that as Zhan Zhao had been promoted to fourth rank of the imperial guard, Sleek Rat should fill the vacancy.

Afterwards the band of men decided to celebrate with a party. The only one missing was Earth Rat, Han Zhang, who was still searching for Sleek Rat, unaware that he had already been captured.

It put a dark cloud over the feasting and drinking. Jiang Ping, River Rat, said morosely: "Five sworn Rat brothers — four of us have been promoted, leaving our second brother alone in the wilderness. As I feel responsible I will go to look for him tomorrow."

The missing brother, Han Zhang, after cleaning up his mother's grave at the God Blessing Temple, left to visit the sights in Hangzhou. He put up at an inn for the night and as he was about to sleep, he heard a boy crying in the room next door and a man shouting and slapping him.

Han Zhang went into their room. "Why are you beating such a little boy?" he asked.

"I bought him for five taels of silver to be my adopted son," the man answered. "But he will persist in calling me uncle and not father and even stopped calling me that when we reached the inn."

The boy was sad but handsome-looking and Han Zhang felt pity.

"He seems to be a nice enough lad. You may as well sell him to me," he said.

He took out five taels of silver plus the interest which the man demanded and the boy was handed over. The man left without a backward glance.

The boy remarked: "He got off lightly. He found me half-dead in the mountains where my uncle had dumped me. My uncle was a bad lot, a robber who had kidnapped the nephew of the prime minister and was going to kill him in revenge for his brother's death. My mother set the nephew free and then hanged herself in shame and because I cried, my uncle lost his temper and beat me up and then left me for dead. The man who rescued me was hoping to sell me and that's why he insisted I call him father."

Han Zhang was excited at finding the missing boy, whose name was Jiuru. He comforted the child and the following morning left him in the care of a kindly old sweet-dumpling seller named Zhang until he finished his business in Hangzhou and was ready to leave for Kaifeng, where he would take the boy.

CHAPTER 59

The Old Man's Debt Is Paid.
A Bully Is Exposed in Giant Village.

THE sweet-dumpling seller was persuaded to take some money for Jiuru's keep until Han Zhang returned from business. Han clasped his hands respectfully to the old man and Jiuru bowed low.

Meanwhile the prime minister's faithful page, Bao Xing, had escorted Master Fang and his daughter to stay with her future in-laws, the prime minister's brother and his wife. He paid his respects to the whole extended family and also visited the prime minister's old tutor, Master Ning.

On his way back to Kaifeng he noticed a tall building surrounded by trees and bushes and wondered who lived in such a formidable place. He thought they must be descendants of an aristocratic family or a retired official. His horse was suddenly startled by a loud bang and he was thrown while the horse bolted. Luckily he was unhurt and he was helped up by his followers. He sent one of them to get his horse, but the varlet returned, saying he had met a man shooting birds who accused him of frightening the birds away. "After I have brought them down, you can have your horse back," he said. When the servant insisted that he return the horse he retorted: "Nobody crosses Giant Village without leaving something behind," and asked for fifty taels of silver to redeem it.

The angry Bao Xing sought out the local magistrate who turned out to be the magistrate of Renhe County and a good friend of the poor scholar Yan Shenmin whom Sleek Rat had once befriended. The magistrate had known of the crimes in Giant Village but his policemen had been bribed and kept him from discovering the culprits. Bao Xing's sudden appearance surprised and shocked him.

He apologised to Bao Xing and sent one of his men to recover the horse. Then he mentioned how the prime minister's protégé, Yan Shenmin, was a good friend and offered his own horse to save time. It was a hundred times better than Bao Xing's own, with an ornate saddle. He accepted it gladly and they went on their way. Later they stopped at an inn called the Immortal Meeting Building. Bao Xing sat at a table to await his meal and noticed two men sitting by the window. One had green eyes and a purple beard; the other was younger and handsome.

The man with green eyes was a northern hero called Ouyang Chun and the younger man was the twin Ding Zhaolan who had been ordered by his mother to prepare Southern Hero Zhan Zhao for his wedding to Ding's sister Moon Flower.

Another young man, about twenty years old, entered the restaurant accompanied by an old servant. They sat down and began to eat.

Suddenly loud footsteps were heard coming up the stairs and another elderly man accompanied by a weeping boy entered and sat down opposite Bao Xing, the boy standing by his side wiping his eyes. More footsteps sounded and another old man came in searching the room and knelt in front of the elderly man.

"I beg you, sir, I'll repay all the money I owe you, only please don't take the boy away. He does not belong to me but is a nephew of a customer."

The man at first ignored him and then said: "You can have him back when you have paid your debt."

It was the sweet-dumplings seller, Zhang, who promised to sell his stall and repay the man.

The man contemptuously gave him three days to find the money.

The young man who had been watching was touched by the moving scene and offered to pay the debt and the boy was returned to Zhang.

The grateful dumpling seller told him he had borrowed five taels of silver from the Second Squire, Ma Lu, of Giant Village but the interest was so high he could never pay off the principal and the boy had been taken as a pledge. The young man, named Ni Jizu, was on his way to sit for the imperial examinations and after he and his servant finished their meal, they clasped their hands in front of the assembled customers and left.

Ding Zhaolan was curious about the incident and asked the dumpling seller to tell him about Giant Village. He told them about the bully called Ma Gang who lorded it over everyone because of his special relationship with a palace major-domo called Chaoxian.

The old man then went over to Bao Xing's table and told him the whole story of how he acquired the young boy. Bao Xing thought: "It must have been pre-ordained that I lost my horse and so found the missing boy," and offered to take the boy with him to Kaifeng.

CHAPTER 60

Uncle Purple Beard Gets Rid of a Bully.
The Ding Twin Meets a Bold Man.

WHEN Bao Xing discovered that old man Zhang could hardly make ends meet selling sweet dumplings, he suggested that he accompany them to Kaifeng. Zhang was very amenable to the idea and told him how the young boy had been rescued by a gallant warrior called Han Zhang — Earth Rat — and placed in his care until the wicked squire Ma Lu took him as payment for the debt.

"So, Lord Han has already been here," Bao Xing said to himself and then changed his mind and decided to place them in the care of the local magistrate who was very willing to please a representative of the prime minister whose horse had been stolen. Before leaving for Kaifeng, Bao Xing said: "When Lord Han returns tell him I am waiting in the Kaifeng Prefecture."

At the Immortal Meeting Restaurant, the Ding twin and Ouyang Chun, the purple bearded man, were still eating and drinking and discussing the wickedness of the local bully, Ma Lu, and his evil servant.

"Good is always rewarded and evil punished," said Ouyang, also known as Northern Hero. "Leave well alone."

Ding was slightly annoyed and thought: "Northern Hero is famous for his skill with weapons and courage but when the opportunity presents itself to prove it, he turns a blind eye."

He retorted: "Gallant men like us should help those in danger
and rid the world of evil and wickedness."

Ouyang shook his finger: "Walls have ears. We'll talk outside."

"A fine hero you are!" said Ding to himself. "What a pity I
haven't brought any weapons with me. I'll suggest sharing a room
with him tonight, steal his sword and show him what heroes we
twins are and what a timid rabbit he is."

After their meal they staggered out and found their way to a
temple where they promised a crippled priest a handsome donation
if he let them stay the night. They were shown to a small com-
pound with three secluded rooms. Ouyang hung his sword on the
wall and the two men began to chat. Now that they were away
from prying eyes and listening ears, the twin referred to Ma
Gang's crimes. "Wouldn't it be a good thing if we removed this
scourge of the people and the state?" he asked.

Ouyang smiled: "He is guarded round the clock. Being too hasty
might wreck our chances."

Ding changed the subject, having decided his companion was
making smart remarks in order to hide his cowardice and in the
still of the night he would show him up.

The priest brought them their supper and the atmosphere between the two men became chilly.

When he saw Ouyang began to yawn and feel sleepy, it confirmed his belief that the title of "Northern Hero" was a ridiculous
description of such a bag of wine and rice. He waited until Ouyang
fell asleep, removed the sword from the scabbard and made his
way to Giant Village.

He began jumping over the walls and entered through the roof
of Ma Gang's residence. Peering down into the main hall he saw a
man surrounded by singsong girls and concubines persuading their
"highness" to drink. Incensed at the debauched scene before him
he went to draw his sword only to find that it had slipped out of
the scabbard when he scrambled down from the roof. Frustrated,
he could only hide himself behind a rockery looking on. Suddenly

the women began shrieking in terror: "Our lord's head has been taken away by a monster!"

The chastened Ding made his way back, saying to himself: "Truly the evildoer has been punished and Northern Hero's prophecy has been fulfilled." As he jumped down from the wall he was confronted by a man wielding a stout staff and as he dodged the blows he noticed another man sitting on the wall who hurled something which knocked his attacker down. His rescuer was no other than Northern Hero holding the missing sword.

The man with the staff yelled out: "It's all over, Butterfly! We must have been enemies in a previous existence."

"My name is not Butterfly," replied the twin. "My name is Ding Zhaolan."

The man rose to his feet and while he was dusting himself down, he noticed bloodstains on his clothes and a human head lying on the ground. The object that Northern Hero had knocked him down with was Ma Gang's head.

The three men left the scene together and the man with the staff told them he was called Long Tao and that he was seeking his brother's murderer who was a notorious womaniser and could be found wherever there were pretty women to be had. "His real name is Hua Chong but because he wears a flower in the pattern of a butterfly by his ear that is his nickname." Long Tao told the two men that Butterfly was due at the Kitchen God Temple in fifteen days' time. The three decided they would meet up there then.

The twin and Northern Hero returned to their room where the latter explained to the perplexed Ding how he had been able to remove his sword when Ding was negotiating his way down the wall.

"I don't understand how the women thought it was a monster who had removed Ma Gang's head," said Ding.

"Gallant men do good deeds quietly and modestly," replied Northern Hero, to which Ding had to agree.

The "monster" turned out to be a mask made from three pieces of leather.

"I now know my brother is two-faced," laughed Ding.

"I may have two faces," replied Ouyang, "but there is only one true one."

"So it's a kind of game," said Ding.

Northern Hero laughed. "You don't understand it yet, brother. Though I disguised myself for killing Ma Gang, it has an advantage."

"What's that?" asked Ding. "Pray let me into your secret."

CHAPTER 61

Earth Rat Meets a Man Called Stingy Elephant.
Iron Rooster Loses His Silver.

"LET me explain," said Northern Hero. "Since this Ma Gang called himself 'Highness' it must be because he has influential friends and if I had killed him without my disguise, his family would have reported the murder to the local authorities. But now the singsong girls can only describe a monster with a blue face and red hair that took off Ma Gang's head, so the authorities will be unable to do anything about it."

Ding Zhaolan was suitably impressed and after chatting for a while they turned in. When day broke they gave the lame priest a donation for incense and left. Ding invited Northern Hero to come with him to his hometown, Jasmine Village, and stay until the Kitchen God Temple opened when they would meet up with Long Tao and together the three men would tackle the evil Hua Chong.

Meanwhile Earth Rat had left the tavern where sweet dumplings were sold, on his way to Hangzhou. As he walked along he heard people referring to "Butterfly" but not being very interested in finding out continued on his journey. He became hungry and found a house with a wine sign and red gourd sticking out from the eaves. It was a pleasant-looking place with a reed hedge covered with bean sprouts and bean flowers in full bloom. Over the doorway was a tablet which read "Minister Tavern" and in the front courtyard there were two tables and the ground was covered with a mat. Next to the house were three thatched cottages. An old man was dozing.

Earth Rat gave a little cough. The old man woke up and hastily took up a dish-cloth and took his order for a warm pot of sorghum liquor and food. He said that as it was such an out-of-the-way place he could only offer stewed bean curd and boiled eggs.

Another man, aged about thirty, entered the room and called out: "Old Dou, warm a measure of wine for me quickly, for I have urgent business."

"Why the rush?" demanded the old man.

The young man sighed. "My niece Qiaojie is missing and my sister is distraught and has sent me with a message to her husband."

Earth Rat was intrigued and invited him over to his table where the young man, named Zhuang Zhihe, insisted on acting as host, bribing the old man with some silver to kill one of the chickens outside and prepare a decent meal for his guest.

Another man entered, sat on the edge of the table and putting his feet on a stool, gave a glance at the two men and called for hot wine. When the old servant brought the wine, he complained it was not warm enough and then demanded some meat dishes to which the answer was the same as Earth Rat had received. He aimed a blow at the old man and lurched out of the room where he smelt the appetising smell of chicken stew.

"What!" he roared. "You said you had no meat and here I find a nice juicy fat chicken."

Dou explained that if he was prepared to pay two drams of silver he would cook him one too.

"Humph," said the man. "I'll eat this first and you can cook another one for those two." With that he scooped the chicken out of the pot and proceeded to eat it, ignoring the old man's protests.

Earth Rat was furious and kicked the plate of boiling hot chicken stew into his face. With scalded face, the bully slunk out of the room, realising he was no match.

Zhuang Zhihe paid the old man for the wine and the chicken, rather crestfallen at having spent money for nothing, and the two men left the tavern.

Old man Dou scooped up the chicken from the ground, washed the dirt off it and stewed it once again. He poured himself out a measure of wine and chuckled to himself: "A nice drink and a tender chicken all to myself."

He was just about to tuck into the chicken when Earth Rat re-entered. "Please sir," said the old man, "I've kept the chicken and wine warm ready for you."

Earth Rat smiled and declined it, but asked who was the lout who had caused all the trouble.

"You don't want to know about that piece of dung," said old Dou. "He comes from a well-off family but they are all mean and brutal. They live in the Bian Family Village. His father Bian Long is known as the Iron Rooster and is so mean, that if he were not afraid of starving to death, he would not eat. His son is even worse and is known as Stingy Elephant. Father and son are so mean that people have changed the name Bian Family Village to Bian Family Pillage. He often comes and eats without paying but I can't afford to upset him."

Earth Rat left the old man and made his way to an inn not far from the Bian Family Village and when night fell he sneaked onto the roof of the Bian house. Looking down he saw an old man with a mouth like a beak and cheeks like a monkey weighing silver and tying it up into four parcels. He then ordered his page to light a lantern and take them into the rear quarters while he remained to pack up his scales.

Earth Rat slid down and as the page stepped over the threshold he stuck his leg out and tripped him up, making the lantern go out. He scrambled to his feet and re-lit the lantern. "Be careful, boy," shouted his master, "the parcels might have broken and some of the silver dust spilt out. Bring them back so I can weigh them again and woe betide you if it weighs less." But the silver was gone and the furious Iron Rooster, for it was he, shook the panic-stricken boy threatening to kill him. His son, Stingy Elephant, also came and dragged the boy back into the room where they saw a note under a weight on the table which read: "Your grandfather passed your home this evening. I hear you are notoriously mean and stingy despite wallowing in money. I have borrowed four parcels of silver and will repay you one day. Don't wrong others. If you don't do as I say, I will put you to the sword, for I often take these measures at night-time."

Trembling with fear, the two men released the boy and knew they could not make their loss public because of the threat. All they could do was keep a good lookout.

CHAPTER 62

Earth Rat Rescues the Kidnapped Girl.
A Fight Takes Place on Iron Mountain.

AS Earth Rat, carrying the four parcels of silver, made his way through a forest, he heard the sound of a wheelbarrow being trundled along. He quickly climbed a tree; the wheelbarrow stopped beneath him.

"This thing has been incarcerated all day," said a man's voice. "As there is no one around let's take it out and give it some air."

"Yes, we don't want it to suffocate," a woman's voice agreed.

They removed a little boy from a trunk and seated him against a tree. Hiding the silver in a fork of the tree, Earth Rat sprang down and confronted the couple. As the man tried to escape, he stabbed him with his sword and the woman collapsed, shaking with fear.

"What are you up to?" Earth Rat demanded. "Tell me quick or you'll die."

The woman confessed they were kidnappers and they were taking the boy to the Prince of Xiangyang who was training actors and singsong girls. For each good-looking child he would pay five hundred to six hundred taels of silver.

The kidnapped child turned out to be a young girl who had been drugged by the couple. Earth Rat tied the woman up and as the girl slowly recovered she told him her name was Qiaojie.

"Is your maternal uncle called Zhuang Zhihe?" he asked.

"Yes," the surprised girl said, and he offered up a silent prayer to Buddha for this happy coincidence. Realising that it would be improper for him to be with the young girl so early in the morning, he told her he was a friend of her uncle's and that she should wait till someone came along and get the local bailiff to take her home. With that he left for Mulberry Flower Town. Soon the female kidnapper was taken by passers-by to the bailiff and the young girl waited to be collected by her uncle who on his way dropped in at the Minister Tavern and told the good news to Old Man Dou. Dou informed him who her rescuer had been.

"He came back after the two of you left yesterday, to ask me about the Bian family," he said. "Now I hear they have lost a lot of silver. Don't you think it a bit of a coincidence? What kind of person is this man called Han?"

A priest came over and bowed to Zhuang Zhihe. "Is this man called Han a tall man with golden complexion and a sparse yellow beard? I am looking for him." The priest was all skin and bone as if he had just recovered from a long illness. But his eyes were piercing bright and his voice was deep.

Old Man Dou was a bit short with him as the priest had only ordered one measure of wine since the morning and had occupied a whole table. "I suppose he's looking for a free meal," he thought to himself. The priest ignored him and said to Zhuang: "It must be fate that I meet you here, patron. Would you treat me to two measures of wine?"

Zhuang ordered the wine for the priest who was in reality Jiang Ping — River Rat — who had promised Prime Minister Bao that he would find Earth Rat and bring him back. He had taken on the disguise of a priest so no one would discover who he really was. The more he talked to Zhuang the more sure he felt that it was Earth Rat who had rescued his niece. He thanked him and made more inquiries at every inn and hotel but in vain. When shadows lengthened he came to the Iron Mountain Monastery. A priest carrying a wine gourd emerged.

Jiang Ping stepped forward and clasping his hands before him asked for shelter. The priest gave him a disdainful look and said: "You're too short and puny to give us much trouble. Wait here until I've bought the wine."

"I love drinking too," replied Jiang Ping and offered to go and buy it for him, bringing back some titbits as well, which impressed the priest who treated him more politely and showed him in. The priest put the wine and some leftovers onto a low table and they sat down. Jiang Ping introduced himself as Zhang and the two began to drink. The abbot of that monastery was swarthy, had a big belly and called himself Iron Arhat. He was very skilful with weapons but flattered anyone who was rich and influential.

The priest became drunk as he gulped cup after cup of wine, and told River Rat: "When the abbot comes, don't speak to him. Let him go to the back of the room and we will continue drinking. When we are drunk we'll have a good sleep and not interfere in anything that happens. You see," the priest said, his tongue now loosened with wine, "this abbot of ours is really a bandit and is hiding here in the monastery. Recently a friend of his named 'Butterfly' came to see him because he is being hunted by someone who luckily got captured and is locked up in the pagoda in the backyard."

Jiang Ping's heart missed a beat. "Who is this man?" he asked.

"He was captured last night and has been accused of some misdeeds."

It turned out that the man captured was Earth Rat. After saving the young girl, he had arrived in Mulberry Flower Town where he heard about the evil Butterfly, a fugitive who had escaped from the eastern capital. When night fell he scouted about for him and noticed what looked like a wisp of smoke entering the temple of the Goddess of Mercy. "Why is a night prowler going into a nunnery?" he wondered.

He saw a silhouette on a window of a man with a butterfly fluttering at the side of his temple.

"I've got him," Earth Rat said to himself and squatted down by the window to listen.

"Please, I beg you, reverend nun, don't spurn me, grant me my request."

"What if I resist?" said a woman's voice.

"No woman who catches my fancy can escape me," answered Butterfly. "I like your looks and don't want to harm you."

"I come from a decent family," the nun answered. "I am only here because my parents could not afford to pay for medical treatment when I fell ill. I pray to Buddha every day for good health in my next life. It may be fate that I met you devil today. Well, well. Let me die quickly." She burst into tears.

"Slut!" Butterfly swore. "I'll kill you!"

Earth Rat saw Hua Chong draw his sword.

"That's enough," thundered Earth Rat. "I'm coming to get you!"

Butterfly blew out the lamp, drew his sword and went out into the courtyard. An arrow just missed him and then they came to blows but the protagonists were hampered by the narrow space. A man was seen jumping down from the wall; he was big and hefty-looking and swung his sword at Butterfly who managed to dodge and jump up to the wall where Earth Rat followed, chasing Butterfly up the street, while the third man rushed out of the gate in pursuit. They reached another temple where Butterfly vaulted over the wall, closely chased by Earth Rat. As Butterfly tried to hide behind a pagoda, Earth Rat felt something hit his shoulder which made it go numb. He realised he had been hit by a poison arrow and managed to get over the wall and make his way to Mulberry Flower Town.

Butterfly was about to tackle the third pursuer when the fat abbot, Iron Arhat, arrived and together they locked him in the pagoda.

As River Rat heard the story he was stunned and wondered what to do next.

CHAPTER 63

River Rat Stabs the Fat Abbot in a Fight.
He Finds Earth Rat.

"NO wonder I can't find Earth Rat," thought Jiang Ping. "He's been imprisoned by these people."

There was a knock at the door, and the priest put his finger to his lips and blew out the lamp.

"Anything happened today?" a gruff voice asked.

The priest, who was by then quite drunk, answered in the negative and the voice then told him to lock the door.

Two men disappeared into the back; the priest returned to Jiang Ping and resumed drinking until he finally fell into a drunken sleep.

Jiang Ping took off his robe, drew a three-edged weapon from the bamboo tube, blew out the lamp and made his way to the backyard where the three pagodas stood. The middle one was the largest and he heard a man shouting from the inside. It was not Earth Rat's voice but nevertheless Jiang Ping released the man.

"Who are you?" the man asked. When Jiang Ping told him his name he exclaimed: "You are River Rat, the fourth lord! I'm so glad to meet you. My name is Long Tao. I've been tracking this Butterfly from the Kitchen God Temple of Renhe County all the way here. I mean to take revenge on him for my brother but thought I was done for until you rescued me."

"Where is my second brother?" Jiang Ping asked.

"I saw a slender man fighting Butterfly, but when I went to help I got caught."

"It sounds like him," thought Jiang Ping. "I wonder where he is now?"

Long Tao told him he had seen two men pass through a door in the wall behind the bamboo grove. Jiang Ping told him to wait while he investigated. At first he could not find a door in the wall but on closer examination he found a button which he pressed. A swivel door swung open and he stepped inside. He found rooms flanked by verandahs and a courtyard with a white marble basin planted with chrysanthemums, a scene of great tranquillity. One of the main rooms was brightly lit and two men sat there conversing. He tiptoed to the window to listen.

"You are too weak-minded, brother," said the voice of Iron Arhat. "You shouldn't bother your head about a slip of a nun. If you go on like this I'll look down on you."

Butterfly retorted: "What do you know of the matter? I became infatuated as soon as I set eyes on her. I can't sleep or eat. She's so obstinate. If she was like one of the others, I would have killed her long before this, but I haven't the heart. What shall I do?"

The abbot laughed. "If that's the case, do me right and I'll guarantee you success."

Butterfly dropped on his knees and promised.

Jiang Ping was scornful. "Normally one kowtows to the mother-in-law for one's wife. This fellow kowtows to a priest for a nun. How shameless!"

"Get up," said Iron Arhat. "I'll get my mistress to visit the convent and burn incense tomorrow. She will put some knockout drops into the food the nun eats and then you can have your way with her."

"Splendid, splendid," laughed Butterfly. "If you help me to succeed, I will regard you as my brother."

"Remember that," said the abbot. "Don't forget that you are a brother and don't do the same with my woman."

"I'll treat her as my sister-in-law," replied Butterfly.

It was hard for the eavesdropper, Jiang Ping, to control his fury but he managed to and instead of breaking in and confronting the evil pair, he shouted at the door, "Amida Buddha!" and hid behind the bamboo grove.

The abbot came into the courtyard and seeing the door in the wall open hastened out. Seeing no one he decided it must have been the priest, drunk again, and went to relieve himself against the bamboo grove. Jiang Ping took out his three-pointed weapon and stabbed the abbot in his fat belly. Iron Arhat gave a groan and fell down dead. He then rushed into the main room and stabbed at Butterfly but only managed to wound him. So the evildoer was able to jump over the wall and make his escape. The disappointed Jiang Ping returned to Long Tao who was recovering from his incarceration in the pagoda and the two left the temple for Mulberry Flower Town.

The hard night's work had left them hungry and they entered a restaurant where they saw the waiter taking a flapping live fish out of a basin.

The waiter refused to sell Jiang Ping the fish, saying it was for a customer who was very ill.

"Strange," thought River Rat. "Carp is the warm element and is not suitable for overcoming illness."

He followed the waiter as he took the steaming, appetising carp to the rear of the tavern and then returned smiling as Long Tao was busy wolfing down plates of cakes.

He questioned the waiter on his return who told him the sick customer was an officer who had previously asked for medicinal herbs. On the second day he was well enough to order live carp which the waiter served each day for a week before he showed signs of recovery.

Jiang Ping guessed Earth Rat had been poisoned and wondered what he had done with the two pills of antidote he always carried with him. "He'll blame me for all the trouble I caused him when we were in the Literary Splendour Building and he looked depressed." He heaved a sigh and told Long Tao that the man he had been seeking was in the back room of the tavern but the waiter had been given orders that if anyone named Jiang was looking for him, he was to say he was not there.

Jiang Ping persuaded the waiter to let him follow when next he paid a visit and pretend to Earth Rat it was a chance meeting. The waiter agreed.

CHAPTER 64

River Rat Makes Peace with Earth Rat.
Sleek Rat Visits the Dragon-Killing Bridge.

THE waiter went into the back room where Earth Rat lay resting.
"I hope everything is to your liking, sir," he said. He stood aside
to reveal River Rat who made a pretence of starting back in surprise. "Aiya! Second Brother! I've missed you dreadfully!" He
dropped onto his knees but the sick man turned his back.

"I know you are angry with me," Jiang Ping sobbed, "but I have
to explain, otherwise I shall die."

He related the whole long story which led to their separation on
bad terms and how everyone missed him and how the emperor and
Prime Minister Bao had given him leave to find him.

Han Zhang, Earth Rat, was greatly moved and wiped a tear
from his eye but he still felt angry at the way Jiang Ping had
tricked him out of his antidote to poison. "Because you stole those
pills from my pouch, I nearly died," he said.

River Rat laughed. "I had to remove the pills to put the note in.
How could I know you would be hit by a poisoned spear?"

Han Zhang forgave him and the air was cleared. Jiang Ping told
him about his fight with Iron Arhat and the evil Butterfly whom
he had wounded.

Long Tao then joined the two men and they promised they
would help him to avenge his brother.

One day while the three were eating, a mutual friend called Shooting Star Feng rushed in and in great excitement told them that Butterfly had fled to Xinyang to seek the protection of the Deng family.

They decided to go to Xinyang in disguise and sent Shooting Star Feng to Jasmine Village to give the news to the Ding twins. They decided to meet at the River God Temple west of Dragon-Killing Bridge.

Meanwhile in Jasmine Village, Northern Hero and the twins were preparing to leave for the Kitchen God Temple. The twins' mother was not at all pleased to see her sons go off again on their adventures but probity forbade her to express her feelings in front of Northern Hero. Instead she ordered a sumptuous farewell feast and took to her bed.

When her sons hastened to her bedside, she lay facing the wall and said: "It's unimportant, go your own way."

They decided to put off their journey until she felt better, which was just as well because the next day Shooting Star arrived and told them of the change of plans. They were all to meet at the River God Temple west of the Dragon-Killing Bridge.

As there were so many now involved in the hunting of Butterfly the twins decided they could stay with their mother. So Northern Hero left Jasmine Village for Xinyang where he recalled the previous occasion he had been there and had heard about a Dragon-Killing sword under the bridge with the same name. He went to the quayside to hire a boat but the boatman charged him an exorbitant fee, hoping it would put him off his quest.

CHAPTER 65

Northern Hero Hunts in Vain for the Dragon-Killing Sword.
Butterfly Goes into Hiding.

MONEY was no obstacle to Northern Hero whenever he wanted to go to a particular place and he would have paid the boatman forty taels of silver.

"I don't mind the cost," he told the boatman, "but I'll pay it only if I see the Dragon-Killing sword."

The boatman agreed and the boat slowly began to move as the haulers on the bank towed it towards the northern bank. The boatman steered with the rudder and Northern Hero sat in the middle. He felt relaxed and happy as he enjoyed the scenery. Reed flowers set off the distant mountains and ancient trees towered toward the sky. Inns and villages lined both banks and the smoke from the kitchens curled upwards. Wild geese and other birds skimmed over the water and he could not help but think of heroes of bygone days and the fleeting passage of time.

Suddenly the boatman interrupted his train of thought. "Up ahead is the flagstaff in the River God Temple. It's not far from the Dragon-Killing Bridge."

The current was rapid and the boat soon reached the bridge and quickly passed under it. Northern Hero looked right and left but could not see any sword and soon the boat was on its way to the River God Temple.

"Wait," he shouted to the boatman. "I haven't seen the sword yet."

The boatman laughed. "Everybody knows you should look upwards," he said. "The current is too fast to go back now."

Northern Hero caught his meaning and offered double the fare. The boat then returned to the bridge but when he looked up all he saw was a drawing of a sword etched into the stonework. Evidently, as the story of the picture of the sword under the bridge had been passed from mouth to mouth generation after generation, it had become exaggeratd into a real sword.

Disappointed, he told the boatman to carry on to the River God Temple where he paid a total of eight taels of silver.

Entering the temple, Northern Hero saw a big man selling flapjacks. "Delicious with onions and sauce," he shouted. It was Long Tao. The two men exchanged greetings and went off to the temple to await the arrival of Earth Rat and River Rat.

One day Northern Hero was playing chess with the abbot Hui Hai when a handsomely dressed rich young man entered the room. He clasped his hands respectfully to the abbot. He was a warrior named Chong and wanted to rent a room to wait for his friend. Northern Hero was impressed with his demeanour but a lecherous look in his eye raised his suspicions. The young man paid a deposit and left saying he would return soon.

Shooting Star then arrived and he revealed to Northern Hero and Long Tao that the young man who had booked a room was no other than Butterfly.

They decided not to do anything until the two Rat brothers arrived.

Evening came but Northern Hero did not light the lamp in his room. He saw a room in the west wing brightly lit. A shadow flashed across which looked like Butterfly but then the light went out and left the room in darkness.

"He's up to no good," thought Northern Hero, and decided to keep a lookout. He saw the door open and a black figure slide out, moving silently, his feet hardly touching the ground, towards the rear quarters.

Northern Hero decided to follow him thinking what a pity such an agile person should have such a bad reputation. When he jumped to the top of the wall there was no sign of Butterfly. He saw Shooting Star and Long Tao, but Butterfly had completely disappeared. They decided to hide in the grounds but waited in vain. At dawn they went to the room in the west wing and found a little bundle which contained the flowered gown, boots and headdress of the young man.

The abbot arrived and asked why they were up so early. "You have lost face," Northern Hero answered.

"We monks abstain from meat and wine, chant scriptures every day and abide by the pure way of life. How can we lose face?" the abbot retorted. "What are you alluding to?"

The men then revealed to the astonished abbot who they really were and that the young man who had booked a room was a notorious criminal.

CHAPTER 66

Butterfly Is Caught As He Tries to Steal the Pearl Lantern.
He Is Freed by Sick Giant.

THE abbot told the men that not far away was a convent in the village of Xiaodan, where a rich man, a retired official, named Squire Gou lived. Being a filial son, he had built his mother a magnificent Buddha Hall so that she could chant scriptures there every day. Inside the building was a priceless Pearl Lantern, decorated with pearls and precious stones. To please his mother, the squire performed many good deeds and gave large donations for incense.

Northern Hero was suspicious and dispatched Shooting Star to the village to reconnoitre.

Earth Rat, now fully recovered, arrived and said River Rat, disguised as a priest, would be there shortly as it wasn't prudent for them to come together.

Butterfly went to Xiaodan Village because it was his friend Deng Che's birthday. As he had not brought anything he decided to steal the Pearl Lantern to give him as a birthday gift.

He was unaware that the lantern was theif-proof, set with all sorts of traps. As he took hold of it, the lantern began to glide into a shrine. Beneath was a hole where two hooks emerged which grabbed his shoulders and despite his struggles raised him high in the air. Bells started to clang and men rushed in. The steward put a key in a lock beside the shrine and brought him down. Butterfly was tied up and imprisoned in the watchtower. As it was rather late, the steward decided to take him to Squire Gou in the morning and meanwhile set a guard on him. Later when the steward went to check he found the watchmen dead. They had been killed by a friend of Deng Che, called Sick Giant, who released Butterfly and carried him off.

News of the escape spread throughout the village and when River Rat finally arrived later that day he decided to go to the Deng family residence right away and scout around. Still dressed in priest's garb, carrying his bamboo cane and the cloth sign of a fortune-teller, he made his way to the home of Deng Che but Butterfly recognised him as the man who had tried to kill him in the bamboo grove and invited him into the hall where, much to his host's surprise, he began to interrogate the priest. "I am just a poverty-stricken priest," protested Jiang Ping. "I make a living by telling fortunes."

Butterfly sneered: "I was nearly killed by you and all you do is tell lies. We'll see what a beating will do!" Butterfly struck him with a whip and Jiang Ping pretended to howl with pain.

Deng Che, astonished at his friend beating a priest, pulled him away. "There are lots of people who look alike, how can you be so sure that this is the man who tried to kill you?"

CHAPTER 67

Uncle Purple Beard Fights Deng Che.
River Rat Catches Butterfly Under the Bridge.

AS Jiang Ping was led away he demanded the return of his belongings. But Butterfly was unwilling and as Deng Che picked up the
cloth sign and bamboo cane, a three-edged weapon fell to the
floor.

"Tie him up!" he ordered his attendants, and Butterfly, happy
that his suspicions had been justified, begged to be allowed to torture him and find out who the priest's masters were.

Jiang Ping was beaten again but protested that as a travelling
priest he needed something to defend himself against bandits.

"He's right," thought Deng Che. "Even the immortals in ancient times carried a sword for protection. So why should a wandering priest not have something to protect himself?"

Finding him wavering, Butterfly was worried that he would release the priest; so he suggested Deng take a rest while he questioned Jiang Ping.

The priest was taken to another room where the beatings continued but still he said nothing. When he was told what Butterfly had
done, Deng Che was annoyed at his guest taking advantage of his
hospitality, especially on his birthday, but he didn't want to appear timid in front of him and instead tried flattery. "Brother,"
he smiled, "have a rest. It's not because I feel sorry for the priest

but you have only eaten birthday noodles today and you must be quite hungry now. The feast is ready and the wine is waiting. Why ruin my birthday because of him?"

Butterfly apologised for his bad manners and told the servants to watch Jiang Ping — he would continue the interrogation the next day.

The servants were not too pleased at being given orders by a guest. They also felt sorry for the priest and brought him some warm wine and loosened his bonds. Evening was drawing near and the servants were hungry.

"Off you go," said Jiang Ping. "How can I escape injured and tied up like this?"

As the servants resented doing a job which was not within their normal duties, they were easily persuaded to go off, little realising that Northern Hero and Earth Rat had arrived and heard them go. These two released River Rat's ropes and because of his injuries Northern Hero carried him into the garden and hid him on a grape trellis.

The servants returned after their meal and finding their prisoner gone warned Butterfly and Deng Che who prepared to do battle, Butterfly with his sword and Deng Che with his iron bow and bag of iron balls. As Northern Hero entered the hall, Deng Che placed one of the iron balls on the bowstring and shot at him but Northern Hero was prepared, raised his sword and parried the shot and the others which followed in rapid succession. Butterfly sprang forward to help his friend but Earth Rat smashed his sword to the ground with one heavy blow and the terrified Butterfly ran out into the garden and squatted under the grape trellis where Jiang Ping was still hidden. Seeing his enemy below him, River Rat bundled himself up into a tight ball and crashed down, sending Butterfly flying into the dust. The evildoer managed to scramble to his feet and lurch away with Earth Rat in hot pursuit. Now Long Tao joined in the chase. Butterfly made his way across a bridge only to find a fully recovered Jiang Ping waiting for him. River Rat threw him into the water and dicked him under until he lost consciousness.

Northern Hero was still fending off the iron balls from Deng Che's bow but when Deng heard Butterfly had been captured, he ran away.

"Who are you?" gasped Butterfly when he recovered consciousness. "Why are you against me?"

Jiang Ping answered: "Everyone has complained about your behaviour, raping young girls and committing various crimes. We were so outraged we were determined to arrest you and take you for trial to the Kaifeng Prefecture. I am also known as River Rat, and these men here are Ouyang Chun, otherwise known as Northern Hero, Han Zhang or Earth Rat, and that is Long Tao seeking revenge for his brother."

The men prepared to leave for Kaifeng, except for Northern Hero who told his friends that he intended to return to Jasmine Village to attend the wedding of Southern Hero to the twins' sister. "Besides," he said, "I don't really like getting involved in officialdom."

They bade farewell and Northern Hero made his way alone to Jasmine Village while the others returned to Kaifeng and their master, Prime Minister Bao.

CHAPTER 68

Butterfly Meets His Just Deserts.
Southern Hero Is Married.

THE men soon reached the eastern capital with their prisoner where there was a grand reunion of all the brothers and friends. Lu Fang — Sky Rat — and Earth Rat were beside themselves with joy and all quarrels and misunderstandings disappeared at the joy of reunion. A grand feast was prepared to celebrate the occasion.

The prime minister's assistant, Bao Xing, then announced that his master was prepared to cross-examine Butterfly in the second hall. There the latter made a full confession and because he had been cooperative it was ordered that he should be given a quick death by decapitation rather than a slow slicing to death.

When the emperor heard of Earth Rat's bravery he was made an imperial guard and joined his other Rat brothers. After Butterfly's execution, a satisfied Long Tao returned home with a hundred taels of silver.

Southern Hero, having married the twins' sister, settled in Kaifeng, while Northern Hero remained at Jasmine Village, unwilling to get too involved with the social life of the city. When the twins returned home after the celebrations, he was restless to go on his travels and left soon after for Hangzhou.

Northern Hero enjoyed the freedom of the road, admiring the scenery of mountains and rivers and soon reached the county of

Renhe. He noticed a banner fluttering in the middle of a dense forest and thinking that it must pinpoint a magnificent monastery, he went to have a look. He saw a gate with a tablet over it proclaiming: "Monastery of the Creator." Inside all was neat and tidy. He put down his bag and dusted his clothes. In the main hall he saw the statues of Three Kings. A young monk greeted him.

"Is your master in?" Northern Hero inquired.

The monk led the way to the reception hall furnished simply, but bright and clean. An old monk of about seventy years entered and introduced himself as Jing Xiu. The two spent a pleasant time talking and partaking of a simple vegetarian meal. The old monk was pleased with Northern Hero's personality and invited him to stay for a few days.

In the evenings the pair played chess because the old man was very fond of the game and they were well-matched. He refused Northern Hero's offer of payment for his keep, saying the monastery had many wealthy patrons who often came to burn incense and were not short of money.

One evening as they were engrossed in a chess game, a ragged scholar, looking like a skeleton, entered the hall and bowed.

"What do you want?" asked Northern Hero.

"I am very hard up," the scholar replied. "Will you pay me for these couplets I have composed?"

The old monk unrolled the parchment and after reading it started to applaud.

CHAPTER 69

A Wanton Woman Flirts with the Scholar.
A Serving Maid Is Accused.

THE old monk was very impressed with the scholar's style of writing as well as his appearance. He felt sorry for the young man and invited him to clean himself up and have a meal.

"He seems to be a man of integrity and not a mere imposter," remarked Northern Hero.

The old monk agreed, saying that with his kind of personality he would not be in an inferior position for long. They carried on with their game and just before it came to an end, the local squire, named Qin Chang, entered looking excited and happy.

"I've been sitting on pins and needles," he said. "You must tell my fortune."

"I don't tell fortunes," replied the old monk.

"Monks never tell lies," Qin Chang said. "I heard of an old man who was worried about his grandson's illness and you told him to choose a word and you would analyse it. But a sudden gust of wind made the old man place a paper-weight on the paper, covering the radical and leaving the rest of it to spell 'death'. You told the old man that his grandson would die and sure enough he did. The fame of your foresight spread everywhere."

Despite his protests, the old monk was persuaded to try again.

Qin Chang chose the character 'easy'.

After careful consideration, the old monk said: "You have chosen a proper word. Being 'easy' on others is a great virtue. Honesty is normal for you and everything you do is aboveboard. But you must be more tolerant, have more patience, otherwise changes will occur and trouble will come. If you are not easy on others, you will cause one of your family to die."

Northern Hero was intrigued and begged the monk to read his fortune and chose the word 'Buddha'.

"That word represents 'kindness'. If you show people kindness, they will show kindness back. If you do evil to others, disaster will follow wherever you go. You have set your heart on doing kindness, succouring the needy, rescuing the endangered and punishing evildoers which is a true kindness. Because of your chivalry, you have renounced your home for twenty years. In another twenty years, you will become a monk like me."

Squire Qin Chang was reading the young scholar's couplets and commented on how good they were. When he heard that the author was poor and needy, he said he was looking for a tutor for his son.

The old monk smiled: "To ask him to be a teacher, you should show respect and not hold him in contempt due to his poverty. All this haste is not the proper way to treat a scholar."

The squire immediately apologised and called for his servant to get a suit of clothes, boots and two saddled horses for the scholar.

The young man was named Du Yong, a well-read scholar, upright and reserved. He readily accepted the offer of tutor to the squire's son.

The son was called Guobi and was eleven years old. Besides the mother of his son, the squire also had a concubine named Bichan. He had many servants and one of them was maid to his wife, Madam Qin. Although Qin Chang was in his forties, his former wet-nurse, now nearly seventy, still lived with them. Though the family was well-to-do the squire was unable to write and was eager for Guobi to study and raise the status of his family.

Heeding the old monk's remarks, the squire treated Scholar Du Yong with great respect. He ate the best food prepared personally by Madam Qin or her personal maid Caifeng. This aroused the jealousy of the concubine Bichan, who decided to seduce the handsome young scholar.

She prepared some special dishes, put them in a round box and instructed her maid to take it to the study. When the maid returned she asked her what the tutor was doing.

"He is reading," replied the maid. "When he saw I wasn't Madam Qin's personal maid, he told me to go away. So I put the box down and went."

Bichan hastened to the study and peeped through a hole in the window. The scholar looked up and saw her.

"Go away," he said.

"There's no one else at home," she replied. "I'm younger than the wife but older than the maid, so I want to see you."

The scholar flushed crimson and threatened to call for help if she didn't remove herself.

"This is a fine state of affairs," he said to himself. "The squire's reputation is tarnished by this hussy. I will have to give him a hint to show my appreciation of his patronage."

Bichan had beat a hasty retreat because she heard the squire coming home.

When the squire entered the tutor's study, the young man refused to greet him. The squire saw a round box full of titbits on the table and picked up his wife's gold ring from the floor. Hot with rage, he stormed into their bedroom where his wife sat chatting with his former wet-nurse.

"Wretched woman," he shouted. "When I said treat the tutor well I meant just his food and not to go into his study. When I saw him just now, he completely ignored me!"

His wife denied ever going into the scholar's room, but her husband flung down her gold ring as proof. She admitted it was hers but said she had given it to Bichan.

When the concubine was questioned, she said the maid Caifeng had stolen it, but 'the maid denied taking the ring.

The squire was at a loss but his wife guessed the truth and dismissed the concubine to her own quarters. She then consulted with the wet-nurse and they decided to put the tutor to the test. Qin Chang agreed.

Later that night he accompanied the wet-nurse to the scholar's study. The nurse knocked on the door.

"Are you in bed, Master Du?" she called.

"Yes, I am," he answered. "What do you want?"

"I'm from the second mistress," she replied. "She has sent me for you."

"This is outrageous," cried the tutor. "She keeps pestering me. No wonder she said she's younger than the wife but older than the maid. It is that concubine. If she keeps on like this, I will have to resign."

The squire now knew the truth of the matter. "'Younger than the wife but older than the maid' proves it's that wretched woman Bichan," he said to the wet-nurse. "She's no use to me any longer and I should finish her off right now."

"Patience," advised the wet-nurse. "If you kill her, you will face a murder charge. Lock her up in the deserted room in the garden and starve her to death."

Qin Chang readily consented.

The next day a manservant called Jinbao was ordered to prepare three empty rooms in the garden and imprison Bichan so that she would die of starvation.

CHAPTER 70

Squire Qin Is Charged with Murder.
Justice Is Dealt Out.

THE squire was unaware that his manservant Jinbao had been the lover of Bichan. Locking her away made it easy for the pair to continue their affair and make plans in complete safety.

They plotted to kill the squire and accuse his wife of the murder, intending to allege that she had a grudge against him. She would pay with her life, thus freeing the pair from their status of concubine and servant.

Master Qin was consience-stricken over his behaviour towards his wife and decided to visit her in her boudoir. Seeing she was already in bed he decided to wait until morning and proceeded to his own bedchamber. Unbeknown to him, the maid Caifeng had sneaked into his bed, hoping to take the place of his concubine. "After all, Bichan was only a serving maid before," she said to herself. As she lay there waiting in the dark, Jinbao, sword in hand, sneaked in and with one blow decapitated the body in the squire's bed.

Jinbao hurried away to change his blood-stained clothes and was startled to hear his master's voice calling him after the squire discovered the maid's body in his bed. Jinbao hid the clothes under Bichan's bed before he rushed into his master's bedroom to find him in such a state of shock that his wife, Madam Qin, had to order Jinbao to inform the maid's mother. Madam Qin said: "We'll give her a sum of money and give her daughter a good funeral, and that will put an end to the matter."

Jinbao had other ideas and persuaded the girl's mother to report her daughter's murder to the Renhe County court, accusing Squire Qin of killing her when she resisted his sexual advances.

The magistrate, Jin Bizheng, ordered that the squire should stand trial for murder, where, to the magistrate's surprise, he admitted the charge. The squire was too embarrassed to say that he and his wife slept in different rooms and reveal the whole scandal of his concubine's treachery. Moreover, he didn't want to force the two women to appear in public. "How can I bear the shame?" he thought. "She's only a slave girl and I may not have to pay with my life. But if I am condemned to death, then it is fate and I am being punished for doubting my wife. It proves the old monk's prophecy that one of my family will die."

The magistrate was not satisfied with such a willing confession and asked the squire the whereabouts of the weapon he had used to do the deed.

"I was in such a fluster, I don't know where I dropped it," was the reply.

The magistrate ordered him to be held in prison. Madam Qin had already bribed the jailer to make sure her husband was comfortable and Jinbao and three other servants were ordered to wait on their master in jail. The scholar Du Yong was put in charge of the squire's household.

One day, the monk Jing Xiu visited the Qin household where the resentful Jinbao told him that it was the scholar who had killed the maid and caused so much trouble.

The monk was mortified at his protégé's treachery and when he returned to the monastery he said to Northern Hero: "What kind of person drops his benefactor when he is no longer needed? Surely he's a beast in human shape."

Northern Hero was not convinced and commented that there

was more to it than met the eye. When the monk retired to his own quarters, he decided to pay a visit to the Qin household during the night.

The first watch had been struck when he reached the main house and heard the voices of a man and woman. The man was saying: "Come on, let's not waste this evening."

"This time you get me cheap, but don't forget the favour I'm doing you," the woman replied.

Northern Hero decided to kill the guilty pair and drawing out his scimitar he pushed open the door and despatched them to the nether world just as they were enjoying themselves. Tying their heads together he hung them over the door and returned to the monastery thinking he had killed the scholar Du Yong and Madam Qin.

Du Yong was sitting in his study balancing the household accounts which he did with great attention to detail, even checking on the number of candles being burned. When the watchman reported that he had discovered two heads but was unable to identify them because he had no light the scholar was forced to hand him some candles and accompanied him to the gruesome scene. He saw the heads of Bichan and one of the servants.

The magistrate was summoned and it was obvious that the murdered couple had been caught in the act. There was a note on the bed and some bloodstained clothes hidden under the bed. Jinbao, who was taking his turn at the prison waiting on the squire, had sent a note via the other servant to Bichan to get rid of the clothes.

The magistrate called his court into session and ordered Jinbao to be brought in.

"I've been making a thorough investigation of your master's case and want you to write an account of the matter," he said with a smile.

When the magistrate saw his handwriting he realized it was the same as that on the note that had found on Bichan's bed and accused Jinbao of engineering the whole plot to save his own skin.

Jinbao finally confessed after several slaps on the face by the court officers but said he knew nothing of the slaying of Bichan or her lover.

That servant, in his eagerness to sleep with Bichan, had flung the note on the bed.

Heaven's vengeance is sometimes slow but always sure.

CHAPTER 71

A Dutiful Son Finds His Long-Lost Mother.
His Faithful Servant Is Rewarded.

SQUIRE Qin Chang was released from prison and Jinbao paid with his life. Scholar Du Yong became a close member of the Qin family and the monk and Northern Hero were much relieved when they heard the whole story.

Northern Hero decided to continue his journey to Hangzhou where he heard people say how glad they were that a new incorruptible governor had taken over.

The new governor was Prime Minister Bao's protégé, Ni Jizu, who had come second in the imperial examination. He decided to go home first to sacrifice to his ancestors before taking up the post. The new governor was the son of a learned scholar named Ni Ren and his mother was the daughter of Old Man Li. Their betrothal gift had been two carved jade lotus flowers, handed down through generations. The young couple each wore one of them. One day they decided to visit relations and hired a boat. The owners were two dishonest characters named Tao Zong and He Bao who habitually robbed their passengers. When they saw the beautiful Mrs Ni they lusted after her and drowned the scholar. His wife was heavy with child and begged them to leave her alone, hoping to gain time by promising to be their mistress once the baby was born. Their hired hand, feeling sorry for the poor woman, persuaded them to hold back, saying that as her husband was dead she had no protector and therefore would not try to escape. He cajoled and plied them with drink until they passed out in a drunken stupor. He told Mrs Ni to make her way quickly to the Convent of the Goddess of Mercy, where his aunt was a nun. As she fled through the forest, she felt the first birth pangs and gave birth to a baby boy. She wrapped him up in her blouse, put the jade lotus flower on his breast, placed the baby under a tree and hurried on to the convent.

The hired hand realised he would get into trouble when the two thieves woke up and so decided to make his escape and shelter at the convent as well. His heart was touched at the distress of the young mother for her son and his aunt ordered him to find out what had happened to the baby.

An old man had found the baby and taken him home to his wife. They were childless and decided to adopt the baby as their own son. By coincidence they had the same surname and named him Ni Jizu.

The old man gave a party for all his neighbours to celebrate his good fortune. The robbers' former hired hand got himself invited to the party and offered to be Old Ni's servant and help with the baby's upbringing. The old man joyfully accepted and gave him a new name: Ni Zhong, which means faithful.

Thus Ni Zhong was carrying out the promise he had made to his aunt, the nun, to stay with the child and paid frequent visits to the convent to report progress.

The child grew to be a very clever young man and a great future was predicted for him.

One day as he was taking a walk, escorted by Ni Zhong, they came to the convent and decided to take a rest. Mrs Ni was praying before the Goddess of Mercy when she heard footsteps and her son entered. He looked so much like his father that she burst into tears and when he saw her, for some inexplicable reason he began to weep as well.

"Virtue be praised," called out the old nun. "Instinct has triumphed over reason!"

The truth was revealed and Jizu embraced his mother and brought out the jade lotus flower he always wore under his shirt, which made her weep even more.

CHAPTER 72

The New Governor Arrives Incognito in Overlord Village.
Martial Arts Are Practised in the Talent-Assembling Hall.

MRS Ni burst into tears once more when she saw the jade lotus flower but refused to accompany her son home.

"I have been too long in the convent to be able to settle in the outside world," she said. Her son pleaded. Weeping he asked how he could fulfil his filial duties if she did not come with him so that he could care for her as a son should for his mother.

At last she agreed, provided he first carried out three wishes. "You must work hard and become an official. Secondly, you must find our enemy and avenge your father's death. Thirdly, you must find the matching jade lotus flower. Only when you fulfil all these tasks will I consent to leave the convent," she said.

As Ni Jizu sadly made his way home he sighed heavily. "Of all these tasks I've been told to carry out, finding the jade lotus flower will be the most difficult."

"The appearance and disappearance of an object is foreordained by God," retorted Ni Zhong. "Securing an official position is more difficult. You must study hard, that is the most important thing."

They decided to keep the secret of his mother from his adopted parents and only reveal it when he became famous.

For the next two years he studied hard and after passing the district civil examinations entered for the national examinations two years later. It was on his way to the capital as a candidate that he met Northern Hero and the twin brother Ding Zhaolan at the Immortal Meeting Building.

Now having passed the national examinations he arrived in Hangzhou to take up his appointment as governor and found a number of indictments waiting for his ruling. They all accused a certain ne'er-do-well named Ma Qiang, who was the younger clan brother of Ma Gang from Giant's Village. Because he had an uncle Ma Chaoxian, who held a powerful position in the imperial palace as major-domo, he felt he could act with impunity. He took over other people's land, raped and pillaged. He had a special building erected called the Talent-Assembling Hall for gallants throughout the country. There were genuine heroes who, having nowhere else to go, had decided to try their talents and prowess at the hall, as well as disreputable characters such as Crack Archer Deng Che and Sick Giant.

The reputation of the Talent-Assembling Hall gradually grew until even the Prince of Xiangyang, Zhao Jue, was eager to associate with Ma Qiang.

Ai Hu was a page-boy who found a position with a hero named Zhi Hua, also known as Black Fox, superior in the martial arts but gentle and kindly, who did not take part in the anti-social behaviour of other members. The young boy was quick to learn from Zhi Hua and soon showed remarkable skill with various weapons.

Trouble came when Ma Qiang kidnapped a young girl named Jinniang from her grandfather Zhai Jiucheng, who was unable to repay a debt. She was pretty with a slim waist and Ma couldn't wait to seduce her. "Don't cry," he said with a lecherous leer. "Satisfy me and I'll keep you in luxury."

She rushed towards him brandishing a pair of scissors she had hidden under her clothes; Ma ducked and the scissors stabbed a chair instead. She was thrown into the dungeon by the angry Ma Qiang.

Meanwhile when the distraught grandfather, Zhai Jiucheng discovered that the scissors were missing from home, he hurried to the Talent-Assembling Hall, fearing that his granddaughter might harm herself or others with the scissors. Sitting under a willow tree for a rest, he mused: "What's the point? If she kills Ma, she'll die and my efforts to bring her up will come to nothing, and such evil men who defy all laws human and divine will punish me."

Sighing heavily, he took off his sash, tied it to the branch of a tree and was just about to hang himself when a voice called out: "Don't hang yourself. Tell me instead what happened."

Looking up, the old man Zhai saw a sturdy-looking man with a purple beard and told him his sad story.

"Since the man is such a bully," said Northern Hero (for it was he), "why don't you go to the law about him?"

"My lord, it's not as easy as you think," said Zhai. "Ma Qiang is an influential and wealthy man. The county court would soon throw out my petition."

"Then go to the eastern capital of Kaifeng," suggested Northern Hero.

"I can't afford that," was the reply.

"No problem," said Northern Hero, and he fished out some silver.

The old man dropped on his knees in gratitude and as he was helped up a man, whip in hand, arrived on the scene.

"You don't have to go to Kaifeng to seek redress," he said. "My master, the new governor, is very honest."

He looked familiar to Northern Hero. When he pointed to his master, Northern Hero drew in a sharp breath. It was Ni Jizu, whom he had known as a student during an earlier adventure. "If he goes into town so openly his life will be in danger," thought Northern Hero. "But I won't be able to persuade him that there are too many powerful enemies about, so I'll have to help him secretly," and he went on his way.

The new governor wrote out an indictment for the old man and, now happy, he started for home meaning to report to the prefecture office in the morning. Unfortunately he bumped into the angry Ma Qiang, who accused him of sending his granddaughter to kill him. He was unprepared for a now confident old man vowing to take vengeance on him.

Ma Qiang, his suspicions aroused by the old man's new courage, ordered his servants to search him, and they found the indictment.

"I wonder who wrote such a well-written accusation," he thought. "I'll have to ferret it out of the old man." He ordered his servants to take the old man to the county office and demand the payment of the debt.

Just then a man on horseback accompanied by his servant approached which gave the evil Ma Qiang an idea.

CHAPTER 73

The Governor's Identity Is Revealed and He Is Placed in Danger. A Maid Helps Him to Escape.

"GREETINGS, brother," said Ma Qiang. "Are you going to Tianzhu to burn incense?"

The man on horseback was Ni Jizu. Greatly intrigued, the incognito new governor asked how he knew.

"I live in the manor nearby and have made a vow that whoever comes to burn incense should be welcome to my hospitality," said Ma Qiang. He nodded to his servants who took hold of the reins of the governor's mount and led him into the manor, with Ni Zhong following behind.

They were hustled indoors and Ma Qiang sat in the Talent-Assembling Hall flanked by gallants and scoundrels alike. "I have just seen old man Zhai who has an indictment against me," he said. "It is too well written for an ordinary man and I suspect it is this scholar who helped him."

He passed the indictment to his cohort, Shen Zhongyuan, who after reading it remarked: "It is very good but I doubt whether the scholar wrote it."

"We'll soon find out," Ma replied. "Hang him from the beam and beat him!"

"No, don't squire," Shen intervened. "Since he is a scholar, you must treat him with respect. Let's ask him first and if he doesn't give a satisfactory answer, then torture him."

Ni Jizu was brought before them. Two of the assembled men were so impressed by his quiet manner and neat dress that they stood up and bowed.

When he told them he had come to Tianzhu to burn incense, Ma Qiang laughed and said it was he who had given him the idea.

Shen was more cunning and asked if he had written an indictment for old man Zhai.

Ni Jizu denied it and he and his servant were led away. As they descended the steps of the hall, they passed a man in a black jacket and travel-worn boots, his face smeared with dust. Ni Zhong's face turned pale. "My enemy has arrived," he muttered to himself.

It was his former employer, Tao Zong, now called Yao Cheng, the boatman who had murdered the scholar's father.

When he and the other boatman, He Bao, sobered up, they discovered their hired hand had absconded and later found out that he had become a servant in the Ni family. But the whereabouts of the scholar's mother was unknown to them. Eventually their crimes caught up with them and they were forced to flee to Hangzhou where they found sanctuary with their friend Sick Giant Zhang Hua. Yao Cheng soon ingratiated himself with Ma Qiang and became his trusted servant. When Ma Qiang heard that a new governor had been appointed and that he was a protégé of Prime Minister Bao, he sent Yao Cheng post-haste to the provincial capital to glean more information so that he would be prepared for any eventuality.

Yao Cheng told him several indictments had been drawn up against him, which made Ma Qiang very nervous and wonder why a warrant hadn't been issued for him.

"Maybe the governor has been delayed on his way here," suggested Yao Cheng.

He had recognised the scholar's servant as his former hired hand and putting two and two together, they realised that they had imprisoned the new governor. Ma Qiang panicked and sought the help of his wife, who was the niece of the imperial eunuch Guo Hai, and the two discussed what they should do. They were overheard by her personal maid, named Jiangzhen, who was the daughter of a poor scholar, Zhu Huanzhang. He had a rare inkstone which Ma Qiang coveted. Ma had accused the scholar of owing him money and he was detained at the county office. Ma Qiang not only took the inkstone but also his daughter Zhu Jiangzhen, but his jealous wife took her for a maid instead and soon she became indispensable and was put in charge of all the jewels, garments and keys.

As she listened to their conversation she thought: "My father has been unjustly treated by this man and imprisoned. If I release the governor, he can rescue him out of gratitude."

She took the keys and unlocked the door of the room where Governor Ni and his servant were incarcerated and helped them escape after exacting a promise that Ni Jizu would release her father.

As they got out of the gate, she called them back. "Wait!" she cried.

CHAPTER 74

A Lecher Saves a Maid from Hanging Herself.
The Dastardly Boatman Meets Purple Beard.

"ONE more thing," the maid, Jiangzhen, said to the impatient Ni Jizu. "When you release my father give him this."

She handed him an ornament which made the governor exclaim in surprise. It was the second carved jade lotus flower. But the maid had hurried back into the manor gate before he could question her.

Her heart beating fast, Jiangzhen ran through the grounds thinking: "I may as well be hanged for a sheep as a lamb." She went to the dungeon and released Jinniang, who had been seized by Ma because her grandfather was in debt to him. Jiangzhen then realised that her own safety and virtue were at risk. "Now that the governor will rescue my father I have fulfilled my promise and will take my life," she said. "If I hang myself in the dungeon people will take me for Jinniang." Untying her silk sash she made a noose and put it round her neck, drifting into unconsciousness. She came round to a voice saying: "How ridiculous! A miserable sneak-thief like you trying to waylay others," and found herself being carried on somebody's back.

It so happened that when Jinniang had tried to kill Ma Qiang with her scissors, she had attracted the attention of another man called Fang Shuo's Equal, a nickname he had given himself after a great scholar, and he was determined to have his way with her. He sneaked into the dark dungeon and finding the hanging body still alive had set her down and carried her off on his back, believing her to be Jinniang. He did not expect to be accosted by a footpad, but when just that happened, he called out "How ridiculous" and took to his heels with the footpad in pursuit. As he pounded ahead he saw a stout hefty fellow blocking his way. "There is a robber chasing me," he shouted. It was Northern Hero who took out his sword to meet the footpad. Fang Shuo's Equal thought he was an accomplice of the footpad and attacked him with his sword but Northern Hero was able to put him to flight. The breathless footpad arrived and thanked him for saving his sack which to their surprise began to move as the maid struggled to get out.

When she was released she told Northern Hero that the footpad was a villain too and the former was just about to take out his sword when the latter fell to his knees and begged for his life.

"I have an old mother of eighty," he implored.

Northern Hero was hard put to know what to do with the girl when she told him her story but when he heard the footpad had a mother he told the man to take her to his mother for safety until he knew what to do.

The robber seemed reluctant but after being threatened by Northern Hero, he carried her to his home, with Northern Hero following closely behind.

Meanwhile the governor and his servant were making good their escape from the Talent-Assembling Hall. As they sat and rested before going on, Ni Jizu wondered how the girl came into possession of the jade lotus flower. His servant was not convinced it was the matching one but suggested that his master should repay the maid by marrying her. "When I saw her in the lamplight I was impressed with her decorum and good looks. Man should repay kindness with gratitude, sir. Don't disappoint her expectations just because of the difference in family status."

As they continued on their way they strayed off the right path and saw men and horses and the blaze of torches ahead of them. The two men split up and ran off in different directions. Later Ni Zhong started to look for his master calling his name. He saw an old man coming towards him.

The two men began to look for the governor together but, tired out, they decided to seek shelter for the night. They came to a cottage and knocked on the door. A woman showed them in and gave them some wine in two bowls. It was drugged and soon the two men collapsed. A voice shouted outside demanding to be let in. It was the robber with Northern Hero. The old woman called out: "Why didn't you waylay these travellers before they got here? I have had to drug them, otherwise you would have been in trouble." She was the robber's wife.

Northern Hero, realising she was a bad lot, took out his sword and when she opened the door he forced her to revive the two men with an antidote. He made the old woman and her footpad husband drink the wine and they collapsed on the floor. As Ni Zhong recovered, he recognised the footpad as the boatman, He Bao, his former master.

The maid Zhu Jiangzhen, who was resting on the bed told them how she had released Jinniang who turned out to be the niece of the old man.

"What is of paramount importance now," said Northern Hero, "is to find the governor." He told Ni Zhong to make his way to the prefecture office and await his master. Zhu Jiangzhen was taken to the home of Jinniang's uncle, while Northern Hero made his way to Overlord Village.

CHAPTER 75

The Governor Is Taken Prisoner Once More.
Black Fox Finishes Off the Wicked Servant.

THE hapless Governor Ni, on seeing the blaze of torches, fled into the night, leaving Ni Zhong to face them. He eventually reached a small shed, lit up from inside, but the occupant refused to open the door. A blaze of lanterns came towards him and in his hurry to get away, he stumbled and fell. Before he could make his escape, Ma Qiang and his men stood before him.

"Who helped you escape?" Ma demanded.

Governor Ni thought: "If I tell him it was his maidservant Zhu Jiangzhen, I shall be betraying her kindness with treachery." Instead he said: "It was your wife who released me."

Ma Qiang swore under his breath. "Shameless slut! She has almost messed up my plans."

The governor was once again imprisoned in the dungeon and Ma Qiang stormed off to tackle his wife. She was sitting on the bed picking her teeth. She listened to his accusations in silence and after a long pause said: "What governor?"

"The quiet scholar and his servant," he replied.

"Nonsense," she replied. "Wasn't I eating with you when they escaped?"

He realised she spoke the truth and apologised abjectly.

She was far more wily than her husband and as they discussed what to do with the recaptured governor, she pointed out that his servant should also be hunted down, otherwise he would make his way to a higher court and report what had happened to his master.

Ma left for the Talent-Assembling Hall to consult his friends while his wife sent for her maidservant Zhu Jiangzhen, only to find that it was she who had released the governor and then disappeared.

Ma Qiang and his cohorts decided that as the fat was already in the fire, they should kill the governor and deny all knowledge of his whereabouts if officials from the higher court came to investigate. If all else failed they would escape to Xiangyang and stage an uprising.

Ma Qiang gave the order for the governor's execution and dispatched Ma Yong to do the deed. Black Fox asked to help him and the two men went off to the dungeon where Black Fox told the guards to have a rest while they stood guard.

"Why let them go," asked Ma Yong, greatly puzzled.

"Because killing a governor has to be secret," he answered.

"That's very thoughtful of you," Ma replied.

"Give me your sword," requested Black Fox, and when he had the sword he promptly cut off Ma Yong's head.

"I've come to rescue you," he told the governor, but when he returned after throwing the body of Ma Yong into the well at the back of the garden, the prisoner had disappeared.

"I wonder if it was Shen Zhongyuan who suspected my motives and followed me?" he thought. But when he peered down from the roof of the Talent-Assembling Hall, he saw Shen talking quietly to Ma Qiang.

He left the hall and outside the manor saw a shadow running into the forest. It was Northern Hero who had spirited away the governor, now resting under a tree.

A clatter of horses' hoofs announced the arrival of Ai Hu, Black Fox's faithful apprentice, who had stolen a horse for the governor. They decided that Black Fox and Ai Hu should return to the manor to allay suspicions while Northern Hero accompanied the governor to his office. There would be time enough next day to arrest Ma Qiang.

As they returned to the manor, Ai Hu told Black Fox how he had followed him to the dungeon and knowing how weak and exhausted the governor would be had stolen the horse.

"That was Northern Hero you just saw," replied Black Fox.

Ai Hu was disappointed he had not recognised the famous "Uncle Purple Beard with the green eyes" but Black Fox reassured him that he would see him again.

When they reached the Talent-Assembling Hall, Black Fox told Ma Qiang that Ma Yong was disposing of the governor's body.

Northern Hero escorted Ni Jizu to his office but refused his entreaties to be entertained, saying that the governor should prepare men to go to Overlord Village. They arranged to meet at the Temple of the God of Plague, two *li* away from the village. At midday, the governor's servant, Ni Zhong, finally arrived after having settled the two girls, Zhu Jiangzhen and Jinniang, in places of safety.

The governor ordered two of his constables, Wang Kai and Zhang Xiong, to take twenty armed men to the Temple of the God of Plague where they would take orders from a hefty man with a purple beard and green eyes.

Ma Qiang waited impatiently for Ma Yong's return and wondered if he was so frightened after murdering the governor that he had taken flight. He was on tenterhooks wondering also whether official troops would come demanding the governor. He gathered his cohorts around him and they began feasting and drinking to raise their morale. "As a murderer, you'll lose nothing but your head, so you will be saved from the endless hardships of striving to get to the top. If you are tortured, just grit your teeth and do not confess, then you will become a hero!"

A servant entered saying that a man from the northern end of the village had come to pay his rent.

"Well, take it," said the emboldened Ma Qiang, "Why bother me with such trivialities?"

He resumed drinking and then found another servant standing before him wanting to speak.

"I've brought you silver from the eastern end of the village," the servant said.

"Fuss and bother," shouted Ma Qiang. "Take it to the accountant. Why is your mouth twitching all the time?"

CHAPTER 76

Northern Hero Traps the Bully with a Silk Braid.
The Matching Jade Lotus Flowers Unite the Lovers.

AS evening drew near and no one came, Ma Qiang relaxed, saying: "Ma Yong must have died in disposing of the governor's body." His wine and meat friends agreed, saying that as he was an old man, it was probably nerves and exhaustion that killed him.

They were so intent on flattery that they overlooked the fact that the imperial government would not let the disappearance of such a high official be forgotten. Only Black Fox and Shen Zhongyuan remained silent while Ma Qiang drank several cups of wine and staggered off to his wife who had to cajole him to write to his powerful uncle, Major-domo Ma Chaoxian. Now completely reassured, they were just about to go to bed when the curtain over the door was yanked up and a man with glittering green eyes entered, sword in hand. Ma Qiang dropped to the floor in fright, begging for his life but Northern Hero cut off the braid from the curtain and tied them up, then clapped his hands for the governor's policemen to enter. "Watch them," he ordered, "while I deal with the other bandits."

Unfortunately a maidservant had watched the whole scene and warned the others. Weapons in hand they confronted Northern Hero who was holding his treasured scimitar. They halted in fear.

"How tall he is," remarked one.

"Look at his scimitar, so bright and sharp," said another.

"Flourish your weapon in his face, brother, and I'll take him from the back," another one said.

Deng Che, the expert in firing iron balls, was no match for Northern Hero, who was able to parry the balls with his scimitar, knocking them to one side and the other and even hitting one or two of the men. Sick Giant, Zhang Hua, then swished his sword at him but Northern Hero was already on guard and with one swish of his scimitar cut his sword in half.

The men took fright and locked themselves in the Talent-Assembling Hall, watched by a gleeful Black Fox and his page Ai Hu, who had taken refuge on the roof.

Ma Qiang's wife was presumed innocent and was released but Ma was tied up and put on a horse to be taken to the prefecture to be sentenced. He was escorted by Black Fox, Ai Hu and Northern Hero.

Day was beginning to break. Ma Qiang, on horseback with his hands tied behind him and a gag in his mouth, sighed as he thought of his so-called friends. "Only Black Fox and his page are still with me," he thought. "The boy must be carrying a change of clothes for me. I shall be kinder to him, if I ever get out of this mess."

As they neared the prefecture office, Black Fox and Ai Hu left Northern Hero to visit Jasmine Village where the Ding twins lived. Northern Hero resisted their pleas to join them, saying he had only recently visited them and was still intent on going sight-seeing in Hangzhou. "Who would have thought," he said, "that I would be side-tracked into rescuing the governor and delivering Ma Qiang to justice. But now I have to deal with the rest of the Talent-Assembling Hall gang."

Black Fox clasped his hands in farewell and the men went on their different ways.

At the Talent-Assembling Hall the bandits waited until Northern Hero and his party had left before they ventured out. They decided to join the Prince of Xiangyang and robbed Ma Qiang's wife of all her jewels, gold and silver. She called the steward Yao Cheng who had hidden outside the manor during the fight and only returned the next day. Together they made a list of all the stolen articles and the robbery was reported to the local authorities. She also wrote a letter to her husband's uncle Ma Chaoxiang and sent Yao Cheng to the capital with it.

Ma Qiang was brought before Governor Ni where he was questioned about the two debtors, Zhai Jiucheng and Zhu Huangzhang. He insisted that the two men had willingly given their granddaughter and daughter to him and denied kidnapping them. He also denied all knowledge of the governor's imprisonment in his dungeon.

Governor Ni angrily ordered Ma Qiang to be beaten but despite twenty slaps on the face and a flogging of forty strokes, he steeled himself and refused to confess. The grandfather and the father were brought in to confront him but he still insisted they had given the girls to him.

The governor was then given the list written by Mrs Ma Qiang which accused Northern Hero of leading a gang to plunder her house. "Northern Hero would never lower himself to doing such a thing," thought Governor Ni, and sent for his two constables, Wang Kai and Zhang Xiong, who recounted to him the true details of the incident. He ordered them to investigate the robbery.

The governor then decided to find out the truth about the carved jade lotus flower brooch which the young girl Zhu Jiangzhen had shown him and sent for her father who told him how he had found the body of a young man floating in the river and out of pity had buried him. He had found the jade lotus flower pinned on his shirt and had given it to his daughter who treasured it.

The governor shed tears as he realised the dead man must have been his father and took out his own brooch. The two were a perfect match.

"The return of the brooch bodes well," said Ni Zhong. "Miss

Zhu saved your life and this jade lotus flower can be regarded as a matchmaker. It is virtually predestined that you two should marry, though you both live a thousand *li* apart."

The governor consented and the father agreed to the match. A suitable marriage was also arranged for the other maid, Jinniang.

Having fulfilled two of his mother's demands, the governor sent Ni Zhong with the jade lotus flower brooch to the convent of the Goddess of Mercy to escort his mother to his new home. When she arrived he would move his father's coffin to its proper place and arrest the enemy of their family. Only then would he conclude the marriage between himself and Zhu Jiangzhen.

CHAPTER 77

Governor Ni Is Relieved of His Post.
Sleek Rat in Disguise Meets the Hero.

THE treacherous Yao Cheng, who had been responsible for the killing of Governor Ni's father and was now steward in Ma Qiang's household, took the letter his mistress had written to his master's uncle in the capital, a powerful man at the imperial court. The letter accused Governor Ni of riding roughshod over the people and ganging up with brigands, robbing and pillaging.

As a result Ma Qiang was removed from the governor's jurisdiction and sent under escort to the capital to stand trial in the supreme court while the governor was temporarily relieved of his post. He handed over the seals and work to another office and travelled to the capital to confront the accuser.

He avoided going to the office of Prime Minister Bao, not wanting to take advantage of the friendship between them, but simply registered at the supreme court where the hearing was to be held before Chief Justice Wen, who had received a letter from Ma Chaoxian asking him to handle the case of his nephew. After hearing Ma Qiang's complaints, he questioned Governor Ni who told him the whole truth regarding the kidnapping of the two young women and how he had been rescued by Northern Hero.

A report was sent to the imperial court who ordered that the imperial guard Sleek Rat — Bai Yutang — should be dispatched to bring Northern Hero to the court.

A farewell dinner was given and one of the gallants, River Rat, or Jiang Ping, warned him that Northern Hero might not be happy about being apprehended by someone he regarded as his friend.

"If you put on the airs of an officer dispatched by the emperor, he won't be lorded over," he said.

"I suggest that when you reach Hangzhou you speak to the governor first and tell him to put up a notice, proclaiming that it is by imperial decree that you are there. That way, Northern Hero will come to you of his own volition and will accompany you without any fuss."

Sleek Rat thought Jiang Ping was too timid and even when Sky Rat, Lu Fang, supported the plan, he just clasped his hands respectfully and made his way to Hangzhou accompanied by his servant Bai Fu.

When he reached Hangzhou he registered at the prefecture office without mentioning his purpose for being there. He sent his man out to find out where Northern Hero was staying but after searching fruitless for three or four days, he decided to disguise himself as a refined scholar wearing a flat-topped cap, embroidered gown and scarlet thick-soled boots. With gold-sprinkled fan in hand, he swaggered out of the inn where he was staying.

It was a summer scene, with farmers working in the green fields and visitors taking a stroll across a scarlet bridge. He discovered a new teahouse called Magnolia Arch, with pavilions and bowers, flowers, bushes and trees, a place well worth visiting. He sat by a rustling bamboo grove and ordered a pot of tea to drink after he had some wine. The sky was overcast and he decided to enjoy the rain while sheltering under the thick bamboo. But the rain became too heavy and he hurried back to his inn which was some distance away. As he ran across a plank bridge he came to the vermilion wall of a temple, the Convent of the Brilliant Sea and Delicate Lotus. He noticed a young boy holding a brush and inkstone calling out for his master. A gate opened at the side of the wall and a young nun told him his master was in the nunnery, so the young boy went away.

"That's strange," thought Sleek Rat. "Why should a man be in a nunnery?" He decided to investigate and knocked on the door. "I'm a traveller caught in the rain," he called. "Please give me shelter."

A voice answered: "This is a nunnery and not suitable for men. Go somewhere else."

Sleek Rat was not to be deterred and decided to take a look for himself. He took off his boots and tucking up his gown leapt onto the wall and landed on the other side. It was dark and he saw a nun with a tray in one hand with steaming hot dishes and a pot of wine in the other, passing through a gate. He followed her into the courtyard where a lamp flickered in a room throwing dark shadows on the window.

"It's getting late," he heard a female voice say. "Have some wine and food then go to bed, young man."

The protesting voice of a man asked: "Why have you dragged me in here and kept me prisoner? This is outrageous. Keep away from me!"

"Don't be so stubborn," answered the female voice. "We've had few occasions to get together. It's a rare chance for us today. 'When there are heavy clouds forming heavy rain is bound to fall.' How can you not see the hidden meaning in that phrase?"

"'A scholar considers his body as jade.' And 'Be upright before cultivating one's mind.' Immoral as your conduct is, I can be compared to the 'cloud in a burning drought', in which there is no rain at all," retorted the man.

Sleek Rat smiled thinking: "What a bookworm to discuss literature with such a woman!"

There was the sound of something breaking as a wine cup fell to the ground.

"I meant to be good to you," said the nun, "but as you appear not to appreciate me, I won't press you. There is another man in here, who is quite ill. He will bear witness to my good intentions."

"Help," shouted the young man. "They're even killing people here!"

Sleek Rat could stay hidden no longer and sprang into the room. "Why make such a fuss, brother. Since they are so amorous, why are you standing on ceremony?"

The man's name was Tang Menglan. He had intended to compose some poetry while walking in Magnolia Arch but he had forgotten his writing utensils and had sent his page-boy back to get them. But the rain had come and he had taken shelter in the nunnery where he was pestered by the nun.

"The fault lies with you, brother," said Sleek Rat. "You are too bookish and not wise to the ways of the world. Being too rigid is as bad as going too far the other way."

"No, no," protested the young man. "I'll never adapt to changing situations. I'd rather die!"

"This man is really a model of propriety. I have to protect him," thought Sleek Rat.

There were two nuns in the room and seeing the virile-looking Sleek Rat they transferred their attentions to him. One was about thirty years old and the other about twenty and both were quite attractive. The elder poured him a cup of wine. "Amorous young man drink this and then we'll go to bed."

He took it and gulped it down. The younger nun then poured him another cup of wine, saying: "Since you have drunk hers, you must also drink mine."

Sleek Rat complied to murmurs of "Shame" from the young scholar.

The two nuns were called Clarity and Sagacity.

"Clarity, if you have no clear head, you'll be befuddled," said Sleek Rat, "and Sagacity, if you're not sagacious enough you will be muddle-headed." He held their hands and asked Tang: "What do you think of my words, brother?"

The young man hung down his head, muttering: "It is you who are muddled-headed. This is outrageous!"

The nuns suddenly yelped out in pain as Sleek Rat crushed their hands.

"You lustful nuns," he snarled. "Seducing decent young men and ruining their lives. How many more lustful nuns are there here?"

"There're only the two of us," they cried. "We've not harmed anyone except the man called Zhou, resting at the rear. He wasn't that good and his health broke down. If he had been as upright as Mr Tang, we would never have violated his privacy. Spare us!"

The young scholar could not bear to see the nuns writhing in pain and begged Sleek Rat to spare them.

Sleek Rat said he would relent, provided they found Zhou's family, got him back as soon as possible and asked for their forgiveness. The nuns agreed and stumbled away.

Tang bowed to Sleek Rat to show his respect as the door curtain was lifted and a hefty fellow accompanied by Tang's page-boy entered. "There you are!" the page cried. "If I had not been helped by this lord, I would not have found you!"

CHAPTER 78

Purple Beard Vanquishes Sleek Rat.
Sleek Rat Visits the Twins.

THE scholar and his page-boy left after expressing thanks for their rescue from the clutches of the lustful nuns, leaving the two men to introduce themselves.

"So you are the man known as Northern Hero and Uncle Purple Beard," said Sleek Rat and thought: "I can't arrest him here in the nunnery but I'll have to wait until we are outside."

Aloud he said: "Let's go to the inn where I am staying and talk."

"With pleasure," replied Northern Hero.

As they went through the gate, Sleek Rat politely stood aside to let Northern Hero go through first. "Please," he said, holding out his arm thinking he could jostle him out. He did not expect to find that it was like a dragonfly trying to topple a stone pillar, and instead he was pushed out first.

As they walked through the night under a sky studded with twinkling stars, Northern Hero asked "What have you come to Hangzhou for, brother?"

"To get you," Sleek Rat replied. He then related how the dastardly Ma Qiang had falsely accused Governor Ni who was now under arrest and that he had been ordered by imperial decree to bring Northern Hero to the capital as a witness.

Northern Hero was not impressed with Sleek Rat's arrogant demeanour, especially when he said he had come to get him by imperial decree rather than just treating him as a brother and friend.

He thought: "If I go with him under those circumstances people will think I am not a real man and will laugh."

He began teasing Sleek Rat who became impatient and suggested that they measure their strength, saying: "When I win, you won't be able to complain I didn't show you sufficient respect."

Sleek Rat took off his embroidered gown, flat-topped hat and vermilion boots and struck up a fighting stance. Northern Hero however remained undisturbed and neither stepped back nor forward but dodged and parried his blows while Sleek Rat lashed out with fists and feet.

After a while as he drew back for another onslaught, Northern Hero suddenly poked him in the ribs with two fingers and he felt all the breath escape from his body, leaving him helpless with mouth open, standing like a wooden statue. He felt a violent shove in the back and he could breathe again.

"Sorry," said Northern Hero, "I was too rough."

Sleek Rat left without a word and reaching his inn he jumped over the wall and entered his room to the surprise of his worried servant Bai Fu.

"How can I face going back to the capital?" he said to himself. "I should have followed River Rat's advice." He took off the silk sash from his waist intending to hang himself, but every time he tried to put his head in the noose the sash fell to the ground. After the third attempt he felt someone pat him on the back. It was Northern Hero who had returned his embroidered gown and vermilion boots, neatly folded. "You are too rash, Fifth Brother," he said.

Sleek Rat realised Northern Hero was by far his superior.

"If you are intent on hanging yourself," Northern Hero said, "let me share the noose with you, because if you die how can I face your four gallant brothers, Southern Hero and the heroes in the Kaifeng Prefecture? Killing yourself, you will also be killing me."

He told the shamefaced Sleek Rat that they should treat the fight as just fun. "You should have consulted me first," he said, "but you were too intent on personal glory. Do as you would be done by — that's my motto."

"What shall I do now to make amends?" Sleek Rat asked.

"Go to Jasmine Village and ask the Ding twins to act as mediators between us. That way it will save you from being called a good-for-nothing and I won't lose face by being taken prisoner by you."

Sleek Rat was not so stupid as not to seize the opportunity. He ordered Bai Fu to saddle the horses and left for Jasmine Village.

He was warmly welcomed by the Ding twins who asked why he had not given them warning of his visit so that they could welcome him properly as befitting an officer of the imperial court.

"I have come on official business," he said, "and need your help." He told them of his defeat at the hands of Northern Hero saying how he had underestimated his strength and skill. "I want you to invite him here and suggest he accompanies me to the capital." Sleek Rat admitted that this was Northern Hero's suggestion.

Three men emerged from behind a screen. They were Northern Hero and his friends from the Talent-Assembling Hall, Black Fox and Ai Fu. Black Fox's father had been a close friend of the twins' father.

Before all of them, Sleek Rat formally asked Northern Hero to accompany him to the capital, to which request the latter consented.

CHAPTER 79

Black Fox Plans to Steal the Pearl Crown.
An Old Servant Dresses Up as a Refugee.

NORTHERN Hero and Sleek Rat left for the capital while the others returned to the hall in sombre mood. Black Fox's young apprentice, Ai Hu, was rather sad as he had become the adopted son of Northern Hero.

Black Fox was first to break the silence, saying: "Governor Ni is a loyal and faithful servant of the state and Brother Sleek Rat often helps the needy and rescues those in danger, yet this dreadful Ma Qiang and his uncle Ma Chaoxian have trumped up these false charges and they are in danger. If we could get rid of his uncle it would be easy to deal with Ma Qiang."

"We ought to try and get rid of them both in one go," suggested one of the twins.

"Then we shall have to do something against our conscience and accuse them of a false crime," said Black Fox. "Ma Qiang is a crony of the Prince of Xiangyang and we can clip the wings of the prince as well. But there are four tasks we need to perform. The first is to steal an imperial object of great value, which I will do. The second task needs the cooperation of an old man, a girl or boy. They need to be brave, resourceful and able to bear hardships as they will accompany me. Third, the stolen object must be taken to Ma Qiang's home and hidden in the Buddha Hall."

"I'll do that task," said the twin Ding Zhaohui. "What about the fourth task?"

"The fourth task is more difficult," said Black Fox. "It needs a person whom Ma Qiang does not suspect is against him and who can go to the Kaifeng Prefecture and inform on him." He looked at Ai Hu.

"I am the right person for the job," said Ai Hu. "I have been in Overlord Village since I was a child. I know everything about Ma Qiang and I was present when his uncle brought a precious object from the court three years ago. I will be able to convince the authorities and I will be famous."

They applauded his enthusiasm but Black Fox was more circumspect. "He doesn't know how awe-inspiring Prime Minister Bao is and it will need more than courage to confront him. There are the frightening instruments of torture which strike terror into the bravest, like the bronze execution axe. If he makes any mistakes he will lose his life and our efforts will have been wasted."

Ai Hu was not to be deterred. "I would rather go up a sword-covered tree or hill than go back on my word. I am determined to rescue the loyal official and chivalrous champion and am not afraid of the imperial bronze axe."

The twins clicked their tongues in admiration but Black Fox said: "Wait. If you can answer this question I will let you go."

Ai Hu dropped on one knee, waiting.

"You will be asked why you didn't say anything about the object at the time it was brought back by Ma Chaoxian," said Black Fox. "Then what will you say?"

"I will tell them I was only twelve at the time and was ignorant of the seriousness of the theft and now that I am older I realise I must report the matter to the authorities," answered Ai Hu.

The twins applauded the cunning of Ai Hu. Black Fox decided to write two letters to make arrangements for his safety and told the twins to make a list of what was needed for the enterprise. They put down a wooden cart, a big basket, tattered quilts, an iron ladle, a yellow earthen bowl — and an old man and a child. Black Fox intended to dress himself and the two as refugees and go to the eastern capital, where he would steal the Nine-Dragon Pearl Crown of the emperor from the Four Treasuries which were in the charge of Ma Chaoxian. He would hide the crown in the basket, cover it with the quilts and as refugees sit beside it and return.

The twins knew of just the person to play the part of the old man. He was a faithful retainer of the family, a man named Pei Fu who was honest and loyal. When the old man heard about the crimes of Ma Qiang, he was incensed and asked why the twins had not removed this evil-doer long before. "Have patience, old man," they said, "you will accompany Black Fox pretending you are fleeing from a famine-stricken area."

Pei Fu had a granddaughter just nine years old who would pretend to be the third generation refugee.

"Her name is Yingjie and she has been pestering me to take her to the eastern capital, so this is as good an opportunity as any."

The party travelled many miles day and night. When they crossed the Yangtze River they found an isolated spot and donned their ragged clothes. They found a place in the market and begged from people walking by. Yingjie, relishing her role as a beggar, wiped her eyes and whined. "I'm starving and haven't eaten for two days!"

As the sun was setting a bailiff told them to go away but a kind-hearted passer-by intervened and suggested they shelter in the Yellow Pavilion. They pulled the cart with their meagre possessions to the place and settled down for the night. In the morning a group of workmen, carrying spades and other equipment, passed the trio and Black Fox asked for alms.

"He looks quite strong," commented one of the workmen, "why should he lower himself by begging? Look at his massive build, he could work like a horse," and he walked towards him.

CHAPTER 80

Black Fox Disguises Himself as a Labourer.
He Climbs Up a Tree to Catch a Monkey.

THE workman was the gang foreman, named Wang, and he was
short of hands. He offered Black Fox a job digging a moat around
the Forbidden City. He would be given three meals a day and sixty
cash into the bargain.

Pei Fu in the role of Black Fox's father persuaded him to take
the job.

The other workmen thought he was a bit of a country bumpkin
and persuaded him to carry their hoes and spades, and laughing
they made their way to the gate of the Forbidden City.

Black Fox worked well and dug up more earth than the rest,
much to the annoyance of the others who told him to slow down so
that the work would take longer and they would get more pay.

Coming from a wealthy background, he was unaccustomed to
the hard work and plain food, but he was so anxious to rescue the
governor that he was not to be deterred.

Pei Fu and his granddaughter got more money from their begging with Black Fox out of the way, so their disguise as famine
victims went smoothly.

The next day, while Black Fox was working, he heard a hubbub
and a crowd of people looking up at a tree where a little monkey
with a chain round its neck was sitting on a branch. Two eunuchs

were rubbing their hands in consternation, worried that they would get into trouble. Although the foreman was reluctant to let Black Fox climb up the tree and get the monkey, he was over-ruled by the eunuchs. He took off his shoes, shinned up the tree and parked himself in the fork of the tree pretending to take a rest while he surveyed the buildings on the other side of the wall, try-ing to find the location of the treasury. Then he reached out his foot, grabbed the chain round the monkey's neck with his toes and pulled it into his hat. To applause from the onlookers, he climbed down and with a bow handed the monkey to the eunuchs who gave him two silver ingots.

Still pretending to be a country bumpkin he pretended he did not know their value. The grateful eunuchs instructed the foreman to give him lighter work in future. Wang was a kindly man and ac-companied Black Fox back to Pei Fu and his granddaughter where, still playing the country simpleton, Black Fox said: "Look Dad, I've got enough silver for us to buy two *mu* of land and two head of cattle and..."

"Enough, enough!" said Wang, "You only have enough to buy a donkey, you silly man!"

The next day, mindful of the eunuchs' request that Black Fox be given lighter work, the foreman assigned him to keeping an eye on the tools. Later one of the eunuchs arrived holding a peach-shaped filigree box inlaid with precious jewels. "My master bid me come to check that you are not working too hard and to take some re-freshment." He handed him the box which held some delicious fried titbits but Black Fox closed the lid saying that he would give such luxuries to his father. The eunuch was impressed at such a fil-ial son and later in the day both eunuchs arrived with a second box of goodies which they insisted Black Fox should eat there and then and watched him while standing in front of the imperial palaces.

They were amused by what they thought was the simple-minded countryman and answered his guileless questions about the various royal buildings.

"That's the Temple of the Loyal and Dauntless Maid and the Temple of Two Champions," they said. "And this one is the Palace of Literary Cultivation and that high building is the Prowess-Displaying Hall."

"What about that building over there?" asked Black Fox all innocence.

"That is the Treasury of Jewels," was the answer.

Late that night during the second watch, Black Fox took a bag with various tools and set off for the imperial palace.

CHAPTER 81

Black Fox Steals the Royal Crown.
The Boy Ai Hu Informs on His Master.

BLACK Fox skilfully jumped over the walls of the Forbidden City, giving full play to his athletic skills as he negotiated the glazed tiles on the roofs, leaping like an arrow and leaving marks so that he could retrace his way back. He reached the roof of the Treasury Building and taking a saw from his bag cut a hole through the rafters. He hooked a metal claw to the edge and shimmied down a rope.

He saw a row of red trunks, each one numbered and with a sealed lock. The first box held the Nine Dragon Crown. He took out a leather pot filled with wine, wetted the seals and gingerly slid them off. Then he took out a key, unlocked the trunk and removed the crown wrapped in yellow cloth, fastened with an ivory pin with the inscription: "No. 1 Nine Dragon Crown presented by your subject so-and-so." Taking the two ends of the cloth, he tied it round his head and then closed the trunk, carefully slipping the seals back and locking it again. He wiped off his fingerprints and any other signs that he had been there and climbed back up the rope. He replaced the rafters and tiles, so as to leave no trace and by the fifth watch had already made his way back to an anxious Pei Fu.

They hid the crown in the basket and covered it with the ragged

quilt. The next morning when the foreman came to pick up Black
Fox, he pretended that Pei Fu had fallen ill and said that they
were therefore returning home. Yingjie cried bitterly, believing
her grandfather was really ill and so Wang was forced to let them
go.

Leaving the area they boarded a boat to take them across the
Yangtze River and eventually met up with the Ding twins and Ai
Hu. Black Fox told them of his daring feat and triumphantly they
returned home to make arrangements for the next part of the
plan.

"I will pretend I am going by the order of my mother to visit a
temple in Tianzhu," said Black Fox. "There I shall find an old
man called Zhou Zeng, who keeps a teahouse, and put up there."

They took out the crown from its wrappings to gaze on its beauty. It was embossed with nine dragons and embellished with magnificent pearls.

Black Fox returned a few days later and related to the twins
what had taken place. He had gone to Ma Qiang's residence and
hidden the crown behind the middle shrine in the Buddha Hall.

He then stared at Ai Hu.

"Your uncles Ding and I have taken risks to help a loyal official.
Now it is up to you to do your part."

"Don't worry," replied Ai Hu. "I will accomplish the task even
if I die in the attempt."

Black Fox gave him a letter for Sleek Rat with the request that
he should help Ai Hu if anything happened.

When Ai Hu arrived in Kaifeng he did not seek out Sleek Rat
but went first to the prefecture's yamen to see what it was like.
Policemen appeared scattering the crowd as they made way for
Prime Minister Bao.

"That's a stroke of luck," thought Ai Hu, "why shouldn't I ac-
cost him?"

As the palanquin approached, he edged his way through the
crowd and dropped on his knees.

"Help me, Your Lordship," he cried. "I have been wronged!"

Despite the attempts of Lord Bao's guards to thwart him, Ai Hu gained admittance to the court and awe-inspired to be brought before such a powerful figure, he dropped to his knees again.

"My name is Ai Hu," he said. "I am fifteen years old, a servant of the squire Ma Qiang, but I have to inform against him."

He then told the prime minister about Ma Qiang's uncle, Ma Chaoxian, who was keeper of the royal Four Treasuries. He had seen him bring a yellow bundle to his nephew telling him that it was the Nine Dragon Crown belonging to the emperor. Ai Hu added that he told his nephew: "When the Prince of Xiangyang rises up in the future, you can present it to him." He then told Prime Minister Bao where the crown was hidden.

"I was very young three years ago," said Ai Hu, "and did not realise until now the seriousness of the case and that is why I am before you now."

After a few minutes' silence, Lord Bao suddenly struck his gavel on the table and roared: "You filthy dog! Who put you up to such impudence that you should accuse the major-domo of the imperial palace and your master?"

CHAPTER 82

The Young Hero Stands the Test of the Imperial Chopper.
An Imperial Decree Is Issued.

THE young Ai Hu was suitably impressed by the redoubtable Lord Bao, who glared at him threateningly.

"You have placed me in a dilemma," Ai Hu stammered. "I am in trouble if I tell and in trouble if I don't. I won't say any more until you question my squire, Ma Qiang."

"You are young but cunning," said Lord Bao. "Don't you realise that servants who inform against their masters have their limbs chopped off?"

The prime minister's attendants brought in the dog-headed chopper and Ai Hu shuddered when he saw the yellowish cold steel. But he thought: "I've come to save the loyal official and the champion Northern Hero. I can become quite a hero if I don't give the game away even if they chop off my legs."

His shoes and socks were taken off by the heroes Zhao Long and Zhao Hu, his feet were placed under the blade and they waited for a sign from the prime minister.

"Ai Hu, who put you up to it?" he demanded.

"No one has," he answered. "Why not send someone for the pearl crown; if it's not where I said it was, I'm ready to plead guilty."

He gave an exact description of the Nine Dragon Crown which

persuaded Lord Bao to stop further proceedings. He was taken to a cell while a report of the case was prepared to be presented to the emperor.

Ai Hu was surprised to find himself being well treated by a sycophantic warder who prepared fragrant tea and tasty dishes. This was organised by Sleek Rat, who had recognised Ai Hu when he appeared in court and had been impressed by his courage. He came to the conclusion that the young boy was here to help Governor Ni and Northern Hero somehow.

He entered the cell and Ai Hu bowed low.

"Nephew," said Sleek Rat, "why are you so bold as to play tricks in the Kaifeng Prefecture?"

Ai Hu related the plan devised by Black Fox and the Ding twins and then gave him the letter they had written asking for his help if their young charge was in trouble.

"The critical moment has passed," he said. "We must wait and see what happens when the emperor receives the prime minister's report."

When the emperor read the case report it reminded him of two instances when his uncle the Prince of Xiangyang had attempted a rebellion.

He summoned his major-domo-in-chief Chen Lin and ordered him to inspect the imperial treasury. Ma Chaoxian, ignorant of the plot against him, opened the red trunk in Chen Lin's presence and they discovered it was empty.

"Where is the Nine Dragon Crown?" demanded Chen Lin.

Ma Chaoxian went pale with fright and was unable to answer.

The emperor was furious when he received the news and ordered Chen Lin to investigate the matter.

Chen Lin decided that uncle and nephew should be tried together in the same court and the emperor sent high-ranking court officials to be present to make sure there would be no corruption. The chief justice Wen Yenbo was appointed to preside over the case. Ai Hu was brought before them and he related the same story he had given to Prime Minister Bao, including the intimation of a plot to involve the Prince of Xiangyang in an uprising.

"Can you recognise the keeper of the Treasury House?" he was asked.

CHAPTER 83

Ai Hu Stands Firm.
The Villains Are Silenced.

AI Hu was worried when he was asked if he could recognise the keeper of the treasury, Ma Chaoxian, as it had been many years since he had visited his nephew Ma Qiang. But the boy was helped by Yan Shenming, one of the court officials who had been asked to help by Sleek Rat. When an old eunuch in chains entered the court, Ai Hu was asked if he was Ma Chaoxian. He saw Yan Shenmin's hat wobble — so he said no.

Soon the crafty Ma Chaoxian was marched in. He denied taking the crown and confronted with Ai Hu's story also denied knowing him, even when threatened with torture. Because of his status the court was unable to take the word of a young boy and he was taken away while his nephew was brought before them. He instantly recognised his young servant and swore at him when he heard his accusation.

"Be quiet!" Chen Lin shouted. "You are in a court of law, not in your own home where you can berate your servants. Have some respect!"

Ma Qiang crawled forward. "It's untrue what Ai Hu is saying. My uncle never gave me the Nine Dragon Crown. If you find it in my home then I'll plead guilty."

Ma Qiang was convinced they would not find the crown and

willingly signed a document affirming that if it was found at his home, he would admit guilt.

When his uncle was shown this document, he realised that he was on shaky ground unless he said the same, and therefore declared that if the crown was found there he would plead guilty.

Ai Hu was questioned about another robbery at the Talent-Assembling Hall of which Governor Ni and Northern Hero had been accused by Ma Qiang and his wife. Ai Hu was able to tell them the whole story of the governor's imprisonment in the dungeon and his rescue by soldiers led by Northern Hero.

"It appears that that robbery has nothing to do with Northern Hero," Judge Wen told the court officials.

The following day a warrant for the arrest of the bandits in the Talent-Assembling Hall was issued and the Nine Dragon Crown was discovered where Ai Hu had said it was hidden — behind the middle shrine in the Buddha Hall. The evil steward, who in his previous occupation as a boatman had robbed and drowned the governor's father, managed to escape. But Ma Qiang's wife was arrested and, deciding to save her own skin, accused her husband of the theft of the Nine Dragon Crown. Faced with such damning evidence, uncle and nephew confessed and they were led away. The judge began to question Mrs Ma about the robbery of her jewels and property.

A commotion disturbed the court proceedings and an old man was brought in pleading for Governor Ni.

"What a coincidence!" Major-domo-in-chief Chen Lin cried. "Let him speak. We still have to clear up the case of Governor Ni. Summon all those involved in the case and then we will present the findings of the two cases to the throne tomorrow."

CHAPTER 84

Governor Ni Gets Married.
Sleek Rat Tackles a Monster.

THE old servant Ni Zhong told the court about his master's imprisonment by Ma Qiang and how the girl Zhu Jiangzhen had helped him to escape and of Northern Hero's part in his rescue when he was recaptured.

Chen Lin commented: "His account tallies with all we have heard from the others, except for those who committed the robbery. Let us question Governor Ni and Northern Hero."

When they checked the times of the rescue and robbery they did not coincide with the account given by Mrs Ma. So the judge ruled that the robbery had been committed by the men of the Talent-Assembling Hall before they fled to the protection of the Prince of Xiangyang. A report of the findings was delivered to the emperor who ordered the execution of Ma Chaoxian and his nephew. He put aside the threatened conspiracy against him by the prince because he was his uncle and it would be against filial piety.

Governor Ni was reinstated and Northern Hero acquitted. Ai Hu, despite committing the crime of disloyalty against his former master, obtained clemency from the emperor.

In a letter of gratitude which Governor Ni Jizu wrote to the emperor, he described how his father had been killed by the river robbers, Tao Zong and He Bao, the sad life of his mother and the history of the pair of matching carved jade lotus flowers.

The emperor was moved by the story and conferred the official title of fifth rank on him and his mother, while his adopted father, the old man Ni, was not forgotten and was awarded the title of sixth rank. The governor's faithful servant was promoted to palace guard of the seventh rank and, because the matching jade lotus flowers were instrumental in bringing the governor and his rescuer Zhu Jiangzhen together, they were to be married.

When he reached home, Governor Ni paid his respects to his mother and his adopted parents, and moved his father's coffin to its proper resting place in Hangzhou. One of the river robbers, He Bao, was arrested and executed. Then an auspicious day was fixed to celebrate Ni's marriage to Zhu Jiangzhen, when a merry time was had by all.

After they were treated as honoured guests, Northern Hero, accompanied by his now adopted son, Ai Hu, left for Jasmine Village.

Although the threatened rebellion by his uncle worried the emperor, he had a more serious matter to consider. Despite a great deal of effort and money spent to prevent the flooding of the area near Hongze Lake, it still happened every year. People were drowned and crops submerged. Prime Minister Bao suggested that the emperor should send Yan Shenmin, an able and learned man, to take charge of taming the rivers. He was promoted to inspecting commissioner and he took as his assistants, Bao's able assistant, Gongsun Ce, and Sleek Rat.

They reached the city of Sishui where Prefect Zou Jia welcomed Yan.

Farmers from Reddish Mound complained about the water monsters who came out of the swollen rivers to rob them and destroy their homes, leaving them with nothing but the threadbare clothes they stood up in. Commissioner Yan promised to inspect the flooded area and accompanied by the prefect and his two assistants, climbed to the top of a mountain the next day to inspect the wilderness of turbulent waters stretching from Reddish Bend to Reddish Mound, where homes and trees were submerged. The villagers from Reddish Mound had made makeshift sheds on stilts in the water, where they eked out a miserable existence, naming the place "Forsaken Life Village".

Sleek Rat was greatly affected by the sorry scene and decided to see what he could do to alleviate the poor people's sufferings. They told him they were unable to build a dam to keep the floods out because of the swift currents and whirlpool at the foot of the mountain. He asked the name of the nearest place to the whirlpool and was told it was a monastery called The Three Kings. He kept it in mind and asked them to describe the monsters that had made their lives so miserable. He gave them two silver ingots to buy food and fuel and told them not to run away but to stay in their huts when the monsters came in the night and make a loud noise — he would then take over.

Late that night, when the moon emerged clean and bright over the rippling water, Sleek Rat waited patiently and at about the second watch he heard a splash and saw something with a tousled head of hair emerge from the water. Without thinking what it might do, he hurled a stone and hit it on the back and then threw another which hit it in the face. Giving out an "Ouch" Tousle Head fell flop to the ground and Sleek Rat pinned him down and carried him into the shed. It was a man clad in a leather wrap, who moaned: "Spare me, lord!"

A voice shouted out that another monster was coming but it managed to escape back into the water. The angry villagers turned on the captive and wanted to beat him up but Sleek Rat managed to stop them, saying he would be tried properly at the yamen.

Now that they saw that the so-called monsters were really only men, the villagers thanked Sleek Rat and went off to search for the others while he took his captive to the yamen.

CHAPTER 85

The Prime Minister's Assistant Is Captured.
The Lake Is Searched for the Robbers.

COMMISSIONER Yan was very disturbed at the flood scene and was unable to sleep. When Sleek Rat returned with the robber, he wasted no time in calling the court into session to try him. It emerged that there were thirteen more robbers who had taken refuge in the Monastery of the Three Kings. They plundered boats during the day and pretended to be monsters at night to frighten off the refugees in Reddish Mound who wanted to protect their land.

Gongsun Ce concluded that the whirlpool must have been caused by an obstacle blocking the free flow of water, so creating the floods, and he went off to investigate. Two boats with their captains, Huang Kai and Qing Ping, and eight sailors accompanied him.

When Sleek Rat asked permission for more help to deal with the robbers and suggested his fourth brother, River Rat, the commissioner agreed.

The next day, Captain Qing Ping hurried back to report that as they were approaching the whirlpool, the boat with Gongsun Ce and Captain Huang Kai was sucked down.

An agitated commissioner ordered the prefect to send men to recover the corpses — but to no avail: there was no sign of any bodies.

Sleek Rat suggested waiting until his brother River Rat arrived to see what he could do.

When he arrived a few days later, Commissioner Yan ordered Captain Qing Ping to accompany River Rat to the whirlpool. Seeing his short scraggy frame, the captain thought: "What can such a weakling do? If he meets the river robbers he's bound to be killed."

When they reached the whirlpool, River Rat put on his swimming costume and holding his three-edged chisel in his hand, told Captain Qing not to panic if he did not emerge for some time.

He dived into the water as if piercing a hole and swam under the water like a fish. He saw a man in a leather suit and weapon in hand swimming towards him. He thrust his weapon into the man's chest, killing him before he realised what had happened and was swept away by the current. River Rat disposed of three more of the robbers in the same way and swam on two or three *li* further until he reached a bank and saw the Monastery of the Three Kings before him. He sneaked into the kitchen where he heard someone groaning. It was an old monk who cried out when he saw River Rat: "It's not my fault, it was my disciple who has let go of that man and captain. Now he has run away and put the blame for their escape on me."

"I've come to rescue them," said River Rat.

The old monk told him that the robbers had panicked when they realised how important their captives were. A group had gone to the Prince of Xiangyang to inform him what they had done. The monk said that after they left he released Gongsun Ce and the captain and was now waiting to be killed by the robbers when they returned.

"Who is their leader?" asked River Rat.

"He calls himself Sea-Guarding Dragon Wu Ze," the monk answered.

He told River Rat that the two officials had gone to a place called Conch Cove, but he could take a short cut by swimming there.

"Set your heart at ease, old man," said River Rat. "Men will come here to capture those bandits tomorrow and you will be safe."

He swam back to the whirlpool where he told the waiting Qing Ping to report back to Commissioner Yan and take fifty soldiers to the monastery and lie in ambush. "If the robbers escape into the water, don't worry, I'll know what to do."

River Rat dived back into the water, leaving Captain Qing now impressed by his prowess.

When River Rat reached Conch Cove he saw a man on a raft casting a net who gave a start when he noticed the strange figure sticking out of the water.

"Wretch," he shouted. "A river bandit with a figure like yours makes a laughing stock. I'm not intimidated by you, so clear off!"

River Rat explained who he was and the fisherman told him that he had given shelter to two officials and they had told him to look out for him. The fisherman, named Mao Xiu, quickly tethered the raft and the two men walked to a little hamlet of thatch and bamboo cottages.

They entered one of them where they were met by the fisherman's father who took them inside to Gongsun Ce and Captain Huang. Old Man Mao knew the ways of the river well.

River Rat was anxious to catch the robbers and the next day he left the two officials in the care of the fisherman and his old father and returned to the river. He swam towards the whirlpool where he noticed two armed robbers. He quickly dispatched them and their corpses were swept away down the river. Another came towards him wielding a lance. It was Sea-Guarding Dragon Wu Ze himself, who had managed to escape the ambush lying in wait for the returning bandits by jumping into the river. A fierce battle ensued, in which the smaller-framed River Rat was up against a bigger and stronger man, but River Rat was the better swimmer and soon overcame the bandit and dragged the drowning man to the bank where Captain Qing Ping and his men were waiting.

Sea-Guarding Dragon Wu Ze and the remaining bandits were then marched off to the yamen to be brought to trial.

CHAPTER 86

The Two Fishermen Are Given Titles.
A Young Hero Lands in Trouble Through Drink.

EVERYONE rejoiced over the defeat of the bandits. After River Rat paid his respects to Commissioner Yan he told him of the invaluable help given by Old Man Mao and his son in capturing the bandits, as well as their sheltering of Gongsun Ce and Captain Huang Kai. A boat was dispatched to Conch Village to bring back the two fishermen.

Sea-Guarding Dragon Wu Ze confessed that because he was a good swimmer the Prince of Xiangyang had sent him and his men to Hongze Lake to destroy the embankments and cause flooding to bring trouble to the country. They had not expected to be beaten by superior forces. They were imprisoned in the county jail and when the river was tamed would be sent to the capital for trial.

When Old Man Mao and his son arrived, Commissioner Yan treated them with great respect, even placing the old man on his left, a high honour indeed. Old Man Mao then produced a map and presented it to him with both hands. It detailed the physical features of mountains and rivers, all neatly captioned. His notes also showed where embankments and dikes should be built and which river and stream should be diverted. When Gongsun Ce saw the plans, he felt as if he had obtained a rare treasure and decided to present it to the emperor for his approval.

The old monk who had been instrumental in releasing the prime minister's assistant and Captain Huang Kai from Sea-Guarding Dragon Wu Ze and his bandits, was rewarded with a hundred taels of silver.

A few days later a royal decree was issued and the flood-taming project began, using Old Man Mao's plans, calculated with minimum cost. The project took just four months; the floods receded and the fields were levelled.

The emperor was so pleased he conferred the title of fifth rank on the old man and his son was given the title of sixth rank. The officials as well as the two captains who were instrumental in solving the causes of the flood were also rewarded.

The conspiracy of the Prince of Xiangyang and the river robbers was relayed to the emperor. He conferred with Prime Minister Bao and it was decided to send undercover men first to Xiangyang to discover the best way to apprehend the prince, rather than use open force which might exacerbate a tense situation.

Commissioner Yan, who had been given the new title of great scholar of the Wenyuan Library, in recognition of his flood control success, was sent to Xiangyang. He was accompanied by Gongsun Ce, who had been promoted to imperial secretary, and Sleek Rat, who had also been promoted to palace guard of the fourth rank.

The Prince of Xiangyang had anticipated repercussions from the palace, after the arrest of the river robbers, and was prepared for their arrival. To the west of Xiangyang was the Black Wolf Mountain which was guarded by a man called Gold-Face God, Lan Xiao. To the east of the area was a stretch of water guarded by Marvellous Trident-Thrower, Zhong Xiong.

Thus the prince and the two men formed a triple watch for any intruders.

After his emissaries left, the emperor discussed with Prime Minister Bao the part which Northern Hero had played in rescuing Governor Ni and expressed his admiration. Bao took the hint and returning to his study, told one of his gallants.

"To find Northern Hero is my job," said River Rat, "as you gallants can't be absent from the Kaifeng Prefecture. I have nothing particular to do."

The gallants agreed and when they reported to the prime minister, he made out an identity card for River Rat who then left for Jasmine Village.

Several days later, hungry and tired, he put up at an inn and ordered food and drink. The tea was delicate and sweet and he drank rather a lot of it which gave him a full bladder. So he was forced to get up in the night to relieve himself.

As he entered the courtyard he heard a silent tapping on a door and saw a man quickly slip through.

It looked suspicious and River Rat jumped onto a wall and listened carefully. It was the innkeeper's room and he heard someone say: "Lend me a hand, brother. I recognise the man in the east wing. He is the very enemy of our squire. He's dead drunk at the moment so it will be easy to strangle him and throw his body into the wilderness."

"Wait till he falls asleep," the other voice answered.

River Rat decided to find out who the intended victim was and tip-toed to the east wing where he pushed through the curtain of the door and looked closely at the now snoring figure. It was the young page, Ai Hu, who had already caused anxiety to Northern Hero with his love of good wine.

"This rascal is too fond of drink. But for me he would be dead," said River Rat to himself.

"I'd better wait here in the dark, and see what ensues."

His bladder was fit to burst but he dared not leave the room to relieve himself. In desperation he went behind the door and released a flood of urine which spread all over the floor. A man entered the room, slipped on the wet floor and fell flat on his face, the second following closely bumped into him and also fell. River Rat jumped on top of them yelling out loud. Ai Hu, roused by the noise, quickly got up and helped to overcome the two men.

"Why are you helping this man with a murder," River Rat asked the innkeeper.

"He is a friend of mine," he replied. "My name is Cao Biao and he is called Tao Zong. He says his master was framed and this young man was responsible."

Ai Hu looked closely at one of the men and exclaimed: "This man is not Tao Zong, he's the steward called Yao Cheng who accused Northern Hero of the robberies."

River Rat handed the two would-be murderers to the bailiffs and ordered them to be taken to the county office where they would be brought before the local magistrate.

CHAPTER 87

Three Heroes Pay a Visit to an Old Friend.
A Gallant Goes to the Rescue.

"WHERE is your master?" River Rat asked Ai Hu.

The boy gave a long account of what had happened after the rout of the rebels from the Talent-Assembling Hall. Governor Ni had insisted that Northern Hero, and his master, Black Fox, stay with him until he got married. They visited Jasmine Village so that the governor could thank the Ding twins in person. The brothers in the meantime discovered that the Prince of Xiangyang had been preparing an armed force against Governor Ni and had enlisted the help of Gold-Face God Lan Xiao and Marvellous Trident-Thrower Zhong Xiong.

"My master and foster-father were worried that one of their close friends named Iron-Face Guardian Sha Long would be persuaded to join the insurrectionists. So they and Uncle Ding decided to go to Sleeping Tiger Gully where their friend lived. They left me in charge of Second Uncle Ding but I was bored because I wanted to go with them and enjoy myself at Sleeping Tiger Gully. I stole five taels of silver from Second Uncle Ding and took off, staying the night here at this inn."

"Young rascal," thought River Rat. "He regards fighting as entertainment."

As Northern Hero, the man he was seeking on behalf of the emperor, had now left Jasmine Village and was making his way to Sleeping Tiger Gully, River Rat decided to go there too. Ai Hu begged River Rat to let him accompany him. He consented only after extracting a promise that the young man would drink no more than three measures of wine at each meal.

The next morning River Rat and Ai Hu packed their things and went to the county seat where River Rat sent in his identity card and arranged for the magistrate to deliver the two criminals to the capital. There, under threat of torture, Yao Cheng made a full confession before Prime Minister Bao, including his part in murdering Governor Ni's father, and gave details of Ma Qiang's conspiracy with the Prince of Xiangyang.

Yao Cheng was then executed.

River Rat and Ai Hu continued on their way to Sleeping Tiger Gully and, sure enough, the boy kept his promise and only drank three measures of wine at each meal. They reached a river and hired a boat to take them across. The boat owner was called Fu San and he had two helpers. Soon Ai Hu dozed off and River Rat sat at the bow to enjoy the scenery. A gale blew up and the boat took shelter at a secluded spot called Goose Head Bluff. River Rat was just about to turn in when he heard someone crying for help. He took off his shoes and placed them on the bow, jumped in, swam towards a man bobbing about in the water and pulled him towards land.

The man was about fifty and was named Lei Zhen. He had a son who was an adjutant in the palace of the Prince of Xiangyang. He lived in Eight Treasure Village and had been on his way to his married daughter's home to bring her clothes and other goods as she and her husband were very poor. He had hired a boat but the owners were evil-doers known as Mi the Third and Mi the Seventh.

They had robbed him of his goods and were just about to kill him when he managed to escape by jumping into the water where River Rat had found him.

"I'll go and get your goods," promised River Rat and dived back into the water and swam towards the robbers' boat. He heard them commenting on the goods they had stolen. He shouted: "Robbers! A lot you care for others!"

He jumped onto the boat and met Mi the Seventh with sword in hand coming towards him. He lashed out with his foot and Mi fell flat on his back, letting go of the sword. River Rat snatched it and dispatched the robber before he could utter a sound. Mi the Third jumped into the water but River Rat quickly caught up with him and seizing his ankles dunked him several times until he swallowed a copious amount of water. Then he was pulled back onto the deck and tied up. River Rat swam back to the old man, gave him the sword and told him to stand guard over the robber until morning. He swam back to where his own boat had been moored, but it had vanished. So he was forced to return to a nervous Lei Zhen. In the morning he kicked Mi the Third into the water, saying: "That's one less robber for innocent travellers!"

When Ai Hu woke up and discovered River Rat was missing he at first accused the boatman Fu San of murdering him, but when they saw his shoes neatly placed on the bow, he realised that he must have gone of his own accord. Tying River Rat's money-bag containing one hundred taels of silver round his waist, he took their luggage and went on his way.

CHAPTER 88

Ai Hu Becomes a Sworn Brother.
A Son-in-Law Is Chosen While Two Men Discuss Literature.

AS he walked along, Ai Hu cried as he thought about the kindness River Rat had shown him, not knowing whether he had drowned and then cheered up when he remembered what a good swimmer he was. He was so preoccupied with his thoughts that it was night time before he realised how hungry and thirsty he was and found an inn. Inside, two fishermen sat face to face playing a finger drinking game. He decided to join in but they scolded him and told him to go away. Ai Hu pleaded: "I've been travelling a long way and am famished and parched."

The fishermen told him to wait until they had finished and he could have the leftovers.

The indignant Ai Hu said he had plenty of money and tried to snatch their wine. This made one of the fishermen so angry he got up and raised his fist to strike him only to find Ai Hu pulling it to one side so that he fell flat on his face. The second fisherman joined in and a free-for-all ensued in which Ai Hu, with his superior fighting skills, was able to fend them off and they took to their heels.

The victorious Ai Hu sat at the table, drained a bowl of wine and polished off the fish and soup. His hunger now stayed, he was about to leave when his head knocked against a big wine gourd behind him. To his joy it was full of wine. He drained the contents, staggered out and lurched along the road for two or three *li* before entering a tumble-down pavilion by the side of the road where he stretched out on the ground and fell fast asleep.

It was daylight before he came to and found five or six men standing round him with clubs in their hands. They were friends of the two fishermen and they began beating him up. One old man told them not to beat him to death but just to teach him a lesson. Ai Hu bore it with fortitude, realising that he deserved it. When they finally stopped, he opened his eyes, got up, dusted his clothes and made to go, clasping his hands before him saying: "Cheerio."

The fishermen still barred his way. "You've robbed us of our fish and wine and broken our gourd and plates. Pay us!"

"That's nothing," said Ai Hu. "I'll give you some silver to buy new ones."

"What do we want silver for?" they asked. "We want the old ones."

"What's done cannot be undone," replied Ai Hu. "You might as well beat me again."

He lay down on the ground like a naughty boy and waited.

The fishermen did not know whether to laugh or be angry.

"He's mocking us," said one of the men. "I'll kill him even if I have to pay with my life!"

As they argued what to do a young scholar came up and pleaded with them not to beat him any more.

Seeing a young gentleman, they bowed and left.

Ai Hu uncovered his face, blushed with shame and then laughed. He got up and brushed himself down.

"I was in the wrong," he said, and told the scholar the story, who was impressed with his honest admission of wrong.

They introduced themselves and the two young men instantly took a liking to each other and decided to become sworn brothers. The scholar was named Shi Jun and was seventeen years old, a year older than Ai Hu.

Outside the pavilion a page-boy was holding two horses and Shi Jun told him that he now had a second young master. He stepped forward and fell on his knees, saying: "The humble servant Jinjian bows before you."

Nobody had ever called him young master or bowed before him and Ai Hu was delighted, but was at a loss what to do next.

He fished two silver ingots out of his purse and said: "Buy something for yourself."

Jinjian only took it after the scholar gave permission, and bowed once more.

The scholar was on his way to Xiangyang to his uncle's home to have a composition corrected and to do some reading. So the two friends bade a fond farewell and went their separate ways.

Shi Jun's father had been a magistrate but blindness and ill-health forced him to retire early and return home. He had two sworn brothers, one a previous war minister named Jin Hui, who had been removed from office for impeaching the Prince of Xiangyang. The other sworn brother was the governor of Changsha and was called Shao Bangjie. The ex-war minister had a lovely daughter. Old Shi hoped she would marry his son one day, so he had sent him there with the excuse of getting his composition corrected.

Jin Hui was impressed with his proposed future son-in-law and suggested the scholar should stay with him for a while and they could spend some fruitful hours discussing literature.

The more he saw of Shi Jun the more attractive became the idea that he should marry his daughter. After settling him in for the night, he went highly elated to confer with his wife in the rear quarters.

CHAPTER 89

The Scholar's Page Hides a Brooch and Brews Up Trouble.
A Careless Maid Loses the Purple Goldfish Pendant.

MASTER Jin Hui's wife was the sister of the magistrate of Tangxian County. She ran a well-ordered household which enabled her husband to have a comfortable stress-free life. He also had a concubine called Clever. When he entered his wife's room he couldn't praise his young protégé enough, remarking what a learned prospective son-in-law they were getting for their beautiful daughter, Peony.

His wife agreed that such a match would be ideal for both families, but her husband decided he needed more time to observe the young scholar before making a formal engagement.

As he was extolling the virtues of Shi Jun, their daughter's maidservant, Jiahui, was eavesdropping and hurried off to her young mistress to tell her what a clever husband she was going to marry. Jiahui had attended Peony since childhood. She was quick-witted, pretty and able to read and write.

"Congratulations, young mistress," she said smiling. "Lord Shi has sent his son to study here and has asked your father to correct his compositions. Your parents intend to marry you to him."

Peony was not pleased, scolded her maid for telling tales and told her to go.

Feeling hurt, Jiahui went to her room, grumbling to herself:

"She may be a young lady and I only a maidservant, but we have been very close and I thought she would be pleased to hear the news, rather than turn me away with a cross word. Maybe she feels that learned men are not handsome and didn't like hearing how clever this Shi Jun is. I'll take a peep and see if he is handsome as well as clever and then she'll be pleased with me."

She sneaked to the study to take a look and, satisfied that he was also handsome, decided to make sure that her young mistress should not reject the scholar.

She got an embroidered handkerchief which Peony had once given her and copied two lines from the *Book of Songs* onto it. They read:

> "*Merrily the ospreys cry,*
> *On the islet in the stream.*"

The next day she entered the study where Shi Jun was dozing over his book, and dropped the handkerchief on the desk and quietly left. When his page, Jinjian, came later, he noticed the handkerchief and mystified, unfolded it and read the two lines of poetry. He waited till his master woke up to see whether he mentioned it, but he didn't and Jinjian decided to find out where it had come from. It wasn't long before the maid returned and he thought the handkerchief was hers. Waving it in front of her he teased: "Have patience, sister. You'll get married some day. What's the hurry?"

Blushing furiously, Jiahui told him the real meaning of the poem on the handkerchief. "Don't you see it means that your master must offer his hand to my mistress as soon as possible?"

Jinjian thought the handkerchief was not enough to achieve the desired end, and the two young servants decided on another plan, which was to have disastrous results. Jiahui took one of Peony's exquisite jade hairpins and gave it to Jinjian. He in turn took a pendant in the shape of a purple goldfish from his master's box, wrapped it in a piece of cloth and handed it to Jiahui who thrust it into her bosom to take to her mistress. On her way she bumped into the maidservant of the concubine Clever and as they talked the package slid to the ground where it was picked up by the concubine's maid and taken to her mistress.

When Clever saw what the package contained her heart filled with exultation. Now she could take her revenge on Peony and her maid. They had discovered her making love in the garden with a young protégé of her husband. Her lover took flight and she was left wondering how she could punish the two women for causing the end of her affair. With the handkerchief and the purple gold-fish she had her chance. She dismissed her maid after promising she would make her a lined jacket as a reward.

One evening Jin Hui returned home rather late and as Madam Jin had already retired, decided to spend the night with Clever instead.

"The humble concubine has something to tell you, sir," she said kneeling down in front of him.

She gave him the handkerchief and the pendant with the lines of a poem from the *Book of Songs*, written in two different styles. Two lines were written in a delicate and graceful style while the other two were thick and slipshod.

His heart missed a beat.

"I picked it up outside Peony's quarters," Clever said meekly.

He turned pale with anger. "The wretch! How could she have done such a thing!" he said.

"Don't publicise it, sir," the concubine added, "for it bears upon the reputation of our family. Find out more first. Maybe it is not the young lady but her maid."

Jin Hui said nothing but nodded and went to his study to sleep.

CHAPTER 90

Peony Runs Away.
Her Maid Plays the Role of Her Mistress.

THE concubine's plan was to pretend that she had Peony's reputation at heart and to put the blame on the maid but in reality to involve both the women and get rid of them. As she expected, Jin Hui was too angry to question his daughter himself and spent a sleepless night in his study. The next day he searched the scholar's room and found his daughter's hairpin hidden in the bookcase. It was one of a pair of jade hairpins he had given her. Now even more incensed he charged into his wife's quarters and demanded that she send one of her maids to their daughter's room to bring the jade hairpins to him. She returned a few minutes later with only one of them, saying that Peony was at a loss as to where the missing hairpin had gone and when she found it would send it.

Master Jin sneered at his wife: "A fine daughter you have produced," and took the missing hairpin from his sleeve and the handkerchief with the pendant, telling her how he had acquired them.

"I give her three days to take her life," he said. "I do not want to see her anymore." He strode off to his study.

Madam Jin hastened to her daughter's room and the two women wept bitterly, unable to fathom the mystery. They sent Peony's old nanny Liang to ask the maid Jiahui whether she could throw any light on the affair of the hairpin and pendant but she had been taken ill and was unable to give a coherent answer. Nanny Liang returned saying she knew nothing.

Calming down at last, Peony was resigned to her fate. "As my father has ordered me to commit suicide, I can't disobey."

They burst out crying again, hugging each other. Nanny Liang knew her young charge too well to suspect her of anything underhand and blamed Jiahui, but as she was too ill to be questioned, time was against them.

She suggested that Peony and her maid take refuge in Madam Jin's brother's home, the one who was a magistrate in Tangxian County, and wait until Jiahui had recovered and then find out the truth.

At first Peony was reluctant to go. She had always led a sheltered life and was afraid of showing herself in public, but she was persuaded when Nanny Liang said that if she killed herself, the truth would never come out. They decided that Jiahui should take on her identity and she would be the maid.

Nanny Liang sent for her husband, known as Good-for-Nothing Wu because he had never been able to father a child. Any job he undertook always ended in failure and thus it was that when he hired a boat to take his charges to Tangxian County, the boatmen turned out to be scoundrels.

Meanwhile, Master Jin could not pretend to be friendly towards the young scholar and treated him with uncharacteristic rudeness. "Isn't it time you went home?" he asked. Shi Jun blushed with embarrassment and told his page to saddle their horses.

The parting was barely polite and Jin Hui sighed as he thought of the misfortune of his old friend in having such a son. He looked at the books on the table and noticed a folding fan left in one of them, the fan which had held the pendant, but the opportunity of finding out the truth by questioning the scholar about the fan was lost in the anger he still felt towards the young man. He went to his wife's room and found her in tears. He sighed and sat down and his wife suddenly knelt before him and confessed that Peony had escaped to Tangxian County.

At the sight of her prostrate form, he was overcome with love for her and helped her up.

"Don't cry any more," he said. "All we can do now is give up all thought of the matter."

The boat Good-For-Nothing Wu had hired was owned by two brothers, Weng Da and Weng Er, who robbed their passengers. The sight of the two young pretty girls aroused their lust. Making a coming storm the excuse, they demanded that they buy sacrifices for the god.

"Where can we buy offerings in the middle of the river?" Good-for-Nothing Wu asked.

"We keep everything on the boat," answered Weng Er, and demanded a large sum of money to pay for a cock, fish, sheep, incense, candles and paper money, which turned out to be a sheep's head without skin or hair, a dead cock minus its wings and dried fish. The paper silver ingots were tarnished and dented and the yellow sheets of paper faded. Even the sticks of incense were used and uneven and the candles just burnt-out stubs. Good-for-Nothing Wu protested and when Weng Da asked for extra money to buy wine his hackles rose. But before he could do or say anything, he was pushed into the water. Nanny Liang saw the scene and shouted out. This alerted Peony who broke a window in the cabin and jumped into the water.

Wang Da seized Jiahui, saying: "Never fear, my beauty, I want a word with you."

She screamed out so loudly that a boat full of passengers heard her and drew up alongside which frightened the robbers and they dived into the river.

"Help us," shouted Nanny Liang who crawled out from under the bed. "My husband and maidservant are lost in the river and I fear they are drowned. My lady is too ill to move."

In reality it was Jiahui playing the part of Peony.

Several servants helped the two women onto the second boat where a lord was sitting in an armchair.

Jiahui stepped forward and introduced herself as Peony, daughter of Jin Hui.

At the mention of the name of the former war minister, the man smiled and announced he was her adopted uncle Shao Bangjie, a sworn brother of her father's. He exclaimed what a happy coincidence it was that they had been passing by and asked where she was going.

CHAPTER 91

The Young Lady Finds a New Father.
Ai Hu Starts Drinking Again.

THE maid masquerading as Peony told her uncle that she was on her way to Tangxian County to see a doctor.

"How can your father send such a slip of a girl with only a nanny and her husband to take you?" he asked. "I ought to send you home, but I've been summoned by imperial decree to attend court and haven't the time. You had better accompany me to Changsha. My wife and daughters will keep you company until you are better."

Their boat sailed to the river junction near Plum Flower Cove; one branch led to Changsha while the other led to Green Duck Beach where there was a settlement of thirteen fishing households. In one of the households lived elderly Zhang Li, an honest fisherman, and his wife. They had no children. One night as he cast his net into the river, he pulled up the body of a young woman clasping a bamboo window frame.

"Woe is me!" he exclaimed and made to throw the body back, but his wife stopped him. "Have patience, man," she said. "Let me see if she is breathing. Saving a life is better than building a seven-storey pagoda!"

Peony's heart was still beating and Mrs Zhang massaged her chest until with a groan and a cough, she came to. She told them that she was the maidservant of the daughter of Magistrate Jin, had leant against the window of the boat which gave way and had fallen into the river.

The childless Mrs Zhang saw a lovely young girl before her and wanted to adopt Peony as her own daughter, to which her husband agreed. She was beside herself with joy and couldn't wait to take her home and get her a change of clothes and food. Peony, accustomed to fine clothes and jewels, now found herself dressed in plain homespun, with hairpins made from thorns to fix her hair, but she didn't want to upset the old lady and ate a little of the millet soup and pickled radishes.

As time went by the old couple began to love their adopted daughter and spoiled her with food they could ill afford, knowing she had been a member of a magistrate's household. Their idea of luxury food was fat pork and rice and Zhang Li worked hard to catch more fish so they could indulge their daughter. Soon the news reached the other households and they all wanted to offer their congratulations to the couple on their luck in acquiring such a beautiful daughter. The leader of the families, a man named Shi Yun, suggested they club together and organise a feast in celebration. "They must be rewarded for their kindness," he said. He was a bold and chivalrous man, fairly skilled with weapons and respected by his fellowmen. They worked as one to get enough fish to sell and buy wine and food for the feast. Under his direction they brought in the food, wine and furniture to the Zhangs. "You're looking happy and smart, mother," said her husband.

His wife replied, smiling: "Yes, my hair has been combed by my daughter."

"Show-off," her husband laughed in reply.

Everyone was impressed with Peony's appearance and good looks, clicking their tongues in admiration and envious of the Zhangs' good fortune.

The women and girls sat round one table and the men round another and soon they polished off all the dishes. As the party progressed, the men began to drink more and soon were daring each other with the finger-guessing game. Suddenly they heard a voice outside shout: "Count me in!"

As all the thirteen families were accounted for, Shi Yun went out and found a young boy with a bundle on his back.

"I've been watching you drinking merrily for a long time and my mouth has been watering," said the youth. "I would like to buy a drink."

"We are not a wine shop or tavern. This is a private party," replied Shi Yun. "Go away."

The youth grabbed his arm, annoying Shi Yun who raised his hand to slap him, but he found himself flat on his back. Now very angry he was about to retaliate when Zhang Li came out and invited the youth to join them in a drink.

The young man beamed, apologised, bowed low and introduced himself.

CHAPTER 92

Ai Hu Gets Drunk.
He Is Involved in a Fight.

"MY name is Ai Hu and I am on my way to Sleeping Tiger Gully," he said. He had travelled many miles, stopping at inns and drinking heavily, using River Rat's money and continuing on his way to find his adopted father, Northern Hero, and his master, Black Fox. When he saw the lights and merriment coming from the Zhangs' house, he gatecrashed and joined in the drinking games. He pressed Zhang to accept two silver ingots as a gift for his new daughter.

Such a big sum of money had never been seen by the poor fisher folk and they were filled with envy. Peony tried to persuade her foster-father not to accept money from strangers, but Ai Hu was adamant and suggested instead they hold another feast the next day. This made everyone happy and they continued celebrating and drinking until only Zhang Li and Shi Yun remained sober to keep an eye on the proceedings. It was just as well, because in the midst of the jollity, two brigands from the Black Wolf Mountain arrived demanding fish and shrimps for their master, Lan Xiao. It had been Zhang Li's turn to provide the tribute but in his new-found happiness he had forgotten. The brigands noticed how attractive Peony was and went back to their master to report the news. As they left, they stumbled over the drunken sleeping Ai

Hu and became angry that he had not greeted them in the same subservient manner as the fishermen.

Shi Yun and Zhang Li managed to pacify them, saying he was only a visitor and they left still angry.

When Ai Hu woke up he was furious. "I'm looking for those mountain brigands," he said. "I am not going to run away as you suggest but will wait for them here."

Zhang Li tried to persuade him to leave, but too late: there was a sound of men's voices and horses' hoofs and when he went out he saw a man on horseback accompanied by more than twenty brigands.

"Old man," called the man on horseback, "I've been told your daughter is very attractive. I'm just the right husband for her and I've come to plead my suit."

"Who are you?" demanded Ai Hu.

"Impudent young whipper-snapper. I am Ge Yaoming the Clam. Everybody has heard of me."

"You are just a nobody," Ai Hu replied. "I thought you were that lout, Lan Xiao."

Ai Hu was quickly surrounded by a group of the brigands who went to tie him up. But Ai Hu sent them flying with flailing fists and feet, turning and twisting, like a tiger rushing a flock of sheep.

Shi Yun applauded and then joined in with a five-pronged lance aimed at Ge Yaoming the Clam who had drawn his sword. It was wrested from his grasp and finding unexpected retaliation, the brigands took flight with Ai Hu chasing close at their heels.

It is always a mistake to chase after a retreating foe and Ai Hu, like a new-born calf who is not afraid of a tiger, thought with his prowess in the martial arts no one could defeat him. He did not notice a rope had been strung across his path and he was felled and quickly surrounded. Ge Yaoming the Clam split his men into two groups, one to get Zhang's daughter while he slowly followed the other group with Ai Hu back to his mountain hideout. As he began congratulating himself on his success, a pheasant suddenly fell from the sky and hit him. He stooped down to pick it up but heard someone shouting: "Put that pheasant down, it's ours."

The speaker was a plain-looking girl about fifteen years old and another girl with a bow in her hand stood under a tree. That one was very attractive. "I'm in luck today," he thought. "First the Zhangs' daughter and now another here. Double happiness has struck me."

His admiring looks towards the girl under the tree made the other girl angry. She struck him and he fell flat on his back. An iron ball shot by as her sister hit him between the eyes and made him bleed. As he tried to get up, the first girl struck out with her foot and knocked him flying again. He took to his heels.

Someone began cheering loudly.

CHAPTER 93

The Fishermen Join the Hunters.
Girlish Talk in Sleeping Tiger Gully.

IT was Ai Hu who, tied up on a horse, had observed the encounter and the ensuing battle when the brigands were driven off.

"Wonderful, wonderful!" he cried.

The plain-looking girl was called Autumn Sunflower and her beautiful sister was called Phoenix Sprite, daughters of Iron-Face Guardian Sha Long, the man Black Fox and Northern Hero were looking for.

A loud voice hailed them from the mountain. Looking up they saw it was the girls' father accompanied by his two brothers, Meng Jie and Jiao Chi. When they heard it was Ai Hu, they came rushing down in great excitement to greet him. Northern Hero, Black Fox and the Ding brother had already arrived and told them of Ai Hu's bravery in standing up to the threat of the imperial execution axe and they had been waiting impatiently to see this young hero.

In particular, Jiao Chi, a quick-tempered fellow, threw down his steel trident and gave him a hug, looking at a bemused Ai Hu wondering who these people were.

"Good, good," said Jiao Chi. "The marriage is settled. Look how handsome he is, brother Sha Long. Decide now, the marriage is settled."

Northern Hero and Black Fox had seen what a crack shot

Phoenix Sprite was and had asked the Ding brother to act as a matchmaker on behalf of Ai Hu. Sha Long had consented, believing that anyone connected with Northern Hero and Black Fox must be an ideal husband for his daughter. But he was also very fond of Autumn Sunflower, the plain one, and said that only after she was married could he consent to the marriage of the younger prettier one.

When he saw what a comely young man Ai Hu was, he couldn't resist shouting out: "The marriage is settled!" Phoenix Sprite blushed and ran away.

Ai Hu persuaded the three brothers to join him in rescuing the Zhangs and their daughter from the second group of brigands. They met up with them at the entrance to the mountain pass as the brigands were returning from the fishing village with the captured Peony hidden in a covered sedan chair. Swooping down on them, Ai Hu and his friends routed the brigands and freed Peony, who was quickly reunited with her foster-parents, the Zhangs, who had been following her.

Now all the families of Green Duck Beach were in danger of the vengeance of Lan Xiao of the Black Wolf Mountain. Sha Long decided that they should all leave for Sleeping Tiger Gully and said he would protect them. Sha Long was a man of great integrity, with remarkable fighting skills. He had gathered all the hunters of the area and taught them the martial arts and they were a match for Lan Xiao and his men on Black Wolf Mountain who had come out the worse in a battle with him.

Impressed with his skills, Lan Xiao had contacted the Prince of Xiangyang to say what a worthy ally his victor would make in the future.

Peony and the Zhangs moved into the quarters of Sha Long and soon the three girls became good friends. Sha Long was impressed with Peony's great composure and refined manners and wondered what her real background was. "She's not a fisherman's daughter but must be a young lady from a rich family," he thought.

CHAPTER 94

Ai Hu Sets Off to Find His Master and Adopted Father. Friendship Is Sacrificed to Ambition.

NOW that the fisher folk were settled in Sleeping Tiger Gully, Ai Hu wanted to join Northern Hero and Black Fox who had left for Xiangyang County three days before he arrived. He was angry with himself for giving way to his drinking habits, which had wasted time. "You can't possibly catch them up," said Sha Long. "Stay a little longer and tell us about your adventures."

They sat down at a table and drank tea with the brothers and with old fisherman Zhang and Shi Yun.

He told them how he had met River Rat and then lost him again, being careful not to drink any wine as he did not want his future father-in-law, Sha Long, to think he was a drunkard.

Afterwards Sha Long dispatched some of his hunters to spy on Lan Xiao's movements, as he wasn't sure of his reaction after he discovered that the fishermen of Green Duck Village had taken refuge in Sleeping Tiger Gully.

They reported back that Lan knew nothing about Ge Yaoming the Clam's attempted kidnapping of the girl and didn't seem to be interested.

Sha Long relaxed his guard and Ai Hu decided to leave for Xiangyang. The next day, he packed his things and for safe-keeping gave Sha Long the identity card that Prime Minister Bao had given to River Rat authorising him to bring Northern Hero to Kaifeng. "If River Rat comes, please return it to him," he said. No mention was made of Ai Hu's proposed marriage to Phoenix Sprite. Her father wanted to wait until Northern Hero arrived to conclude it.

Ai Hu was tempted into drinking several cups of wine before he left for Xiangyang.

River Rat in the meantime had safely delivered Lei Zhen to his destination and continued on his way. He was walking along a lonely road when it began to rain and he took refuge in a tumble-down monastery. He sheltered behind a statue where it was dry and when the rain stopped, he was just about to leave when he heard two men talking.

They were the two boatmen, Weng Da And Weng Er, who had tried to abduct Peony on the boat. They were scheming yet again to rob another passenger, a man named Li Pingshan, who wanted to get to Nine Immortals Bridge in Xiangyin County. Unluckily for them, their plans were overheard by River Rat who sought out Li Pingshan and offered to share the boat fare with him as he was going the same way. Li was impressed by River Rat's good manners and warmed to him even more when he realised that he spoke in the dialect of his own home district.

The next morning they boarded the boat and the Weng brothers pushed off. River Rat entertained Li with amusing anecdotes and time passed pleasantly.

Suddenly the sails began flapping and Weng Da suggested they pull the boat in, to shelter from the wind. River Rat was suspicious but as it was blowing hard, they found shelter in a quiet deserted corner of the bank, which made Li Pingshan uneasy. Fortunately loud gongs sounded and an official ship approached, also sheltering from the gale. Relieved he called over: "Do you have a Mr Jin over there?"

"Yes," was the reply and the boat drew alongside. "Our lord has been promoted by imperial decree to be Governor of Xiangyang," said the other boatman.

"That's wonderful," said Li Pingshan, and asked to be taken to him.

The official was Peony's father, Jin Hui, the former war minister, who at Prime Minister Bao's suggestion had been made Governor of Xiangyang to lay the way for the subjugation of the Prince of Xiangyang. The job called for a devoted and loyal official, and as Jin Hui had previously tried to impeach the prince and lost his post as war minister as a consequence, the emperor felt he could be trusted.

After a time, Li Pingshan returned to his boat, swaggering and puffing out his cheeks with self-importance. He cut River Rat dead and could hardly take the trouble to answer when asked who the official was. "He's the high-ranking official, Jin Hui," Li said. "I'm getting my luggage transferred to his boat tomorrow, so you can go off on your own."

River Rat could now see what a low person his companion was and asked for his part of the fare, saying he was a poor man and could not afford to pay all of it.

Li Pingshan glared at him. "We met only by chance. Now you want to borrow money off me. If you don't stop pestering me, the governor will hear of it and you will be turned over to the authorities."

There was a sound of footsteps on the gangplank and Li went out. River Rat hid behind the cabin door to listen.

CHAPTER 95

A Treacherous Man and Woman Are Secretly Put to Death.
Two Murderers Are Finished Off by a Chivalrous Knight.

A page delivered a note to Li Pingshan saying it was from the second mistress. After reading it, he said: "Tell her I'll be there late tonight." It so happened that Li Pingshan was the concubine Clever's secret lover, who had fled when they were discovered by Peony and her maid.

"So, he's that kind of a man," thought River Rat and lay on his bunk pretending to be sound asleep. Li Pingshan pored over the note in a transport of joy and reclined on his own bunk to wait. When night came, he quietly got up and crossed over to the boat where Mistress Clever lay waiting. River Rat followed and slid the gangplank into the water after boarding the boat. He crept to the cabin where the two lovers were and listened to their love-making.

"Thief," he shouted in a loud voice. "There's a thief on the boat!" He then slid back into the water while the chief steward, Jin Fulu, and the other attendants searched the boat. Li Pingshan hurried onto the deck to make his way to his own boat only to find the gangplank was missing. He was captured and taken to Jin Hui who noticed his clothes were all in disarray and guessed what had taken place.

He walked to Clever's cabin and called out: "Are you asleep, Madam Clever?" He entered and by the lantern light saw his concubine's tousled hair and flushed cheeks. A pair of men's boots were by the side of the bed. Jin Hui pretended not to notice but asked: "Where is your maid Xinghua?"

"I thought you might join me so I sent her to her own quarters," she answered and kicked Li's shoes under the bed.

"That's very thoughtful of you," he answered. "Let's go and see her, because there is a thief about and then we'll return together."

They went on board and suddenly he gave her a push and she fell into the water. Only when she did not come up again, did he shout out: "Help! The madam has fallen overboard!" But it was too late.

He then ordered his steward to return Li Pingshan to his own boat, knowing full well what had taken place. But he did not want the scandal to get about and decided to let him go. When Li Pingshan got back to his cabin he noticed River Rat's clothes on the bed and said to himself: "Has he got a lover as well?" But soon, with a lot of noise and shouting, River Rat appeared, shivering with cold. "I went to relieve myself and fell in the water," he said. River Rat changed into dry clothes while Li sat rubbing his hands, shaking his head and wiping his eyes. He regretted that the escapade had lost him the chance of a position with the governor, and blamed himself for Clever's death. He had been too impatient and should have waited until his position was assured. There would have been plenty of time then to resume relations with Clever, he mused.

He told River Rat that he had decided against the position with Governor Jin and would be going with him to Xiangyin after all. "The poor wretch," thought River Rat. "He's still talking big. Such a low person chopping and changing all the time should be done away with."

The boat set sail with Li Pingshan sighing, neither eating nor sleeping. At sundown the two Weng brothers hid the boat in the reeds and Li, now very tired, decided to turn in early.

"You'll sleep soundly tonight, I can assure you," muttered River

Rat. "I should save him from those two boatmen but he caused the death of a woman. I may as well let those two finish him off and then I'll kill them. This way I'll kill three birds with one stone."

He went onto the roof of the cabin and after a while the two boatmen entered the cabin. He heard a thud and knew Li Pingshan was done for. As Weng Da emerged from the cabin, River Rat flung a padded coat over his head, took the struggling man's sword from his hand, struck him with it and he fell into the water. The other brother was so intent on looking for his second victim that River Rat was able to thrust the sword into his throat and kill him.

He entered the cabin and found Li's body sprawled on the bed. He sighed and wrenched open his box. It contained a hundred and sixty taels of silver.

"I'm sorry, Pingshan. I'm not taking the money for nothing. I've revenged your death so you ought to thank me for it."

He put the silver into his bag, satisfied that he had made up for the money he had lost on the boat when he was with Ai Hu. He packed his bags and sculled the boat over to the bank where he jumped off and pushed the boat adrift.

The sky was getting light as he strode along the road. It became windy and clouds of dust began to blow up which blinded him. Tired out from a sleepless night he looked for somewhere to rest. He came to a cemetery surrounded by tumbledown walls and decided to take shelter. He saw an emaciated and haggard boy, cheeks wet with tears, making a noose.

"What do you want to hang yourself for?" he called.

"I'm just a mere boy and not worth anything," he answered.

"Well, you shouldn't hang yourself in a cemetery," River Rat said.

"I'll have to hang myself somewhere else then," the boy replied and made to leave.

"Come back," called River Rat, "and tell me why you want to kill yourself."

The boy wiped his tears and told him his story.

"Young as he is," thought River Rat, "he has high aspirations."
He said: "If I give you some travelling money, will you kill
yourself?"

"If I have money, what do I want to die for?" he asked.

River Rat fished out two silver ingots and handed them to him.

"Don't say any more," said River Rat. "Get to Changsha as
soon as possible."

The boy left and River Rat continued his journey to Sleeping
Tiger Gully, where Sha Long told him that Northern Hero and the
others had gone to Xiangyang to help the imperial inspector Yan
Shenmin to apprehend the prince. River Rat decided to cut his
losses and return to Kaifeng where he reported the latest develop-
ments to Prime Minister Bao and the emperor. "His chivalrous behaviour really is admirable," commented the latter and dispatched
his royal guards, Southern Hero, Royal Cat, Sky Rat and others
to Xiangyang. The order for Northern Hero to attend the Kaifeng
Prefecture was temporarily rescinded.

CHAPTER 96

The Young Scholar Is Arrested on Suspicion of Murder.
The Body of the Drunken Victim Is Found.

THE boy whom River Rat had saved from suicide was the scholar Shi Jun's page, Jinjian. After they were framed by Mistress Clever, and Lord Jin had rudely told them to go home, the scholar was so upset that he fell ill with typhoid fever and they were forced to put up at an inn. Jinjian kept vigil night and day, nursing him and spending all the money they had on medicines and payment to the avaricious innkeeper. When Shi Jun recovered, his young page fell ill and it was his turn to be nurse. Most of the money had gone and he had to pawn his clothes and sell his horse. By the time he had paid off the innkeeper, he had only a tael of silver left.

He was on his way from the pharmacy when he met a grain merchant, named Li Cun, and his friend Zheng Shen. It was market day and they were drinking in a tavern. They invited the scholar to sit with them. When they heard about his troubles, Li Cun generously lent him ten taels of silver with a promise of more if it was needed.

Zheng Shen became very drunk and his friend, knowing he carried a vast sum of money, was worried he would not reach home safely. The grateful Shi Jun offered to see him home and as Li Cun had other business to attend to, he happily accepted.

Verily, trouble often results from being too eager to please. Shi Jun should not have seen Zheng Shen home because as a result he got into trouble with the law.

As they neared Zheng Shen's home, he persuaded Shi Jun that he was able to make the last few steps unaided, and as the scholar was anxious about his young page, he reluctantly left him.

With the money he had been given by Li Cun, he was able to send for the doctor and buy more medicine and Jinjian rapidly recovered.

Two days went by and they were preparing to continue their journey when Shi Jun was arrested and taken to the magistrate's office where he was accused of doing away with Zheng Shen.

Magistrate Fang was impressed with Shi Jun's honest answers to the questions put to him and instead of having him tortured, imprisoned him.

The young page Jinjian felt there was nothing he could do. He had no money, was too weak to travel back to his master's family and was on his way to seek the help of the honest and upright governor in Changsha but gradually became too weak to carry on and in despair decided to hang himself. That was when River Rat found him and lent him the money. Truly, money boosts a man's morale: he reached Changsha in no time and lodged an appeal with the governor, Lord Shao, who was the sworn brother of Shi Jun's father.

He lost no time in hearing Jinjian's story and ordered the magistrate who had imprisoned Shi Jun to organise a search party to find the missing Zheng Shen. As they scoured the countryside they noticed a flock of ravens above the Fragrant Emerald Pond which led them to a body.

Zheng Shen's wife identified it as her husband's. He had finger marks round his neck and had been strangled before being thrown into the pond. There were seven households including Zheng Shen's which were situated near the Fragrant Emerald Pond and Magistrate Fang decided to bring them all to Changsha to be questioned before Lord Shao. They knelt before him and waited. "A wronged person came to me last night and lodged an appeal," he said. "He told me who the offender was. I have marked the name on this list. All of you get up except the guilty one." He pretended to make a mark.

They all rose to their feet except one named Wu Fu.

"Now make a full confession," ordered Lord Shao.

CHAPTER 97

The Scholar Gets Married. The Emperor's Emissary Is Captured by the Bandits of Black Wolf Mountain.

THE thief Wu Fu confessed to throttling Zheng Shen and throwing his body into the pond. He had taken the sack of silver and buried it. He was taken away to await execution and the silver was recovered and restored to the widow. The rest of the villagers, including Li Cun, were released but the governor discovered that Shi Jun was the son of his best friend, the blind Shi Qiao, and made him stay so he could hear all the news of his friend as well as of his other friend, Governor Jin Hui.

Jinjian warned his young master not to reveal the reasons for quarrelling with Jin Hui, the newly promoted Governor of Xiangyang. So the scholar gave an account of his recent adventures and made Jin Hui's recent promotion to governor the excuse for leaving suddenly.

Governor Shao was much taken by the his old friend's son, his modesty and gentle demeanour, and was happy to hear of the proposed marriage with Peony, the daughter of his other great friend.

He clapped his hands with excitement and said: "It so happens that your fianceé is here with me. I rescued her from the river robbers and as she is the daughter of my sworn brother and you the son of another sworn brother it falls to me to arrange the marriage."

He instructed his wife to make the arrangements. The maid Jiahui, still pretending to be Peony, was plunged into grief as she thought of her poor drowned mistress and the trouble she herself was now involved in, but was too frightened to admit that she was only a servant.

The nuptial day arrived and guests assembled for the sumptuous feast. Shi Jun was decked out in bridegroom clothes and the bride sent to the bridal chamber. The young Jinjian decided to have a peep at the new bride, who quickly tried to hide her face behind a fan.

"Ho, ho," thought Jinjian. "Why, it is the maid Jiahui."

He was about to call out when she put down the fan and told him how Nanny Liang had persuaded them to change places for safety's sake.

"What's done cannot be undone," she said. "If by good fortune, my mistress is alive, I will gladly give up the pretence."

Jinjian said no more and decided to search for the whereabouts of the real mistress.

When Governor Jin Hui heard of the marriage between what he thought was his daughter Peony and Shi Jun he was most displeased and thought that his old friend Shao had taken advantage of their friendship. But as he was on his way to take up office in Xiangyang, he could do nothing except smoulder with anger.

They were approaching an area called Red Stone Cliff when a number of bandits blocked their way. In the middle of the line was a sallow-complexioned man on a tawny horse. He had a sunken face, golden eyes under bushy eyebrows and a chin covered with a curly yellow beard. He held two maces in his hands. No wonder he was known as Gold-Face God. The governor's steward, Jin Fulu, and the entourage with the governor's wife all fled, while their master and his companion, Ding Xiong, were captured. "Lan Xiao is inviting you to the mountain for a talk," bellowed Gold-Face God, and he took them to his mountain lair. There Lan Xiao was seething with rage at Sha Long's rescue of the fishermen and the lady Peony. When Ge Yaoming returned and reported that Sha Long had also rescued the governor's wife and her entourage, he placed the captive Governor Jin Hui in a secure place and together with his men made his way down to Red Stone Cliff.

On seeing his adversary, Lan Xiao roared: "Squire Sha, I've treated you generously. Why are you meddling in my affairs? I have a grudge against Governor Jin and now I hear you have snatched his dependants and placed them under your care."

Sha Long retorted: "Governor Jin is a fourth-rank official of the government. You have no right to intercept him and his party. Release him to me and I will intercede on your behalf for mercy."

This only made Lan Xiao even more angry and he shouted: "I'll fight you until only one of us is left!"

A desperate battle took place. Sha Long had the help of the two warrior maidens, Autumn Sunflower and Phoenix Sprite, who dispatched Ge Yaoming, first blinding him with iron shot and then smashing his head with an iron staff. "That will teach him to flirt with us and steal our pheasant," said Autumn Sunflower.

Despite the help of his brothers and daughters, Sha Long — Iron-Face Guardian — and his group were outnumbered by Lan Xiao's men and were trapped in Red Stone Cliff.

CHAPTER 98

Mother and Daughter Are Reunited. Black Fox and the Gallants Go to the Rescue of Iron-Face Guardian.

GOVERNOR Jin's wife and entourage were escorted to Sleeping Tiger Gully where the fishermen and hunters crowded round to see the august persons rescued by Sha Long. The old fisherman, Zhang Li, and his wife were entrusted to take care of Madam Jin and her young son. Mrs Zhang was very proud of her beautiful adopted daughter Peony, and lost no time in taking her to see Madam Jin, who instantly fell into her arms, weeping with joy at finding her long-lost daughter.

As mother and daughter related all their adventures, Northern Hero, Black Fox and the Ding brothers arrived. They had reached Xiangyang only to find that the prince had entered an alliance with his followers. He had pinned the agreement on top of a high tower and deployed his men in the shape of eight triangles as guards below. Traps had also been set. They hastened to Sleeping Tiger Gully to enlist the help of Sha Long and together they hoped to return to Xiangyang to protect Imperial Inspector Yan who only had Sleek Rat as his guard. When they heard that Sha Long had not returned from his fight with Lan Xiao, they took reinforcements which included Shi Yun, the head fisherman, and hurried off to Red Stone Cliff.

Lan Xiao descended down the cliff and demanded to know who

they were.

"I am Northern Hero, otherwise known as Ouyang Chun," was the answer. "How dare you intercept an imperial government official of the fourth rank? This is a rebellious act!"

Northern Hero swung his rare seven-treasure scimitar and Lan Xiao met it with his spiked mace which spun into the air, making him lose his balance. Northern Hero seized him by his leather belt and handed him over to Shi Yun who tied him up. While the fight was taking place, the Ding twin and his followers rushed up the mountain, routed the others and freed Jin Hui. Sha Long's brothers, Meng Jie and Jiao Chi, then finished off the rest of the bandits before the triumphant men returned to Sleeping Tiger Gully.

CHAPTER 99

Father and Daughter Are Reconciled.
An Engagement Is Announced.

AS soon as Governor Jin reached the manor house he was reunited with his wife, but not before the curious villagers noticed his dishevelled appearance, his gauze hat minus a wing, worn-out black boots and his white jade-ornamented belt broken in the struggle with his captors. He presented a sorry figure and the onlookers covered their mouths to suppress sniggers.

When his wife told him that Peony had been found he retorted: "That is impossible. How can there be two Peonies?" He showed her the letter Lord Shao had written.

The mystery was solved when Madam Jin showed him the clothes that Peony had worn when she was rescued — clothes which had belonged to her maid Jiahui.

Governor Jin then realised how unjust he had been to suspect his daughter of impropriety and guessed the part his concubine had played in implicating his friend's son Shi Jun with the handkerchief and goldfish pin.

"What a fool I have been," he thought and felt conscious-stricken at ordering his daughter to commit suicide on such flimsy evidence.

He sent for Peony but she refused to come. So he went to her room where he saw her standing with her back turned. He felt a pang in his heart when he saw her dressed in the simple homespun clothes of a fisherman's daughter.

"Peony, my dear. Your father has wronged you. Anger made me thoughtless."

She remained unmoved until her mother pleaded: "Daughter, please be reasonable. How do you think it would look to your adoptive parents if you treat your own father in this way?"

Peony had no choice but to comply and dropping to her knees she cried out: "Now that you represent the imperial government, please judge any case like mine which come before you clearly and with impartiality. Ordering a girl to commit suicide before finding out the facts is unjust."

Jin Hui reddened with shame but he accepted her criticism with dignity and promised to heed her words. He then left to thank Northern Hero and the others for rescuing him and apprehending the bandits. He arranged for Lan Xiao to be incarcerated at Sleeping Tiger Gully until he reached Xiangyang where he would get proof of his conspiracy with the prince and then have him sent to Kaifeng and Prime Minister Bao. It was decided that Sha Long, Northern Hero and the Ding twin should remain to guard Lan Xiao in case the prince sent men to rescue him. Governor Jin and his party should proceed to Xiangyang accompanied by Black Fox.

There was much sadness at the imminent departure. Peony's adoptive parents, Zhang Li and his wife, wept at losing their newly-acquired daughter but quickly recovered when Madam Jin suggested they accompany them to Xiangyang. Peony, Autumn Sunflower and Phoenix Sprite were also heartbroken at being separated but Governor Jin honoured Sha Long by adopting Autumn Sunflower as his daughter, which also made Sha Long a sworn brother of the governor, and as Phoenix Sprite was promised to Ai Hu, it didn't need too much for her uncle Jiao Chi to suggest to Sha Long that they speed up the official engagement.

A grand feast was arranged before the governor and his party left for Xiangyang.

Sha Long as the host said: "We are celebrating four happy events today. First, the governor is reunited with his family."

"I'll drink to that," said Jiao Chi.

"Second, as brothers Northern Hero and Black Fox are with us, we can decide on our son's and daughter's wedding today. From now on we three families are related. Betrothal gifts can be settled later."

"Wonderful, I'll drink to that too," replied Jiao Chi. "In fact, I'll drink two bowls. One for brothers Northern Hero and Black Fox and the other for Brother Sha Long."

"The third happy event," continued Sha Long, "is that the governor will be taking up his new office tomorrow."

"Brother Sha is getting his money's worth, I'm thinking," remarked Jiao Chi, "but I'll drink to that too."

"What's the fourth?" asked Meng Jie.

"The governor who has adopted my daughter Autumn Sunflower has also become a relative of ours and Phoenix Sprite is now the daughter-in-law of brothers Northern Hero and Black Fox, so we three families are related. Mr and Mrs. Zhang adopted Peony so those two families are related as well. All our families are assembled today, isn't that a happy event?"

This time Jiao Chi did not drink but looked sour. "Where do I come in, in this happy family?" he asked.

"Don't you see," laughed the Ding twin, "when the girls are married, their fathers will become fathers-in-law and we'll be uncles of their daughters."

Everyone laughed and the merry-making continued until late.

The next day, Governor Jin and his party set out with Black Fox for Xiangyang, while Northern Hero and the others stayed behind to wait for the memorial to the emperor to arrive to escort Lan Xiao to the capital.

CHAPTER 100

The Treacherous Prince Sends Out His Assassins.
Young Ai Hu Encounters the Scholar's Page.

YOUNG Ai Hu, who left Sleeping Tiger Gully for Xiangyang, had abstained from alcohol while he was with his future in-laws in order to make a good impression, but now free from restraint, he put up at an inn after travelling for half a day and drank so much wine he did not come to his senses until three days later.

"This is not good enough," he said to himself. "If I slip back to the time when I was on my way to Sleeping Tiger Gully, I shall never find Northern Hero and the others." He was full of remorse and in his hurry he took the wrong road and lost his way.

When he finally reached Xiangyang, he asked at every inn whether they had stayed there, but to no avail. He did not know that his friends had avoided staying in public places and had lodged at monasteries and temples to put the prince off the scent.

The people of Xiangyang were waiting for the new inspection commissioner, Yan Shenmin, Prime Minister Bao's protégé, so they could bring up their grievances against the prince. They also talked of the prince's alliance with renegades and bandits. Ai Hu, from his vantage point of a two-storeyed restaurant opposite, noticed the Sky-Scraping Building which the prince had built with a formidable trap beneath made of a brass net.

One day as he was keeping watch on the prince's mansion, he

noticed two men arrive on horseback. A man came running out and started whispering to them. It looked very suspicious and Ai Hu decided to follow the two men when they left. At the fork of the road, one said to the other: "We'll meet at the Ten-Li Fort outside the city of Changsha." They then galloped off, one to the east and the other to the west. Ai Hu recognised them as former acquaintances in the Talent-Assembling Hall. One was the evil-minded Fang Diao, who had lost his fight with Northern Hero and escaped to Xiangyang to join the treacherous prince, while the other was Shen Zhongyuan, who had decided that he would be more useful to the imperial court if he pretended to support the prince, paying lip-service to all the evil doings and plans so that his inside knowledge would be of value to the emperor. He was a brave and intelligent man, hiding his true chivalrous qualities. While Southern Hero Zhan Zhao, Northern Hero Ouyang Chun, twin brothers Ding Zhaolan and Ding Zhaohui and Ai Hu openly succoured the needy and rescued those in danger and were praised for their heroic deeds, Shen Zhongyuan had to hide his true colours.

He was in the Talent-Assembling Hall when the prince heard of Lan Xiao's arrest and was debating what his next move should be. "I haven't started the insurrection yet," he said, "but a wing has been clipped. I had hoped that Lan Xiao would kill Governor Jin but now Northern Hero has thwarted my plans, what other way is there?"

"There's no point in killing just Jin Hui," said one of his co-horts. "The emperor has dispatched Yan Shenmin as inspector to Xiangyang and appointed Shao Bangjie as Governor of Changsha."

"They are like tigers waiting to pounce on us. If you plan on murder you might as well kill all three."

The prince decided this was a good idea. Jin Hui would have to pass through Changsha before reaching Xiangyang where the local authorities greeted officials in a place called Ten-Li Fort. If Jin

Hui was assassinated there, the governor Shao Bangjie would be blamed, the inspecting commissioner Yan Shenmin would also be implicated and this in turn would reflect on the character of Prime Minister Bao.

The plan highly delighted the prince and he decided to send Fang Diao to carry out the deed. Shen Zhongyuan stepped forward and volunteered to accompany Fang Diao, pretending that it needed two men to make sure the assassination was carried out successfully. The prince was very pleased to have such a loyal man to serve him and told them to saddle two horses from his stables. They rode to the fork in the road where Ai Hu recognised them as his former acquaintances at the Talent-Assembling Hall and decided to hurry to the Ten-Li Fort ahead of them. When he got there he found the place adorned with lanterns and festoons to welcome the Governor of Xiangyang, Jin Hui. The local governor, Shao Bangjie, looked forward to meeting his old friend.

Ai Hu was worried about how he could protect the two governors from the imminent danger. As he walked the streets he bumped into the young page Jinjian who greeted him warmly, remembering how kind Ai Hu had been when his master Shi Jun had fallen ill. "But for the silver ingots you gave me, how could my young master have recovered from his illness?"

Jinjian then told Ai Hu about all their adventures after he left them, including the incident when, on the brink of suicide, he had been rescued by River Rat — Jiang Ping — and thus had been able to make his way to Changsha.

Ai Hu was beside himself with joy when he heard that River Rat was safe. Jinjian also confessed to Ai Hu his part in deceiving his master into marrying the false Peony. Ai Hu little knew that the daughter adopted by Zhang Li at the Green Duck Beach was in fact the real Peony. The two men returned to where Shi Jun with his wife, the maid Jiahui, were staying and the group decided to make sacrifices on the bank of the river for Peony's soul.

CHAPTER 101

Mistress and Maid Meet Again and Are United in Marriage.
Assassins Lie in Wait for the Governor.

THE group changed into white mourning clothes and prepared to make sacrificial offerings on the river bank. Jiahui wept as she thought of her beloved mistress Peony, and her husband Shi Jun also wept. After the offerings were burnt to ashes, they calmed down and began to enjoy the scenery around the river. A boat passed by carrying Governor Jin Hui and his family. Madam Jin thought she recognised the party on the shore and her heart missed a beat, but she dismissed them from her mind, not wanting to upset her daughter or husband any further.

"There are many people in the world who look alike," she said to herself. The boat went on and berthed at Changsha, where Governor Shao welcomed his old friend and brother with great affection. Later that evening the two men reminisced about old times and Shao Bangjie told him about the marriage of Shi Jun and Jiahui and the reasons why the maid had pretended to be Peony.

Shi Jun was surprised and happy when Governor Shao told him of Peony's reappearance. "I've explained to Brother Jin today about your marriage to Jiahui and he is very sorry for all the misunderstanding and wants to conclude the marriage agreement between you and Peony as soon as possible."

Shi Jun readily consented and bowed his thanks. He went to his own quarters and told Jiahui about her mistress's rescue and she in turn explained why she had taken Peony's place and said she was ready to resume her old position and serve them both. She knelt down and kowtowed. Shi Jun hastily raised her from her knees.

It was late that night when Black Fox emerged from the monastery where he had been hiding out with Northern Hero and patrolled the streets. He went to the side of a house where he caught sight of a figure on the roof. He crouched down and sprang silently onto the roof where he noticed a man sitting with his back towards him. In the opposite direction he noticed another figure lying across the eaves looking downwards. It was Fang Diao.

"This looks very fishy," Black Fox said to himself, but before he could move, another figure, short but very agile, appeared and silently removed a brick from under the left foot of the man lying across the eaves. It was Ai Hu who swung his sword and hit the man's shoulder. The latter gave a cry and fell, which alarmed the other man. "Stop assassin!" Ai Hu cried and gave chase as the second man leapt from the roof and over a wall into the surrounding wood. There he saw his master Black Fox holding the man. It was Shen Zhongyuan. There was a happy reunion when they recognised each other and Shen had nothing but praise for the young Ai Hu. "His movements are really agile. How quick and dextrous his hand when drawing the blade out of the scabbard," he said.

Black Fox agreed but added that his protégé had been a little too rash and if he hadn't been on the roof and had got Shen Zhongyuan before Ai Hu, his young brave would have been ambushed.

Shen explained the reasons why he had joined the Prince of Xiangyang and Black Fox had to agree that his decision to stay could be valuable in eventually defeating the treacherous prince.

Shen Zhongyuan then took his leave of the two men and returned to Xiangyang while Black Fox and Ai Hu took the captive Fang Diao before governors Shao and Jin. Fang confessed he had been sent by the prince to assassinate Governor Jin Hui.

The marriage between Shi Jun and Peony was formalised and bridegroom, new bride and the maid — now given the position of concubine — prepared to leave for the scholar's home, accompanied by his page Jinjian and Ai Hu to protect them on their journey.

CHAPTER 102

Sleek Rat Reconnoitres the Sky-Scraping Tower.
Black Fox Takes a Second Look at the Brass Net Trap.

WHEN Commissioner Yan Shenmin arrived in Xiangyang, he at once began receiving the complaints of the victims of the prince. The prince had taken their land and kidnapped their wives and children, training some of them as actors and actresses. Commissioner Yan comforted them and promised he would look into their grievances, but asked them to be patient and not to publicise their meeting with him, lest the prince hear and take measures to silence them. But spies told the prince what the commissioner was planning and he was furious. "I am the uncle of the emperor. Just because he is a protégé of Prime Minister Bao, how dare Yan have the audacity to try to apprehend me?"

He racked his brains to find ways of trapping the commissioner and of consolidating the uprising against the emperor. "My influence has spread far and wide," he thought, "and the Imperial Government has got wind of it. I must make the alliance with the insurgents more secure and make sure that no one can prove anything against me."

He ordered his followers, gallants and knaves to guard the Sky-Scraping Tower day and night and made ready every contrivance leading to its trap. Archers and spearmen were at the ready at all times. If there was any unaccountable noise, the tower alarm gongs would sound. But they underestimated the resourcefulness of Bai Yutang — Sleek Rat. He heard of the Brass Net Trap in the shape of eight trigrams and in the still of the night jumped over several walls until he reached the Sky-Scraping Tower and felt its walls, built of wood on a stone base. Above, embrasures bristled with sharp spikes. In the middle of the wall there were three tightly shut doors. He went to the other side where there were also three tightly shut doors. All the sides were the same.

"There are eight sides in all," he thought to himself, "and each side has three doors. Every three doors must stand for one pattern of the eight trigrams. What a pity I don't know what the date is today, otherwise I would know which door will open." He was about to leave when he heard a gong sounding and the beats of a clapper. He hid behind the watchmen's shed and listened in to the watchmen as they argued who should do the rounds. As none of the doors were likely to be opened that day, Sleek Rat returned home.

The next day, Governor Jin Hui arrived in Xiangyang and reported to Commissioner Yan Shenmin on the capture of Lan Xiao and the assassin Fang Diao, giving him the proof he needed to implicate the prince. Yan immediately sent men to take the two murderers to Changsha for trial and wrote a memorial to the throne.

Now his task of escorting Governor Jin Hui to Xiangyang was over, Black Fox had some time on his hands and together with the old fisherman, Zhang Li, took a walk. They reached a precipitous mountain covered with dark luxuriant trees. It was called Square Mountain and on the top stood a monastery surrounded by vermilion walls topped with green-glazed tiles. Under the mountain was a deep winding pool with clear rippling water. In a bend of the pool there was a terrace and a stone path leading to a pavilion from which, the local people told them, an immortal had emerged. Although the buildings were dilapidated, there was a certain charm about the place, as if some celebrity long past had resided there.

Black Fox thought it was a good hiding place for putting up people bold enough to speak against the prince and for the governor in
case of emergency. He told his plan to the governor who thought
it a good idea and immediately organised workmen to start renova-
tions.

Black Fox decided to take another look at the Sky-Scraping
Tower and the Brass Net Trap. At midnight he reached the wood-
en tower and noticed the three doors that Sleek Rat had seen the
night before, except that in one set of three doors the middle one
was open; another set had two doors open with the middle one
shut. "Now I see," said Black Fox. "The doors are spheres repre-
sented by varied permutations of eight trigrams: Heaven, Earth,
Mountain, Thunder, Water, Fire, Wind and Vapour. I'll go into
the middle door and see what takes place."

Inside he found plank walls, slanted and upright in different
shapes and sizes. There were numerous doors set along tortuous
and winding walls. He meant to go east, but actually he was led to
the west. When going south, he was stepping towards the north.
Some of the doors were genuine, some false, some opened, some
closed. One of the passages led through but the other was blocked.
One was open the other concealed. There were all kinds of different obstacles.

"Really redoubtable!" said Black Fox. "It's lucky no one else is
hiding here. If I was attacked I wouldn't be able to find my way
out."

He heard a snap and something hit the plank wall, then dropped
to the floor as if someone had thrown a brick or a tile from the
other side. He looked but found no one and marched forward until
he reached a door. Something came whizzing toward him and fell
on the ground. He picked it up and found it was a small stone.

He recognised it as the kind that Sleek Rat used and he crouched
down and hid behind the door, in case more stones were thrown.

"It's me, Zhi Hua," he called out.

Sleek Rat then emerged from his hiding place. Both men admitted that they were completely lost in the labyrinth. They were discussing what to do when another voice called out. It was Shen Zhongyuan whose turn it was to be on guard duty. He guided them through many doors until they reached the Sky-Scraping Tower.

"We can rest here a while," he said. "It's lucky I was on guard duty today." He warned them of the contrivances and traps the prince had set for any unwary intruder which would kill them.

"Do you want us to give up just because of those traps?" asked Sleek Rat.

"We must bide our time," said Shen, "and wait until I have discovered how to break the traps; then we can storm the tower."

He added: "It's the fifth of the fifth today. That means the Heavenly Stem Thunder represents male; Vapour female, the eighth trigram. We should turn left and go on until we find the way out. Thunder is the fourth trigram. Should we turn right and go wrong, we would find all the doors shut and we would never escape from here. Although the outside is constructed with the eight trigrams, the inside has sixty-four hexagrams. They are so designed in order to indicate Halt, Life, Wound, Block, Sunlight, Death, Shock and Opening. Every hexagram has a distinctive pattern; you'll find no fault in them."

He saw them safely to the exit and bade farewell and Sleek Rat made his way to the commissioner's office while Black Fox returned to the inn where he was staying.

Commissioner Yan still had many accusations against the prince to settle but knew he had to be very careful. Gongsun Ce had discovered that the prince knew of their movements and was guarding himself from any possible attack. "We must be vigilant at all times," he said to Sleek Rat, who was feeling rather low at not being able to penetrate the Brass Net Trap.

He turned to Gongsun Ce's page Yumo, warning him to safeguard the commissioner's seal at all costs, telling him how easy it would be to steal it, as easy as when he had stolen the three rare treasures from the Kaifeng Prefecture.

Sleek Rat then said goodnight to Commissioner Yan, Gongsun Ce and Yumo and returned to his own room.

CHAPTER 103

Sleek Rat Is Annoyed and Leaves the Commissioner's Office.
River Rat Searches for the Lost Gold Seal.

SLEEK Rat spent two sleepless nights, tossing and turning, labouring under a sense of foreboding. His mind raced over past events and wondered what the future held. Finally on the second night he rose from his bed, got dressed, slung his bag of pebbles over his shoulder and with sword in hand patrolled the courtyard from east to west. A hubbub of voices cried out: "Fire!" He rushed toward the blaze and saw a man standing on the roof of the main hall. He took a pebble from his bag and aimed it at the figure who fell but then stood up again. It was a dummy made of leather and was a decoy.

"Curse it," he said to himself.

Yumo was in the middle of the people trying to put out the fire.

"Why aren't you guarding the seal?" Sleek Rat called out.

Yumo slapped his hand to his brow with a cry of anguish. They hurried to the hall. Too late — the box with the seal had gone.

Sleek Rat rushed out of the yamen and saw two men fleeing before him. He fired one of his pebbles and it hit the box which one of the men was carrying. He fell and Sleek Rat pinned him down with his foot. At the same time he aimed another pebble at the second man who took to his heels leaving his companion to the tender mercies of Sleek Rat.

The thief with the box holding the seal was marched off to Commissioner Yan and Gongsun Ce, with a trembling Yumo standing beside them.

The thief was called Cloud-Rending Petrel or Dumpling Shen Hu, a short dumpy man with a bloodstained face. His companion was no other than Crack Archer Deng Che.

They decided to open the box to check that the seal was safe. Sleek Rat was a little contemptuous of Gongsun Ce's naivety. The latter had suggested that quite a period of time elapsed after the box was stolen and it seemed a little too heavy to hold just a seal. Sleek Rat retorted: "I'm just a rough fellow, not as prudent and thoughtful as you. Let's see what is inside."

Yumo opened the box and removed a yellow bundle which he unwrapped. He then relapsed into another fit of trembling as it revealed a piece of scrap-iron.

Sleek Rat, furious, wanted to torture the truth out of Cloud-Rending Petrel but Gongsun Ce was far more cunning and decided to worm out the whereabouts of his companion by flattery and soft words. He had the man's shackles removed and said: "It's a pity such a man as you should be sold."

"I came here on the orders of the prince," Cloud-Rending Petrel replied. "Why do you say I have been sold?"

"Why," replied Gongsun Ce looking surprised, "both of you were ordered to do the same job, but why were you given the box while Crack Archer Deng Che took the seal? He'll get the credit while you were captured with a worthless piece of iron. He didn't even try to rescue you."

Gnashing his teeth, Cloud-Rending Petrel saw what a fool he had been and wanted to get his own back on his treacherous friend.

Gongsun Ce ordered snacks and wine and sat with Cloud-Rending Petrel who told him that they had overheard Bai Yutang tell Yumo to guard the seal and they had started the fire to draw him away. "If I had known Crack Archer Deng Che had removed the seal and put in a piece of iron, I could have thrown the box away and escaped."

He told Gongsun Ce that the prince planned to throw the seal into Dongting Lake where there was a Counter-Current Spring so deep that no one would be able to retrieve it.

Commissioner Yan and Gongsun Ce were dismayed, at a loss what to do and even more worried when they discovered Bai Yutang had disappeared saying that he was off to find the seal and would not return without it.

For the next few days, Commissioner Yan was unable to eat or do anything, sighing all the time. If Gongsun Ce had not been on hand, his public duties would have suffered.

Five days later, Southern Hero, Sky Rat, his brothers Earth Rat, Mountain Rat and River Rat arrived. "Where is that fifth brother of ours, Sleek Rat?" asked Lu Fang — Sky Rat.

When he was told that Sleek Rat had left after the loss of the seal, River Rat managed to reassure everyone saying that he would be the ideal person to hunt for the seal in the Counter-Current Spring in Dongting Lake. Sky Rat went as his companion and when they reached the lake, River Rat took off his clothes and gave them to Sky Rat to look after while he plunged into the water. Sky Rat decided to wait by a nearby monastery where there were five gods of wealth. He put the bundle of clothes on the altar and sat on the threshold to enjoy the mountain scenery.

CHAPTER 104

Sky Rat Rescues a Countrywoman in Distress.
He Hears Tragic News.

SKY Rat's quiet contemplation of the mountain scenery was suddenly disturbed by the screams of a woman running towards him, being chased by a soldier.

As the woman ran into the monastery, Sky Rat felled the soldier with a mighty kick and then stamped his foot on his chest.

The terrified soldier begged for mercy and said he was only teasing the woman and hadn't meant any harm.

"I am Liu Libao, petty officer of the fourth rank in the Marvellous Trident-Thrower Chieftain Zhong's Fortress. Two days ago, the prince sent an urn containing the bones of Bai Yutang — known as Sleek Rat — ordering my master to take good care of it. As Bai Yutang is famous as a chivalrous gallant, he is buried under the Five-Peak Mountain by the Nine Pine Trees. I have been ordered with sixteen of my colleagues to make sacrificial offerings at his grave, but the rest went on ahead and I lagged behind and saw this woman."

Sky Rat stood dazed at what he had heard. His brother Sleek Rat dead? He did not hear the rest and the soldier was able to roll away from under his foot and run off. His men were waiting for him at the grave laden with sacrificial offerings. Liu knelt down and burst into tears.

"Fifth Lord Bai, Fifth Lord Bai," he sobbed, "I have come to visit your grave by the order of our chieftain. But for your supernatural powers I would have been beaten to death!"

His men were impatient to finish the sacrificial ceremonies and eat the offerings. They packed the food in boxes and followed the still weeping Liu Libao. Some armed hunters approached the party and Liu quickly made himself scarce. The leaders were two brothers called Lu Bin and Lu Ying and the woman who had been chased was Lu Bin's wife. They were furious and smashed their boxes. "Tell your chieftain that Liu Libao has had the audacity to waylay my wife. If it wasn't for the high regard we have for your chief, we would have wiped you out. Now go!" The men scampered away.

Lu Bin's wife was skilled in weapons and a good huntress. When Liu Libao accosted her she had pretended to run off in a panic but meant to shoot an arrow at him at a convenient place to teach him a lesson. But Sky Rat had thwarted her plans and she went home and told her husband and brother-in-law. After they saw off the chieftain's men, they continued on to the monastery and found Sky Rat distraught with grief. He put off their invitation to go back with them until he found his brothers. He clasped his hands respectfully to them and then headed for the Counter-Current Spring. In the evening he saw a blaze ahead and standing there was Han Zhang — Earth Rat.

"How is River Rat doing?" he asked quietly.

"He's been in twice," replied Earth Rat, "and is chilled to the bone. I have lit a fire to warm him up."

The water was indeed very, very cold and Sky Rat shivered as he gazed sadly into the lake, waiting patiently for River Rat to emerge. After some time, River Rat came spluttering to the surface, struggling to gain a foothold against the strong current. At length he was able with great difficulty to cling to a stone. Earth Rat reached down and dragged him to the bank and then to the fire to recover.

"Don't go in again. Give up the search," Sky Rat begged.

"No, I won't ever go in again," replied River Rat and held out the seal.

"Congratulations!" said voices from beyond the firelight. They were the brothers Lu Bin and Lu Ying. They had followed Sky Rat, worried at his rather depressed state.

They pressed on them to stay at their house to recover, where food and dry clothes were provided and they became better acquainted.

The brothers had been told about the seal by Lei Ying who had confessed to them how he had been ordered to throw the seal into the Counter-Current Spring. They had warned him of the consequences of what he had done and he was sorry but now relieved that River Rat had been able to retrieve the seal

"Does this Lei Ying live in Eight Treasure Village?" asked River Rat.

"Yes," replied a surprised Lu Bin. "Do you know him?"

River Rat said he only knew him by name, having remembered he had rescued a man called Lei Zhen, in an earlier adventure.

Sky Rat had been rather silent during their conversation but suddenly asked: "Is Five Peak Mountain nearby?"

Lu Bin asked why.

Tears coursed down Sky Rat's cheeks as he told the shocked gathering that Sleek Rat was apparently dead and his bones lay at that peak in the Nine Pine Trees area.

River Rat at first thought it was just a rumour and suggested that they hasten back to the commissioner's office and make enquiries.

Early the next morning the three brothers left for the office without delay and returned the seal to a delighted commissioner and a relieved Yumo. But the officials' joy soon turned to tears as they heard about the death of Sleek Rat.

CHAPTER 105

Sleek Rat Meets His Death in the Sky-Scraping Tower.
The Treacherous Prince Feels Threatened.

RIVER Rat made his way to Eight Treasure Village to question Lei Ying about Sleek Rat's death.

"It's a very sad story," said Lei Ying, sighing.

Sleek Rat had decided that if there were men bold enough to steal the commissioner's seal, why couldn't he, with all his brilliance, capture the prince's agreement fluttering defiantly on top of the Sky-Scraping Tower? He did not believe Shen Zhongyuan's warnings about how dreadful the Brass Net Trap was and decided that he was well able to overcome the various contrivances and traps it held.

At the second watch he entered the wooden fortress and managed to get in through the water door. When he came to an obstacle he turned another way, throwing up a rope and pulling himself upwards. He was quite cheered at his success and soon came in view of the Sky-Scraping Tower. He remembered Shen Zhongyuan mentioning a staircase in the northern part of the fortress and sure enough soon came to a narrow staircase. He was about to ascend when a voice challenged him. It was Sick Giant Zhang Hua, who was on guard duty.

He drew out his sword but Sleek Rat was able to trip him up and grab the sword. Though it was extremely heavy and hard to wield he managed to place it against Sick Giant's throat and plunge the weapon in, dispatching him in a trice.

He was observed by another guard named Little Devil Xu Bi who hid behind an iron door. Sleek Rat carried on, using the tip of the sword to prise open a window. It gave access to the inside of the tower, where a bright light shone in the distance. He threw down a pebble which landed with a slight thud on wooden planks, so he leapt down from the window, landed softly on the other side and glided towards the light which came from another eight-sided window frame, smaller and brighter than the last one. He was about to prise it open again when it opened of its own accord and he saw a beam of light which lit up a small case suspended from a beam.

"So the agreement of their alliance is kept there,'" he said to himself. But before he could take another step, the plank beneath him gave way. Dropping the sword, he tumbled over and over downwards until he landed on a contraption which pierced every part of his body with excruciating pain. Sharp blades protruded from every part, from head to toe.

Alarm gongs sounded everywhere and voices called out. "A man has been caught in the Brass Net!"

An order was given to shoot and a swarm of arrows was sent flying into the net until there was no movement left and the body looked like a hedgehog.

Blood dripped down from the net and Little Devil Xu Bi ordered the body to be pulled up. But as the Brass Net was raised, the heavy sword fell through the mesh on Xu Bi's head, cutting him in half.

The prince was informed of Sleek Rat's death in the Brass Net but because Little Devil Xu Bi was dead no one could identify the bloodied corpse at first until Deng Che saw the bag of pebbles which he knew Sleek Rat always carried and cried out: "It's none other than Sleek Rat, Bai Yutang, who wreaked havoc in the eastern capital. He is one of Commissioner Yan Shenmin's assistants."

The prince was happy and ordered Sleek Rat's remains to be put into a stone jar and handed over to Zhong Xiong to bury.

River Rat shed more tears as he realised that what Liu Libao had told him was true. Sleek Rat was well and truly dead.

"Brother," he said to Lei Ying, "what is that treacherous prince's next move?"

"At the moment," he answered, "he is wallowing in sensual pleasures of the flesh but hasn't forgotten about his vow to kill the commissioner."

River Rat returned to the commissioner's office and confirmed the death of Sleek Rat. Sky Rat, who had remained very calm and quiet until that moment, now broke down completely and wept inconsolably.

"It's very sad," said River Rat, "but he was always a little too ruthless and cruel and now he has died a tragic death."

While they lamented and wailed over the death of their Rat brother and were discussing how to avenge him, a messenger appeared with a letter from the Prince of Xiangyang. Gongsun Ce read it and said it was not official. "He is only wondering why nothing is happening, but really he is sounding us out about the seal," he said. "I shall send back an acknowledgement and he will be very surprised to find it will be stamped with the seal which he believed lay for all time at the bottom of the lake. He will then be even more determined to take the commissioner's life so we must be extra vigilant."

As expected, the prince was in high dudgeon when he saw the stamp of the official seal and demanded an explanation from Deng Che.

"I stole that seal with great difficulty," he said. "Why not question the man who took the seal to the Counter-Current Spring?"

"Fetch Lei Ying," commanded the prince.

CHAPTER 106

The Attempt on the Commissioner's Life Is Thwarted.
Crack Archer Deng Che Is Captured.

THE prince threw the letter bearing the impression of the seal before the kneeling Lei Ying. "Explain this, if you can," he demanded. "I ordered you to fling the commissioner's seal of authority into the Counter-Current Spring."

Lei Ying replied that as a loyal servant of the prince he wouldn't have dared to disobey. When he was told that it was Deng Che who had accused him, he said sneeringly: "That man! It is he who has been tricked into stealing a worthless piece of iron. He was in such a hurry to be a hero he didn't even check. All my trouble therefore has been for nothing."

Crack Archer Deng Che hung his head in shame and swore that he would kill Commissioner Yan Shenmin with his own hands.

Lei Ying now told him in a mollified tone: "Don't feel bad. It was an easy mistake to make. Let's put our heads together and see what we can do."

Deng Che, however, was still too angry to think clearly and was determined to kill the commissioner. Shen Zhongyuan volunteered to go with him and the prince gave a feast in the Talent-Assembling Hall before they left.

After the first watch the two men made their way to the commissioner's office. Shen was to be on lookout while Deng did the deed. But at the entrance, Shen disappeared. "Hmm," thought Deng Che, "Old Shen talks big but fades away when it comes to danger. No matter, afterwards I can mock his cowardice."

He made his way to the back of the office and saw the east room lit up. He moistened the paper window, poked a small hole and peeped in. He saw the commissioner reading a file, occasionally gazing up at the ceiling to reflect on the case.

Deng Che felt a slight twinge of conscience, thinking that his victim looked like a loyal member of the government and wondering if it was right to make such a move. But he was eager for success and suppressed his scruples.

He tiptoed to the door, drew out his sword, levered it between the crack and slid open the bolt. Putting his sword between his teeth, he pushed open the door and sidled into the room. He was unaware that Sky Rat was waiting for him with his sword at the ready until he noticed the danger by the dim light from a candle. He had but a few seconds to back-track and make a quick getaway, with Sky Rat in hot pursuit. Once over the walls of the commissioner's residence, he hid behind an elm tree as Sky Rat searched the area. A voice whispered: "Brother Deng, don't hide there, hide behind this pine tree."

As Deng Che ran towards the second tree, Sky Rat was able to follow him, wondering at the same time who was the man who had given Deng Che away. Again a voice said: "Brother Deng, you are doing the right thing but be careful of his concealed weapons."

It was Shen Zhongyuan who was warning Sky Rat in this roundabout way of the iron balls which Deng Che had concealed on his person. He shot a dart at the running figure which hit Deng in the shoulder. The Crack Archer ran a little way before his shoulder became numb and he began to grow dizzy as the poison from the dart began to take effect. He collapsed to the ground.

He was carried back to the office where Sky Rat prepared an antidote. As he gradually regained consciousness, Deng muttered:

"Shen Zhongyuan, you have betrayed me and have caused my death."

"Friend Deng," he heard someone say: "You and I are brave and not sentimental men. We should adapt to different circumstances. Take this drink of warm wine."

He opened his eyes and saw a group of men surrounding him. A scrawny-looking man squatted beside him with a cup of wine. "Who are you?" he asked.

"My name is Jiang Ping. Are you brave enough to take this drink from me?"

Deng Che laughed. "So you are the Water Rat. If I am not afraid of swords and axes, why should I fear a cup of wine?" With that he took the cup and drank it down in one gulp.

Another man came forward calling him friend Deng. It was Gongsun Ce, who had dressed up in the commissioner's clothes to trap him. The other members of the group were Sky Rat, Earth Rat and Mountain Rat. "His Excellency the commissioner is being guarded by Royal Cat in another part of the building," Gongsun Ce said.

"Your names are well known to me and I have longed to meet you," said Deng Che.

He was helped up and joined them in drinking and exchanging pleasantries.

When Royal Cat entered the room, Gongsun Ce asked if the commissioner had spent a restful night.

"Not so bad," replied Royal Cat, "but he sometimes dreams of Sleek Rat and then he sheds tears."

At the mention of Sleek Rat, Mountain Rat could not control his anger and yelled at Deng Che: "How did you murder my brother? Own up quickly!"

He was restrained from any further action by his other Rat brothers, unaware that Gongsun Ce was sounding out Deng Che more subtly to get information about the death of Sleek Rat and the prince's plans.

Deng Che, drinking more and more among what he thought were his friends, soon revealed the secrets of the Sky-Scraping Tower. It was the Marvellous Trident-Thrower Zhong Xiong who protected the tower and if he was overpowered, the prince would be destroyed.

Gongsun Ce, now with the knowledge he needed, had Deng Che marched off to prison and retired to his rooms.

The Rat brothers discussed how to retrieve the bones of their murdered brother Sleek Rat and bury them in his native place.

It was River Rat who suggested that he and Earth Rat should be the ones to go as Sky Rat was too emotional, and Mountain Rat was too short-tempered. This did not go down well with Mountain Rat who looked daggers at his brother.

They decided to leave the next day for the Five-Peak Mountain by the Nine Pine Trees where Sleek Rat was buried.

CHAPTER 107

Mountain Rat Begs Royal Cat for Help.
River Rat Falls Ill on His Way to Get the Bones of Sleek Rat.

MOUNTAIN Rat was still seething with anger the next day as River Rat and Earth Rat made preparations for their journey. He felt alone and ignored as Sky Rat was still too grief-stricken to be of much help.

"I'm one of their sworn brothers," he thought. "Why can't I go with them to help? They really don't care about me."

He barged into Royal Cat's room and flung himself down on his knees before him. "Aiya! Brother Zhan. I'm really very upset. Help me please!" He then burst out crying.

The astonished Royal Cat tried to help him up but Mountain Rat refused until he had exacted a promise that he would help him.

"Very well, I promise," said Royal Cat. "Now get up from your knees."

"Since you've promised, you can't back out," said Mountain Rat. He stood up and bowed.

"I'm not being treated as a sworn brother by the others, so I want you to accompany me to the Five-Peak Mountain to get the bones of Sleek Rat."

Royal Cat felt he had been pushed into a corner. "How can a man with such a fiery temper embark on so delicate a task? Now I've promised him I shall have to go with him." He said out loud:

"When shall we go?"

"This very night," was the reply. "My brothers intend to leave the day after tomorrow, so we will leave a day earlier."

Royal Cat left messages telling the others what Mountain Rat was planning, but because of the promise he had made, he was forced to go with him. He suggested that they follow slowly so as not to embarrass Mountain Rat.

Before he left, Mountain Rat went into Deng Che's cell and gouged out his eyes. When the others heard, they were deeply shocked and ordered the jailers to nurse him well, while they discussed the incident into the small hours of the morning.

Later in the morning, Northern Hero and one of the twin heroes, Ding Zhaohui, arrived. After they had taken Gold Face God Lan Xiao and Fang Shuo's Equal Fang Diao to Kaifeng, they had returned to Jasmine Village before setting off to join them. Unfortunately, they had been delayed by the twins' mother's illness. The second twin, Ding Zhaolan, had remained with Madam Ding while the other two set off for Xiangyang. They first paid their respects to Governor Jin Hui at his office where Black Fox told them about the tragic death of Sleek Rat. He then accompanied them to Commissioner Yan Shenmin. The twin Ding Zhaohui and Sky Rat wept together as they reminisced over Sleek Rat. Even Commissioner Yan Shenmin seemed inconsolable and was indisposed.

When River Rat told them of Mountain Rat's cruelty in blinding Deng Che, the newcomers were shocked. "He's been unjustly treated," said Black Fox. But the Ding twin said: "Deng Che has done many things offensive to God and reason, so losing his eyes should not be considered an injustice."

The men decided that they would leave Earth Rat behind to protect Sky Rat and the commissioner's office, make their way to where Sleek Rat's bones had been interred and capture the Marvellous Trident-thrower Zhong Xiong.

On the way, River Rat became ill and decided to rest for a few days while the others continued on their way. He told them to wait for him at a place called Chenqiwang, not far from Dongting Lake, where they could stay with his friends, the brothers Lu Bin and Lu Ying.

River Rat made his way slowly and was forced eventually to seek shelter at an inn where a small wicker basket hung outside the gate.

"Is anybody in?" he called.

A quavering voice answered.

CHAPTER 108

Travellers Are Murdered and Robbed by the Innkeeper.
The Importance of Choosing the Right Husband.

THE gate was opened and River Rat saw an old woman holding a lantern. "I'm too old and weak to stable your horse," she said. He pulled it in and was told to tether it in the courtyard. As he unsaddled the horse, the old woman prepared a room for him. Named Mrs Gan, she was about fifty, and the place was called Divine Tree Crag. She told him that his destination, Chenqiwang, was over forty *li* away towards the west.

He ordered some warm wine which she brought to him in a bowl. River Rat drained it in one draught — and collapsed almost immediately. Who would have thought a ship would capsize in a ditch? Though resourceful and skilful with weapons, he was no match for the old woman. She smiled as she reached out for his bag of money, but a voice called from outside:

"Is anybody in?"

Mrs Gan scolded herself for not removing the white paper lantern from the gate. "I can't drive him away now," she thought. "I'll put him in the other wing."

A young man with his servant stood at the gate. She took them to rooms in the wing of the house away from the north room where River Rat lay drugged.

Mrs Gan was impressed with the young man's graceful figure

and delicate skin and went off to prepare food for him. She took down the lantern from the gate, lest more visitors should turn up demanding rooms. She went to see her daughter and told her about the young man accompanied by his servant. "Put this bag away," she said. "We'll prepare some food and liquor. We have a couple of young pigeons here."   .

Her daughter was called Jade Orchid, distinguished in needlework and skilful with weapons. Although she was already twenty years old, she was not yet engaged to be married. She was ashamed of her mother's criminal ways and often remonstrated with her to stop. Mrs Gan promised that River Rat would be the last one.

As Jade Orchid prepared the food, her mother spoke in praise of the handsome young man. Curious, she took a peep and saw a young man with a fair and smooth complexion, lips red and moist as if with rouge, but he was frowning and looking worried.

"He doesn't look a commoner, more like of noble birth," she thought.

Even the servant with his bushy eyebrows and big eyes was attractive looking.

"You haven't eaten anything today," the servant said to his master. "Why not eat a little now?"

The young man sighed and said he had no appetite.

Mrs Gan entered and suggested he take some wine instead.

Jade Orchid was angry at her mother's knavery and angrily went to her room.

Soon Mrs Gan entered in triumph holding a money bag in her hand.

"Our fortune is made," she said. "This bag is heavier than the last one. Stow it away and help me finish them off."

Jade Orchid turned her back and started to cry. "Father left us enough money to live on. Why do you offend god and reason? Father always said there were three sorts of people we should not drug: monks and priests, convicts and men in distress. We are bound to be found out one day!"

"We live in reduced circumstances," replied her mother. "We need money for your trousseau, to say nothing of a decent coffin for me when I die."

Her daughter was not to be pacified. "How can you rob that young man who is looking so distressed?"

"So that was the reason for my daughter's change of heart," thought Mrs Gan. "Why shouldn't I take him for a son-in-law? That way I'll marry off my daughter and have a man to rely on in future."

The two women decided to revive River Rat, and ask him to act as go-between for Jade Orchid and the young man.

They poured some cold water into River Rat's mouth and he gradually came to. The old woman apologised, saying that she was just a poor old widow woman trying to do her best by her daughter. When she told him her dead husband was called Gan Bao, River Rat said: "Not Gold Head Giant Gan Bao?"

When she said that was indeed her husband and that he had died three years before, River Rat got up at once and bowed. "Elder sister," he said, "your husband was once my guest on Hollow Island, and he and the Fair-Complexioned Judge Liu Qing once helped me in a very difficult matter regarding the imperial court." He bowed again and when Mrs Gan asked him to help in arranging a match between her daughter and the young guest, he readily agreed.

CHAPTER 109

A Corrupt Magistrate Snares a Gallant.
River Rat Acts as Go-Between.

MRS Gan was unaware that she had been overheard by the young man and his servant. They were delighted to see River Rat because in reality they were the sisters Autumn Sunflower and Phoenix Sprite.

Life at Sleeping Tiger Gully had become rather tame after the battle with the prince's co-conspirator Lan Xiao, and when he was captured and sent off to be tried, the sisters and their father, Sha Long, and their uncles had whiled away the time hunting in the mountains.

One day, Sha Long was invited by the local magistrate to be his guest at the county office where he was treated so royally that he became as smug as a cat who had swallowed a canary. What he did not realise was that the Prince of Xiangyang had promised the magistrate ten thousand taels of gold if he could capture him. The magistrate plied Sha Long with wine until he was so drunk that he was unable to stand, let alone walk. So the magistrate gave Sha's page some money and told him to go back without him and let Sha Long stay the night to recover. In the night, the mountain chief was taken to the Prince of Xiangyang while the magistrate chose to make himself scarce, anticipating that the brothers Jiao Chi and Meng Jie would start looking for him.

Once Sha Long was in the prince's hands it was very likely that he would send men to attack Sleeping Tiger Gully, so Autumn Sunflower and Phoenix Sprite decided to disguise themselves as men and make their way to Xiangyang to find their father, while their uncles and their supporters stayed behind to protect the manor.

Fortunately the prince admired Sha Long's gallantry too much to have him put to death; he hoped instead to persuade him to join him in the uprising. So Sha Long was just confined in four rooms. The sisters hoped to enlist the help of Northern Hero and Black Fox who were already in Xiangyang. Phoenix Sprite pretended to be her future husband Ai Hu, while Autumn Sunflower was her page. As they were mountain girls, used to living like men, their feet had not been bound, so the disguise was quite easy to assume and when they put up at Mrs Gan's inn, she was easily duped into thinking they were men.

River Rat was most surprised to see them and after hearing about their father's capture and the reason for their disguise, he fell in with the deception, telling Mrs Gan that Phoenix Sprite was his nephew Ai Hu, the adopted son of Uncle Purple Beard and the disciple of Black Fox.

"My goodness!" exclaimed the old woman. "Truly, the Dragon King Monastery has been inundated with the flood of the Dragon King himself; men of one family did not recognise one another. Northern Hero and Black Fox were friends of my late husband. No wonder Ai Hu is so handsome."

She placed food and drink before them, chatting busily as she plied to and fro, assuring them there was nothing wrong with the wine this time.

River Rat said: "Sister, I haven't seen my nephew Ai Hu for a long time and want to have a good talk with him. So you need not stand on ceremony. If you have business to attend to, please go."

Mrs Gan thought she understood what he meant, that he was going to discuss the betrothal of her daughter to Ai Hu, and left the room.

They talked all through the night on how to resolve the problem. Eventually the practical Autumn Sunflower said: "There are many men who have concubines. I don't think my sister cares very much who will be the wife or the concubine, if Dame Gan's daughter marries Ai Hu as well. I don't think he'll mind either, so we'll all have a jolly time together!"

They all had a laugh and when Dame Gan came in with tea and refreshments, River Rat told her that he would announce the engagement to Northern Hero and Black Fox and they would send betrothal gifts. He gave the excited woman some money to buy paper money to burn for her husband while Phoenix Sprite, still in the guise of Ai Hu, gave her a packet of silver, saying: "This will help you, mother-in-law, to eke out your livelihood, but be sure not to rob anymore."

The old woman blushed and said: "It would be impolite to refuse such a good sum. Set your heart at ease, son-in-law."

The sisters and River Rat then prepared to leave for Chenqiwang to find Northern Hero, Black Fox and the twin Ding Zhaohui before making their way to Xiangyang to rescue Sha Long.

CHAPTER 110

Royal Cat Is Trapped.
Sleek Rat's Bones Are Recovered.

THE two sisters and River Rat made their way slowly towards their destination of Chenqiwang. As Phoenix Sprite was more delicate than her robust sister, Autumn Sunflower, she rode the one horse, while the other two walked behind. They reached Chenqiwang just as the sun was setting and the brothers Lu Bin and Lu Ying came out to greet them.

Northern Hero and the others were already waiting for River Rat rather impatiently and he had to explain the reasons for his delay, including who the two disguised "men" were. Phoenix Sprite was rather tearful as she told them she was seeking their help to rescue her father. The two girls then went to the women's quarters where Lu Bin's wife helped them change into their proper clothes.

River Rat entertained the gathering with his account of Dame Gan and they were sad to hear of her husband's death, as he had been a friend of theirs.

They were about to go to bed when the two pages of Southern Hero and Mountain Rat arrived in haste to report that their masters had been captured by the bandit chief Zhong Xiong. Mountain Rat had rushed up Five Peak Mountain regardless of traps in his eagerness to retrieve Sleek Rat's bones and had fallen into a pit in the shape of a plum flower which had been dug in front of the grave. Southern Hero, following him, had also stumbled into the pit. Zhong Xiong's men had tied them up and taken them to their master.

Zhong Xiong's stronghold was the Dongting Water Fortress in the Army Mountain, strongly fortified with a strong and lethal bamboo palisade. The bamboos were so tough that they could withstand swords and guns and only the highest grade steel blades could cut through them.

They decided to enter the fortress using the Ding twin's steel sword to cut their way through.

The rescue of Sha Long was postponed as he was in no immediate danger from the prince, who was still hoping he would come over to his side.

The four men — River Rat, the Lu brothers and the Ding twin — then made their way across the water by boat to the bamboo palisade. One of them hacked down some of the bamboo but they left sharp points and it was impossible to dig them up, so River Rat slipped into the water and found a narrow gully where a swift current carried him onto the bank. Seeing a light approaching he jumped up into a tree and looked down.

Two men passed by, plotting what they would do with the captive they had been sent to escort to their chief to be killed. River Rat followed them and hid behind a rock to await their return with their prisoner. Soon he saw the light coming towards him. Drawing his sword, he stretched out a foot, tripped up the man with the lantern and with one slash, killed him. He waited for the second and finished him off as well. The prisoner was no other than Mountain Rat, bound in chains, who offered to accompany River Rat to the Water Fortress to rescue Southern Hero. But River Rat was worried about his brother's foolhardiness and therefore told him that he had already been rescued and was safe at Chenqiwang. He was also concerned that Zhong Xiong wouldn't be too happy about Mountain Rat's rescue at his hands and would resent his interference. That was why he lied and said that Southern Hero was already waiting for them at Chenqiwang. They made their way through the bamboo grove and to the boat where the others were waiting for them. The Ding twin also lied to Mountain Rat, telling him that Southern Hero had gone to help rescue Sha Long, which satisfied the gullible hothead.

The next day they discussed how to get into the Water Fortress and win over Zhong Xiong as well as retrieve the bones of Sleek Rat. They sent out scouts to reconnoitre the area who reported that after Mountain Rat's escape, Zhong Xiong had collected his followers, as well as those guarding the grave of Sleek Rat, to search for him. This made it easier for the heroes to organise a party to make their way to Sleek Rat's grave. They would then prepare a proper ceremony with sacrificial offerings to show their respect for their dead friend.

A group headed by River Rat, which included the twin Ding Zhaohui and the Lu brothers, left for the Nine Pine Trees and Five Peak Mountain, going a roundabout way to put off any suspicion, and reached the back of the mountain. Clambering to the top of the highest of the five peaks they found the nine dense green pine trees encircling a deserted mound. River Rat felt a piercing pain in his heart and tears coursed down his cheeks as they dug up a porcelain urn. They were on their way back when they heard someone weeping.

CHAPTER 111

River Rat Is Challenged to Steal a Hairpin.
The Heroes Disguise Themselves as Fishermen.

THE men stopped for a second. "That weeping sound must be the ghost of Sleek Rat making his presence known," said River Rat sadly.

By the light of the moon they saw it came from a man resembling a woodcutter. He looked familiar to River Rat who couldn't place him at first. "Sleek Rat didn't count woodcutters among his circle of close friends," he thought, "so why is he making such a fuss?"

The mourner was saying: "When Fifth Brother Bai was alive, he was famous for his gallantry and high aspirations. What a waste of such a noble being. Where are his sworn brothers who should be avenging his untimely death? Who mourns over his grave? Only me, who disguised himself to come to pay homage."

River Rat then recognised the woodcutter as the Fair-Complexioned Judge Liu Qing. "Brother Liu, do not take on so," he said.

"Don't call me brother," the judge retorted. "Since you are his sworn brother, why haven't you avenged his death?"

"Brother Bai was too impatient and foolhardy and that's why he lost his life," River Rat replied. "We came here first to retrieve his body and take it back to his native home so that his soul should be at peace. Then we will decide how to avenge his death."

Fair-Complexioned Judge Liu was annoyed at his friend Sleek Rat being described as foolhardy. He said angrily: "All you can do is snatch his body like a thief in the night and ignore his courageous deeds." Lu Ying wanted to step in between the two men, but was restrained by the Ding twin Zhaohui. "Let's hear what River Rat has to say to him," he said.

"I am not a learned man, I know," replied River Rat, "but my skill at removing objects is second to none, almost like magic."

"You have just been lucky," sneered the judge, "and you wouldn't be able to put one across me."

"He is an honourable man," thought River Rat. "If I can win him over, he will be useful to me in the future." Aloud he said: "Let's have a wager and see what I can do."

The judge took a pin made of smooth turtle shell from his hair and said: "If you can steal this without my knowing, you can have it."

The two men decided that after the judge had finished his mourning, River Rat would visit his manor and be given three days to steal the hairpin.

Both clasped hands rather coldly to each other and the judge went down the mountain.

The Lu brothers were worried that the judge had set a trap for River Rat and tried to dissuade him from taking up the wager. But River Rat said that the judge was only trying to display his high regard for Sleek Rat. Picking up the urn containing the bones of their friend the men descended the mountain and returned to the manor where Northern Hero was the first to make sacrificial offerings. Afterwards they took refreshments and turned in.

The next morning a letter arrived requesting the Lu brothers to provide some fish for Zhong Xiong, as it would soon be his birthday. Black Fox, who was standing nearby, thought this was a splendid opportunity for him to accompany the brothers into the fortress and reconnoitre.

Black Fox and the Ding twin dressed up as fishermen to accompany the Lu brothers to go by boat into the Water Fortress. They smeared their legs with mud and put on shorts, an apron and straw sandals. Ding even stuck a flower into his hair to make himself look as unlike a warrior as possible. When the Lu brothers saw them dressed in such ragged clothes they burst out laughing, saying: "You look like a rustic Second Brother Wang and a smart Li the Fourth."

"So be it," replied Black Fox. "You can address us as such."

As lowly fishermen they followed the Lu brothers onto the boat taking the crates of fish and shoved off for the Water Fortress. As the boat neared the Five Arch Bridge, they could see banners and flags fluttering round the fortress which bristled with lances and halberds. The fortress and even the rampart and gate were built of huge bamboos. A voice hailed them from inside threatening to shoot, but Black Fox stood up and announced that they were bringing the fish which had been requested by Zhong Xiong.

On the gate he saw a notice asking for strong able-bodied men and thought that they needn't have bothered going through all the rigmarole of being fishermen; he and Ding could just have volunteered.

A drum sounded in the Drum Tower, the gate opened and a little boat scudded out and let them through a phalanx of boats on either side with armed men standing in them and archers behind them. The Lu brothers disembarked, followed by Black Fox and Ding Zhaohui carrying the crates of fish.

They had to register in the Officer-Receiving Hall and were questioned about their business before being given passes. They returned to their boat and were allowed to proceed to the living quarters of Zhong Xiong. It was a magnificent mansion, with three palatial gates guarded by armed men. As Black Fox and Ding carried in the crates of fish they glanced around them. The mansion was surrounded by water. In the middle was a flat, smooth road; on the south side was a huge mountain, the very Army Mountain. They noticed that the actual Water Fortress nestled among hills on which flags and banners flew from numerous trees and shrubs where the Land Fortress was located.

They ascended the steps and entered the grounds of the mansion.

CHAPTER 112

The Heroes Meet the Bandit Chief.
They Become Blood Brothers.

AS the two men carried the fish in, they noted the magnificent buildings, terraces and richly ornamented halls. "Zhong Xiong has gone too far," they thought.

As they waited on the steps for the Lu brothers, Black Fox and Ding Zhaohui joked with some of the servants and received the tip of silver with due humility and gratitude. When the brothers finally emerged from their audience with Zhong Xiong, they followed the servants back to the boat, which took them through the various fortresses. Only after they had sailed under the Five Arch Bridge did they all heave a sigh of relief. Ding burst out laughing. "Whatever Brother Black Fox dresses in he really looks and behaves the part," he said. He then told the Lu brothers how they had deceived the servants with their disguises.

Black Fox was far more serious and did not take it so lightly. "Normally, we are Black Fox and Ding Zhaohui, but when we pretend to be someone else, we must become that person in every way."

They reached the Lu brothers' residence without further mishap and told Northern Hero and the others who were waiting for them that Zhong Xiong was looking for able-bodied men. They decided that Northern Hero and Black Fox should volunteer and try to persuade the bandit chief to join them against the Prince of Xiangyang.

They managed to persuade a reluctant boatman to row them back across the water and when they reached the Water Fortress were taken to the Officer-Receiving Hall.

When Zhong Xiong heard that Northern Hero was no other than the famous Uncle Purple Beard he demanded that he first see his seven-treasure scimitar before receiving them.

"No problem," said Northern Hero and he took off his scimitar and handed it to the servant.

A few minutes later, the servant returned and very respectfully addressed them as "lords" and they were taken through the palace gate along a flowery gravel passage way set with stones leading to the moon platform flanked by five wings and seven side palaces built of carved beams, painted rafters and glazed tiles, resplendent in green and gold. Above them was a gold tablet decorated with dragons inscribed with three ebony characters on an indigo-blue background which read: "Silvery Peace Palace".

A guard lifted the door curtain and a man entered. He was seven-foot tall and wore an embroidered hat ornamented with dragon-patterned silk wings and a purple top-coat with loose sleeves embroidered with dragons and medallions. Round his waist was an iridescent yellow sash with tassels hanging from it and he wore black satin boots. He clasped his hands respectfully in greeting and bade his attendants to serve tea. The two men returned the salute, and sat down as Zhong Xiong measured them with his eyes.

"So you are Mr Ouyang," he said to Northern Hero.

"That is correct," replied Northern Hero. "I hear you are recruiting able-bodied men so that is why I am here."

"I have long heard of your illustrious name," Zhong Xiong said. "Your weapon is really a rare treasure worthy of admiration."

Black Fox, who had been ignored, butted in: "It may be a treasure but it is not an invaluable one."

Zhong Xiong looked at him: "What do you mean?"

"Treasures exist everywhere," said Black Fox, "but even more invaluable is benevolence. Filial piety is the other. Land, people and government affairs are another three. Compared to those why do you set such store on a scimitar? We came here to join you, not to present a scimitar. Praising a mere blade shows that you, a chieftain, set too much store on material objects and too little on mankind. Only when you accept this belief can you prove worthy of recruiting men of talent."

"Your words describe the principles for governing the country and serving the people," replied Zhong Xiong. "I am not a high-ranking official, nor of noble birth. So what use is morality to me?"

"So why do you wear a dragon-embroidered top-coat and preside in the Silvery Peace Palace?" asked Black Fox.

His remarks reduced Zhong Xiong to silence for a few moments. Then he said: "I have learned much and you have made me see the light, Brother Zhi."

He bowed to both men and ordered his servants to prepare a banquet while he took off his ornate clothes, changed into a simple blue gown and tied a flowered bandanna round his head in the style of a warrior.

He placed his guests in the seats of honour and sat in a lower place. "Thank you, Brother Zhi, for a hard lesson. My palace...," he scolded himself before resuming: "It's too presumptuous of me to say palace. I mean the title for the tablet in my hall should be changed too."

Black Fox suggested he change the name to Emulation Hall, meaning "to emulate those superior to you", but he hastened to add that he did not mean that he was superior.

"You are too modest, Brother Zhi," replied Zhong Xiong and he ordered that the tablet be changed immediately. He was eager to become a sworn brother of such heroes and bade his men to prepare incense and candles so they could swear an oath of brotherhood before god.

Black Fox and Northern Hero then retired to their quarters and drank and chatted until late into the night, discussing how to rescue Sha Long and Southern Hero, before finally turning in.

CHAPTER 113

The Marvellous Trident Thrower Seeks to Recruit a Man of Talent. River Rat Gets Caught in the Rain.

THE next day the three men discussed military matters, trying to decide who was the worthiest hero of the time.

"I know of a man," Northern Hero said. "It's a pity he's tied down by his official position."

"Who is he?" asked Zhong Xiong.

"He is the armed guard of the fourth rank of the Kaifeng Prefecture, named Zhan Zhao, otherwise known as Southern Hero, or Royal Cat," answered Northern Hero.

Zhong Xiong burst out laughing. "I have him here! When the Prince of Xiangyang ordered me to bury the remains of Sleek Rat — Bai Yutang — I trapped Southern Hero in one of my pits, while his companion, Mountain Rat, managed to escape. I tried to persuade him to join me but he refused, so he is incarcerated under the Green Cloud Cliff."

Northern Hero rejoiced at hearing the news and suggested that he should talk Southern Hero round.

Black Fox then remarked that he knew of someone else who should join them.

"His name is Sha Long, of Sleeping Tiger Gully."

"Isn't he Squire Sha, who captured Lan Xiao?" asked Zhong Xiong. "I wanted him to join me but he refused. I even suggested to the Prince of Xiangyang that he would be a worthy man to guard the Black Wolf Mountain, but I have not had a reply."

"Then I shall go to Sleeping Tiger Gully tomorrow and persuade him myself," replied Black Fox.

The next day, instead of going to Sleeping Tiger Gully, Black Fox went to Chenqiwang and told River Rat and the others about Zhong Xiong's potential value if only he could be persuaded to join them against the prince. Black Fox decided that Sha Long's brothers, Meng Jie and Jiao Chi, who were guarding Sleeping Tiger Gully, should take the fishermen and hunters to the residence of the Governor of Xiangyang to await further orders. Black Fox had already anticipated the number of people to be housed and that was why he had prepared the houses in the Square Mountain of Hangao and put the old fisherman, Zhang Li, in charge.

Zhong Xiong's birthday was due in two weeks' time and Black Fox and River Rat decided that would be the right time to win him over to the righteousness of their cause in defending the emperor.

The twin brother Ding Zhaohui suggested that they send River Rat to persuade Squire Liu to bring his soul-draining incense and to use it, if necessary, in their plan.

River Rat decided to leave in the next few days while Black Fox persuaded Zhong Xiong to send a message to the prince suggesting that Sha Long be escorted to Army Mountain where he would be persuaded to join his camp.

Southern Hero was only persuaded to leave his prison in Green Cloud Cliff after he was personally escorted to the Emulation Hall by Zhong Xiong himself, which the latter did with good grace.

The prince was only too happy to accede to the request and despatched Sha Long under escort to Army Mountain. When he arrived, Black Fox suggested that he see him first in the Officer-Receiving Hall to tell him how much Zhong Xiong honoured and respected him. "I have no doubt that then he'll come over to our side," he said.

Black Fox pretended that it took a lot of persuading for Sha

Long to join them, but after he saw Zhong Xiong and Northern
Hero and Southern Hero standing together to receive him, he pre-
varicated no longer, saying: "It's a rare privilege to see Southern
Hero and Northern Hero together. It must be because of the
chieftain's prestige. How lucky I am to follow their lead."

Zhong Xiong was flattered and led the party into the Emulation
Hall where they took their seats and received their commissions.
Northern Hero was put in charge of the Water Fortress, Southern
Hero to take charge of the Land Fortress, while Black Fox would
be superintendent and oversee the fortresses, thus giving more
time for Zhong Xiong to spend with his new friend Sha Long.

Within five days, all the affairs of Army Mountain were put in
good order and soldiers as well as officers were loud in their praises. Ignorance is bliss, and Zhong Xiong revelled in his new-found
freedom, unaware of what complicated plans had been engineered
to gain his support against the Prince of Xiangyang.

River Rat then took leave of his friends and set off for the Liu
Family Village. It was late autumn and he trudged along kicking
over the fallen leaves and scattering chrysanthemum petals. The
sky clouded over and it grew dark as the rain began to fall heavily,
soaking him to the skin. It was another forty-five *li* before he
reached his destination and he looked for shelter. He came to a
monastery where he drummed on the gate asking to be let in. Opposite was a bean-curd shop from which an old man holding a broken umbrella emerged and offered him shelter.

"Come in," he said. "Make yourself at home."

CHAPTER 114

River Rat Enrols More Men for the Water Fortress.
He Meets the Challenge of Stealing the Hairpin.

THE old man lit some rice stalks so that River Rat could dry off his wet clothes and said goodnight. After he was warm and dry, River Rat also lay down to sleep but his stomach was rumbling with hunger and at last he got up and went out into the courtyard.

As he was taking in the night air he heard the sound of clashing metal, like the clashing of swords. He forgot his hunger and followed the sound, which came from the monastery opposite. Jumping over the wall he heard a woman crying from inside one of the rooms and entered. She told River Rat that she and her brother had taken shelter in the monastery from the rain but the monk had felled her brother with a blow and wanted to have his way with her after he had dealt with another man. The fighting was what had alerted River Rat in the first place and he quickly went to help. The monk was soon overcome and dispatched with his own sword.

The second man was no other than Long Tao who had been instrumental in seizing Butterfly Hua Chong and bringing him to justice. He had then returned home to become a farmer and also to visit his aunt. On his way he had taken shelter in the monastery and had been attacked by the monk.

"But for your intervention, I would have been killed," Long Tao said.

The two men went to free the woman and her brother. After introductions were made, Long Tao discovered that the brother and sister were relations of his and their name was Yao.

As they ate and refreshed themselves before continuing their journey, River Rat told Long Tao how the gallants and heroes were hoping to win over Zhong Xiong and that he was on his way to Liu Family Village to get Liu Qing's soul-draining incense.

Long Tao volunteered to join them, saying that he would persuade Mrs Yao's husband, Yao Meng, to come as well after he had escorted the brother and sister home.

The two men agreed that Long Tao would collect Yao Meng and set off for Chenqiwang where the other heroes would be waiting for them. River Rat continued on his way to the Liu Family Village and reached his destination as the sun was setting.

He was not greeted very civilly by Liu Qing's servants, who had been warned that he was coming to prove that he could steal the hairpin without Liu's knowledge. So he was announced with the greeting: "The thief has arrived."

Liu Qing greeted him rather coldly. "So you are bold enough to come here, eh?" he said.

"I didn't want to keep you waiting in suspense, brother," replied River Rat.

He was shown into a suite of three rooms in which there was nothing but a lamp and a bed.

"I've put you in the west wing while I will wait for you in a room in the east wing," Liu Qing said. "My servants have been ordered to avoid you. When you have stolen my hairpin, give me a call saying: 'Liu Qing, I have it.' Only when you have returned it unbeknownst to me will I give you credit for your skill and receive you as my brother and go through fire and water for you."

"Very well," Jiang Ping smiled. "I just hope you keep your word."

Liu Qing snorted. "As a gentleman, how could I break a promise?"

CHAPTER 115

River Rat Outwits Liu Qing. More Men of Valour Flock to Join the Heroes in the Water Fortress.

LIU Qing ordered his servants to prepare a fire and refreshments for himself in the east wing, warning them to keep a sharp lookout for their possessions in case River Rat was tempted to steal them.

Settling down in his room, Liu Qing grumbled to himself: "I won't be able to sleep properly tonight. The charcoal fire isn't giving out enough heat and the tea is getting cold, while I keep my wits about me wondering what River Rat will steal."

A shuffling sound of footsteps revealed River Rat entering his room.

"What are you grumbling about, brother?" he said. "You have a nice warm fire and tea, with quilts and sheets on the bed, while I have to sit in an ice-cold room with no heating or bedding to keep me warm. So I've come here for a bit."

He wore slippers with the heels turned down and his head was uncovered.

"If you are feeling so cold, why don't you wrap your bandanna round your head?" retorted Liu Qing.

"Because I'm using it as a pillow and I didn't even get a cup of tea when I came, so I thought I'd come in and see you," River Rat replied.

"Why should I prepare tea to welcome a would-be thief?" Liu Qing asked.

"Stealing the hairpin from your head is not difficult — if you really are wearing it," said River Rat.

Liu Qing took off his bandanna with the hairpin and threw it on the table. "There it is," he snarled. "Do you imagine I am low enough to cheat you? If you are so clever, let me see you take it away."

River Rat picked the hairpin up and put it up his sleeve. "Thank you very much, brother," he said and made to go out of the room.

"What a fine river rat you are, " Liu Qing sneered. "You are not so cunning after all."

River Rat, abashed, took out the hairpin and tossed it on the table. "Take care. I shall steal it from you," and went out.

Liu Qing quickly pinned it back into his hair, leaving his bandanna on the table.

He then heard a voice calling from the west wing: "Liu Qing! I have stolen your hairpin."

Startled, Liu Qing took off his hairpin. "You must be mad," he said. "I still have it."

"That's not the real one," River Rat called out from across the courtyard. "I have the genuine one here. Look on the back and you'll find the character 'Longevity' is not incised on the one you are holding."

River Rat had substituted Liu Qing's hairpin for a copy and Liu Qing marvelled at how difficult it was to tell them apart.

"He just got a glimpse of it in the moonlight on Five Peak Mountain," he thought to himself. "He really commands my respect and I blame myself for being too rash and foolhardy. If he can restore the hairpin without my knowledge, I swear I won't lose my temper again."

For a while nothing happened. He gave the fire a poke and heated up some wine. River Rat shuffled in again, yawning. "Let me have a cup of your wine, brother."

"Help yourself," was the reply, "but don't forget to restore the hairpin to me."

"I will," answered River Rat, "if you will grant my request."

"I'll do whatever you want," Liu Qing said.

River Rat then told him how all the gallants had assembled in Chenqiwang to take up arms against the Prince of Xiangyang, and that they were hoping to persuade Zhong Xiong to come over to their side if Liu Qing would give them the soul-draining incense.

"Only after we have won Zhong Xiong over can we seize the treacherous Prince. It's a state affair by imperial decree and the prime minister's order. So you must come with me."

"He's playing another trick on me," thought Liu Qing. "I refuse to get angry and give him a chance to return the hairpin." So he said with a smile: "That's a matter for officers of the state. I am just an ordinary man. All I want is the return of my hairpin."

River Rat picked up the bandanna, placed it on his head and shuffled away in a huff.

"That bandanna won't serve as a quilt or keep out the cold," Liu Qing said. "Stealing such a thing only proves how worthless you are!"

River Rat took it off and flung it at his face. The jubilant Liu Qing placed it back on his head and poured himself out a cup of wine.

River Rat, back in the west wing, called out: "Liu Qing, your hairpin has been returned to you!"

Sure enough, the hairpin was in his bandanna and he had to concede defeat.

River Rat entered the room and the two men bowed low to each other.

"Now will you help us?" he asked.

"Set your heart at rest," Liu Qing replied. "I will help you to persuade Zhong Xiong to join you in the battle against the prince."

The next morning, the two men set off for Chenqiwang.

In the meantime, Long Tao had collected Yao Meng and they had made their way to the Water Fortress where they reported to Black Fox. He presented them to Zhong Xiong at the Emulation Hall who was impressed with their soldierly bearing. Northern Hero, who already knew Long Tao from the occasion when the two of them captured Butterfly Hua Chong, asked why they had come and was pleased to hear that it was River Rat who had sent them. They all decided to keep quiet about their plans regarding Zhong Xiong until the right time came, which was to be his birthday.

Black Fox in his capacity of superintendent inspected everything and was soon familiar with the whole of Army Mountain. He particularly cultivated the friendship and admiration of Zhong Xiong's brother-in-law, Jiang Kai, an upright young man, with golden cheeks, a flat nose, bushy eyebrows and a big mouth with a moustache. His nickname was Young Demon-Fighting God and he was very skilful with his three-pronged stick. The middle prong was five-foot long and all three were tipped with iron. Two trusted followers of Zhong Xiong also became close to Black Fox. They were called Wu Bonan and Wu Bobei.

With Zhong Xiong's birthday only three days off, Black Fox went to Chenqiwang and met with River Rat and Liu Qing.

"Have you got the stuff ready?" he asked Liu Qing. He nodded. "Then I know what to do next," Black Fox said.

CHAPTER 116

The Bandit Chief Inhales the Soul-Draining Incense.
A Careless Move Creates More Problems for the Heroes.

AS Black Fox took Liu Qing into the Water Fortress, he suggested that he pass himself off as a fortune-teller and beguile Zhong Xiong with flattery until his birthday.

The Lu brothers came the next day and presented some fine fish for the party and Zhong Xiong thanked them not only for the present but also for recruiting Long Tao and Yao Meng to his fortress. "I have appointed them upper servants," he said.

Sha Long, Northern Hero, Southern Hero, Black Fox and the Lu brothers were now all assembled at the Water Fortress to attend the birthday party which took place the following day. The grounds were decorated with festoons and lanterns, concerts and theatricals were staged, creating a very lively atmosphere, the like of which had not been seen there for many a year. The soldiers and officers were told by Black Fox that they could drink as much as they wanted and even if they became the worse for liquor, it would not be regarded as a breach of discipline. Everyone was filled with joy.

In the Emulation Hall a sumptuous banquet was given and birthday gifts displayed. Everyone was dressed in their brightest clothes. Zhan Zhao — Southern Hero — wore his official garments of the fourth rank of the imperial guard. The men took it in turn to bow respectfully to their birthday host despite his modest objections. "I should be bowing to you all for you have done everything for me and taken a lot of trouble," he said.

The wine flowed freely. Soon Zhong Xiong became very drunk as each of the warriors and guards proposed a toast to him and he had to drain several cups to show his appreciation.

Liu Qing, the Fair-Complexioned Judge, wrote a birthday couplet for his host which read: "Only a great hero can show his true self; a celebrity with unconventional ways is a man of taste."

"Mr Liu's handwriting is beautiful," said Zhong Xiong, bowing to him.

Black Fox prevented Liu Qing from returning the bow by suggesting he offer three cups of wine instead.

After much persuasion, Zhong Xiong was prevailed upon to drink more wine and soon he could no longer sit up straight. Two of the heroes then carried him into his room where he was laid on his bed while Liu Qing lit his soul-destroying incense in the belly of a miniature bronze crane and let the smoke waft into the nostrils of the sleeping Zhong Xiong. He sneezed twice and his respiration became weak.

The plan had previously been worked out between Black Fox and Southern Hero. The latter was to display his officer's uniform of the imperial guard to the whole assembly and then leave quietly and take off his uniform in Zhong Xiong's bedroom where Black Fox would dress Zhong Xiong in them while Southern Hero would make his way back to land. The exchange was soon effected and Black Fox called out in a very loud voice: "The imperial guard is drunk! Take him to the Land Fortress at once!" The unconscious Zhong Xiong was carried down to the shore where a boat carried him and the others through the various palisades to Chenqiwang.

Black Fox then ordered Sha Long and Northern Hero to wait until Zhong Xiong recovered consciousness and then to persuade him to join them in their fight against the prince. He would return to the Water Fortress and inform Mrs Zhong and the family where her husband was.

It was already too late. Mrs. Zhong had prepared a feast in the rear hall to celebrate her husband's birthday and when they found he was nowhere to be found, she became extremely suspicious. She mused: "Southern Hero is an imperial government officer of the fourth rank, so why should he submit himself to my husband a mere chieftain? It is a trick instigated by him and his friends to seize my husband. If anything happens to him, the whole family of Zhongs will die out!"

She began to panic and all she could think of was to send her children to a place of safety and then to kill herself. She sent for the family retainers, Wu Bonan and Wu Bobei, and told them to take her son Zhong Lin and daughter Yanan to a place of safety. Going out through the back gate of the Water Fortress, the four headed for the mountains, leaving Mrs Zhong and her brother Jiang Kai to await their fate.

CHAPTER 117

Black Fox Sets Off to Find the Missing Children.
A Loyal Servant Encounters a Beast.

WHEN Black Fox returned to the Water Fortress to inform Lady Zhong of her husband's whereabouts, he was set upon by an angry Jiang Kai and injured with a blow to the foot.

"Stay where you are, brother," he shouted. "I have important news for your sister."

Jiang Kai, thinking it must be about his brother-in-law Zhong Xiong, lowered his weapon and took him to the rear quarters. They were just in time, because Mrs. Zhong was preparing to hang herself. Black Fox hastened to tell her the whole story of why her husband had been whisked away. "We were afraid his reputation would be sullied by supporting the Prince of Xiangyang and wanted to persuade him, without loss of face, to deliver him from such a fate. We had to plan carefully and secretly to avoid any mishap which would force him to make a wrong move. He is now safe in Chenqiwang with other friends and hopefully he will be persuaded to see the light."

Mrs Zhong was relieved but regretted sending her children away. "Uncle," she said to Black Fox, "I was so worried after my husband disappeared, I told my retainers Wu Bonan and Wu Bobei to take my children to a place of safety."

Black Fox stamped his uninjured foot in frustration, blaming himself for not revealing the whereabouts of Zhong Xiong earlier, and hurried off to find them.

He had gone several miles before he heard voices and found the boy Zhong Lin accompanied by Wu Bonan but no sign of his sister and her escort.

"Go to her rescue, quickly," Wu said. "That wicked Wu Bobei pushed us down the ravine because he wanted to kill the two children. Luckily we landed on a pile of leaves and we were unhurt, but he has carried off the young mistress."

Black Fox left them and despite the pain from his injury, raced ahead to the rescue. After several miles he came across two herbalists who told him that they had seen a man lashing a young girl with his whip. They had tried to stop him but he chased them off. They took him to a spot where Black Fox saw Wu Bobei threatening Yanan with his sword. He picked up a stone and hurled it, hitting Wu on the head making him fall back. Black Fox picked up the sword and dispatched him.

"He wanted to present me as tribute to the Prince of Xiangyang," Yanan sobbed. "When I refused to cooperate he threatened to kill me."

Black Fox comforted her and said her father was safe in Chenqiwang and he would take her there.

The herbalists took them along obscure mountain paths and when they reached their destination safely, Black Fox placed Yanan in the care of Lu Bin's wife and the sisters Phoenix Sprite and Autumn Sunflower, telling them not to tell her father. Only after her brother was found could they be reunited with him.

Meanwhile, Wu Bonan carried his young charge on his back for several miles and then collapsed exhausted beside a stream. He caught sight of a small boat in which there were two men fishing and asked to be taken to a place he knew called Divine Tree Crag. He did not realise that they were two villains, one being no other than the infamous Huai Bao, who had figured in earlier adventures. The other was called Yin Xian. The two of them lived with a loose woman, Madam Tao, in a place called Infant Ravine. All three lived on the proceeds of their robberies, drinking and gambling away their ill-gotten gains.

As Wu Bonan and Zhong Lin were being rowed across, they pushed the servant into the water, drugged the boy and took him back to their house.

When Zhong Lin recovered they told him that Wu had gone to buy refreshments but when they discovered who he was, they were extremely worried.

"This is too bad," said Yin Xian. "He's the son of the cheiftain Zhong Xiong. He was probably kidnapped by that man we pushed into the water."

"What's the problem?" said Huai Bao. "He's a prey that has fallen from the jaws of a tiger only to be picked up by the wolf. We'll take him back to the Water Fortress tomorrow and tell them we rescued him from a bad lot who jumped into the water to make his getaway. We'll get a big reward."

Yin Xian was not convinced. "Zhong Xiong is a mountain bandit; he'll turn against us and show no mercy. Suppose he demands the kidnapper from us and we can't produce him? He'll kill us! We would get much more from the Prince of Xiangyang."

As they lived rather close to Army Mountain, Yin Xian suggested they leave in the dead of night. Madam Tao agreed with the idea but quietly twitched at Yin Xian's sleeve and he caught her meaning.

"I have a terrible stomachache," he groaned and Huai Bao suggested he go first and wait for him in Xiangyang when he recovered.

Huai Bao then went to the room where Zhong Lin was resting and suggested they look for Wu Bonan.

CHAPTER 118

Our Wine-Loving Young Hero Appears and Vanquishes the Plotters. He Goes to the Rescue at the Divine Tree Crag.

YIN Xian looked at his mistress with admiration. "You really are an old hand at it indeed," he said. "I'd much rather stay at home with you."

"We can't go on like this for ever," said Mrs Tao. "Huai Bao is bound to find out we are having an affair."

"Don't worry," said Yin Xian, "if we get the reward from the prince, my share will be one hundred taels of silver at least. Enough for us to be off to distant parts."

"It would be better to kill him," she answered, "then we can live as husband and wife for ever."

No one in the world can be more cruel than a woman. Yin Xian was evil but she was still more so.

They were so pleased with their plan that they were taken unawares as the door curtain was suddenly yanked off and a man entered who lifted up Yin Xian, threw him to the floor and trussed him up with his belt. He then grabbed hold of Mrs Tao, tied her up and gagged her.

"Where's Chenqiwang?" he demanded.

The terrified Yin Xian blabbered: "Go out of the door and turn east. After crossing the Small Stream Bridge, you'll reach the Divine Tree Crag. Then go south and you'll reach Chenqiwang. I'm only too willing to take you there. "

"Now that I know the way, what's the use of you guiding me?"

He tore the lapel from his jacket, gagged him, took a huge mill-stone and placed it on top of the couple. He found a bottle on the table, poured himself out some wine and greedily partook of the dishes.

It was the wine-loving Ai Hu who, after escorting the young scholar Shi Jun home to his blind father, had stayed with them while Shi Jun entered the prefectural examinations. Ai Hu spent the days with his friend Jinjian who was always in a state of anxiety in case he drank too much. When Shi Jun passed, getting third place, Ai Hu left for Xiangyang to tell Lord Jin that he should conclude the marriage between his daughter Peony and Shi Jun.

Ai Hu wasn't interested in waiting around for the marriage celebrations and left to join his master and mentor, Black Fox, and his other friends at Chenqiwang.

He was in such a hurry to get there that he paid no heed to the best route to go and soon lost his way. He eventually fell fast asleep and only woke up when the moon was high in the sky and he felt hunger pangs. He had begun to look for somewhere to eat and sleep when he came to Mrs Tao's house and heard them plotting.

He finished the food and drink by which time the evil couple had been suffocated by the heavy weight of the millstone. He left the house as if nothing had happened but did not find the Small Stream Bridge because he went the wrong way again. He came to a pile of timber stored up in a shipyard and saw a light coming from a shed. As he neared it he heard someone complaining: "You are being very unreasonable. I have let you warm yourself by the fire, and now you want my clothes. "

Ai Hu peeped in and saw a man looking like a drowned rat shivering before a fire. "Just give me your worn out rags and when mine are dry, you can have them back. "

But the shed-keeper was not to be moved. "If you don't shut up, I'll drive you away from the fire. You have disturbed my sleep!"

"If you are supposed to be watching, why are you going to bed," shouted Ai Hu, and he yanked off the door mat, giving the watchman a start.

Ai Hu took some clothes from his bundle and gave them to the wet man, who told him that he had been pushed into the water by two fishermen. Luckily he could swim but had lost his young master.

Ai Hu then knew that the man's name was Wu Bonan and together they decided to make their way to the Divine Tree Crag, after telling the cowed watchman that they would be back for the clothes.

Wu Bonan was able to give all the up-to-date news of Ai Hu's adopted father Northern Hero, his mentor Black Fox and all the other heroes who were waiting for Zhong Xiong to come over to their side.

When they reached the Divine Tree Crag, Wu Bonan looked up an old acquaintance of his, who was no other than Mrs Gan, the widow of Gan Bao. When she heard who was with him, she let out an exclamation. "How come he is also called Ai Hu?"

A voice then called from outside. "Mrs Gan please let me in."

CHAPTER 119

Ai Hu Rescues the Chieftain's Son. The Chieftain Is Finally Won Over to the Side of Righteousness.

MRS Gan was about to open the door when Wu Bonan took her arm and said: "If it is a man carrying a boy on his back, be sure to keep him here."

Sure enough it was Huai Bao who found carrying Zhong Lin on his back was more tiring than he expected. Moreover, the child was crying and screaming for Wu Bonan. Fearing that the noise would alert others, Huai was afraid to use stronger methods to silence him. Consequently the journey was taking longer than he planned and as a result Wu Bonan and Ai Hu were able to reach Mrs Gan's before he did.

"Are you kidnapping the boy?" Mrs Gan asked.

"Don't talk nonsense," replied Huai Bao. "This boy is a relative. He was kidnapped by someone else and I have rescued him and am taking him back home."

She put him and Zhong Lin in a side room where the exhausted pair fell fast asleep.

Mrs Gan then locked the door and went to the waiting Wu Bonan and Ai Hu and the three sat drinking some wine before making a move.

Ai Hu drank three cups of wine before he asked Mrs Gan why had she said there was another Ai Hu. She then told him how a young man and his servant had put up at her inn and River Rat had consented to act as a go-between for her daughter and the young man.

Ai Hu was mystified. "Since River Rat acted as a go-between, he can't have made a mistake," he pondered. Out loud he said: "This is very odd."

"I don't care how odd it seems," retorted the old lady. "What is my daughter to do? Ai Hu told me he would report to his adopted father Northern Hero and his mentor Black Fox and send betrothal gifts to me and I have been waiting ever since."

"I have an idea," said Wu Bonan. "Why not betroth your daughter to this Ai Hu?"

Ai Hu protested, saying no girl could be promised in marriage to two men and that he was already engaged.

Mrs Gan's heart missed a beat, for she had taken quite a fancy to the present Ai Hu, whereas the other Ai Hu was a little effeminate and delicate and not so virile and heroic as this one, and she was all in favour of Wu's suggestion.

"It's all River Rat's fault," she complained. "I'll have an account to settle with him, when I see him."

"Don't fret," Ai Hu comforted her. "We'll go to Chenqiwang tomorrow and see him. Write a letter and ask for an explanation." Mollified, the old lady went to her daughter to write the letter for her.

After she left, Wu Bonan asked what they should do about Huai Bao.

Ai Hu thought it would be bad for business if they killed him in Mrs Gan's hotel and that they should waylay him on the road.

"You are too naive," smiled Wu Bonan. "That old woman is a ruthless tigress. When her husband was alive, goodness knows how many poor creatures they slaughtered here."

Mrs Gan then entered with the letter and asked what they were going to do with Huai Bao.

When they told her they intended to waylay him outside, she

went out and woke Huai Bao and Zhong Lin up and saw them out to the road. Ai Hu and Wu Bonan followed them out, taking a slip road, so that they would meet them head on.

When Huai Bao saw Wu Bonan walking towards him he shook with fear, while Zhong Lin threw himself into Wu's arms. Huai Bao tried to run away but he was tripped up and a foot stamped down on his back. As Wu Bonan led the boy away, Ai Hu took out his sword and dispatched Huai Bao without more ado, and the triumphant trio made their way to Chenqiwang.

At Chenqiwang, Zhong Xiong had drunk so much wine and soul-destroying incense that it wasn't until the fifth watch when a cock was crowing that he began to stir. A large group, including Northern Hero, Sha Long, Southern Hero, the twin Ding Zhaohui, River Rat, Liu Qing, the brothers Lu Bin and Lu Yin, Long Tao and Yao Meng, as well as Black Fox, gathered round his bedside waiting. The room was thick with people but they all kept silent as they heard him muttering: "I'm thirsty, bring me some tea, quickly."

Black Fox handed him a cup of strong tea and he gradually opened his eyes and saw the whole assembly of warriors and heroes. He sat up quickly and saw he was in a strange room and dressed in fisherman's clothes.

"Where am I?" he shouted.

"You are at Chenqiwang in the drawing room of Brother Lu Bin," said Sha Long.

Black Fox then gently explained: "Everybody knows that the emperor is highly regarded in the empire. We came here by his imperial decree and the order of Prime Minister Bao to pacify Xiangyang and seize the treacherous Prince Zhao Jue. We knew you were involved with him but did not have the heart to destroy the good with the bad. You are an outstanding hero. You are too proud to condescend to others, so that is why we played a trick on you because we love the state and you, our friend. I hope you will pardon me, as it was all my idea."

He dropped down on his knees and the others followed suit. Zhong Xiong hastily stood up and fell down on his knees saying: "What prestige have I that you should show me such favour? I am not equal to it. I never dreamed you set such store by friendship instead of relying on your strength. If I do not turn over a new leaf now, I am not a real man."

At this all the men stood up pleased that Zhong Xiong had resolved to mend his ways.

CHAPTER 120

Heroes and Gallants Gather Together.
Peace Comes to Army Mountain.

THE bandit chief Zhong Xiong lost no time in breaking away from gangsters and joining the side of good. His good resolutions spoke volumes for his sincerity and generosity. He vowed not to go back on his word and likened himself to oil on boiling water. The water, representing low life, bubbles, while the oil drifts to the rim of the cauldron and looks on — boiling oil remains quiet and never shows off and if a drop of water falls into it, it will splutter and spit. Zhong Xiong compared himself to unpurified oil able to blend with the oil of friendship as depicted by the gallants and heroes.

A feast was held to celebrate the alliance and much wine was drunk as Zhong Xiong was told about the parts each of the heroes had played in his capture. Laughingly he joked saying: "If I get drunk again, where will you lot carry me?"

The answer was he would be taken back to Army Mountain. But his good intentions were sorely tested when Black Fox confessed what had happened to his son and daughter. "Your daughter is safe here," he said, "but I don't know the whereabouts of your son."

Zhong Xiong was confident that his son, Zhong Lin, would be safe in Wu Bonan's care, though Black Fox was full of remorse.

But as morning came, Ai Hu and Wu Bonan arrived with the boy and Black Fox went wild with joy.

Ai Hu went down on his knees to his mentor and Black Fox presented him to Zhong Xiong who found him a handsome and valiant young man.

After River Rat read Mrs Gan's letter, he explained how it was his idea to pretend Phoenix Sprite was Ai Hu and Autumn Sunflower as his servant in order to protect their honour. But now all could be cleared up and Mrs Gan and her daughter should settle in Square Mountain in Xiangyang. Zhong Xiong should return to Army Mountain with his family, escorted by some of the heroes while the rest went on to Xiangyang to prepare for battle.

So ends the story of the Seven Heroes and Five Gallants.

(The original text consists of more than half a million Chinese characters in its entirety. The editors have shortened it for an English-speaking readership by cutting out unnecessary details and repetition.)

图书在版编目（CIP）数据

七侠五义/(清)石玉昆,(清)俞樾著;宋绶荃译.—北京:外文出版社,2003.7
（熊猫丛书）

ISBN 7-119-03354-9

Ⅰ．七...　Ⅱ．①石...②俞...③宋...　Ⅲ．英语–语言读物,小说

Ⅳ．H319.4：I

中国版本图书馆 CIP 数据核字(2003)第 055137 号

外文出版社网址：
  http://www.flp.com.cn
外文出版社电子信箱：
  info@flp.com.cn
  sales@flp.com.cn

熊猫丛书

七侠五义

作　　者	石玉昆　俞　樾	
译　　者	宋绶荃	
责任编辑	陈海燕　李　芳	
封面设计	唐少文	
印刷监制	张国祥	
出版发行	外文出版社	
社　　址	北京市百万庄大街 24 号	邮政编码　100037
电　　话	(010) 68320579（总编室）	
	(010) 68329514/68327211（推广发行部）	
印　　刷	北京中印联印务有限公司	
经　　销	新华书店/外文书店	
开　　本	大 32 开	
印　　数	0001—2000 册	印　张　16.25
版　　次	2005 年第 1 版第 1 次印刷	
装　　别	平	
书　　号	ISBN 7-119-03354-9	
	10—E—3565P	
定　　价	28.00 元	